"When I clos
face."

His words, so gravel-rough, had her heart racing.

"You're driving me crazy. Taking over every moment of my life."

She couldn't breathe. Because what he was saying—that was the way she felt. As if he'd taken over her life.

"I tried to walk away. I tried to be strong." He lowered his head.

"Gunner…"

"There are some lines that if you cross them, you can't ever go back."

"I don't want to go back." There was nothing in her past to go back to.

"I won't be able to let you go."

She wouldn't let him go. Before Gunner could say anything else, Sydney wrapped her hands around his neck and pulled his head down toward her.

SHARPSHOOTER

BY
CYNTHIA EDEN

First published in Great Britain 2013
by Mills & Boon, an imprint of Harlequin (UK) Limited,
Eton House, 18-24 Paradise Road, Richmond, Surrey TW9 1SR

© Cindy Roussos 2013

ISBN: 978 0 263 90368 3
ebook ISBN: 978 1 472 00734 6

46-0813

Harlequin (UK) policy is to use papers that are natural, renewable and recyclable products and made from wood grown in sustainable forests. The logging and manufacturing processes conform to the legal environmental regulations of the country of origin.

Printed and bound in Spain
by Blackprint CPI, Barcelona

I wanted to offer a huge thank-you to all the wonderful folks at Mills & Boon Intrigue. It is always a pleasure! And for my friend Joan, a woman who loves her strong heroes, I hope you enjoy this story.

Prologue

The thunder of gunfire erupted around her as Sydney Sloan ran through the remains of the enemy's camp. Voices were calling out, screaming, but she didn't stop. She couldn't.

Her focus was on the man before her. The man lying so still in the middle of that nightmare scene.

"Slade!" Her own scream joined the others as she fell to her knees beside him. She grabbed for his shoulder and rolled him toward her.

His chest was a bloody mess. His eyes—those dark eyes that she'd stared into so many times—were closed. "Slade?" she whispered hoarsely. No, this couldn't happen. They were supposed to get out of there together. They were going to start their life together back in the States. They were going to get married.

"I'll get you out of here." He *would* be fine. She'd get him to the helicopter. Fly him out of there. He'd get patched up, and everything would be just as they'd planned.

More gunfire erupted. Her breath choked out when a bullet drove into her shoulder. The pain burned her, terrified her. If she was hurt too badly, how would she get Slade to safety?

She grabbed his arms. Started to drag him.

More gunfire. This time, the bullet hit her in the side. She stumbled but refused to fall. Slade needed her. She wasn't going to let him down.

"Sydney!" The roar of her name had her jerking up her head. She saw Gunner Ortez then, running toward her and his brother.

Gunner and Slade. They were so different. Slade was always laughing, so easygoing. Gunner was intense, almost… frightening to her.

But she knew Gunner would do anything for his brother. "Help him!" Sydney called as her knees buckled. She hit the ground, still holding tight to Slade.

Why weren't her knees working? Why did she feel so cold? It was so hot in the jungle.

Then Gunner was there. He was curling his body around hers, shielding her from the hail of gunfire that just wouldn't stop.

A trap. They'd walked right into this hell because they'd been going after Slade. A rescue mission. They'd had to take the risk of infiltrating the area, against orders.

Gunner's fingers—long, tan, strong—went to Slade's throat. She felt the thick tension in the big body behind hers as Gunner checked for his brother's pulse. Then Gunner swore.

No. *No.*

His hand pulled back. She grabbed his fingers. Held tight. "You have to help me," she whispered. "Gunner, please, we have to get him out of here!"

More gunfire. Gunner curled his body even tighter to hers. She heard the thud of the impact and knew he'd just taken a bullet.

For her.

"He's not here anymore," Gunner rasped. His eyes—as dark as Slade's but lined with gold flecks, stared into her own. *"He's not here."*

She shook her head.

The *rat-a-tat* of gunfire came again. Gunner yanked out a handgun with his left hand. He began to fire back, even as the fingers of his right hand twisted and locked with hers. "We have to get out of here! We're damn sitting ducks!"

"Not without…Slade…" Her side *hurt*. A deep, agonizing burn, and she wondered just how bad the hit was. But she'd make it, she'd hold on, until they got Slade out of there. They'd come to rescue him, and they'd never failed on a mission before. *"Help me."*

The gold in his eyes seemed to blaze. "How many times have you been hit?"

Two? Three? What did it matter? "Slade…"

Then she heard the roar of engines. Coming toward them. The enemy closing in. There wasn't any more time. "Just… *take him.*" Because she wasn't sure that she'd be able to get out on her own steam. She couldn't make her legs work, and as she pulled her fingers from Gunner's, she realized that she was shaking. She'd run out of ammo, and the blood was pumping down her side. "Take him…please." Her voice broke and her body began to sway. She was already on her knees, but Sydney was pretty sure she'd soon slump forward and crash face-first into the dirt.

Hold it together. Stay strong, just until Slade is safe.

But Gunner's hands didn't wrap around Slade's body. His hands reached for her.

She screamed then, and lunged toward Slade.

But Gunner pulled her back. The bullets were hitting the ground around her, sending chunks of dirt flying into the air. They had no cover, no backup and it sounded as though more enemy reinforcements were coming in.

Shouldn't have been here. Shouldn't have happened. How had everything gotten so messed up? Their cover had been blown pretty much from the get-go.

"Gunner, no." She tried to pull away from him. "Can't... leave..."

Another bullet hit her. Driving through her upper shoulder and sinking into Gunner.

She choked, barely managing to breathe as the pain swamped her.

"He's dead," Gunner gritted out. She was in his arms then. He was holding her tight, bruising her. "You...*won't* be."

Sydney fought him, using all the strength that she had, but she didn't have enough. Gunner was wounded, too, but nothing stopped him. Not ever.

So he ran right through the gunfire, holding her in arms like steel. He ran and ran, and then they were in the heavier, denser part of the jungle, evading the men who chased them. No jeeps could follow them here.

Gunner wouldn't let her go, no matter how much she begged him.

He didn't speak to her again. Didn't say a word.

And behind them, in that nightmare, Slade remained in the dirt.

Dead.

His eyes had never opened. From the time she'd fallen by his side, he hadn't moved. Hadn't spoken. Hadn't even been able to open his eyes.

They never would open again.

GUNNER GOT HER out of that jungle. Patched her up. Stopped the blood flow. She wasn't helping him. Sydney was barely moving at all.

"Shock," Gunner told her, voice terse.

Yeah, that was it. She had to be in shock. Because she'd just seen her fiancé die in that trap. She and Slade had fought before, and for him to die with that anger between them...*I'm so sorry.*

"You lost too much blood." Gunner's fingers curled around her chin. She didn't know where they were now. Some kind of hut? A run-down shack? Just some shelter he'd found them. Gunner was good at finding shelters. "You *won't* die."

Hadn't he said that before? It was hard to remember. Her tongue seemed so thick in her mouth, but after three tries she managed to say, "Slade..."

Gunner's fingers tightened on her. "He's gone."

A tear leaked down her cheek.

Gunner's jaw clenched. That hard jaw. That dangerous face. "I've got you, Syd. I'll take care of you."

She was breaking apart on the inside. The mission was over. They'd failed.

He pulled her into his arms. Held her against his chest. Gentleness? He'd never seemed the kind for that. "I've got you," he said again, voice deepening.

And it was there, in his arms, that she finally let herself go.

She cried until there were no tears left to shed.

Chapter One

Two years later...

The kidnapper had a gun pressed to Sydney's head.

Gunner Ortez stopped breathing when he saw Sydney's beautiful face fill his scope. So perfect. Delicate, high cheekbones. The soft curve of her nose. The full, red lips...

And the green eyes that stared straight back at him. Seeming to *know* where he was. Her green gaze that showed no fear even as that soon-to-be-dead man jammed the gun harder into her temple.

"Do you have the shot?" a low voice asked in his ear. The earpiece wouldn't even be noticed by most people. Uncle Sam was great at inventing gear that his soldiers could use anytime, anyplace.

With a minimum of fuss and a maximum of damage.

Gunner's finger was curled over the trigger, but he wasn't taking the shot. "Negative, Alpha One," he told his team leader. "Sydney isn't clear."

And he was sweating, feeling a tendril of fear—when he *never* felt fear. There was no room for emotion on any of their missions.

He worked with a group far off the grid. The Elite Ops Division wasn't on any books anywhere in the U.S. government. They took the jobs that the rest of the world wasn't meant to know about. In particular, his EOD team—code-named the Shadow Agents—had a reputation for deadly accuracy when it came to taking out their targets.

And this guy…that jerk with the trembling finger, he was going down. The man had kidnapped an ambassador's daughter. Held her for ransom, and when the ransom had been paid, he'd still killed her.

He'd thought he could hide from justice.

He'd thought wrong.

Sydney's intel had led them to Jonathan Hall. Led them to his hideout just over the border in Mexico.

Sydney had volunteered to go in, to make sure that Hall was holding no civilians.

Now she was the one being held.

"He can't leave the scene," Logan Quinn said, the faint drawl of the South sliding beneath the team leader's words as they carried easily over the transmitter. "You know our orders."

Containment or death. Yeah, Gunner knew the drill, because the ambassador's daughter hadn't been the first victim. Hall liked to kill.

Gunner stared down at the man, at Sydney. *You won't kill her.*

Sydney's face was emotionless. Like a pale canvas, waiting for life. That wasn't her. She was always brimming with emotion, letting it spill over onto everything and everyone.

It was only on the missions that she changed.

How many more missions would she take? She seemed to be putting herself at risk more these days. He *hated* that.

He shifted his position, testing the wind. Hall wouldn't see him. He was too far away. Gunner's specialty was attacking from a distance.

There was no target that he couldn't reach.

He could take out that man right now. A perfect shot…

if he hadn't been worried that Hall's finger would jerk on that trigger at impact.

"I want the gun away from her head," Gunner snapped into his mouthpiece.

But even as he said the words, he saw Sydney's lips moving.

Take. The. Shot.

Hall was outside the small house, his gaze frantically searching the area even as he kept Sydney killing-close. The man wasn't stupid. He'd eluded capture for over a year because he understood how the game was played.

Hall knew Sydney hadn't come in alone. The guy just didn't see her backup. When he hunted like this, Gunner's prey never saw him, not unless he wanted to be seen.

This time, he wanted to be seen because that gun *was* coming away from Sydney's head.

Take. The. Shot. Her lips moved again.

He shook his head, even though he realized she'd never see the movement. Then he took two steps to the right. He knew that, in this particular position, the sunlight would glint off his weapon. When he saw that flash of light, Hall would fire—

And he did. The man yanked the gun away from Sydney's head and shot at Gunner.

Too late.

Gunner had already taken his own shot.

The second the gun moved away from her temple, Sydney shoved back against Hall with her elbow, and then she'd jerked away from her captor and threw herself down.

Before she even hit the ground, Gunner's bullet slammed into Hall. The man stumbled back and fell.

"Converge," Logan's hard order came in Gunner's ear.

The other EOD team members rushed from the shadows. Not that they needed to rush. Hall wasn't going to be a threat to anyone, not anymore.

Gunner's breath eased out. He watched as Sydney pushed to her knees, then rose to her feet.

Cale Lane, the newest team member, crouched over Hall as Sydney looked toward Gunner's position.

He'd put the weapon down, so he couldn't see her face clearly, not with the distance that separated them. But he was aware that his heart beat too fast. His hands had been sweating.

A sharpshooter wasn't supposed to get nervous, wasn't supposed to *feel* on the mission.

But whenever he was close to Sydney, all he could do was feel.

He packed up his weapon and hurried down to her. Because lately, it was always about her.

Day and night. Whether he was awake or asleep, he was obsessed with the woman.

Cale and Logan had secured the scene by the time he got down to the front of the house, and Cale was leading some sobbing redhead from the cabin. So Sydney had been right. Hall had already taken his next victim. If they hadn't moved then, would she have been dead by nightfall?

"Good shot." Sydney's voice was quiet.

Gunner's body tensed. He knew he should hold on to his control, but...*the gun had been at her temple.* If Hall hadn't hesitated, Gunner would have watched while the man put a hole in her head.

So he ignored the wide stare that Logan gave him and stalked to Sydney. He grabbed her wrist, pulled her against him. "You took too much of a risk."

Her short blond hair shone in the light. Her cheeks stained red—he didn't know if that red was from fury or embarrassment.

"I did my job," Sydney said through gritted teeth, lifting her chin. "I told you that my intel indicated a new hostage. She was hidden in the closet. If I hadn't moved in—"

He pulled her even closer. "He could have killed you."

Then what would I have done?

Her voice dropped. "You say it like that matters to you." Her words were whispered, carrying only to his ears.

Damn it, she did matter. "Sydney..."

"You're the one who wants to be hands-off," she snapped with a hard flash of her green eyes. "So why are you holding on to me so tightly?"

He was. Too tightly. He dropped her wrist as if he'd been burned.

"I'm not waiting any longer," Sydney told him as she straightened her shoulders. "Death can come at any moment, and I told you once...I'm not crawling into the grave with Slade."

Yes, she'd told him that, when he'd made the mistake of getting too close to Sydney on their last case. They'd been trapped during a storm, forced together in a small cabin, and all he'd been able to think was...

I want her.

But he'd—*barely*—managed to stop himself from taking what he wanted. He did have some self-control. Unfortunately, with her, that self-control was growing weaker every day.

"I'm going to start living my life on *my* terms," Sydney told him. "Consider yourself warned."

Then she spun away. Sydney headed toward Cale and the redhead. More backup had swarmed the scene. Other EOD agents who'd come to lend their support for the rescue-and-takedown operation.

Gunner stared after Sydney, feeling...lost.

Then Logan cleared his throat. "I've seen that look before."

Gunner glared at him. Logan might be the team leader for the Shadow Agents, and Gunner considered him as a friend most days, but the man should know not to—

"Better watch yourself, or you might just lose something important."

Sydney had already walked away. Logan didn't understand.

She was never mine to lose.

THE BAR WAS too loud. The place was packed with too many people, and coming there, well, it had been a serious mistake.

Sydney huffed out a hard breath and pushed her barely sipped drink away. She'd gotten back to the States just hours before—finally gotten a break for some serious R & R time, and she'd gone home to Baton Rouge.

But it didn't feel like home anymore.

So many missions. So many places.

They were all blending together into a hail of gunfire and death.

"A pretty lady like you shouldn't be sitting alone." The voice, marked with the Cajun that she loved, came from her right.

Sydney's gaze rose, and she found herself staring at a tall, blond man. He was handsome, with the kind of good looks that probably drew women all the time.

So why isn't he drawing me?

She'd come to that bar to find someone like him. It seemed as if she'd been living in a void for the past two years of her life, and she wanted—so desperately wanted—to start feeling again.

The blond glanced at her drink. "Don't you like it?"

Sydney shook her head. "It's not what I wanted."

He pulled up the bar stool next to her, leaned in close. "Why don't you tell me what you want?"

A stranger, a guy who didn't know her at all, and he looked at her with more warmth than Gunner did.

Don't think about him. This was not supposed to be another Gunner night.

She forced a smile on her face. Gunner was miles away. He always had been. This man, he was right in front of her. She wanted to live, and here was her chance. "I'm really not sure," she said softly. The words were the truth.

What did she want?

Gunner.

That wasn't happening. Time to consider other options.

The guy leaned toward her. "How about we start with a dance, then? Maybe that will help you figure out just what you want."

How long had it been since she'd danced with someone? Too long.

"I'm Colin," he said, giving her a broad smile. "And I promise, I'm a good guy."

As if she could believe a promise from a stranger. She'd met far too many dangerous, lying men for that.

"I'm Sydney." She took the hand that he offered to her. "I guess one dance—"

She broke off, her words stuttering to a halt because she'd just met the dark gaze of the man who'd entered the bar. A man who should *not* have been there.

A man whose stare was hot enough to burn.

Colin stiffened beside her as he followed her gaze. "Problem?"

Yes. No. Maybe. If Gunner was there, then there could be a new mission. There *had* to be a new mission. There was no other reason for Gunner to be in Baton Rouge instead of up in D.C.

But why hadn't Logan just called her?

Gunner was stalking toward her.

"I thought you were here alone," Colin said softly.

"I am." He still had her hand, and that felt wrong all of a sudden.

Maybe because Gunner's gaze had dipped to their hands. Hardened.

"Then you want to tell me why that guy looks like he's about to rip me apart?"

Gunner did look that way. But Gunner *usually* looked tough. It was his face. Not handsome like Colin's. Not perfect. It was full of hard angles and dangerous edges. With his golden skin and that jet-black hair, he always looked like walking, talking danger to Sydney.

Danger wasn't supposed to draw you in, but Gunner seemed to draw her more and more.

Even as he kept pushing her away.

"He's a friend," Sydney said, giving a shrug that she hoped looked careless. "An old friend."

Then Gunner was in front of them. "Sydney." His voice was a deep, rumbling growl when Colin's voice had been soft and flirtatious. Did Gunner even know how to flirt? She doubted it. "We need to talk."

A mission. Right. Just as she'd suspected. Sydney cleared her throat and glanced at Colin. His hold was light on her wrist. "Can you give us just a minute?"

One blond eyebrow rose, but he nodded. "I'll wait for you." She noticed that when he glanced back at Gunner, Colin's face hardened, losing some of its easygoing appeal.

Gunner didn't wait for the guy to back away. He grabbed Sydney's hand—his grip much tighter than Colin's—and pulled her into the nearest dark corner.

"Gunner!" His name burst from her. "What are you doing?"

He caged her with his body. "What are *you* doing?"

"Getting a drink? Getting ready to dance?" Some things should be obvious to a superagent like him.

His teeth snapped together as he leaned in, even closer. The wooden wall was behind her, and Gunner's muscled form wasn't leaving much space in front of her. "You know what he wants."

She was in some kind of weird alternate reality. Sydney shook her head. "What's the mission? Why didn't Logan call—"

"There is no mission."

She didn't have any kind of comeback. She couldn't think of what to say. If there was no mission, then Gunner shouldn't be in Louisiana. Her family's old home was there, but Gunner had a place in D.C. Not here.

"I could see it in your eyes," he growled.

"See what?" Her voice came out huskier than she'd intended.

Gunner flinched. "After the last mission, I knew you'd do something like this." He glanced over his shoulder. Since Gunner was big, easily six foot three, with wide shoulders, she couldn't see what he was looking at when he glared behind him.

But she had a pretty good idea.

Colin.

"Any man?" Gunner asked as that hard, dark gaze came back to her. "Is that what you're—"

Her cheeks felt numb. "Don't say another word." She wanted to slug him. "You don't have the right to say anything to me, to judge me." She'd wanted Gunner, had let him become too important to her in the past few years, but *enough*. "Slade is gone. I've moved on." She pushed at him.

Gunner stepped back.

Good. She marched away from him and didn't look back.

Colin stood as she approached. "I want that dance," Sydney said, and she pretty much dragged him onto the small floor.

She didn't know what Gunner's game was. But he wasn't controlling her. He didn't want her. He'd made that clear when she'd tried to kiss him on that case in Texas.

Colin's hands settled along her hips. She was wearing a pair of jeans, a top that was a little low and strappy sandals that pushed her a bit higher than her normal five-foot-six height. Colin was big, not as tall or muscled as Gunner, and—

"You don't want to come between us."

Gunner was *there*. Again. On the dance floor. And he'd just pulled Colin away from her.

This was insane.

"Sydney, come with me," Gunner said in that low growl of his.

Colin shook his head. "Look, buddy, I don't care if you are her friend, you don't—"

"Is that what I am, Sydney?" Gunner asked, his voice flat. "Your friend?

He had been. After that nightmare two years ago, he'd become her rock. The man she depended on. The one who'd pulled her through her darkest time.

But she wanted him to be more than that.

She wanted *more*.

He didn't.

"I don't know what you are," she told him. "But you should leave." Because she was tired of living only for the job. She'd find happiness. Everyone else did. She wanted to have a real home one day. A family.

Not just mission after mission.

Why couldn't someone be waiting on her when she came home? Someone who loved her? Wanted her?

"You heard the lady," Colin muttered.

But Gunner wasn't moving. He *had* started to give Colin a killing glare.

Colin made the mistake of stepping toward Gunner. Of shoving against his chest. "You need to *back off*—" Colin began.

Definitely a mistake.

Gunner grabbed that shoving hand and twisted it. Colin's words choked off, and the dancers around them froze as they realized what was happening.

In less than three seconds, Gunner had Colin on his knees...all from that hold that Gunner had on Colin's hand. Sydney knew the twist that Gunner was using could be incredibly painful, and if Gunner just pulled a little more, Colin's bones would snap.

This scene was turning into a nightmare.

"Gunner, let him go!" Sydney grabbed his arm. "You're making a scene!"

"No, *he* did that when he shoved me." But Gunner let the other man go.

Colin scrambled away, eyes wide, cheeks flushed. He headed for the door as fast as he could.

Well, so much for that dance. So much for the whole night. Sydney turned from Gunner and started marching for the door. The plan had been stupid, anyway. As if she was going to find some kind of Prince Charming in a bar like this.

She pushed open the front door, and the night air rushed over her. Sydney took two more steps, then...

She stopped. "Tell me that you aren't following me home." Because she *knew* he was behind her. As a rule, Gunner could move pretty soundlessly. That was one of the reasons he'd been so good during his time as a SEAL sharpshooter. But she could *feel* him, so she knew he was trailing her.

"We need to talk."

Fabulous. "I thought there wasn't anything to say. I mean, you had your chance at Whiskey Ridge…" When she'd ditched her pride and told him that she needed him.

But he'd stayed aloof.

Gunner always held back with her. Always saw the ghost of her fiancé, *his half brother,* between them.

She knew now that he wasn't ever going to let that ghost go. She might want Gunner. Want him so badly that her heart had seemed to break when he kept pulling away, but she'd survive his rejection.

She'd survived much worse than not being wanted by Gunner Ortez.

"What do you want from me?" Gunner asked her.

Everything.

Sydney turned toward him. "I want you to look at me and just see a woman. Not a ghost."

A muscle jerked in his jaw. "You're pushing me too much."

She shook her head. "I'm not pushing you at all. You're the one who came here, to *my town*. You're the one who showed up in the bar." Frustrated, she demanded, "How did you even find me here? Did you follow my GPS location?" All of the EOD agents had trackers installed on their phones. But if he'd used that tracking system… *Stalker much.* "Now I'm the one walking away."

Only she didn't get to walk far. Four steps was all she took. Then Gunner's hands were on her shoulders. He spun her back around and lifted her up on her tiptoes.

"When I close my eyes, I see your face."

His words, so gravel-rough, had her heart racing.

"I don't see a ghost, I just see you." His eyes were on her mouth. "You're driving me crazy, taking over every moment of my life."

She couldn't breathe. Because what he was saying—that was the way she felt. As if he'd taken over her life.

"I tried to walk away. I tried to be strong." His head lowered. "But I don't want you to be with anyone else."

Sydney didn't want to be with any other man. "Gunner…"

"There are some lines that if you cross them, you can't ever go back."

"I don't want to go back." There was nothing in her past to go back to. Only death.

Gunner was life.

"I won't be able to let you go."

She wouldn't let him go. Before Gunner could say anything else, Sydney wrapped her hands around his neck and she pulled his head down toward her.

The kiss wasn't easy or gentle. Wasn't the tentative kiss of soon-to-be lovers.

It was hard and deep—consuming. The touch of his lips sent need spiraling through her. Then she was crushed against him. Holding on as tight as she could as he tasted her, and she tasted him, and all of the longing that she'd held inside so tightly broke from her control.

This was Gunner. This wasn't a dream. This was real.

And there was no going back.

HE SHOULD LET her go. Gunner knew he shouldn't have followed her to Baton Rouge, but he'd been afraid.

I don't want to lose her.

Sydney Sloan. The woman he'd wanted since the moment he first met her. Even when she'd been planning to marry his brother, Gunner had wanted her.

They were back at her house. He'd followed her from the bar, feeling the hunger for her burn just beneath his skin.

She stood on the porch now. The swamp waited behind her, and the sound of crickets filled the air.

He was closing in on her. There was still time to pull back, still time to do the right thing.

But he wasn't sure what was right anymore. Slade was gone, buried in a jungle in South America. Sydney was alive. There, just a few feet away, and wonder of wonders, the woman actually wanted him.

She knew about his darkness. About the sins that marked his soul, but she still wanted him.

He would die for her.

So he followed her up the steps to the home that she'd once loved so much, before her family had passed away and left her alone. She opened the door for him. Light spilled out onto the porch.

Onto her.

There would be no going back.

The wooden porch creaked beneath his feet. Her hand was up, reaching for him, and Gunner was pretty sure he'd had this same dream before. Only then, he'd wakened alone, sweating and tangled in his sheets, with her name on his lips.

Make this good for her. Give her pleasure.

Because he only wanted Sydney to know pleasure. She'd known too much pain in her life.

He crossed the threshold with her. Pushed the door shut behind them.

Her breath came a little too fast, and she shifted from her right foot to her left. He'd been in this house before. It carried her sweet scent, light vanilla, and he knew just where her bedroom waited.

Down the hallway, second door on the right.

Could he make it that far?

"Gunner..."

He loved the way she said his name. Breathless. Eager.

Can't make it that far. He'd done well to make it out of the street and into her house.

Gunner pulled Sydney against him, breathed in that vanilla scent and locked his hands around her waist. Those jeans had been driving him crazy. "I—I can't go slow."

"Good."

She surprised him. Always.

Then his mouth was on hers. He thrust his tongue past her lips, and she was the sweetest thing he'd ever tasted.

Before, he'd told himself to stay hands-off, but in Mexico, when she'd walked away and hadn't looked back, he'd realized that she was too important to lose.

Now his hands were most definitely *on* her.

Her breasts were pressed against his chest. Her hips arched against him. He wanted her naked. He wanted to kiss every inch of her.

And he would. The second time.

The first time—the time that *should* have been perfect—need was controlling him. Raw lust.

So he stripped her. He couldn't take his mouth from hers. His hands learned her body and slid over her silken flesh even as he shoved down her jeans.

He heard her kick off the sandals that had made him ache. He would have liked for her to keep them on—*another time.*

Then they were falling together onto her sofa. He was kissing her neck now, inhaling more of that wonderful scent, even as his hands went between her thighs. He meant to pull away her panties, but his fingers were too rough and the silk tore.

Sydney just laughed.

He loved her laugh.

After Peru, it had taken too long for her laugh to come back.

No. He slammed the door on that thought and instead enjoyed the soft heat of her flesh. She was pushing up against him, whispering his name.

His head lifted. He stared at her and told her the simple truth, "You are the most beautiful thing I've ever seen."

Her lips curled in a smile.

Take.

He yanked open his jeans, pushed his body deeper between her thighs. Waited right there at the entrance to her body. This was the moment. No going back. No—

She arched toward him, and he sank inside her.

The pleasure was so incredible that he had to clench his teeth together to hold back a groan. Nothing, *nothing,* had ever felt so good.

Or so right.

He began to thrust. Withdrawing slowly, then plunging back inside her. She was paradise to him, the best dream he'd ever had, and he kissed as much of her body as he could.

Her nipples were tight, pink, and when he licked one, she tensed beneath him.

Gunner felt the pleasure rock through her.

Her legs lifted, locked around his hips. Then she started pushing up with her hips.

He couldn't hold back. His own thrusts became even harder. He caught her hands and laced his fingers with hers.

He stared into her eyes.

Saw her climax. Her green gaze went wide, then wild as the pleasure crested through her.

His release swept him away on a wave so intense that he

shuddered and pushed deeper into her. The release shook his whole body. Seemed to gut him and never end.

I don't want it to end.

He wanted to keep holding her to make the perfect moment last as long as possible.

He kissed her again because he needed to taste her pleasure, to taste all of her.

And he swore that before the night was done, he would.

Chapter Two

The ringing of her phone woke Sydney. Her hand flew out automatically, reaching for her nightstand—for the phone. But instead of scooping up her phone, her fingers collided with warm, strong flesh.

Not a dream.

Her eyes snapped open, and she found herself staring straight into Gunner's dark gaze. There was no sleepiness in that gaze, just a deep hunger.

For her.

Then he reached out and grabbed the ringing phone from her nightstand. Silently, he handed it to her.

"S-Sydney Sloan." Her fingers tightened around the phone. Gunner's tanned fingers were sliding down her arm.

Goose bumps rose on her flesh as she remembered the night before. The things he'd done to her. What she'd done to him.

More, please.

"Sydney?" Logan barked. "Sydney, are you okay?"

She shot up in bed, clutching the sheet to her chest. "I'm fine. Just…sleeping." Gunner didn't stop stroking her. He raised himself, and his lips brushed over her shoulder.

She shivered.

"Look, I know you were due to have a few weeks off, but

we've got a case that we can't refuse. I've got you booked on a jet to Peru at three today."

Peru.

"I'm going to call Gunner and Cale. They'll be meeting up with you there."

I can tell Gunner. He's right here kissing me, lying naked next to me. She cleared her throat. "What's the case?" She hadn't been back to Peru in two years. Not since Slade had died in that jungle, and the place had nearly become her own grave, too.

"An American is being held hostage by a group of rebels."

Hostage rescue. That was what their team did best.

"He needs us," Logan said. "So be on that plane."

"I'll be there," she whispered, and then, because Logan would figure the situation out when he had to make reservations for Gunner—and those flight reservations had Gunner leaving from Baton Rouge, Sydney said, "Now hold on, and I'll get Gunner for you."

Gunner's gaze rose to hers. She knew that her cheeks flushed; she could feel the burn. But this wasn't the time for secrets. They had a case to work. And when a civilian's life was on the line, there wasn't room for embarrassment.

Gunner took the phone from her but didn't look away from her eyes. "Gunner."

There was a beat of silence. Then Sydney rolled away from Gunner and climbed from the bed before she could overhear Logan's response to the discovery that Gunner was so close she could just, ahem, hand him her phone first thing in the morning.

She grabbed for a robe. Her body ached in a way that felt so good, and she hated that their time together was already ending.

No, not ending. They were just beginning. They'd turned a corner last night, and there would be no going back for them.

"I'll be there," she heard Gunner say, and she looked up as he ended the call.

No man should look as sexy as he did. His hair was a little tousled. A line of stubble coated his square jaw, and his eyes blazed as they raked over her.

"We have at least six hours," Gunner told her.

Six hours.

She nodded.

"I want you."

Her fingers clenched around the belt of the robe. "Again?"

"Always."

She dropped the robe and climbed back in bed with him. Six hours.

This was perfect. What she'd hoped for.

And this time, things would end well for her in Peru. She wouldn't lose Gunner. Not the way that she'd lost Slade.

Gunner's lips pressed to hers, and she shoved away the fear that wanted to rise within her.

Peru. The last time she'd been to Peru, her lover had died there.

It won't happen this time. She'd finally gotten her chance with Gunner. It wouldn't slip through her fingers.

LOGAN STARED DOWN at the phone in his hand. Gunner was with Sydney.

He'd seen the sexual awareness between the two of them. Had known that Gunner wanted Sydney, and that the sniper had held back with her. He had clung so tightly to his control and his rule that Sydney was off-limits.

But it looked as if Gunner had broken his rule.

Logan tossed aside the phone and stared at the photographs in front of him. The tip he'd received could be wrong. He shouldn't *want* it to be wrong, but he did.

Because Gunner was his friend. Gunner had been through hell. The man deserved some happiness.

But if the intel was right—and this intel had come right down from Bruce Mercer, the man who'd formed the EOD—then Gunner's life was about to be ripped apart.

"Enjoy her while you can," Logan whispered. Because Gunner would need some good memories to hold tight to in the darkness that was coming.

PERU WAS JUST as hot and beautiful and wild as Sydney remembered. When the plane touched down, and she headed out on the tarmac, the heat was the first thing to hit her.

Cale was inside the airport, waiting for them. Gunner walked right beside Sydney, his hand lightly pressing at the base of her back.

To any onlookers, they probably looked like a vacationing couple.

That was their cover, after all. Lovers. A cover they'd used before.

Only this time, they weren't pretending.

When they entered the airport, Cale approached them with a broad grin. Again, another cover. The reuniting friends. He slapped Gunner on the back and hugged Sydney.

"Ready?" he asked quietly, keeping his smile in place.

She always was.

They went outside together and tossed their bags into the back of Cale's jeep.

Sydney climbed into the front seat next to Cale, while Gunner jumped in the back. In moments, Cale was driving them away from the airport.

"Where's Logan?" Gunner asked, his voice rising over

the growl of the engine. "I thought he was meeting us down here."

"He's doing recon," Cale said, keeping his eyes on the road. Cale was an ex–Army Ranger, one who'd actually been targeted by the EOD for takedown.

He'd been framed for the murders of three EOD agents. He'd proven his innocence and earned his way onto their team.

"Have you seen a picture of the target?" Sydney asked. She was trying hard not to glance back at Gunner, but she was so aware of him. She was hyperaware of every single move that he made.

Had they really spent the night together? She'd wanted him for so long that part of her wondered if it had all just been a wonderful dream.

An erotic dream.

She couldn't help herself—she glanced back at him.

And found Gunner's dark eyes locked on her.

There was such heat in that gaze. She swallowed and forced her eyes away from him as Cale said—

"No, I haven't seen any visuals on him yet. I just know that the order for extraction came down from the top."

She caught the brief grin that flashed over Cale's face.

"Seems Mr. Mercer thinks this rescue is priority, and he wanted *only* the Shadow Agents to take point on this one."

The Shadow Agents. Sure, there were other teams in the EOD, but *their* team had earned the moniker of Shadow Agents because of the way they handled their missions. They went in soundlessly and attacked before their enemies even realized they were there. Then they vanished, disappearing like shadows.

Gunner was especially good at being a shadow. If Gunner didn't want you to know he was there, you wouldn't.

Sydney knew Gunner's grandfather had been the one to

first train him to track and hunt on a reservation. Gunner was the best hunter she'd ever seen, even better than Slade.

Slade's body was in Peru. That knowledge was sitting heavily on her now that she was back in the area.

The EOD had tried to recover his remains again and again, but the rebels they'd fought that day had taken his body away from the scene. Despite the EOD's efforts, they hadn't been able to bring him home.

Slade had a grave, an empty one, one that honored him as the soldier he'd been. But he'd actually never made it back home.

"Logan told me that you and Gunner had been in Peru before," Cale said.

She cleared her throat. "A...few times."

"Logan has set us up in a resort near the beach. You and Gunner are supposed to look like honeymooners."

Because sometimes it wasn't about hiding in a hut or sliding through the jungle. Blending in plain sight could work so much better. The EOD knew this well.

"And I'm your single friend, enjoying some R & R myself." The road was bumpy and the jeep bounced. Once, twice. "Sure is a long way from Texas," he murmured, and she heard the faint drawl in his voice.

Cale's home was in Texas, and the EOD agent he'd replaced—Jasper—was currently living in Texas with Cale's sister.

"When are we looking at extraction?" Gunner asked as he leaned forward. His fingers were on the back of Sydney's seat. It almost felt as if he was playing with her hair. Was he?

"Logan said this was a fast-moving mission. We want the civilian out of there within twenty-four hours."

Sydney nodded. Definitely doable. As soon as Logan returned, she'd start her own reconnaissance work. She could uplink to satellites and get aerial maps of the area to find the best places for them to venture in as they started the rescue operation. As long as she had a good computer and the necessary uplink, she'd be able to access anything that the team needed. Tech had always been her specialty.

Then the jeep turned and headed through the high gates of the resort. Sydney put a smile on her face. She could pretend to be a happy honeymooner. With Gunner at her side, she could do anything.

And she *was* happy, even if painful memories were trying to push their way into her mind. Peru had been a nightmare for her once, but it didn't have to be again.

The valet hurried over to the jeep. Gunner was already out and reaching for Sydney. His hand curled around hers, swallowing her fingers. His hold was strong, possessive. And the kiss that he brushed over her lips—it felt possessive, too.

Just for show…or was that something more?

Cale was laughing and saying something, playing his part. Gunner responded, but Sydney was lost.

She actually wished that this moment could be real. That she was just a happy honeymooner. A woman with Gunner.

But this wasn't her life. She had a mission. A rescue. A civilian who needed her. She'd get the job done.

She'd get her man, too.

Gunner's arm wrapped around Sydney's shoulders. He steered her toward the entrance to the resort. She took a deep breath and slipped into her role.

LOGAN'S BODY WAS pressed tightly to the ground. He kept only his head up as he peered through the binoculars to get a visual on the small camp that sat at the base of the mountain. Not a typical rebel group, from what he'd been able to tell. These guys were armed to the teeth, patrolling constantly, and that one tent to the back…the one that housed the hostage…

There'd been no movement from that tent for the past four hours. Logan knew that fact for certain, because he'd been unmoving in his own position for that time.

He shouldn't have come out alone, he knew that, but before he brought Sydney out there, before Gunner got the rebels in his sights, Logan just had to be sure of his target.

An armed guard headed toward the tent, lifted the flap, and went inside. Logan stopped breathing.

Then the guard came out again, leading the hostage. Logan's fingers tightened around the binoculars as he stared at that prisoner. Long hair and a beard that hadn't been trimmed in what looked like months. The man was walking with a faint limp.

This wasn't a hostage who had been taken a few days ago. This was a man who had been held for a very, very long time.

Logan stared at the man's face.

And knew the mission was going to be personal.

GUNNER TIPPED THE bellman and shut the door. Then he flipped the lock and turned his attention to Sydney.

She stood in front of a big bed, her blond hair framing her face. Her eyes were wide and fixed on him, but she wasn't smiling.

Sydney looked nervous. An unusual situation for her. As far as he knew, Sydney was never nervous.

He took a step toward her, and she tensed.

What the hell? "Sydney?"

She shook her head. Then she smiled and gave the light laugh that always made his chest ache. "I swear, I feel like I'm on a real honeymoon."

If only. He wouldn't say he hadn't thought about what

it would be like to marry her, because he had. Too many times. Even when she'd been planning to marry his brother, he'd thought—

She should be mine.

Then Slade had died, and he'd hated himself for the jealousy he'd felt.

"Are you…are you okay with being back here again?" Sydney asked him quietly.

He strolled toward the window, then looked out over the lush resort. Within the resort's walls, everything was beautiful, perfect. But there were other parts of Peru that were savage. Dangerous. Once you left the city and journeyed into the jungle, civilization truly faded away. "I've been back here a few times since his death."

"You have?" Surprise lifted her words.

He knew she'd stayed away. But he'd had to come back. "I tried to find him." Again and again. "My grandfather would have wanted him brought back." *I wanted him back.* He shrugged, trying to push away the past. "But I couldn't find Slade."

The floor creaked behind him, and then Sydney's soft hands were on his shoulders, curling over him. Her touch was warm, soft, and he remembered all the ways that she had touched him during their night together. The ways he'd touched her.

The ways he would touch her again.

He had Sydney now, and he didn't plan to let her go. Gunner turned toward her. His fingers skimmed over the curve of her cheek. He'd spent the past two years guarding her, determined to protect her from any danger that came their way.

Because Sydney seemed drawn to the danger.

She was the strongest woman he'd ever met, and her brain—hell, the things the lady could do with a computer amazed him. She'd been in the air force, he knew that. A lieutenant colonel. So in addition to her computer skills, there was no plane the woman couldn't fly. She'd flown their team out of more than a few hot spots around the world.

Slade had been a pilot, too. Not in the air force, though. His brother had done a stint in the army, then gotten civilian flying lessons after his tour of duty.

On a charter run to South America, Slade's plane had crashed in the wrong spot at the wrong time.

Against orders, Sydney and Gunner had gone in after him.

But they'd failed to bring him home.

"Gunner?" Her voice was soft.

He'd pulled her out of the jungle in Peru. He'd been so afraid she'd die on him. Her blood had stained his hands. She'd shuddered and jerked, cried out desperately.

For Slade.

But Gunner had been the one there for her. He'd always be there for her.

He offered her a smile, when he wasn't normally the type to smile. He wasn't like Cale or Logan. They could flirt and charm at will. He knew he had a dangerous edge. One that frightened more than it charmed.

But Sydney didn't seem frightened. He shook his head and asked, "Why?"

She blinked; then her blond eyebrows rose in confusion.

"Why me?" he asked her. He should have probably just kept quiet, but, hell, he was no prize. His body was scarred…sliced open, literally. He'd been caught by the enemy more times than he wanted to count. And during one bloody, pain-filled capture, he'd been sure that death would take him.

His captors had tied him up and come at him with a

knife. They'd wanted information. He hadn't given it to them, so they'd sliced him over and over on his stomach, his chest. Cuts meant to break him.

But he'd gotten away.

They'd died.

There was nothing light or easy about him—nothing safe.

So why in the hell did Sydney want to be with him? She could have anyone.

"What do you mean?" Sydney still seemed confused.

She was so beautiful. Fragile, though that delicacy was a deception, he knew.

"Why was it me…and not someone else?" Not that guy in the bar who'd had his hands all over her. Sydney could have taken another lover over the past two years. She hadn't. He knew because he always watched her too closely.

If she had tried to take another lover, what would he have done?

Better not think about it.

With her, his control could be a delicate thing. If she'd actually turned to another, Gunner wasn't sure that his control would have lasted. That *other* guy would have found himself in a battle.

"I'm with you because you remind me that I'm alive." Her smile seemed bittersweet. "When I'm with you, I feel. I want. I need."

He felt too much when he was with her. That was dangerous—for them both.

"I don't like being back here," she told him quietly, "but I'm glad that I'm with you." She rose onto her toes. Her lips brushed over his. "I've wanted to be with you for a long time."

He'd been rough with her before, so hungry and desper-

ate. This time, before the mission started, he was determined to use care with her. She deserved care.

Gunner lifted her up. Held her in his arms and then took
her to that big, giant bed. He laid her down, slowly stripped
her, kissed every inch of flesh that was revealed to him,
and he kept a stranglehold on his control.

This time, he'd show her the way things were supposed
to be between them. This time, it would all be for her.

He kissed her breasts, loving the tight peaks of her nipples. Like candy. So good and sweet and perfect for his
mouth. Her stomach dipped down, and he explored all of
her, sliding his fingers gently over her skin, over her sensitive core.

She arched against him, whispering his name.

He kept touching her, kissing and enjoying the silken
feel of her skin.

"Gunner, *I want you.*"

Those were the words he needed. He'd never be a stand-
in for a ghost, but Sydney wasn't asking for a stand-in. She
wanted him.

He pulled away from her just long enough to push down
his jeans. Then he positioned his body between her thighs.
One strong thrust—*yes*—and he drove into her, pleasure
pulsing along his aroused length.

Her legs wrapped around him. She urged him to thrust
deeper, harder, and he gave in to her. Moving quickly, wanting to give her as much pleasure as she could stand, wanting to give her everything.

When her body tensed beneath his, he knew her release
was close. His spine tingled, his body tightened, but he
forced himself to hold back.

He needed to feel her pleasure first.

Then she was gasping, calling his name, and her nails were scoring his shoulders. The pleasure washed across her face, brightening her eyes and flushing her cheeks.

Only then did he give in to his own need. He drove into her and let go.

The climax ripped through him, just as strong as the pleasure he'd gotten the night before.

He'd always known that Sydney was a dangerous woman, but he hadn't realized that once he'd had a taste of the paradise she offered, there would be no turning back.

THE RAP SOUNDED on their door an hour later. Gunner glanced up to see Sydney coming out of the shower. Her hair was still wet, and her clothes clung tightly to her body.

"Must be Cale...or Logan," she said, glancing toward the door.

Logan would know what they'd been up to. Even though they'd tried to fix the wrecked bed, Gunner knew that the minute Logan looked into his eyes, he would know.

Logan was his friend, and the man could read him too well.

Logan also knew well enough not to say a damn word that would make Sydney feel uncomfortable.

Gunner rose and headed for the door. He checked through the peephole and saw Logan staring straight ahead. After opening the door, Gunner stepped back so that Logan could enter.

Their team leader stalked inside, his body tight with tension.

Frowning, Gunner locked the door behind him.

"Did you get a visual?" Sydney asked as she approached him.

Logan gave a grim nod.

Then Gunner saw Logan's gaze sweep from Sydney, to the bed, to Gunner.

Logan's stare was…guarded. No emotion.

Gunner's gut clenched.

"Is Cale coming in for the update?" Sydney glanced toward the door. "I'm sure he needs to hear—"

"I need to talk to the two of you first." Logan's words were emotionless. Just like his eyes.

Gunner didn't like where this scene was going.

"Mercer…Mercer is the one who handed down this job. He asked *specifically* for our team to handle the mission."

"We are the best," Sydney said, grinning a bit.

Logan didn't smile. "He had a tip about the hostage, and he wanted us to follow up. *I* wanted to get a visual before I passed on the suspicions to the team."

"Just what kind of suspicions are we talking about?" Gunner crossed his hands over his chest and waited.

Sydney came to his side. Her grin was gone. Her shoulders brushed against his.

Logan's watchful gaze noted that light touch. His eyes narrowed, and he blew out a hard breath. "Mercer had intel that an American pilot was being held. A man with strong ties that could potentially be…manipulated by the group holding him."

"What kind of ties?" Sydney asked.

"Military ties to a covert team." Logan's shoulders straightened. "To *our* team."

Gunner's heartbeat kicked up.

"I saw the hostage earlier." Logan's hands were clenched. That wasn't a good sign. Not good at all. His gaze came back to Gunner. "I got the visual confirmation that we needed."

Why wasn't he just coming out and *saying*—

"The hostage…it's Slade."

Sydney's body swayed next to him, and Gunner automatically reached out, wrapping his hands around her shoulders.

Then he froze.

Slade?

"He's thinner. His hair's longer. He's got a beard and a limp but…*it's him*."

"Slade is dead." Sydney's voice was hushed.

Logan's gaze drifted to her. "No, he's not."

"We *buried* him."

Gunner felt like ice was wrapping around him. "We put a tombstone over an empty grave." He stepped toward Logan. "I saw him die. I was there." This couldn't be happening. "There was no pulse," he growled out the words. "I checked. There was no surviving the hits that Slade had taken. With that much blood loss…"

He'd been dead.

Because Gunner never would have left him if he thought his brother had still been alive.

"I saw him, Gunner. I. Saw. Him." Now Logan raked a hand through his hair, and Gunner realized just how agitated the team leader was. "The features are the same. Hell, I'm not one hundred percent on this…we'd need DNA for that…but the intel Mercer has…what I just saw…it *looks* like him."

"G-Gunner?" Sydney sounded shocked. Lost.

He couldn't look at her right then. Because he was afraid of what he might see in her eyes.

He'd had her beneath him on that bed, been inside her…

While his brother had been held captive in a camp.

Slade's fiancée.

"We're going to do more recon tonight. We don't have

time to waste. We need to use the darkness while we can," Logan said. His voice was stiff. "Syd, I'll need you to get working on the satellite imagery. We'll all go in to sweep the area. Then we'll plan for extraction at 0600."

Extraction.

His brother's extraction.

The silence in the room was too heavy.

"Gunner, I want to talk to you alone." Logan's words held the snap of command.

And Gunner realized he was staring at Logan, but seeing nothing.

But he gave a rough nod and turned toward the room's door. He brushed by Sydney—*can't look at her yet, can't*—because he didn't want to see the regret in her eyes.

She loved Slade, not him, and to find out that he might still be alive, after everything, had to be tearing her apart.

Logan shut the door after them. They were in the hallway. Alone. There was no sound from the room behind him.

Nothing at all.

"You gonna be able to handle this?" Logan whispered.

This? Finding my brother? Losing Sydney? Gunner nodded. "I'll get the mission done."

Logan grabbed his arm. "I saw the way you looked at her. I know you were *with* her in Baton Rouge." His voice was a bare whisper of sound. "Man, I'm so damn sorry."

Sorry that Slade was alive? They should be celebrating that miracle. Sydney would be celebrating.

And Gunner *was* glad. His brother's death had weighed on him for two years. They'd fought just before Slade's plane went down. Fought because...Slade knew how Gunner felt for Sydney.

Gunner had known that Slade didn't deserve her. He'd caught his brother cheating on Sydney, twice. He'd threatened to tell her the truth.

"You don't deserve her." That had been his snarl to Slade. But the truth was…

Neither of us deserved her.

But it looked as if one of them would still get her.

"Mercer wanted you on this mission because Slade's your blood, but the boss didn't know about you and Sydney—"

"There is no me and Sydney." He forced himself to say the words. There couldn't be a he and Sydney. Not now. Maybe after the mission, maybe after—

Stop lying to yourself.

His dream had ended, just as he'd known it would. But he'd just wanted more time with her.

More.

"Gunner…"

He shrugged away from Logan's hold. "We'll do the mission. We'll get him out—if he's Slade, if he's someone else…we'll get him out, either way." Because that was what they did.

The mission.

Always.

He hated the pity in Logan's eyes. He'd rather have seen the guarded mask come back.

"She wants you," Logan said.

Gunner stiffened. "She wanted to marry him."

Maybe it's not him. But Logan wouldn't have said that he thought it was, not unless the evidence he had was compelling.

Logan exhaled on a rough sigh. "We go out in an hour."

Gunner's head jerked in a nod.

"Gunner—"

He held up his hand. "Let's just get him free." That was all he could think right now. Do the mission. Save the hostage.

Let everything else go to hell.

"Okay." Logan's sigh was rough. "But you're to stand back on the actual extraction, got it? You'll provide the cover for the team."

The way he always did. Shooting, killing, from a distance.

"I'll need you and Syd to survey the area more. When I left, it looked like they were bringing in more men." He paused. "Are you going to stay in control?"

Sydney was the only one who could make him lose control. Sydney…who wasn't his.

"Yes." He didn't want the word to be a lie.

And maybe it wouldn't be.

He didn't walk back into the room with Sydney then. He walked down the hallway, went outside.

I shouldn't have touched her. I should have stayed away.

Because now—now he knew what he'd be losing.

What he'd lose, even as he found his brother again.

I'm sorry, Slade. Because he'd just taken the one thing that his brother loved most.

HER EAR WAS pressed to the door. The resort might be fancy, but the room doors were thin, and Sydney could hear every word that Gunner and Logan said.

There is no me and Sydney.

The words hurt her, pounding through the numbness that had surrounded her ever since Logan had said that Slade might be alive.

Alive? How was that even possible? Gunner had been so sure that he was dead, and she'd seen Slade's injuries. Too many injuries. Too much blood.

Slade had been dead. She'd been sure of it. If he hadn't been…

We left him alone? For two years?

A tear trekked down her cheek, and once more, she heard
Gunner's gruff words echo through her mind.

There is no me and Sydney.

Chapter Three

Gunner wouldn't look at her. Sydney crept quietly through the jungle, stepping so that she wouldn't so much as snap a twig, and she was too aware of the silence that came from the man behind her.

Cale and Logan were scouting on the west side of the area. She and Gunner were alone on the east side. The chirps and calls from the insects and creatures in the dark jungle drifted in the air.

And no sound came from Gunner.

She stopped. Took a deep breath, and turned to face him. "Say *something*."

The moon shone down on him, but she couldn't read his expression. Like Logan, Gunner was too skilled at hiding what he felt.

"Are you happy? Stunned? Talk to me!" Didn't he realize that he was her best friend? When she had a secret to share with someone, she always went to him.

He was her rock.

Her...lover.

Slade's alive.

"It was a mistake," Gunner told her.

Her heart slammed into her chest. "You don't think it's Slade?" Her voice was quiet, so she stepped closer to him.

So close that she could feel the seductive warmth of his body. "Logan's wrong and—"

"We were a mistake."

Her body trembled, but she kept her chin up. She kept her eyes on him only because she *wouldn't* break there, not in the jungle. Not in front of him. "Is that really how you feel?"

She didn't feel that way. Being with him had been the only thing that seemed right in her world.

Something that felt so amazing, no, it couldn't be a mistake.

"It won't happen again. We won't be together again."

A bullet wound would probably hurt less. Actually, she knew from personal experience that it would. "It might not even be him." Her hoarse voice. But it was true. She'd given up on Slade, put him to rest and moved on.

"And if it is?" Now Gunner was the one to take a step toward her. "I *left* him. I thought he was dead. If he was alive, for all this time, do you know the hell he would have been put through by his captors?"

She didn't want to think too much about that. She *couldn't* think about it now.

"I'm his older brother. I was supposed to keep him safe." Disgust tightened his mouth. "Not screw his fiancée."

Pinpricks of heat shot across her cheeks. "Is that what you did? Because I thought we'd been making love."

Her mistake.

"We need to finish scouting so we can secure the area. "Now isn't the time to talk about this."

Right. Of course. But would there ever be a time when he wanted to talk? "It was more to me," she said, and turned away.

That was when she realized...all of the chirps and calls had stopped. The jungle was eerily silent around them, and clouds were starting to drift across the surface of the moon, making the shadows even darker.

Sydney brought up her weapon, and she knew Gunner was doing the same. She stepped forward, her body tensing now. Something had changed in the jungle. Shifted.

She and Gunner had been hunting before, but now she had the feeling that they were the prey.

The rebel camp should have been about a mile away. No one should be in their immediate area.

But the brush was so thick and heavy.

Sweat coated Sydney's back and slicked her fingers as she held her weapon.

Then she heard it. The snap of a twig. Twenty feet to the left. She swung around with her gun.

Another twig snapped.

That snapping came from thirty feet to the right.

Trouble.

She felt, rather than saw, Gunner's movements as he swung to the right. One word whispered through her mind: *surrounded.*

Her breath barely left her lungs. She reached up with her left hand and tapped the communicator near her ear. "Alpha One…" Her words were a whisper as she signaled Logan. "We've got movement in our perimeter. There's—"

Footsteps thundered toward them, coming fast and hard. She took aim, ready to shoot, but then she saw the hostage. A man who was being pushed through the jungle, with some kind of brown sack over his head. His hands were bound in front of him, and a gun was pressed to the top right side of that sack, just where his temple would be. A flashlight was held on the man, the better for them to see just what trump card the captors held.

"Deje caer sus armas!" The shout came from the man who held the gun. *Drop your weapons.*

Sydney took aim at him. *"Deje caer sus armas!"* She snarled right back at him.

He wasn't alone. There was another armed man who'd come out from the right side. Sydney had heard his rushing footsteps. Gunner hadn't fired on him, because, like her, he had to be worried about the hostage.

An innocent getting injured in a firefight wasn't on the agenda.

But neither was getting captured.

A radio crackled behind her. The other man was calling for backup. If they didn't do something, soon, this mission was about to go bad.

I shouldn't have gotten distracted. This is my fault. I should have kept walking, kept searching the area. But I was too caught up in Gunner.

Now they were both in trouble.

The man near the hostage laughed and shook his head. *"Voy a disparar contra él."*

I will shoot him. Yes, she'd just bet that he'd shot plenty of men in his time.

"Please!" The broken cry came from the hostage. "Help me!"

"We will," Sydney promised him, but she wasn't dropping her gun yet.

Only…a weapon *did* hit the ground. She turned at the thud. Gunner had tossed away his gun. His hands were up. What was he doing? Surrender wasn't the way the team operated.

"Sydney?" It was Cale's voice in her ear. If she could hear him, Gunner could, too. They were all on the same comm link. "We're coming for you."

But would he come soon enough?

Gunner walked forward, putting his body before her.

Sydney didn't know if he was protecting her or blocking her shot, but either way, the result was the same.

"No dispare," Gunner said, voice loud and carrying easily. With the transmitter so close to his mouth, Cale would hear every word and understand exactly what was happening to them. *"Puede tener tres rehenes en lugar de dos."*

Don't shoot. You can have three hostages instead of two.

That was a terrible plan.

But then she felt the cold metal of a gun being shoved against the base of her neck.

It looked as though it was their only plan, for the moment.

Sydney let her weapon drop, and she lifted her hands in surrender.

Cale, hurry up, she thought.

Because she wasn't sure how much time they had.

HE'D MADE A deadly mistake.

Gunner sat in the old chair, his hands tied behind him, his ankles lashed to the wooden chair legs. A heavy black sack covered his head. When he strained his eyes, he could just make out a form across from him. The shadowy outline of— "Sydney?" he rasped.

"Yes."

He'd been distracted by her in the jungle. Too aware of her every move. He should have been on the lookout for the enemy, but they'd gotten the drop on him.

On Sydney. As if they were both rookies.

Now the hostage was gone, taken to another tent, and he and Sydney were about to be interrogated.

The last time he'd been interrogated in a South American jungle, he'd had to spend six hours getting enough stitches to close all of the wounds in his body.

Those stitches had been given to him by a relief worker

on the edge of a river. There'd been no anesthesia. He'd roared at the pain.

And called Sydney's name.

Something he'd never told her. What would have been the point?

"It was his voice," Gunner growled as he yanked against his bonds. "You know it was him." There were guards right outside their tent. Guards who'd foolishly thought that they'd taken all of his weapons.

Not that Gunner needed a weapon to kill. He was very good with his hands.

As his last interrogators had discovered.

"I—I can't remember his voice." Her words were soft. Sad. "It's been too long for me, Gunner."

He stilled. That *had* been his brother's voice, hadn't it? Because if it hadn't, then he'd dropped his gun for no damn reason.

I could have taken them out. But he wouldn't have been able to do it without hurting the hostage. If that had been his brother, then Slade had already been hurt enough. Gunner wasn't going to add to the man's pain.

Gunner cleared his throat. "Are you bound?"

"Tied like a pig, with a sack over my head."

He'd thought so, but they'd been separated on the way to the camp. Then he hadn't heard her voice for a while, and he'd...worried. "We're gonna get out of here." His comm transmitter was gone. Taken and smashed in the jungle, just as hers had been.

But this camp wasn't in the location that they'd been told of. Either Logan had been given bad intel or the group had a second and, from the sound of things, much larger base. Because they'd walked east. Been dumped into the back of a vehicle, and they'd zigged and zagged through the jungle before they'd stopped.

Good thing he and Sydney were both equipped with a special GPS locator, courtesy of Uncle Sam. They both had trackers inserted just beneath their skin. Cale and Logan would be able to find them; it was just a matter of time.

"We'll get out of here," Gunner told her as he twisted his wrists. The ropes were rough, and he could feel them tearing into his skin. So what if he got cut? The blood would just make it easier for him to break loose.

Then he heard voices outside. The group leader's voice— that would be the one who'd come for them in the jungle. The one who'd held the hostage and laughed as he stared into Gunner's eyes.

"Sounds like the fun is about to start," Sydney said. There was no fear in her voice. She could have been terrified, and he wouldn't have known. She was in her mission mode now.

"We'll get out of here." He needed her to understand that.

He heard the rustle of the tent's opening. Footsteps came closer. He listened carefully and counted the tread of those footsteps…two men.

One man went to stand behind him.

The other— "You shouldn't have come into my jungle." Heavily accented English, and Gunner knew it was the leader. The guy was standing right in front of him. He could make out the outline of the man's body through the fabric of the sack that covered him.

He could see the guy's body and see the weapon that the man lifted and pointed toward Sydney. "Coming here was a terrible mistake for you both."

"Stop!" Gunner barked, heart racing.

Laughter. Low. Sinister. From the man with the gun. The rebel behind Gunner didn't make a sound.

Rebels…what cause were they fighting for? As far as he

could tell, Logan thought this group was little more than drug runners. Weapons dealers.

"I am not going to shoot the señorita yet. Not just yet." But he still had the weapon near her head. "First, you talk, *si?* You tell me all about your team. About the men who think they can come into my jungle and take what is mine."

The rope cut deeper into Gunner's wrists. "There is no team. Just us."

Silence. Then, "I can start by shooting her in the knee, if you want."

"There is no team!" Sydney snapped at him.

But Gunner didn't speak. The man's words were replaying in his head. *"I can start by shooting her in the knee."*

"You both wore...what are they? Ah...transmitters of some sort. That means you were talking to someone else."

"There is no team," Gunner said woodenly, because that was the response he had to give. When the enemy caught you, you didn't turn. You didn't reveal your intel, and you didn't jeopardize the others still out in the field.

"So sad." Now the man's voice had deepened. Behind him, Gunner heard the other rebel shifting from foot to foot. "He must not care for you at all, señorita."

Gunner yanked on the ropes. They weren't giving. Not yet.

"I don't like hurting women. It's not in my nature, but..." A regretful sigh drifted in the air. "If I do not learn what I must know, there will be no choice for me."

"Let her go!" Gunner demanded as fury swirled inside him. "That's the only choice you need to make."

"No, I need to know about your team. About your... EOD."

Gunner's mind whirled. The rebel—no way should he have known about the Elite Ops Division. They were off the books for a reason.

Classified cases. Classified kills.

"How many EOD agents are in Peru?"

"I don't know what the EOD is," Gunner told him.

A growl broke from the man behind him, and Gunner felt the blade of a knife slice through the sack and press right against his throat.

"Ah…I'm afraid my companion is more impatient than I am."

The companion…he'd moved quickly but wasn't getting a reprimand of any sort by the guy Gunner had pegged as the leader. Unusual. Very unusual. Leaders didn't usually like it when someone jumped the gun.

Maybe he isn't the leader.

Maybe the real leader was the man getting ready to slice open his throat.

The man with the knife hadn't said a word, but the other guy kept talking, throwing out, "Her life doesn't matter to you, but what about your own? Care to tell us about the EOD…now?"

"We don't know what you're talking about!" The angry words came from Sydney. "We can't tell you when we don't know!"

Sydney had been trained not to break, too. They'd both learned how to hold out against torture.

But would he really be able to sit there, while Syndey was hurting? If he heard Sydney in pain, Gunner was afraid that his control would shatter.

The ropes began to give way even as the knife blade pressed deeper into his skin.

"We have intel…that is what you call it, *si?* We have intel of our own, and we know who you both are. We lured you to us because we have…interests…who are after the EOD."

Interests? Would that be the same interested party who had sent out hits on the EOD agents in the U.S. a while back?

"You cannot tell, señorita, but your friend's throat is bleeding. There's a knife against his jugular, and if I don't learn what I must know, then I will tell my associate to kill him."

Gunner heard the sound of Sydney's sharply indrawn breath. Then… "Gunner?"

"It's a scratch," he told her, keeping his voice flat. "I do worse than this when I shave in the morning."

The knife pressed harder.

Gunner laughed. "You think this is torture? You boys need to up your game."

"Perhaps we will," the man said, voice snarling. "But I do not think that we need to keep both of you. We already have one hostage, why keep two more?"

Hell. He'd been afraid of this.

Logan and Cale need to hurry the hell up.

"So, which will we eliminate? The lovely lady or the man who thinks he can laugh at death?"

Gunner knew exactly what choice they needed to make. So he laughed again, mocking them, wanting to draw their attention and do anything necessary to ensure Sydney's survival. "You aren't killing us. You're all talk and—"

Blood slid down his neck.

"—and when I get out of here," Gunner continued, voice roughening, "you'll be the ones to die." The words were a promise. "So, what you need to be doing is running, while you still can."

Was the gun still pressed to Sydney's head? He hoped not. He wanted that gun—and the attention of the two men—focused just on him.

He'd buy Sydney as much survival time as he could. Cale and Logan would come, sooner or later. She just had to live until then.

My fault. I dropped my guard in the jungle. I got distracted by her. She won't be dying for my mistake.

"Who is your hostage?" Sydney's voice came, louder and sharper than he'd expected. She should have stayed quiet. Didn't she realize what he was trying to do?

"You come into my jungle," their captor said, "trying to rescue a man you don't even know?"

"It's my job," Sydney snapped.

"You shouldn't have done this job. You should have just left him to die." There was the rustle of clothing, and Gunner saw the shadow of their captor's body shift. He thought the man was coming toward him, but—*no*. He heard the man step closer to Sydney.

And the knife was suddenly gone from Gunner's throat. The guard's footsteps shuffled behind Gunner as the man moved back.

They were told, "It's time to lose a hostage. Do you want a moment to say your goodbyes?"

Both men were near Sydney now. He could see the dark outlines of their bodies through his mask. "Don't you even *think* of killing her!"

"As if you could stop us…"

"It's all right, Gunner," Sydney said at the same time. "It's all right."

No, it wasn't. They should be turning their attention on him. Not her. "What kind of coward holds a woman prisoner like this?"

The men didn't speak.

Sydney did. "Gunner, can you close your eyes?"

Because she must have on a covering just like his. She'd be able to see a little bit, just as he could. And Sydney didn't want him seeing her die.

"Yes," he said, even as he kept his eyes wide open. This wasn't happening. He wouldn't let it happen. Not to her.

He yanked on the rope that bound his wrists. Felt it give way. Just. In. Time.

"Thank you," Sydney said softly. "And, Gunner, I—"

An explosion rocked the tent, and Gunner's chair fell to the side. He yanked out with his hands, shattering the chair legs and pulling free from the ropes that bound his legs.

Voices were crying out. Yelling. And more explosions—they sounded like thunder, but he could feel the heat from the blasts—blasted through the camp. Footsteps pounded out of the room. More shouts.

More fire. He could smell the acrid scent.

"Sydney!"

He yanked the sack off his head and rushed to her. She'd fallen back, too, and, at first, he didn't think she was moving at all. Had they killed her before the explosion? Had that sick jerk with the knife hurt her?

But then she groaned, and he saw her hands come up. She'd worked her wrists free, too. Of course she had. That was his Sydney.

He clawed away the ropes that bound her feet and jerked that sack from over her eyes. With his breath heaving, he stared down at her, desperately looking for blood.

Her eyes were wide and bright. As always, she was the most beautiful thing he'd ever seen. He wanted to kiss her so badly that he ached.

Slade's alive.

He swallowed and pulled Sydney to her feet. "What the hell were you doing?" Gunner demanded. "I wanted their attention on me."

She blinked, and some of the brightness seemed to leave her gaze. "Sorry, I was just doing my part to keep you breathing." She bent down and picked up a sharp chunk of wood, one of the remnants from her chair's legs. "You're welcome."

His hold on her left wrist tightened. "Next time, try to keep yourself alive instead." Because to him, she was the priority.

Gunfire burst out into the night then, firing with a *rat-a-tat* that was too familiar to him. "Our backup is here." Just in time. He'd have to thank Cale and Logan with a round of beer later.

After they all got out of that jungle.

First order of business…get better weapons. That wood of Sydney's wouldn't last long. They'd get weapons, then hurry out there to provide support to the other EOD agents.

Moving like shadows, he and Sydney slid to the front of their tent. Their guards were gone. From what Gunner could see, chaos had taken over the camp. Men were running everywhere, shooting wildly.

Cale wouldn't be positioned close, and those shots being fired so wildly from the rebels *wouldn't* hit him. The guy was a sniper, too. Not ex-SEAL like Gunner, but a Ranger sniper who'd survived some of the deadliest places on earth.

Cale's shots were deliberate, timed perfectly. Gunner realized that the explosions had been his handiwork, too. Cale knew far too much about demolitions.

Gunner scanned the area and found his target. Fifteen feet away. The man who was holding up his gun and staring into the jungle, not even glancing around to cover his back.

"I've got you," Sydney said. "Go ahead."

She'd be covering Gunner's back. He knew he could count on her.

He might be a sniper, but he could still handle up close combat just fine. He'd learned those fighting techniques long before he'd let Uncle Sam talk him into being all he could be.

Gunner rushed silently forward. His target never had a chance to fight him, much less to fire his weapon. Gunner swiped out with his hands, an attack designed to take out his opponent, and before the man's body fell, Gunner had the fellow's gun in his hand.

One weapon down.

He looked up, saw that Sydney was close. She gave him a grim nod.

Just then one of the guards ran out of another tent, screaming and aiming his gun at her head.

No. Gunner lifted his gun instantly. Sydney must have read the danger in his eyes because she dropped to the ground, giving him the perfect shot.

But as he fired, another blast thundered.

Two bullets hit the guard, stopping his attack.

Cale? Probably. The other sniper was doing his job and making sure they got out of there alive.

Sydney didn't stand. Instead, she crawled quickly toward the downed man and took his weapon.

Now that they were both better armed, it was time to search. Because they weren't running out of that camp, weren't fleeing. They'd come there for a reason.

Find the hostage. They'd complete their mission.

We're coming, Slade.

Most of the rebels were fleeing. Some jumped into old trucks; others just ran into the jungle. The explosions had scared them. It looked as though they weren't quite up for trading their lives for their cause.

The more of them that left, well, the easier the EOD's mission became. He and Sydney searched the tents, one after the other. Deserted. Burning. No sign of Slade.

But he *had* to be there.

Or...maybe he was close by. Just through the patch of jungle on the right, Gunner could see the outline of old stones. Big, sprawling, the structure looked like some kind of deserted temple.

Sydney was already nodding, because she'd spotted the structure, too. Gunfire erupted behind Gunner, and he turned, firing back. "Go!" he ordered Sydney. If Slade was out there, they had to get to him. He could be hurt, dying…

Gunner saw Logan appear, and the team leader joined the firefight. Sydney rushed toward the temple.

The bullets kept coming. A lucky shot grazed Gunner's left arm, and he clenched his teeth at the flash of pain.

Then he took aim at the men coming for him.

Chapter Four

Sydney's heartbeat echoed in her ears as she ran toward the narrow entrance to what she could only guess was some kind of crumbling temple. Giant slabs of white rock were turned, forming the sloping entrance. But…there was light coming from inside that temple. And where there was light…

Sydney lifted her gun and went in low. She didn't know what kind of angry reception she'd find waiting for her, but she had to do this search and get back to help Gunner. She had to—

A man was tied to a chair, bound, the way she'd been moments before. He looked like the same man she'd seen in the jungle, because he was wearing that same brown sack over his head. A lantern sat near his feet, revealing his old, ragged pants.

She approached him cautiously. No one else appeared to be in the area, but she didn't want to take any chances. She checked every shadowed space, then eased closer to the bound man.

He stiffened as she drew nearer. His sagging head snapped up. "Who's there?" he demanded.

She wanted to say the voice was familiar to her. Gunner had been so sure it was Slade's voice that they'd heard in the jungle. But Sydney just didn't know. The only voice she knew by heart?

Gunner's rough, rumbling drawl.

"I'm here to help you," she whispered to him. She'd shoved that sharp chunk of wood in her belt, and now she pulled it out and began to saw against his binds with it. "Don't move."

But a shudder ran the length of the man's body. "Talk to me again. I know…"

She frowned at him. She should just take off the sack, find out for certain who this man was. But she was afraid.

And she wasn't usually afraid.

"What do you know?" Sydney asked him.

"I know…" A heaving breath. *"You."*

Her makeshift weapon cut through the binds on his wrists. There was no rope on his ankles, and he surged to his feet. As he turned toward her, he yanked off the sack that covered his head. In that dim lantern light, Sydney got her first look at the hostage's face.

The world seemed to slow its spinning.

His hair was longer, his beard heavy, but…those cheekbones. That hawkish nose.

"Sydney…"

He yanked her into his arms. His mouth pressed to hers, and she was so stunned that she couldn't respond, couldn't move at all.

Slade?

He'd been alive. They'd left him, and he'd been…alive.

His mouth was hard on hers. So hard.

She pulled back, staring up at him in shock. "Slade?"

She realized the gunfire had stopped. *A good sign…or a very bad one.* Sydney pushed away from Slade and glanced toward that sloping entrance.

A man stood there. Tall, with wide shoulders, armed. A man who'd been watching them.

He stepped forward, and the lantern light spilled onto Gunner. It was too dark for her to see the expression in his eyes, but his body looked tense.

"Slade?" Gunner's voice was hoarse as he lowered his weapon.

Slowly, Slade turned to face his brother. Slade was thinner—*much thinner*—than he'd been before.

Two years.

Gunner began to walk toward Slade with slow, hesitant steps. "I—I thought you were dead."

Slade shuffled toward him, limping slightly.

Gunner lifted his arms to embrace his brother.

Slade drove his fist into Gunner's jaw.

"Slade!" Sydney shouted.

But Slade wasn't stopping. He attacked Gunner, pummeling him with his fists, kicking him with his legs. Again and again.

Gunner didn't fight back. Didn't try to land a blow, didn't try to block any of the attacks. Gunner fell, and Slade kicked his ribs. Driving in hard with his boot-covered feet.

"Stop!" Sydney grabbed Slade's arm. But he swung around and shoved her back, so hard that she slammed into the rough wall behind her.

"Sydney?" Gunner's growl. And he was rising then.

Even as Slade stood over *her* now, with his fist drawn back as if he'd strike her.

He's been through hell. He doesn't realize what he's doing. Sydney cleared her throat. "You have to calm down, Slade."

Gunfire burst again, sounding as if the blasts came from just yards away.

Sydney shook her head and rose fully to her feet. She

kept her gun in her hand. She'd do whatever was necessary to stop the men from tearing each other apart. "We have to get out of here. Do you understand?"

Slade's breaths sawed in and out of his lungs.

"Slade, do you understand?" There wasn't time to waste. The rebels who'd fled before...what if they'd gone out to get reinforcements? Their EOD team was good, but it was just the four of them against a small army.

Slade nodded. "I...understand."

Gunner was on his feet. Blood dripped from his busted lip.

"Then you stay between me and Gunner when we go out of here. You do exactly what we say."

Slade glanced at Gunner. Even in the dark, she could feel Slade's rage.

Rage? At the brother he'd loved so much?

More gunfire. Then...silence.

"Let's go," Sydney whispered. She had to focus on just getting Slade out of there. They'd deal with everything else once they were in a secure location. The temple looked as if it would fall on them all any second. Not secure at all.

She led the men out, and Gunner closed in behind Slade. She searched first, making sure it was clear to run, and then they were moving, rushing forward and staying within the cover of trees as much as possible.

And she saw Logan firing at a man who'd rushed up toward him. The man fell, and Logan kept running, motioning for Sydney and her group to join him.

She was more than happy to follow him out of that place.

They went to the left, to the right, following a trail that only existed in Logan's mind. Then, beneath the hanging vines of a twisted tree, she saw a jeep, half-hidden by the foliage. Logan jumped in the front of the vehicle.

"Get in!" Logan yelled.

She grabbed Slade's arm and helped hoist him inside and as soon as his feet touched down—

Gunner knocked Sydney to the ground. Two *cracks* of gunfire sounded, and a bullet slammed into the jeep, exactly where she had been about two seconds ago.

His gaze bored into hers. The sun was just starting to rise, still not giving her enough light to gauge the expression in his eyes, and she wished that she could see so much more.

Logan returned fire on the enemy.

Gunner hauled her up, shielded her with his body, and all but tossed her into the jeep.

Then Logan was taking off and rushing away from the battle. Yanking on the wheel, finding a road—well, not a road so much, just a space between trees that most would never have known existed.

The jeep slowed for an instant, and Cale jumped from the shadows and slid into the back.

Then they kept going.

Faster, faster.

Until the gunfire sounded like fireworks in the distance. Until Sydney could breathe without tasting smoke.

She looked around her slowly. Gunner was pressed tightly to her side, and he had a hard grip on her wrist, as if he were afraid that she was going to try to get away from him.

Slade was on his other side. Not speaking. Barely seeming to move at all.

She stared down at Gunner's hand. Very slowly, his hold eased.

Then he wasn't holding her at all.

"Slade Ortez?" Logan said as he gripped the steering wheel.

"Yes." A word that barely rose above the roar of the motor.

"You're going to be safe now," Logan told him. "We're going to get you home."

Gunner wasn't touching her now, wasn't looking at anyone.

She frowned at him, and realized that she could smell blood.

Sydney's hands flew over Gunner.

"Stop!" he told her.

She wasn't going to stop touching him because, right there, high on his left shoulder, she'd just felt something wet and sticky. Blood. "You were shot."

His fingers curled around hers. Pushed her hand away. "It's nothing."

Yes, it was a *bullet wound.* Not some nick. "Is the bullet still in you?"

He didn't answer, and that silence *was* an answer for her.

"You deserve more than that!" came Slade's snarling voice. *"Brother."* The word sounded like a curse. "You deserve to die."

Sydney gasped at the words. "Slade, you don't even know what you're saying!" She remembered Gunner shoving her to the ground. The bullet that had hit the side of the jeep. Only…hadn't she heard two shots then? Two shots, but only one bullet had gone into the jeep.

The other bullet had been meant to go in her.

Gunner took a bullet for me.

"I know…exactly…what I'm saying," Slade growled.

No, he didn't. He'd been in captivity. Been hurt, tortured, but the man talking, that *wasn't* the man she knew. "Gunner just risked his life for you."

They all had.

"The bullet has to come out," she whispered to Gunner. She tried to inspect the wound again.

He gave a grim nod. But...he pushed her hand away once more.

The move just hurt.

"When we're secure," Gunner said, no emotion slipping into his voice. "I can handle it 'til then."

Of course he could. Gunner could handle anything. Handle it, and keep on going. Never showing emotion.

While emotions were about to rip her apart.

They didn't immediately head for civilization. If they were being tailed, they didn't want anyone following them.

They changed vehicles. Once. Twice. Logan picked up the emergency cash that had been sent ahead for the mission, and only *then* did they head back for the coast. The sun was rising in the sky, and Sydney glanced over to see the haggard lines on Slade's face.

He'd aged ten years in two.

The laughing man she'd known was gone. He'd never be coming back.

And as for Gunner...

His eyes weren't meeting hers. He talked only when he had to do so, and the scent of his blood was still heavy in the air.

She pulled her gaze from his. The jungle was behind them, the gunfire just a memory. They'd all changed clothes at their last stop. Gunner had shoved a makeshift bandage over his wound, to stop the blood from leaking through to his clothes.

They didn't look as if they'd just spent the night in the jungle. More as if they'd just been partying too much.

Except for Slade. New clothes hadn't been able to change his appearance that much. Gaunt, grizzled. He would need more care than a five-minute pit stop could give him.

They weren't headed back to their original resort. No, she'd made different arrangements for their accommodations postrescue. It was always important to switch bases—the better to throw off the enemy—and she'd planned for the switch.

They were headed to villas now, private villas on the beach. High-end, far away from anything but luxury. Not a place the rebel group should think to look for government agents. And that was why it would be such a perfect hiding spot.

Not that they'd be hiding for long. Soon enough, they'd all be heading back for the U.S.

Logan and Cale took care of getting the keys to the villas. Three of them, all far away from the rest, nestled on a secluded strip of beach.

Slade climbed from the vehicle, and, for a moment, he just stared at that long, stretching coast.

Gunner followed him out, and Sydney caught the faint tremble of his body. *Get the bullet out.* Her gaze met Cale's, and the ex-Ranger gave a quick nod.

They forced Gunner into the first villa. Literally had to drag the guy in.

But they got him in.

"I can handle this!" Gunner muttered.

Logan tossed Sydney a first aid bag. She caught it easily and shot a glare at Gunner. "No," she said definitely, "you can't." She sucked in a breath, then ordered, "Now take off that shirt."

Slade, Logan and Cale were all in the villa, but it was a big space, with a living area, a kitchen and two bedrooms.

Gunner stripped off his shirt, and the breath she'd just sucked in burned in her throat at the sight of his bloody shoulder. "Lie down, Gunner. Go get on the bed." She hurried to the bathroom in order to get soap and water.

When she came back, Gunner was lying tensely on the

bed. Logan and Cale had Slade in the living area, giving her some privacy to work on Gunner.

She leaned over the bed, her knee dipping into the mattress.

Gunner caught her hand. "Don't tell him," he growled.

Her eyebrows lowered. "What are you talking about?" But the tightness in her gut told her even before he said...

"Don't tell Slade about us." The words seemed so cold. Or maybe she was just cold. "He doesn't ever need to know."

He could have just slapped her. "What about what I need?"

His jaw locked. "You need *him,* right?" he gritted out. "He was the one you loved. The one you were going to marry."

She pulled her hand from him and went to work cleaning his wound. She would *not* look into his eyes. Now she was the one who didn't want to see what expression stared back at her.

"I—I don't have anything to numb the area."

"Pain doesn't matter."

Always so tough. "Why do you have to pretend you don't feel?" The words tore from her. "When we both know that you do."

"Feeling can be dangerous."

She hadn't expected that answer, and, helplessly, her gaze flew back up to his.

His dark stare was burning with emotion, with *feeling.*

"So dangerous," he whispered.

Her heart slammed into her ribs. She put her left hand on his shoulder, carefully; then she used tweezers that she'd sterilized to go into the wound. She was lucky. No, he was. The bullet hadn't fragmented. She pulled it out, wincing for him, but of course, the man made of steel didn't even flinch.

She cleaned the wound, got a better bandage and finished patching him up.

Then she kept…touching him.

Why was touching him such an addiction to her? Warm skin, hard muscles.

"Don't, Sydney." His warning.

A warning that came too late for her.

She stared at his face. At his lips. She'd heard another woman once say that Gunner had cruel lips. Tight. Hard. She'd never found them to be cruel. She'd never found him to be cruel at all. Controlled and dangerous, yes. Cruel?

Not Gunner.

"Your lip is busted." She reached for another cloth, blotted the blood away. "You didn't even try to defend yourself."

Voices rose and fell from the outer room. Logan and Cale, questioning Slade.

Slade.

For months, she'd dreamed of him being found alive. Of him coming home to her. And she was glad, so glad, that he'd been rescued. She would have risked her life a dozen times to get him out of that camp.

But…

She would also risk her life a dozen times—gladly—for Gunner.

That wasn't right, was it? A woman shouldn't feel so torn between two men.

A man she'd once said she'd marry.

And a man…a man who had carried her through the darkness. A man who made her ache, even now, for *him.*

The door she'd shut banged open against the wall. "Sydney!"

Slade's voice.

"Get away from him," Slade ordered.

She blinked and realized that, yes, she was pretty much

draped over Gunner. Her hands were on him, and he—he wasn't touching her with his hands. His hands had flattened against the bed.

Slowly, she eased back and stood on her feet, deliberately positioning herself near the bed. Near Gunner.

"Did you get the bullet?" Logan asked her, voice cautious.

Sydney nodded. "He's good now."

"No, he's *not!*" Slade lunged forward, and Cale actually had to grab him and hold him back. Slade had been going forward with his hands clenched into fists and rage blazing in his eyes. "He's a bastard who deserves to suffer!"

"He just saved you," Logan said, putting his body right in front of Slade's. "Listen, I understand that you've been through hell—"

Slade's brittle laughter broke through his words. "You understand *nothing. You hear me? Nothing! You think that guy over there is your friend? That you can trust him? Hell, no,* you can't. He'll turn on you, just like he turned on me." Spittle flew from his mouth.

Gunner eased from the bed. He was shirtless but still wearing his pants and boots.

His body brushed by Sydney's as he headed toward Slade.

"Yeah, yeah, *come on!*" Slade dared him. "Fight me like a man. Take me on…and don't just leave me to rot in a jungle like you did before!"

Leave me to rot…

"He didn't!" Sydney cried out, shaking her head. "Slade, we thought you were dead! That was the only reason we left. If we'd known the truth, we would never have left you in that jungle."

His twisted grin called her words a lie. "*He* knew."

What?

Slade pulled away from Cale and pointed one shaking finger at Gunner. "That bastard, my *brother,* knew."

Sydney shook her head.

Gunner just stared back at Slade.

"It's easy enough to tell if a man's breathing or not," Slade continued. "Especially for someone with Gunner's special training."

Sydney took a step forward. "We *both* thought you were dead! We were in a firefight. You went down, and there was so much blood…"

Slade yanked open his shirt, revealed the scars on his chest. She knew those marks. Bullet wounds. "I was down, not dead." Then he looked back up at Gunner. "But you were hoping I'd die, right? Just leave me to bleed out, and that way, you never had to get your hands dirty."

This was crazy.

She met Logan's stare. Logan looked…angry? But guarded. Why? He was Gunner's friend. He knew better than to believe these accusations. They all knew better. "You're traumatized," she told Slade. "Not thinking clearly. When we get back to the States, everything will be—"

"He wanted you."

The words fell heavily into the room.

Gunner tensed. She saw the muscles of his chest and shoulders tighten.

She cleared her throat. "I—I know things are confusing for you, Slade." *Two years of hell and pain.* "But Gunner loves you. He would never have left you if he'd known—"

"He. Wanted. You."

Slade's blazing stare seemed to scorch her skin with his rage.

Sydney shook her head.

"I was in his way," Slade said. His eyes were bloodshot. Wild. "So he saw a way to take me out."

"This is crazy! We were in Peru back then to *save* you. Your plane went down. We came in to get you out! Why come in at all if we just wanted to leave you to die?" Surely he'd realize that his words didn't make sense. He'd start to understand, to see reason.

But his hands were fisting again. "*You* wanted to save me. He followed you here, because he couldn't stop you then. He was waiting for his moment, just waiting…willing to do anything to get you."

Gunner had asked her not to tell Slade about them. But Slade was acting as if—

"He got you, didn't he? I can *see* it in his eyes."

Her cheeks burned.

"Enough." Gunner's snarl.

"Not even close," Slade fired right back. "They tortured me, for *two years*. And during all those months, just how many times did you make love with my—"

Gunner lunged forward. This time, he was the one who had to be pulled back. Logan grabbed him and held on tight.

"Let him come at me! Let him take me on…instead of running away with *my* girl!"

"Stop." The quiet word broke from Sydney. Her head was throbbing. For all of the times that she'd imagined Slade's rescue, she'd never imagined *this* scenario. "Just…*stop*." Then she was marching toward Slade. "He had to drag me out of the jungle. I almost died, too. He was shot, so many times, we were both barely moving." Why couldn't he understand what had happened?

Slade glared down at her. "You moved well enough to survive."

Her chin lifted. "Search parties were sent after you. Again and again. We kept looking."

"Not hard enough."

The rage in him seemed to burn past any control.

"Get him out of here," Logan ordered, giving a jerk of his head toward Cale. "Put him in the second villa, guard him and make sure he cools down."

Cale put a hand on Slade's shoulder.

Slade immediately jerked away from him. "Don't believe me?" His voice rose. "None of you believe me? You think you can *trust* him? That I'm crazy?" He laughed again. The sound was rough and wild. "Then just...*ask him.*"

She glanced at Gunner. Logan had released him, and now Gunner stood as still as a statue. The white bandage was a stark contrast to his tanned skin.

"Ask him, Sydney. You do it," Slade urged. "Because it's all about you, right?"

"No, it isn't." The throbbing in her head was getting worse.

But Slade kept talking. This wasn't the man she remembered. So much rage. "Ask him!" Slade yelled. "Ask him if he wanted you, even then."

She stared at Gunner. His eyelashes lifted and his gaze held hers.

She couldn't bring herself to ask the question.

"Take him out," Logan ordered again.

"I saw the way you looked at her then. The way you look at her now! I was in the way!"

Cale pulled Slade toward the door.

Slade kept shouting. "You saw your chance, and you took it. You played hero to her, but you left me to die! You got just what you wanted—*her!*"

Sydney flinched.

"Tell her!" Slade was fighting against Cale's hold. "Tell her the truth. She deserves it! We both do! Look at her. Look at Sydney and tell her how you felt about her...tell her about all the times you'd watch her when you didn't think anyone saw." His voice dropped. "But I saw. I always saw."

His voice was ugly and mean and he was so far from the Slade that she'd remembered. Captivity could twist a man— or a woman—she knew that. It would take months, maybe even years of therapy before the Slade she knew returned.

If he ever did.

"I knew you wanted her, but she wanted *me!* She wasn't going to you, not while I was there. So you got me out of the way." Slade's chest heaved.

She stared at him, seeing past the long hair and beard. His nose had been broken. She could see the rough bump along its bridge. There was a long, thin scar under his right eye. Another scar bisecting his left eyebrow. And that limp…

"Tell her!"

But Gunner wasn't talking.

Cale had Slade near the entrance to the villa now, but all of a sudden, Slade stopped struggling. His cheeks were flushed dark red, his eyes glittered, but his body just froze.

Then he looked at Sydney. "Shouldn't he be defending himself?" Now his voice was flat. From screaming to flat.

Sydney shivered.

"Shouldn't he be trying to tell you that I've got it all wrong?" His voice seemed hoarse. "Why isn't he talking?"

Why wasn't she? Sydney cleared her throat. "You're confused, Slade." She tried to make her voice sound soothing. But her words broke because her control was fracturing.

"Did he wait a few months…or did he go after you right away?"

The question had her gasping. "It wasn't like that!" Gunner hadn't gone after her at all. Not for two years. Not until…

The last mission.

When she'd told him that she'd moved on.

They'd been moving on, together.

"You're wrong about him," Sydney finished, voice quiet. "You'll see that, soon."

Gunner still hadn't spoken.

"No," Slade exhaled on a low breath. "You're the one who's wrong, and *you'll* see that…soon."

Then he was leaving the villa. Cale followed on his heels. The door shut behind them with the softest of clicks.

Silence.

Sydney was still staring at that shut door. Her body was tight and aching, as if she'd just been through another vicious battle. Maybe she had.

"Gunner…" Logan's voice. "Gunner, you know it's the stress. Slade is going to have PTSD, he's going to—"

Gunner shook his head. "He meant what he said."

"Yeah, well, if he meant it, he was wrong." Logan was adamant. "I know you, and that…hell…that's not the way you operate. You don't leave a man behind, especially not your brother."

She couldn't read Gunner's expression.

"But I did leave him behind," Gunner said softly. "Isn't that why we're all here now?"

She wanted to grab him and shake him. "You tried everything you could!" If it hadn't been for Gunner, she would have died on that mission. He'd barely managed to get them both to safety.

"Rescue teams went back. They saw no sign of him." Logan's sigh was ragged. "Stop beating the hell out of yourself over this."

"You already let Slade beat the hell out of you." Sydney didn't even know why she said those words, but…

Gunner glanced at her. The darkness of his eyes was a banked heat. "Why didn't you ask me?" Soft.

Logan whistled. "Okay, I'm going to check in with Mercer. Syd, you, uh, finish up in here, and then we'll talk about our exit strategy."

Then he was gone. Pretty much rushing in his haste to get away.

Gunner rolled his shoulders, as if pushing away a painful memory. Then he stalked toward her.

She didn't move, even though she had the urge to flee.

"He told you to ask me," Gunner said. "So why didn't you?"

Because she hadn't wanted the others to hear his answer. Because some things should be between the two of them.

"You thought he was right, didn't you?"

"Not about you leaving him," she whispered. Logan was on the phone in the outer room, but still close enough that she worried he'd overhear them.

A muscle flexed in Gunner's hard jaw. "You thought I wanted you."

This was the hard part. The part that would tear her pride to shreds, but what did pride matter now? "No, but I knew I wanted you." That was her secret shame. She'd been with Slade; she'd met him first…

Then she'd met Gunner.

And in the beginning, Gunner had made her nervous. He'd put her on edge, every time that she was near him.

Slade had been the one to offer quick compliments. To take her out on fun dates.

She hadn't exactly had a whole lot of fun in her life up to that point.

Her parents had always been so strict, her dad an ex-colonel who ran a tight ship.

Then her mother had died. A sudden heart attack when Sydney was just fourteen. Her dad and his tight ship…they became lost after that. Broken. She'd had to be the caretaker, growing up too fast.

Until her father had slipped into a bottle and not come out again.

She'd been eighteen when he crashed his car.

She'd joined the air force just two weeks later.

Slade had been the Ortez brother she met first. The one with the ready smile, the big dreams.

But it had been Gunner whom she was always so intently aware of. Gunner who put her on edge with his heated stare.

She'd agreed to marry Slade, though, because she *did* love him, and he'd said that he loved her.

While Gunner…back then, he'd barely seemed to tolerate her at all.

Gunner wasn't saying a word now. Just staring at her. And she'd already said enough for them, hadn't she? "Get some rest," she told him, and turned away. She was supposed to stay in another villa, the one on the far end. Only she wouldn't be going there first.

She needed to talk to Slade. Alone.

She headed for the door. Logan had his back turned to her as he talked into his phone, but she had no doubt that he'd heard every word she said to Gunner.

"You don't have to lie." Gunner's flat words. Stopping her.

Insulting her. "Is that what you think I'm doing?" Her fingers curled around the doorknob. "Then maybe you don't know me half as well as I thought."

And she left him.

"CALE, DO YOU mind if I speak to Slade alone?"

Cale stood in the doorway of the second villa, his broad shoulders stretching to take up the space. He stared down at her with hooded eyes. "You sure that's what you want to do? He's pretty messed up right now, Sydney."

"I need to talk to him." To find out what had happened to him. Where he'd been all that time.

Cale gave a slow nod. "Okay, but if you need me, I'll be right outside."

Her eyebrows climbed. She was EOD; she could take care of herself.

But Cale's lips curved in the ghost of a grin. "You just look so delicate..."

A lie. But she used that delicate trap to fool many of her enemies.

"Sydney?" Slade's voice sounded subdued. Good. Maybe he was calming down.

"Right outside," Cale murmured as he slipped past her and gave her the privacy that she needed.

Slade came toward her, his steps uncertain. Only fair, considering how uncertain she felt right now.

"I thought about you," Slade said as his gaze slid over her face, "so much." Then those slow steps of his were coming toward her. He wrapped his arms around her, pulled her tight against his chest.

Why did being in his arms feel wrong? Sydney forced her own arms to lift. To hug him back. "I'm glad you're alive." That was the truth.

He tensed. "At least one person is."

She eased back so that she could stare up at his face. "Gunner is glad, too. He's your brother—"

"*Half* brother."

A distinction that Slade had pointed out before, but Gunner...he never had.

"He didn't know that you were out there," Sydney whispered to him. "Search parties went back to recover you—" She'd almost said *your body.* "But no one found any sign of you." She shook her head. "Where were you, Slade?"

"I don't know." Gruff. Lost. "The first few months were

a blur." He stalked away from her, began to pace the living area. "Different camps. Shacks. They dragged me through the jungle so many times."

"And they never tried to ransom you?" Why not? It didn't make sense to her. If you've got a valuable hostage, you use that hostage.

"I wasn't the only prisoner they had. Some were ransomed." He stopped his pacing. "Some were killed."

She rocked forward onto the balls of her feet. "Are there others still being held?" If there were, they needed to get another rescue team ready.

"No. I was the last." He swung to face her. His chin shot up. "Look, I don't know why they didn't kill me, too. I don't know why they dragged me around. Sometimes I wished that they *would* kill me."

"Slade—"

"Sometimes I just wanted it all to end." His throat moved as he swallowed. "They would…they would ask me questions some days about my life—about you."

Her heart was pounding faster. When she and Gunner had been held, their captor had asked them about the EOD. "Did you tell them about Elite Ops?" Slade hadn't been in the group, but he'd once gotten clearance to work as a liaison on a mission with the group.

"Yes." Hushed.

That was how the leader had known about their division.

"I told them. I would have told them *anything* for food and water."

The mercenary who had come after EOD agents a little while back…that mercenary had been hired by someone in South America. Someone who had learned about the EOD from Slade?

No wonder his captors left him alive. They knew they could use him in order to get us.

"I want him investigated, Sydney."

There was a sharp edge in his words now. He'd seemed almost…calm…a moment before, but now Slade was marching back toward her, his limp barely noticeable. "Did you hear me?" Slade demanded. "I want Gunner investigated. He left me to die. He's not getting away with what he did to me."

She had to make Slade see reason. "We both thought you were dead. Slade, we had your funeral." It had nearly ripped her apart to stand there with the scent of flowers choking her.

But Slade laughed. "I'm sure that was exactly what he wanted."

No, it hadn't been. Gunner's eyes had been haunted at the grave site.

"I'll tear the whole EOD down if I have to do it, but Gunner won't get away with what he's done." Then he was standing right in front of her, glaring down at Sydney. "I'll make him pay, I swear I will."

His eyes looked…wild. And his hands were shaking.

"Slade, are you all right?"

"You were with him, weren't you?" Angry, low, biting.

Sydney squared her shoulders. "You've been through—" Hell. "I don't want you getting so worked up, okay?"

"Worked up?" he yelled.

She winced.

"You have no idea just how 'worked up' I can get." His smile was mean. Not the flirtatious grin that she remembered. "But you're all about to find out."

The door opened behind her. She figured it was Cale, coming back inside to check on her because he'd heard Slade's raised voice.

Slade's eyelids flickered. "Sydney, do you still love me?"

The man's moods were shifting constantly. Too fast. A

break because of his captivity? Or something more? His eyes were bloodshot, lined with deep shadows.

"Sydney?"

"Of course," she said, and it was true. "You have to know that a part of me will—"

The door closed again.

Not Cale.

She spun around, yanked open the door and saw Cale standing to the side and Gunner stalking toward the beach.

"Now he knows," Slade said, sounding satisfied, "and now it's time for *his* world to be ripped apart."

SLADE STARED OUT at the pounding surf. He couldn't remember the last time that he'd seen the ocean. The scent of the salt water was strong, and a million stars glittered down on him.

He'd shaved his beard and used a knife to cut his hair. He still didn't feel quite human, but then, he hadn't felt so for a very long time.

Sydney was gone. She'd headed back to her villa.

But not back to Gunner.

He wouldn't let her go to Gunner. His brother actually thought that he hadn't realized how Gunner felt about her. Slade had known. He'd always known.

I had something you wanted. He'd enjoyed keeping Sydney on his arm, showing Gunner what he'd never have.

His big brother, the one who was supposed to be so strong and tough and perfect.

Sydney would now see that Gunner wasn't perfect.

They'd all see.

Slade was a survivor. He was the strong one. And Gunner...

He was the one who'd be destroyed.

and the moonlight shone down on her. She couldn't see anything in

Chapter Five

Chapter Five

She couldn't sleep. Sydney threw off the sheet that she'd
yanked over her body, and climbed from the bed. She was
wearing a pair of old jogging shorts and a T-shirt.

Sydney ran a hand through her hair. She'd been in that
bed, tossing and turning, for hours. Every time she closed
her eyes, she saw Gunner.

And Slade.

"It's time for his world to be ripped apart."

No, no, it wasn't time for that. Sydney hurried toward
the sliding door and left her villa. She wasn't going to be
able to sleep until she talked to Gunner. Things were going
to be rough for them all, but they would get through this.

He'd heard her say that she loved Slade. She *did* love
him, but her feelings weren't the same as they'd been two
years ago. She wasn't just going to abandon Slade, but she
also wasn't planning on losing Gunner.

He meant too much to her.

Her footsteps were quiet on the sand. Any sounds that
she made were instantly swallowed by the pounding surf.
Cale and Slade were in the second villa, Logan and Gunner in the third.

She walked past that second villa.

The moonlight shone down on her. There were no clouds

tonight. No dense jungle. Just beauty, stretching all around her and—

A sharp retort cut through the night, the sound popping like a firecracker. Sydney knew exactly what that pop was, and even as her arm burned from the bullet as it grazed her flesh, she was diving down into the sand.

Gunfire.

Had the rebel group found them? They'd put so many miles between them, switched vehicles, made a false trail.

They shouldn't have found us.

Then more gunfire came, kicking up the sand near her. She tried to hunch down, to make her way closer to the shoreline so that she'd have at least the slope of the sand to hide behind.

She hadn't even thought to bring a weapon with her. Amateur mistake. But she'd just been going to see Gunner. Taking a quick stroll had seemed safe enough.

Now she was a target.

The shots were coming from the right, from the dense shadows just past Gunner's villa. Her breath heaved in her lungs. The bullet had just grazed her. She'd been lucky.

Very, very lucky…especially considering the big target she must have made as she walked down the beach.

Then there were more shots, but not coming from the right near the last villa. Her team was rushing to help.

Cale was beside her in seconds. He crouched down, even as he kept his gun aimed at the spot where the shooter had been. "You all right?"

What was a little scratch? "Fine… Slade?" Because maybe he was the real target. Maybe the group wanted their hostage back.

"He was gone. He went out for air." His head lifted, just a bit, as he scanned the area. "Logan was going round, trying to get behind the shooter." His words were a mere whisper.

Silence. The pounding surf kept pummeling the beach. She expected to see Gunner come rushing up to join the fight.

He didn't.

After a few more minutes, Logan appeared. "Get to better cover," he ordered, and they rushed for the nearest villa.

Gunner still wasn't there. Neither was Slade. Sydney licked dry lips. "Gunner?"

Logan glanced toward the door. "He needed some time alone."

Her heart was racing too fast. "We have to find him! If he's out there, he could be in danger."

"It looks like the shooter is already gone." Grim. Only there was something about Logan's eyes, that hard, brittle glare that had Sydney on edge. "Just one shooter," Logan muttered. "Just one, and he cleared out fast."

"You think he tailed us?" Cale asked as he glanced carefully through the blinds.

Logan gave a quick shake of his head. Then his gaze fell on Sydney's arm. "He hit you."

"Barely a scratch," she whispered. "Look, we have to find Gunner and Slade!" They were the priority, not her flesh wound.

Logan's fingers curled around her good arm. "You were in the moonlight, walking on the beach?"

She knew where this was going. "Good thing he was a bad shot, huh?"

Logan didn't speak.

"Incoming," Cale murmured.

Then Gunner was there, rushing inside. "I heard gunfire!" His gaze flew to Sydney, dropped to her arm. "You're hit!"

She pulled away from Logan. "It's nothing."

Slade followed behind him, rushing in just a few seconds later. His chest was heaving. "Shots...there were shots..."

She straightened her shoulders. "I think it's safe to say that this location has been compromised."

But Logan wasn't saying that. Logan was staring at both Gunner and Slade, and she knew suspicion when she saw it.

Neither man was armed.

And Logan shouldn't be suspicious of them.

Should he?

Where were they?

Her arm throbbed.

"We're moving our departure up to *now*," Logan snapped. "I'm calling in some favors and getting us the hell out of here."

Gunner was glaring at her arm. Slade was breathing too hard, and a knot was forming in her stomach.

Because she wasn't sure...why would a lone enemy follow them? Why just take shots at her and leave?

The attack almost felt...personal.

As her blood dripped onto the floor, Sydney realized that the danger from this mission was far, far from over.

FOUR WEEKS. FOUR weeks had passed since the team had come back to the United States.

Gunner stared down at the street below him. He was in D.C., at an office most wouldn't ever know existed. He'd been called in, along with the rest of the Shadow Agents, for a briefing with the big boss himself, Bruce Mercer.

Four. Weeks.

Once they'd gotten back onto U.S. soil, Slade had been taken in by other EOD agents. He'd been sent to a hospital, examined, monitored.

And Sydney had been at his side.

His back teeth ground together.

Slade had insisted that Sydney come with him, even as his brother had yelled for Gunner to be investigated.

Locked up.

He'd tried to talk with Slade, over and over, but his brother wouldn't answer his calls. His brother wouldn't talk to him at all.

When he'd been six, he'd discovered that he had a little brother. A boy only two years younger than he'd been.

His father had never believed in commitment of any kind. Gunner's parents hadn't been married, and when his mother had contracted a deadly strain of pneumonia when he was a toddler, his father hadn't been willing to keep his son.

So his father had gone to the doorstep of Gunner's *shinali,* his Navajo grandfather, and he'd just…left Slade there. Gunner had been two years old.

For a long time, he'd thought that his father would come back.

Then he *had* come back.

But only long enough to drop off his second son.

"His mother died in childbirth. You know I can't handle kids. Let him stay here, with Gunner. They're family."

Those words still whispered through Gunner's mind, as if they'd been said just yesterday, instead of over twenty-seven years ago.

His grandfather had been an honorable man. He'd taken in the second child, and, blood or no blood, he'd loved Slade.

They'd become a family. Gunner's father had signed away custody of both his boys. Then he'd just…vanished.

Gunner had always been glad to have a brother. *I wasn't alone then.*

But as they grew older, his relationship with Slade had changed. Slade had pulled away from their grandfather.

He'd seemed to resent the small house, the sparse lifestyle that they led.

He'd seemed to resent Gunner.

And he hates me now.

The door opened behind Gunner. He looked back, too fast, thinking it might be Sydney because he knew she'd been called into the office, too.

It wasn't Sydney. Bruce Mercer stared back at him. The light glinted off Mercer's bald head, and his eyes, a dark brown, studied Gunner.

Not much was known about Mercer, if that was even the guy's real name. But the man was connected to nearly everyone in Washington, and he knew exactly where all the bodies were buried. Figuratively and literally.

"I've been told that I have to investigate you," Mercer said as he crossed the room.

Gunner stiffened. "If that's what you have to do."

"The thing is I don't *like* being told what to do." Mercer lowered himself into the leather chair at the head of the conference table. "I especially don't like being threatened."

Who would have been dumb enough to threaten that guy?

"Slade Ortez has said that if you aren't taken into custody, he'll go to the media and expose the EOD."

What. The. Hell? Slade knew that secrecy was the only way that the EOD could get their missions done. If any of the agents currently out on missions lost their covers, the results would be disastrous.

"He still knows names and faces from his time as a free-lance agent." Mercer's eyes narrowed. "He gave all of that intel to his captors, you know."

Yeah, he knew.

"Now he's ready to tell anyone in the media who will listen to his story." Mercer shook his head. "I can't let that happen. You understand, right? I'll take any steps—do anything necessary—to protect my division."

Even if I get locked up?

Mercer's fingers drummed over the manila file that he'd brought into the room. "Sometimes we *think* that we know a person, but it turns out we really don't."

"Sir, I don't understand." Was Mercer saying he thought Gunner was guilty?

Mercer's head cocked as he studied Gunner. His fingers kept drumming. "What do you value most in this world?"

Sydney. Her name whispered through his mind, but he didn't speak. Couldn't.

Mercer nodded. "And just what would you be willing to do in order to protect what you value?"

Anything. Even let her go. Before he could answer, a knock sounded on the door.

Mercer held his gaze for a moment longer. Then he said, voice cool and calm, "Come in."

Sydney came in first. Gunner tried to school his expression. He'd stayed away from her, tried to give her the space that she needed. She loved Slade, so that meant he was supposed to step aside, right?

Then why did it feel so damn wrong?

Logan followed her inside the office, with Cale right at his heels.

Gunner's gaze, almost helplessly, drifted over Sydney. She looked too pale, and she seemed thinner.

His lips compressed.

"Glad you could all join me," Mercer murmured, "because it seems that we have one very big problem on our hands." His fingers had stilled over the manila file. "Just what are we going to do about Slade Ortez?"

"Do?" Sydney repeated as she crept toward the table. Since when did she creep any place? "What do you mean by that?" She waited a beat, then added, "Sir," as if she realized she was coming across too hard.

One of Mercer's dark brows rose. "You know he's threatening to go to the media."

"Every damn day," Logan muttered, taking the seat closest to Mercer. "It's getting harder to keep him in check. I thought his behavior would settle down the longer he was here, but that's not happening."

"We have to stop him." Mercer motioned for the others to take their seats. When Cale sat near Logan, Gunner had no choice but to sit near Sydney. Her scent rose up, filling his nose. So sweet. That light vanilla that haunted him.

"Just what do you have in mind?" Cale asked cautiously.

Mercer pursed his lips, but instead of answering, he flipped open the manila file. "Have any of you heard about a drug called *muerte?*"

Death. Gunner leaned forward. He made sure not to touch Sydney. "It's a black-market drug from South America." He'd heard rumors about the drug for a few months.

"One that's supposed to be highly addictive," Logan added.

Mercer studied the papers before him. "Highly addictive, and very deadly to its users. It can cause increased aggression, paranoia and even hallucinations." He glanced up at them, letting his gaze drift over the group. "The DEA believes that *muerte* first appeared in Peru, but now it's being transferred all the way up the chain to Mexico." He paused, then said "It hasn't made its way to the U.S. yet."

Gunner waited, knowing there was more to come. Mercer wouldn't be telling them about the drug unless it related to the case. To Slade.

Increased aggression. Paranoia.

"We ran a tox screen on Slade Ortez shortly after he was brought back to the States." The papers rustled in Mercer's hands. "The screen showed that he had high levels of the drug in his system. More tests indicated that he'd been using for...quite some time."

Gunner felt as if a fist had just slammed into his chest.

"You think..." Sydney's voice was hesitant. "You think his captors made him take the drug?"

Mercer's bald head tilted to the side. "They could have used it to keep him better controlled. Controlled prisoners are the easiest to handle," he said, and Gunner knew the man was talking from dark experience. Then Mercer sighed. "The way the man is making these threats, the way he's fighting every shrink I send to help him...I think the *muerte* is still affecting him."

"Can it have an impact after so long?" Cale asked. "He's been here for weeks."

"*Muerte* is one of the most dangerous drugs that the DEA has seen." Flat. "Its effects are far-reaching, and our government researchers think that some of the behavior changes can be permanent for the users."

Gunner shook his head.

But Mercer wasn't done. "Once a user's on it, it's nearly impossible to break free."

"B-but he has been free," Sydney said. Gunner saw her hands fist in her lap. "Slade's been here for weeks, and he hasn't used—"

"The shrinks say his behavior is becoming even more erratic. He needs help, the kind that he can't get without the government's help." The lines around Mercer's eyes deepened. "We have a special facility that we're going to send him to—"

"You're locking him up?" Sydney asked, voice rising.

"For his own safety."

And for the good of the EOD. Gunner understood, without Mercer having to say the words.

"I want you to convince him to go into treatment willingly," Mercer said as his attention focused on Sydney. "You're the one he trusts. You tell him that we can help him."

"Can you?" she fired right back.

"Maybe." A brutal answer because of its honesty. "Or he may be so far gone that there is no pulling him back."

Gunner wouldn't flinch. His brother, the kid he'd promised his grandfather that he would protect…this was how he'd wound up? "Make him better," Gunner growled. "Help him to heal."

Mercer's stare shifted to him. "If I can, I will."

"And if you can't?" Sydney pressed. "What then? You can't just leave him in this—this *treatment* facility indefinitely—"

"If he doesn't get better, we'll explore the next step."

What would the next step be? If the behavior changes were permanent, if there was no way to stop the aggression and the threats and the—

"He's here now." Mercer was back to looking at Sydney. "I had him brought in."

Gunner knew that Mercer had actually been keeping a guard *on* Slade. Making sure that Slade didn't carry through on his threats to speak to the media.

"I want you to go and talk to him. Get him to understand that we aren't the enemy, Sydney." Again, another flicker of the man's gaze toward Gunner. "That *none* of us are his enemy."

Sydney rose. "I want to see that file first."

Mercer pushed it toward her. Her gaze scanned the reports, and Gunner heard her suck in a deep breath. "If he doesn't get treatment?"

"According to my doctors, his behavior is just becoming worse. The paranoia and aggression have only increased while he's been back in the U.S." His lips tightened. "If he doesn't get some serious intervention and treatment, he'll become a danger to himself and others."

If he wasn't already. The way Mercer was talking, the guy *already* thought Slade was a threat.

"He needs your help," Mercer said, his voice softening. "Are you going to leave him—"

Her head jerked up at that even as Gunner shot to his feet. *Low blow.*

"Or will you help him?"

Sydney's fingers were trembling as she pushed the file back toward Mercer. "I'll help him."

"Good." Mercer had obviously gotten just the outcome that he'd wanted. "He's one floor below us, second room on the right."

She headed for the door.

"Convince him, Sydney," Mercer ordered, the words heavy with an unmistakable command.

"I just want to save him," she replied. Then she was gone. The door closed quietly behind her.

Mercer's gaze swept over the agents in the room; then his stare rested on Gunner. "Make sure your brother understands the situation."

Gunner gave a jerky nod even as he headed for the door.

Once he was away from them, his steps picked up and he hurried down the hall. Sydney was already gone on the elevator, so he took the stairs, three at a time, and he was standing in front of that elevator when the doors opened.

Her eyes widened in surprise when she saw him.

Before she could speak, he caught her arm and pulled her toward him. He knew this floor well. He'd spent enough time at the EOD facility to know every inch of the place. He didn't take her to Slade—he knew Slade was in the room with the guard stationed at the door.

Instead, he took her back and to the left. To the old conference room that would be empty.

"Gunner." She started to dig in her heels. "I have to talk to him."

"You're talking to me first." He pushed her inside the conference room and secured the door shut behind him.

Then he turned around and just…stared at her. She was pale, and he didn't like that. There were a whole lot of things he didn't like just now. "What are you going to do?"

She huffed out a breath. "I'm going to get Slade help. That's what we're both going to do."

Through gritted teeth, he asked, "Are you still marrying him?"

Her eyes widened. "That's what you want to know?"

"Are you?" Because if she was, he would back away. No, damn it, his brother was hurting. His captors had strung him out on their poison. He *would* back away, no matter what. "He's the one who loves you." Gunner forced the words out.

If possible, she seemed to become even paler. "And you don't?"

His chest ached. "We had a good time, Sydney." He didn't let emotion slip into his voice. He couldn't weaken. "But he's the one you promised your forever to."

She took a step back. "A…good time?" Her voice faltered. "That's really all I was?"

No, she'd been everything, to him.

She still *was* everything to his brother. "Slade needs you," he said.

"And I'll be there for him. I'll help him." Her voice was tight. "I always planned to help him."

Then she was marching forward.

Gunner stepped out of her path.

She reached for the door, then stopped. "Did you really have to pull me aside just to tell me that you didn't love me?" The pain in her voice seemed to tear into him. "Trust me, Gunner." She glanced back at him, and he saw the sheen of tears in her eyes. "I already knew that."

She left him.

I never said I didn't love you.

He sucked a deep breath. One. Another. When his hands were steady, he left that room. A turn down the hallway showed Sydney just slipping past the guard.

Gunner's stare slid over the hall. Slade was being held in an interrogation room. That meant the area adjacent to that room would be designed for surveillance.

Gunner's steps were silent on the heavily carpeted floor. After about ten feet, he stopped, going not in the room with Slade, but into the surveillance room.

The surveillance room was dark, but he didn't bother turning on the light. Through the big wall of glass—a two-way mirror—he could see perfectly into the area next door. He could see Sydney. See Slade.

Mercer had sent him after Sydney because the boss had wanted to make sure that Slade went in for his treatment.

But Gunner knew that Slade didn't want him anywhere close by, so he'd keep his distance.

He'd just taken the first step to keeping that distance. When his brother was well—and he *would* be well; Gunner would do everything possible to make that happen—Slade would have his chance with Sydney.

After his years of captivity, Slade deserved happiness.

Gunner would make sure he got it.

"WHY THE HELL am I here?" Slade demanded as he crossed his arms over his chest. "I'm sick of this EOD crap. You hear me, Sydney? *Sick of it.*"

She swallowed and eased into the chair across from him. Mercer's words replayed in her mind. *Increased aggres-*

sion. Paranoia. Yes, she'd sure seen that with him. But how much was due to the drugs? And how much was a result of the torture that she feared might have fractured his mind?

"Slade, you need help." She kept her voice soft and easy, trying to soothe him.

He shoved out of his chair and leaped to his feet "What I *need* is to have my brother locked away, but the EOD isn't doing that." His cheeks flushed. "I gave them time. I gave you all time, and that time's run out. I'm going to the press. I'm telling them everything."

She stood, reaching for his hands. "You know the EOD's work is classified."

"I don't care." He yanked away from her.

"The man you used to be—he cared."

"That man died in a jungle."

She flinched. "I think…I think that man is still inside." She had to be very careful. "I want to help you get him back. I want to *help* you."

His eyes searched hers. "How you gonna do that?"

This was the tricky part. "Mercer has a place for you to go. The doctors there can get you well."

"You think I'm sick?" he snarled.

Yes. "I think…" She inhaled a heavy breath that seemed to chill her lungs. "I think your captors gave you something while you were down there. They made you…take some drugs, didn't they?"

He stilled.

So she kept talking. "The drugs are changing you. Making you do things, say things, that you wouldn't normally do. But we can help you—"

"You're not going to stay with me." His flat words had her floundering.

"Slade, I—"

"Whenever I touch you…" He came closer and touched her cheek.

She flinched.

"You do that," he said, and his hand dropped. "You can't *stand* for me to touch you anymore, can you?"

"Slade…" She locked her knees and refused to give in to the urge to back away from him. "You need the help—"

"I *need* you, but he's between us. Always between us."

"This isn't about Gunner!" It wasn't. "It's about getting you back to normal. Getting your life back."

"What life?" Spittle flew from his mouth. "Without you, what the hell am I supposed to do?" Then he moved quickly, faster than she'd anticipated, especially with his limp, and his hands grabbed her arms, right under her elbows. He yanked her up on her tiptoes, forcing her body close to his. "Tell me, are you going to marry me, Sydney?"

"We can't—we can't even think about that now. We have to get you well. That's the priority, that's—"

"Are you going to marry me?" He was yelling at her.

This wasn't the man she'd known. "I want him back," she said, lifting her chin. "I want the man I knew back. We're getting you help. No matter what else happens, we're getting you help."

His hold tightened. "You won't answer my damn question." His hold was so hard that she knew he would leave bruises on her arms. "Have you been with him?"

"Slade—"

"You had sex with my brother."

She flinched. *I made love with him.*

"And you won't marry me. Back in Peru, you said…you said you still loved me, but you didn't mean the words, did you? Just trying to keep me calm, controlled." He said the last word as if it were a curse.

Sydney shook her head. "That's not what I was doing! I care about you, Slade. A part of me will always love you."

He dropped her. She stumbled, almost fell when her knees wanted to wobble. Her heart was racing fast, as fast as it did when she was in combat.

Slade turned away from her. "I don't want your help, Sydney. I don't want Mercer's help. I don't want anyone's help." He strode toward the door.

She rushed after him, grabbed his arm.

Slade spun around and hit her. Sydney wasn't expecting the move, so she didn't have time to block the blow. This time, her stumble wasn't from weak knees. Then he was shoving her, slamming her against the wall. "You think you're getting away from me? You'll *never* get away from me!"

She tried to kick out at him, but he trapped her legs and—

"Let her go!" A roar. Gunner's roar. The door banged against the wall, and in the next breath, Gunner was grabbing Slade and throwing him across the room.

Sydney tried to suck in deep breaths. She'd been in fights before. She'd been on battlefields, but…but this was different. This was Slade.

Gunner.

Gunner caught her hands and tucked her gently into his side. "Are you okay, baby?"

Slade snarled.

Gunner put his body in front of hers. "You know better than to *ever* raise a hand to her. Our grandfather taught us…you never hurt a woman. You *know* that."

"That fool didn't teach me a thing!"

Sydney peered over Gunner's shoulder. Saw that the guard was holding Slade in a tight grip.

"He was a good man." Gunner's voice boiled with fury. "And you were once, too."

But Slade...laughed?

"You will be again." Now that booming voice—that came from Mercer. He'd just appeared in the doorway, right behind Slade and the guard. "We're getting you help, son."

Slade broke away from the guard and lunged for Gunner. *"I'll kill you!"* His fist flew toward Gunner's face.

But Gunner caught that fist. Caught it and shook his head. "No, you won't. And you *won't* ever hurt her again, either." He grabbed Slade, twisted his body around and held him in an unbreakable hold. "You're going in for any kind of help that the doctors can give you."

"It's a treatment facility," Mercer murmured, watching them all carefully. "For veterans. They can give you what you need."

Slade was trying to break away from Gunner. But Gunner held him in a tight grip.

The guard came forward and Mercer gave him—handcuffs?—to put on Slade. More guards entered the room, and they all started dragging Slade out.

Her heart was still racing too fast. Her hands were trembling, so she balled them into fists.

"You think you're safe with him?" Slade shouted. He wasn't going easily. Kicking, head-butting. "You don't know what he's really like!"

At that moment, she felt as if she didn't know what anyone was really like. Her jaw hurt from where he'd hit her, and her arms throbbed. Nausea rolled in her stomach, and her cheeks seemed to be going numb.

"He wanted you, so he took you!" Slade's voice was just getting louder. "He got me out of his way once, and he's doing it again now!"

"Damn it, I'm trying to get you *well!*" Gunner snapped.

"He won't let you go—he won't! If he can't have you, then he'll make sure…he'll make sure that no one else does, either! That's why he's sending me away, that's why—"

The guards pulled him through the door. Sydney kept trying to suck in some much-needed oxygen. The room was spinning on her. Why was the room spinning?

"I'll take care of him," Mercer said as he slipped away to follow the guards and the sound of Slade's yells.

Her cheeks didn't feel cold anymore. Pinpricks of heat were shooting across them.

"Sydney…" Gunner turned back to face her. His face was locked in tight, angry lines. "Did he hurt you?" His gaze locked on her jaw. "Hell, of course he did. I see the mark he left on you."

She shook her head. "I—I'm fine." The words were such a lie. Sydney took a step forward. *Don't fall apart now. Don't. Soldiers never fall apart.* That was what her dad used to tell her. *"A good soldier never falls. You carry on, no matter what."*

She took another step, trying to carry on.

But the spinning wouldn't stop. And the room got dark so fast. She tried to grab for Gunner, but then she couldn't grab anything. Her body went limp, and Sydney felt herself crashing to the floor.

She couldn't even cry out Gunner's name.

Couldn't do anything…but collapse.

"SYDNEY!" GUNNER CAUGHT her before she hit the floor. He dived forward and wrapped his arms around her. He pulled her up into his arms, against his chest, holding her as carefully as he could. "Syd?"

Her head sagged back. Her eyes were closed.

Fear stabbed into him as he rushed for the door. "I need

help, *now!*" His bellowing voice seemed to echo down the hall.

Slade was near the elevator. He turned, and his face went slack with shock when he saw Sydney in Gunner's arms.

"What did you do?" Slade shouted.

Slade had been the one to hit her. The one to hurt her. And Gunner had never wanted to attack another man more in his life.

His brother.

And he could have ripped him apart. When he'd seen Slade punch Sydney…

"Get a medic!" Mercer barked; then he was running toward them. "What happened to her?"

The guards pulled Slade onto the elevator.

Gunner kept his tight hold on Sydney. "She passed out." She'd been trying to reach for him. There had been confusion and fear in her eyes. She'd wanted him.

He hadn't been able to get to her fast enough.

He pulled her closer, held her tighter.

Nothing could be wrong with Sydney.

As he stared down at her, desperate, Sydney's eyelashes began to flutter.

"Open your eyes," he whispered. *Please.* Because he needed to see that green gaze again. Needed to see her, without the fear in her eyes.

Slowly, her eyes opened. She stared up at him in surprised confusion. "Gun…ner? What's happening?"

The medic was running down the hallway toward them.

He wanted to kiss her, wanted to bury his face in the soft curve of her throat.

But more than that…he wanted to find out what the hell had caused her to faint. What was wrong? He had to find out, and he had to make her *better*.

Because he could take torture, betrayal, any number of

sins and punishments tossed against him, but he couldn't take anything happening to Sydney.

Not. Her.

"I DON'T FAINT." Sydney knew her words sounded angry, but *she* was angry.

And a little scared.

She was in the med room at the EOD. The doctor, a brunette with wire-framed glasses, was a woman whom Sydney actually considered a friend. So she figured she could just be blunt with Tina.

"I've been in combat zones. I've been shot. I've been under attack from all sides." She was currently sitting on an exam table. "I have *never* fainted before."

"Well, you did about twenty minutes ago." Tina offered her a small smile. "So I guess there's a first time for everything."

Sydney shook her head. "That wasn't me." She didn't want to be weak. With everything going on with Slade and Gunner, she couldn't afford any weakness.

"Sure it was." Tina lifted her clipboard. "I know you like to think you're pretty much Superwoman, but no one can be strong 24/7." Her eyebrows arched. "Not even you."

Sydney sucked in a deep breath. "I feel fine now."

"Except for that shiner on your jaw? Want to tell me how you got it?"

Slade punched me. He went crazy. He was coming to hit me again, but Gunner stopped him.

"No? Okay…" Tina drew out the word. "Then let's start focusing on what might have made you faint." She put down the clipboard. "Have you sustained any head injuries lately?"

The back of her head was throbbing now. "I hit my head when I…fell."

"You mean when Slade hit you." Crisp, without any emotion.

"If you knew, then why'd you ask?"

"Because we're friends, and I thought you might want to talk." Her fingers were carefully sifting through Sydney's hair searching for the injury. "A slight concussion could explain your fainting spell." A pause. "At least this way, I don't have to ask if you're pregnant."

Pregnant.

Sydney's heart stopped. "What?"

Tina's fingers carefully probed the bump on the back of Sydney's head. "Pregnant. You know, as in, with child? That's usually the reason most women get light-headed. It happens pretty early in term."

Sydney caught Tina's hand and pushed those probing fingers away, even as she frantically counted up the days in her mind.

"Uh, Sydney, why are you looking like that?"

She swiped her tongue across lips that were way too dry. "Can you test me here?"

Behind the lens of her glasses, Tina's eyes widened, but she quickly schooled her expression. "Of course." Then she hurried away only to return with a specimen container in her hand. But before she gave it to Sydney, she asked, quietly, "Are you okay?"

Sydney slid from the table. Took the container and didn't answer her.

Five minutes later she had the results. Was she okay? Not exactly.

Tina stared at her, waiting. A friend, not a doctor.

She was pregnant.

Chapter Six

Sydney kept a small house just outside D.C. It was about a forty-five-minute drive, but the quiet privacy she received out there was well worth the trip.

Considering all that was happening with Slade, Mercer hadn't wanted her to leave the area yet. No trip to Baton Rouge, no returning to her *real* home, not yet, anyway.

It had been three weeks since she found out about her pregnancy. Tina had done some additional testing and taken some blood samples, and she'd told Sydney that all seemed well. The changes in Sydney's body were small. Some increased sensitivity in her breasts, a little light-headedness in the mornings. Nothing too extreme so far.

And so far, only Tina knew about her condition.

She hadn't told Gunner yet, because she didn't know how he'd react.

The fact that he'd been avoiding her as if she were some kind of plague? Yes, well, that didn't exactly make telling him any easier.

Sydney sat on her porch, staring at the setting sun. The sky was red and orange, the hues stretching for as far as she could see. Her fingers were lying over her stomach. Just…there.

A baby.

Her baby.

A vehicle's engine growled, the sound too close. She tensed as her gaze darted toward the road. This was a dead-end street. Her house *was* on the end, and her only neighbors were out of town for a second honeymoon.

She wondered just who her visitor could be.

Then she saw Gunner's truck, coming slowly but steadily toward her.

Sydney didn't rise to her feet. Didn't rush out toward him, the way she had done too many times in the past. She just kept swinging, nice and casual, and soon Gunner was in her driveway. He climbed out of the truck and headed toward her porch.

As he approached, he didn't start speaking. Just stared at her with those dark eyes. What had made him come visit her? Had he finally decided that he just couldn't live without her? Because she'd had that fantasy a time or twenty in the past two weeks.

She forced her hand away from her stomach. "Gunner, I—"

"Slade's better."

Sydney blinked. "That's wonderful." She'd called for updates but hadn't learned much. The doctors had sequestered Slade during his treatment.

"They did an experimental therapy with him, to help push him through the worst of the withdrawal symptoms. Mercer says that while it won't be one hundred percent, Slade should soon be more like the man we remembered." He climbed onto the bottom porch step. The old wood squeaked beneath his boot. "He's going to have to deal with PTSD, but he can get through this, Sydney. He can be the man we knew."

She rose to her feet. "That's so good to hear." Because she was tired of seeing nightmares in which Slade came at her with fury on his face and with his fists swinging. "I hope he can find some peace."

"He wants to talk to you."

Now, that surprised her. "And what? You're his errand boy? Last I heard, he was screaming that you were the enemy."

"We're making progress on that." A pause as his gaze seemed to linger on her face. "He's out now, still under supervision from the EOD, but he's in his own apartment. He—he said you won't talk to him."

Because he'd attacked her. Because she knew this was a delicate situation, and with the news of her pregnancy, she had to do everything possible to protect her baby. "I've called and talked with Mercer and the doctors."

"But you don't want to talk to *him,* not anymore?"

She clenched her hands into fists so she wouldn't touch her stomach again. "Things have changed for me. And I already told Slade, a future for the two of us just won't be happening." It would be impossible.

"So that's it…you're walking away?" Confusion deepened the faint lines near his eyes. "I thought you were going to marry him."

Gunner actually sounded angry. Her own anger bloomed, but she choked it back. Anger couldn't be good for the baby. And the baby was what mattered. "Two years ago, I agreed to marry him." Even when she'd had her doubts. "We weren't perfect then, you know. Or maybe you don't." Her laugh held little humor. "I'll help him transition back to life here, I'll do what I can, but he attacked me. I can't be around anyone who will be a physical threat to me right now."

Even if it hadn't been the drugs, there was no future for them. She was in love with Gunner, not Slade. She was having Gunner's baby.

Gunner stood just a few feet away, and she so badly

wanted to tell him how she felt, but he seemed so wooden. Sydney found herself asking him, "Why did you want to be with me?"

His eyelashes flickered, a tiny movement. "Because you've been an obsession for me."

Obsession wasn't the same thing as love—wasn't even close.

She gathered her resolve and asked another painful question. He was here, talking to her, so she might as well take the chance while she could. "What do you want, Gunner? You came here to talk about Slade, I get that, but what do *you* want?"

"I can't have what I want."

Helpless, she stepped toward him. "How do you know?" Her voice softened because this was the chink she'd wanted to see in his armor. "How do you know you can't have it?"

She ached to touch him.

He retreated off that bottom step, moving away from her. "You're the only thing that matters to Slade. I think you're the only thing keeping him going."

She shook her head. Why did he continue making everything about Slade? "I'm talking about you. About me. Not him."

"But he's there."

She could feel him, standing between them. Would Slade always be there?

"He's getting his sanity back, and I can't take away what he wants most."

"You can't take it away?" Now her spine straightened. "I'm not some kind of prize to be given or taken away. I'm a person, and I choose my own path in this world." A path she'd wanted to take with him. "Tell your brother that I'm glad he's better, but there isn't going to be any marriage."

Not to either brother.

She'd already made arrangements to return Slade's ring, the ring she had locked away for so long. She couldn't keep it, because there was no future for them.

Sydney turned on her heel and marched back inside her house.

THE SUN HAD SET. Night had crept over the area, sealing everything in darkness.

Sydney's house sat at the end of the lane, lights still blazing in a few of her windows.

Gunner was helpless to look away from that sight.

"What the hell am I doing here?" he muttered in disgust, sitting in the shadows, watching her house.

He just hadn't been able to leave her. He'd tried. He'd driven nearly all the way back to D.C.; then he'd turned around and come back.

There had been pain in her eyes. Pain that he knew he'd caused because he wasn't giving her what she needed.

He opened the door of his truck just as her upstairs lights switched off.

Should he still go to her? Knock on the door—and do what?

Ask his brother's fiancée to be with him? Slade had just gotten back on his feet. He'd apologized for his accusations and behavior. Thin, pale, looking shaken, Slade had told him that he *would* get better.

Slade was out of the treatment facility. Mercer hadn't wanted to let him out yet, but the doctors had said that with continued rehab and counseling—therapy that he could receive as an outpatient—Slade would keep progressing. As a precaution—because Mercer was a man who believed in precautions—a guard was stationed at Slade's new apartment.

And Gunner was standing in front of Sydney's house.

Like some kind of lovesick fool. She was sleeping. They could talk later. He didn't have to—

He could smell smoke. Gunner stiffened even as he inhaled—and yes, that was the scent of fire.

The scent was coming from Sydney's house. As he turned his horrified gaze on her house, he saw the flash of flames on the bottom floor. Flames...

"Sydney!" He ran for her house, rushing up the steps and kicking in the front door. The old lock gave way easily, and he saw the flames inside, growing fast, as they raced around her living room and toward the stairs.

Toward Sydney.

"Sydney!" he yelled again even as he leaped forward. The flames were trying to lash out at him, but he jumped over them and took those stairs as fast as he could. How had the fire started? Why was it spreading so rapidly?

Where was—*"Sydney!"*

Her door swung open. She stood there, wearing a small pair of shorts and a T-shirt. She was coughing and trying to cover her mouth. "Gun...ner?"

He grabbed her. He hurried toward her bed, snatched up her covers and wrapped them around her. Then he turned back for the door.

The fire was already climbing up the stairs. Gunner hesitated. He wasn't sure if he would be fast enough to get her through the flames. They were burning so bright and hot.

He backed into her room. Slammed the door shut with his booted heel and whirled to face the window.

Sydney struggled in his arms. "Gunner, I can..." She coughed. "I can help..."

He put her on her feet. Only long enough to shove open her bedroom window and stare down below. A one-story drop. Maybe a broken leg, depending on how he landed. Could be much worse, though, if he—

"I can't go through that window." Sydney had backed away. "I can't jump!"

He caught her arms and pulled her right back against him. "You can't go down those stairs, baby. You wouldn't make it." Not without receiving burns all over her body.

There were tears in her eyes. "I *can't* take that drop, I—" Then her eyes widened. Her hands twisted in his grasp, and her short nails dug into his skin. "The storage room down the hall. There's a lattice leading down from the window there. We can go on that!"

If the lattice held them.

Sydney scrambled and jerked on a pair of sneakers

Giving a grim nod, he grabbed for the blanket and bundled her up once more.

"Gunner, stop, I can—"

He had her in his arms. If the fire was coming, it would get him first.

He rushed down the hallway, holding her tight. The rising smoke was so thick now that every step burned his lungs. He coughed hard, trying to clear his throat and chest. Not working.

Then he was at the other door. Inside that storage room. Carefully, he put her down on her feet. The window didn't want to open, as if it had been sealed shut, so Gunner just used his fist to break the glass. The glass rained down on the ground, his fingers bled, but he didn't care. He could see the lattice, just to the side. It looked old and shaky, and he sure didn't have a whole lot of faith in it.

It wasn't going to hold them both at the same time, that was for sure. But he'd already planned to get her out first.

She'd dropped the cover. It was smoldering, smoking. Sydney's glance locked on his.

"Go," he told her. "Get to safety, and I'll be right behind you."

She nodded and then she—kissed him.

He hadn't expected the move and it was all too brief. A frantic brush of her lips against his, and then Sydney was climbing through the window holding tight to that lattice.

As she climbed down, Gunner realized that he was holding his breath.

Then the lattice started to crack. He heard the wood groaning.

Hurry, Syd. Hurry.

Her feet touched down on the ground. "Come on, Gunner!"

He was already out the window. He grabbed the lattice and double-timed it, and when the wood snapped, when the lattice broke in two, he leaped the rest of the way to the ground.

No broken bones. No burns. They were both damn lucky.

He caught Sydney's hand, and they rushed away from the fire, heading toward Gunner's truck. The hungry blaze was destroying that house, burning higher and higher with every moment that passed.

If he hadn't come back, would Sydney have been able to get out on her own? He hadn't heard any alarms sounding in her house. If she'd been sleeping...

She might never have wakened.

He pulled her into his arms, held her close against his chest. His heart was racing, and fear had sent adrenaline spiking in his blood.

Too close.

He never wanted Sydney that close to death again.

THE FLAMES WERE sputtering out. Sydney stared at the charred remains of her home. Gutted. The firefighters were still using their hoses, and the scent of ash filled the air.

Sydney stood by Gunner's truck, her shoulders hunched.

The blaze had spread quickly. She'd been in bed, drifting off to sleep, when she'd heard Gunner shouting her name.

Her eyes had flown open. She'd run to her bedroom door, and only *then* had she felt the heat of the flames and smelled the smoke.

"You're sure that you had fresh batteries in your smoke detector?" The question came from Logan. As soon as he'd heard about the fire, he'd raced out to the scene. Good thing he'd still been in D.C. Logan and his new wife, Juliana, divided their time between D.C. and Juliana's beach home in Biloxi.

"Yes, I'm sure." She'd checked it a week ago. The smoke detector had been working fine then.

It had just failed her tonight.

"Good thing Gunner was here," Logan murmured. "I think he saved your life."

Again.

She nodded.

"Uh…just why *was* Gunner here?"

Her gaze slid to the right. To Gunner. He was talking to some of the firefighters and looking pretty angry.

"Sydney?"

She snapped her attention back to Logan. "He was… He came out earlier to tell me that Slade was doing better, that he was doing outpatient rehab and counseling now."

Logan nodded. "He is. I saw him at EOD headquarters just yesterday. Seems like a different man…" His words trailed away. He tilted his head to the right. "So…Gunner came out and just…decided to stay with you?"

Why was he asking her all of these questions? "No, he left. I didn't even realize he was back until—until I heard him yelling my name." Her gaze slid back to Gunner.

He was staring at her. He started to make his way toward her.

"You can ask Gunner if he saw anything or anyone before the fire started. I sure didn't see anything. I thought I was alone."

"Yet Gunner was here."

Yes, he had been. *Why?* It wasn't as if she'd stopped to ask him when they were rushing out of the burning house.

"The chief says it looks like arson. The way the burn marks are sliding across the rooms..." Gunner drew closer as he spoke. "An arson investigator will be out tomorrow to start the investigation."

"Arson?" Her hand was on her stomach. She dropped it. "Why would someone torch my house?"

"With you in it?" Gunner growled.

She flinched.

"You know the EOD has plenty of enemies." This came from Logan.

Sydney nodded. Yes, she knew that.

"You're thinking someone is targeting us again?" Gunner demanded as his stare turned to the other man.

Logan shrugged. "We never found out the identity of the man who sent out the hits before. Just that he was based in South America. We've got agents in the EOD who are digging for more intel on him even now." He paused, glanced toward the charred structure that had been Sydney's house. "This isn't random chance, we all know that. I'm going to send out word that all of our agents need to be on alert until we can learn more."

Sydney was sure that the EOD's own investigators would be joining the arson crew tomorrow.

"In the meantime, Sydney, do you want to stay with me and Juliana?" Logan asked her.

"I—"

"She can stay with me," Gunner said instantly.

That sounded like a very bad idea to her. Sydney shook

her head. "Thanks, both of you, but I'm perfectly capable of getting a hotel room. Or maybe even going back to Baton Rouge—"

"No." Gunner was adamant. "If you leave the area, you'll be on your own."

In the EOD, you were never supposed to be on your own. The other agents were there to always have your back.

The way Gunner had protected her tonight. He'd fought the flames to get her out.

Tell him. She had to tell him about the baby. Gunner had a right to know that he would be a father.

"I've got an extra room," he told her, voice stilted. "You'll have plenty of privacy."

Logan just looked between them.

She thought of her baby. She thought of the night someone had tried to shoot her on the beach in Peru. She thought of the flames that she could still feel against her skin.

If someone was after her, and it sure was starting to look that way, she wanted protection.

Gunner was the best agent she knew. "I'll stay with you," she said softly.

In the moonlight, she could see the expression of relief flicker across his face.

Just what expression would he show when she told him about the baby?

When they were alone again, she'd find out.

HE WATCHED THEM from the woods. The firefighters were still running around the scene like ants, spraying everything down with their hoses.

But no one had started to search the area.

They were too busy working on the fire.

His jaw ached, and he realized that he'd been clenching his teeth. Gunner shouldn't have been there. He'd watched

Gunner drive away before. Had *followed* Gunner out there, then waited until he had left.

It had been easy enough to sneak into Sydney's house. She'd been in the shower. She hadn't even heard him.

Not when he'd poured the gasoline all over the ground floor of her home.

Not when he'd lit the matches and started that blaze.

He'd escaped, running to his shelter in the woods to watch the flames, but then he'd seen Gunner running into the house.

Always playing the hero.

Always screwing up his plans.

So Sydney was safe now. Or so she thought. But this wasn't the end. Not even close.

He watched them. Her and Gunner. Their bodies brushed against each other as Gunner led Sydney around the truck and opened the passenger door for her.

Where would Gunner take her? Back to his place?

Bastard.

But he was going to make Gunner pay. By hurting Sydney, he'd be striking blows against Gunner.

He knew Gunner's weakness, and he was ready to use that weakness against him.

He slipped deeper into the woods. He would attack again, and the next time Gunner wouldn't be in time to ride to the rescue.

"DON'T WORRY," GUNNER told Sydney as he unlocked the door to his third-floor condo. "The EOD will find out what happened at your place."

She brushed by him as she headed inside. She was still wearing just her shorts, T-shirt and sneakers. There was ash on her cheek. Her hair was tousled. Her eyes were huge.

She was so beautiful that he ached.

Gunner squared his shoulders, then shut and bolted the door. "You'll be safe here. I promise."

"Are any of us ever really safe?" The quiet question caught him off guard. "You know as well as I do that this world is a very dangerous place." She turned away from him and paced toward the large glass window that over-looked D.C. "Safety is what we make of it."

He stared at her back, at a loss. He knew he'd do any-thing possible to keep Sydney safe, but—

"Why did you come back?"

He took a cautious step toward her. "Because there was more to say between us."

"More?" She wasn't looking at him. "Yes, you're right, there is more." Then she turned to face him. "There's some-thing that I need to tell you."

He braced himself. *There's something that I need to tell you*...usually didn't foreshadow anything good.

What was she going to say? He hoped she hadn't changed her mind and decided to go back to Baton Rouge. He knew Mercer had been pressuring her to remain in the area.

Gunner needed to stay close and keep an eye on Slade, but he couldn't just let Sydney go off on her own when someone as threatening her.

"I'm pregnant."

He hadn't heard her right. Gunner shook his head.

Sydney's lips tightened. "Don't look at me like I'm crazy. We both know you just heard what I said." She spun away. "Jerk."

He rushed toward her and spun her right back around. His hands were wrapped around her shoulders, but he kept that grip as careful as he could. "Say that again."

"Jerk?"

"Sydney—"

Her breath blew out. "I'm pregnant." Her gaze held his.

Right then, he finally understood what people meant when they said the world seemed to stop for them.

His eyes dropped to her stomach. Flat, smooth. He shook his head.

"Tina says I'm in the first trimester, and if I go back and count to when we were together in Baton Rouge—"

"I didn't use any protection." He'd been so desperate for her.

And…he knew everything about Sydney. Just as she knew everything about him. They had blood work run all the time for the EOD. They'd both been all clear in terms of health, and he'd been desperate, so desperate, that he hadn't held back long enough to protect her. "I'm sorry, I—"

"I'm a big girl, you know. I could have told you to stop. I wanted you, just the way you were." She paused, then whispered, "With nothing between us."

The woman was about to shatter his control, and he'd been trying so very hard to stay in control. For her.

"This is why you fainted," he said. *Sydney's pregnant with my baby.* The joy was there, building in his chest, but he didn't know how she felt. And—

Slade.

Slade wasn't going to handle this well.

"This is why I fainted," she agreed.

He wanted to drop his hands, to caress her stomach. Slade was going to be furious. He'd betrayed his brother, taking a risk that he should have never taken but…

My baby.

He couldn't stop the spread of joy.

"I thought you deserved to know."

The fire tonight hadn't just put her life at risk. It had put their baby's life at risk, too.

"Looks like you're going to be a father," she whispered, and she stepped back from him.

He didn't know what to say. In that heavy silence, her lips trembled and she gave a little nod. Then she was walking away, heading into the guest room. Of course, Sydney knew where his guest room was. She'd been in his condo many times over the past two years, and the place always felt better, brighter, when she was there.

"Looks like you're going to be a father." Her words rang in his ears.

In that instant, he thought of his own father—the way the guy hadn't been able to get away from him fast enough. His father had ditched him and hadn't looked back.

He'd ditched Slade, too. Gunner's grandfather had taken him in. Had raised them both, in that house with the threadbare carpet and the sagging roof. His grandfather had taught them to fish, hunt and hike.

They hadn't had much money. No fancy clothes or cars. But...

Grandfather took care of me. Loved me.

Gunner sucked in a deep breath and wondered about his own child. The child that was so small now, barely more than a dream, growing inside Sydney.

Girl? Boy? Would she have Sydney's smile? His eyes?

"Looks like you're going to be a father."

His hands were clenched into fists. He would be a father, but he would *not* be like his old man. He would not abandon his child.

Never.

SYDNEY'S EYES FLEW open as the last of the nightmare ripped through her mind. "Gunner!" His name tore from her, even though she was more asleep than awake. But she could still see the nightmare. The flames coming for her, trapping her.

And the baby.

Gunner burst into the room, flipping on the lights. He

had a gun in his hand and his body was tight with tension. "Sydney?" He searched the room, looking for a threat.

But there was no threat here.

Only a fading nightmare.

She sucked in a deep breath. What was happening to her? "Sorry. Bad dream." He'd been in the dream. He'd died trying to get her out of that fire. She'd watched him burn.

Then she'd been alone with the flames.

Her hands fisted around the covers.

Gunner took a steadying breath of his own, then carefully put the gun down on the nightstand. "Want to talk about it?"

She shook her head. "I'm fine now."

He stared at her, then gave a slow nod. "Aren't you always?"

Sydney wasn't sure what that was supposed to mean.

"I'm...sorry, for earlier," he said gruffly.

Her head tilted back. "You mean when you got all quiet and looked like you might run from the room?"

His eyes widened. "I didn't."

Okay, he hadn't fled. His face had just gotten even harder, even darker.

"You know...my father abandoned me and Slade."

Yes, she knew.

"My mother died when I was two, so it was just me and my grandfather for a long time. I used to...used to see the other kids with their dads, and I was so damn jealous."

She held her body perfectly still. Gunner didn't talk about his past much. Neither did Slade. Slade had just told her once that his childhood had been a waste, that he'd *never* go back to a life like that.

She hadn't pushed him for more. If his past was painful— if Gunner's past was painful—then she didn't want to be the one stirring up old wounds.

"Gunner, you don't have to tell me—"

"Yes, I do. You're having my baby. You deserve to know everything about me." He came toward the bed, hesitated, then sat down beside her, immediately taking up so much space and making her feel hyperaware of him.

What else was new, though? She always seemed to be hyperaware of him.

"Until I was ten, I kept hoping that one day he'd come back. That he'd realize he wanted me and Slade. That he would try to make us into a family."

Her heart ached because she could only imagine the pain he'd felt then.

"But at ten, on my birthday, when another year passed and there was no letter, no phone call, I knew it wasn't happening. He didn't care about me. He never would."

She reached for his hand and twined her fingers through his. "That's his loss."

"That's what my grandfather said." The ghost of a smile lifted his lips. "But when you're ten and your father can't be bothered to find out if you're alive or dead, it can still make you feel worthless."

"You're not—"

His fingers pulled from hers and then pressed over the covers that shielded her stomach. "I don't ever want this baby to feel the way I did."

She had to blink away tears. "She won't." She? He?

"I don't want to be like him."

"You aren't." He had to see that.

"I want to be there, in this baby's life."

Why hadn't she told him sooner? This man before her, the man whose fingers were trembling as he stroked her stomach, he wasn't a man who'd run from fatherhood. He was a man who seemed to want it almost desperately.

"I don't want the baby to feel… I don't want the baby to be like me."

He was breaking her heart. She wrapped her arms around him and pulled Gunner down onto the bed with her. She just…held him. "This baby is wanted. Loved already."

He held her tighter.

She hadn't expected this from Gunner. He'd—

He kissed her. She shouldn't kiss him back, not with everything that was going on between them, but she did.

Because she still wanted him.

The nightmare memory of his death was too strong in her mind.

So her lips parted beneath his. She tasted him as he tasted her. The kiss wasn't rough or wild, but sensual and heavy with need.

As if he were savoring her.

Her body shifted restlessly against his. She'd thought about him so many nights in the past few weeks. Every night. Wanted, and been afraid that she'd never have him close like this again.

It had just taken the little matter of fire and near death to get them together again.

He kept kissing her. He held her carefully, as if he were worried that she'd break.

She was the one to push down the boxers that he wore. She was the one to stroke his body.

He kept kissing her.

Then, still so carefully, his hands began to trail down her body. His mouth went to her neck. Licked, sucked and then he found the sensitive spot just behind her ear….

She squeezed her eyes shut and moaned.

He tossed aside her T-shirt. Licked and kissed her breasts. The touch of his mouth on her nipples, with their increased sensitivity, had her trembling.

Sydney lifted her hips. Helped him to ditch her shorts and underwear, and then she parted her thighs.

Gunner started to thrust, but then he hesitated. "I don't—"

No, he'd better not say—

"I don't want to hurt you," he finished, voice rumbling.

She tried to smile for him. "You won't." Physically, she trusted Gunner more than she trusted any man.

With her emotions? With her heart? She wasn't sure; the pain might come again.

At that moment, she was willing to risk it.

He thrust into her. She met his rhythm eagerly, lifting up with her hips, arching against him. He filled her, stretched her perfectly, and she gasped at the heavy feel of him inside her.

Her hands curled around his shoulders. Her legs wrapped around his hips. He thrust into her, again, deeper. The rhythm swept her away, made her forget fire and fear and nightmares.

So that she knew only him and the pleasure that washed over her and made her cry out.

He held her tighter. Gave in to his own release with a growl of her name.

Then he just…held her, cradled her against his heart and kept his hand on her stomach.

Held her, and the nightmares didn't come back.

THE RINGING OF the phone woke Gunner. He could hear the peal, calling out from down the hall. Swearing, he opened his eyes. He saw Sydney, still sleeping next to him.

Beautiful Sydney.

He eased from the bed, trying not to wake her. The dawn's light spilled through the blinds. She hadn't gotten enough sleep, and in her condition, he wanted her to get all the rest that she could.

He slipped down the hallway. Found his phone. "Gunner."

Silence, then, "Are you *whispering?*"

Crap, he had been. He just hadn't wanted to wake Sydney. Gunner closed the door of his bedroom and cleared his throat. "What do you want, Logan?"

"I *want* to alert you to a security breach." His friend's voice held a tight edge now. "I just got the call from Mercer. Someone's been trying to hack in to the computer system at the EOD."

Hell. The EOD agents *were* being targeted again. The attack on Sydney's house must be the first launch.

"The thing is…our tech guys are saying that it looks like the breach came from inside."

Now, that wasn't what he'd expected. "Another agent?"

"Not sure." Static crackled over the phone. "But the person used the computer system *at* the main EOD office. Support staff, techs—they're all being investigated now. The office is under lockdown until we can figure out what's happening."

Gunner huffed out a hard breath. "What do you want me to do?"

"Stick like glue to Sydney's side. If she's the first target in this mess, there could be another attempt on her." Logan's voice hardened. "The files that were accessed? They were linked to Guerrero."

"What?" Guerrero—now a dead man—had been a Mexican arms dealer. He'd kidnapped Juliana James, the woman who had recently married Logan. When she'd been attacked, Logan had damn near gone crazy.

So how did Logan have to be feeling now?

"Someone was trying to dig into the classified documents that we have on him. That same someone…he or she was looking at Sydney's file. And yours."

Son of a—

"I'm getting a guard put on Juliana, too." Because Juliana had been instrumental in bringing down Guerrero—and because Gunner knew that Logan would never risk the woman he loved. "If someone is looking for some payback, they *aren't* getting it," Logan vowed.

No, they weren't. Gunner would make sure that no one hurt Sydney.

Not on his watch.

She was too important. The baby was too important. The life that he might just have with them—if he hadn't already screwed things up too much—*it* was too important.

SLADE ORTEZ STARED across the city. He'd chosen this apartment deliberately, though no one seemed to have realized that fact. The EOD. They thought they were so smart.

Clueless jerks.

Once upon a time, he'd wanted to be one of them. But he hadn't made the cut into the precious program. Good enough to risk his life on freelance missions, but not good enough to be brought into the fold.

Sydney had made the cut. Gunner had. Of course Gunner had.

But not Slade.

Never as good as big brother.

The EOD was paying for his apartment. Actually, Uncle Sam was paying for anything he wanted right now. After what he'd been through, they were giving him...what had they called it? *Compensation.*

There'd never be enough compensation.

He stared through the window, looking out at the city, and looking right over at the building that housed his brother.

Yes, he'd chosen this location for a reason.

To keep a watch on Gunner.

The fools at the EOD didn't realize what a threat Gunner was. They thought he was a hero. Their mistake. He'd make sure they fully realized the error of their ways.

Sydney had made a mistake, too.

She'd turned from him. Refused to go back to the way that things had been.

She should have been grateful to be with him. Of all the women—and he'd been with plenty—he'd agreed to marry her.

Sure, he'd kept a few girls on the side, the better to stop the boredom of being with just one woman, but he'd offered to marry *her*.

As payback, she'd slept with his brother.

At first, the rage had been so strong that he'd been sure it would consume him. Last night, it had come close. He'd given in to his darker urges.

But now, with the rising of the sun, he realized that there could still be hope for Sydney, if she could be made to see Gunner's true colors. Gunner would slip up, Sydney would turn from him, and Slade would be there.

It was all a matter of time.

He kept staring across at Gunner's place.

He tried not to think about the light that had flashed on in the middle of the night. He'd been watching then, too. Through his binoculars, he'd seen that light come on. The blinds had been open. He'd seen Sydney...

Gunner...

His jaw locked.

A matter of time.

Gunner would get the payback that he had coming.

Chapter Seven

"I need clothes." Sydney curled her toes into the thick carpet
in Gunner's living room. "As fun as it is to keep wearing
your T-shirt…" Her hands lifted the hem of his navy T-shirt.
"I need to go out in public with more than just this on."

But she looked so sexy in his shirt. With her long legs
stretching forever. Gunner cleared his throat. "That's, um,
being covered—"

His doorbell rang. Right. That should be her clothing.
Logan had told him that he'd be sending over some articles
for Sydney. Gunner hurried to the door. Glanced through
the peephole. Swore. Then he looked over his shoulder.
"Why don't you…uh…wait in the bedroom? I'll bring the
clothes to you." Because he didn't want the man on the
other side of that door seeing Sydney when she looked so…

Tempting.

Sydney shook her head, threw her hands into the air and
stomped off toward the bedroom.

Schooling his features, Gunner opened the door. Cale
stood there, shopping bags in his hands and a pained expression on his face. "Send me out to rescue a hostage in
the jungles of the Amazon," he drawled, the Texas slipping
into his voice as he stepped over the threshold, "but please
don't send me shopping for women's clothes ever again."

Gunner almost smiled. He *almost* smiled, would have, if he hadn't heard the returning tread of footsteps.

"Gunner," Sydney called out, "I'm going to need some shoes, too—*Cale?*"

Cale gave a low whistle. Then he choked because Gunner stepped into his path. "I, um, brought you some clothes, Sydney."

Gunner snatched the clothes from him. "Keep those eyes up," he ordered.

Cale's lips twitched. Gunner's own eyes narrowed. Cale was about to get on his—

"Relax, Gunner. I'm sure that Cale has seen a woman's legs before, plenty of times," Sydney said, a thread of humor in her voice.

But she wasn't just any woman. She was—

Mine.

Wasn't that the way he'd always thought about her?

Gunner forced himself to take a deep breath. "Eyes. Up." He gave the order once more; then he turned briskly and marched toward Sydney.

Her eyes were…twinkling. "If I didn't know better," she whispered, "I'd say you were almost jealous."

Almost? Not even close. Cale was one of those annoying pretty boys you saw in magazines. The guys who could easily wear tuxes and blend in anyplace.

Gunner knew what he looked like. A walking bad dream most days. With all the scars on him and a face that was too rough and hard, he was hardly the man women wanted to take home to meet the family.

He never had been.

"There's no need to be jealous." She took the bags from him. "Maybe you should learn to trust me." Her steps were quiet as she headed back into the bedroom to change.

He stilled. He did trust Sydney. In the field, he always

knew that she had his back. If you couldn't trust your team members on a mission, you couldn't trust anyone.

Logan, Sydney and Jasper Adams—the man whom Cale had only recently replaced in the Shadow Agents—they were like his family.

They *were* his family.

"I don't blame you for watching her walk away. That woman is a looker."

Gunner spun around.

Cale had his hands up. "Easy there, big guy. You don't have to worry about any threat from me." His lips twisted. "Not that the woman would be interested. Hell, I knew from day one that she was hung up on you." Then, softer, "Though hell if I can figure out why."

Gunner frowned at that.

"Maybe there's a charmer hidden under the grizzly bear exterior." Cale's hands dropped. "Some women go for the guys who growl."

Once more, the jerk almost made Gunner want to smile. Mostly because he'd said, *"I knew from day one that she was hung up on you."*

"How are you going to handle things with Slade?" Cale asked him, still keeping his voice low. "Because I'm going to assume that the ridiculous plan of giving her up—"

Gunner's brows climbed. Had that plan been so obvious?

"Yeah, I figured out that martyr bit earlier. Forget that. I'm going to assume that's over now?"

Sydney was pregnant. There was *no* way he'd leave her now. "I'll always be there for my brother."

"And for her?"

No one could make him leave Sydney. Last night, hell, he still couldn't believe she'd opened her arms to him last night. That she'd given him such pleasure.

Did it mean that she still cared? Just how *much* did she care?

The real question...*can I make her love me?*

"I'll stay close to Sydney," he said, trying to keep any emotion from his voice.

Cale raked his face with his gaze, considering. "That was the order, right? Logan said you were to keep her at your side, and I'm to do backup duty, watching you both." Cale's stare drifted around the condo. "This isn't the most secure place, you know. All of these windows..."

But Gunner liked the windows. After he'd been held prisoner and tortured on a mission gone bad, he'd needed to find a place that let him look out and feel free.

It was the same reason he'd helped his brother get settled in another nearby building. One that would give Slade views so that he knew he wasn't trapped.

Free.

"Just know that I've got your back, man, okay?" Cale said. "I'll be there for you and Sydney."

That was good to know. Gunner nodded.

Cale hesitated. "Logan told you about the Guerrero file?"

"Yes."

"You know...you and Sydney were on the list of EOD agents who were targeted for takedown."

Gunner rolled his shoulders. A few months back, Cale Lane hadn't been working for the EOD. In fact, the EOD had been hunting Cale. They'd thought that he was responsible for the murders of three EOD agents.

Cale was an ex-Ranger and an ex-mercenary. His psych profile had shown that he was prone to highly aggressive tendencies and that he could prove to be unstable.

Too late, they'd found out most of that profile was garbage, and then they'd realized that Cale was being set up. They'd started working together, and they'd tracked down the real killer—a man who was systematically working his way through a list of EOD agents who needed to be eliminated.

The killer had never had the chance to finish his kills. Never had the chance to take out Sydney or Gunner.

"This could be related to those attacks. Guerrero, the EOD agent hits...it could all tie together," Cale said, voice tight.

Gunner nodded. He feared, suspected, the same thing.

"If this is the case, then the EOD has one powerful enemy, one with a grudge against you and Sydney."

The bedroom door squeaked open. Gunner looked over his shoulder. Sydney was clad in jeans and a fresh shirt. She'd put on her sneakers and was coming toward them with a smile on her face.

"You haven't told her," Cale murmured.

No, not yet, he hadn't.

"Better update her on the way," Cale said, "because Logan wants us all in for a briefing in an hour."

Figured.

Sydney's smile faltered. "Gunner? What's going on?"

He exhaled slowly. He'd never sugarcoated when it came to a mission. Of the Shadow Agents, Sydney was the best at gathering intel. There was nothing that woman couldn't get a computer to tell her, so Gunner knew that Logan would want her in the office, working with the other techs to recover data and try to pick up a trail on the hacker.

So he just told her the plain truth. "The EOD may have been compromised."

Her eyes widened.

"And it looks like the breach came from the inside."

SYDNEY HURRIED OUT of Gunner's building, her steps too fast, but adrenaline was pulsing through her. First the arson at her house, and now someone had hacked into her file? Definitely a personal attack, and she wasn't about to stand by and do nothing.

She was going hunting.

"I'll follow you," Cale said as he exited the building after them. Sure enough, she saw his car waiting a few feet down the road. Cale and his cars. The man loved the classic rides. His vintage Mustang was parked at the edge of the street. Gunner's truck waited in his reserved spot. Being a special agent did have its perks, and having your vehicle close by in case of a government emergency, well, that was important.

Sydney nodded. "Thanks, Cale, I'll see you at the—"

Gunner slammed into her. Sydney's breath was knocked from her body as she tumbled toward the ground. Gunner twisted, trying to cushion her as she fell, and in that split second she just wondered…what the—

A loud *crack* sounded.

Gunfire.

She reached for her own weapon, a weapon she'd taken from Gunner's stash in the condo. Gunner had taken her down behind the truck, giving them cover behind that vehicle. As she pushed up into a crouch, his hands flew over her.

"Are you hurt?" he demanded.

Sydney gave a quick shake of her head. Not hurt, just *mad.*

Another hit? In less than twenty-four hours?

Gunner yanked out his phone. An instant later he was saying, "Logan, get a team on my street *now.* A shot was just fired." His gaze glittered as it held hers. "It came from the northwest corner, the James Fire Building. I saw the damn glint of light right before the bullet came at Sydney."

Gunner was a sharpshooter, one of the best she'd ever seen, so *of course* he'd know where that shot originated.

"Cale's clearing civilians now, and you get that team

here ASAP." He shoved the phone back into his pocket and yanked out the gun that had been holstered beneath his jacket. They'd both left the condo armed, just in case. When you knew you were being targeted, you never went anywhere without a weapon at your side.

"I want you to stay down," Gunner told her. "Stay behind this truck until backup arrives."

She knew what he was planning, and it was not going to fly with her. "While what? You race up to that building and face the shooter on your own?"

"I can't let him take any more shots! Civilians could be at risk."

The street had been nearly deserted when they came out. Just a young couple, walking down the sidewalk. Cale had gotten them clear, but what if someone else came out?

"You need cover," she told him. "I can provide it for you."

He shook his head. "You're the target, and I'm *not* letting him take another shot at you." His gaze dropped to her stomach. "Neither of you."

Her heart was racing too fast. "You can't go in alone."

Sirens were wailing. Yes, thank goodness. Someone had called the cops—could have been someone from the building, could have been Logan. Logan knew how to get the local officials to instantly jump into action.

"The cops are going to be here any second," Gunner said as he tilted his head to listen to that approaching wail. "They're going to scare the shooter off."

Because most shooters ran at the first sign of cops, except for the shooters who'd staged the attack to bring local enforcement *into* the danger zone.

In Gunner's eyes, she saw that same knowledge.

"I have to make sure no one else is at risk."

Because he was Gunner. And that was just what he did.

Sydney nodded grimly. "I won't be able to give you much cover. He's too far away."

Gunner pressed his lips to hers. "I just want you to stay safe."

Then he was gone. Damn him, he was rushing right out into the open. She lifted up, keeping as shielded as she could, and raised her gun. If she saw the glint of that weapon coming from the northwest, she *would*—

There was no glint from a weapon. And the sound of gunfire didn't break the stillness of this morning. Gunner kept to cover as much as he could as he ran toward the building.

No shots were fired.

Sydney still didn't relax her guard.

She stayed there, armed, ready to do anything necessary if she saw Gunner get threatened.

Soon the cops were pulling up and rushing toward her, rushing for the building on the northwest corner. Logan *had* already briefed them. Now it was just a matter of seeing if they could catch the shooter.

She glanced toward the building. *Gunner.*

THE JAMES FIRE Building was abandoned, due to be demolished in just a few weeks so that a new apartment complex could be built in its place. Isolated, private, it was the spot that Gunner would have picked himself if he had to take out a target on the street below.

So as he'd led Sydney to his truck, Gunner's gaze had automatically risen to that building. A reflex act. He'd scanned the windows, then seen the glint—a glint that didn't belong. He'd pushed Sydney to the ground.

Just in time.

He'd actually felt the bullet rip right past his skin.

Now he was in the building, moving quickly but quietly,

just the way his grandfather had taught him. The element of surprise was what he needed. If his prey was still inside, stupidly waiting for another shot…

I'll get you.

But then Gunner heard the thunder of footsteps. His prey was running down the stairs. If he wanted to escape, the shooter *had* to take the stairs. The electricity in that place had been cut off weeks ago, and judging from where Gunner had seen that rifle glint, the man would have been up on the tenth floor.

That was a whole lot of stairs to take. And if the man was armed with just that rifle, he wouldn't be able to aim that thing well as he ran down the stairs.

A grim smile curved Gunner's lips as he started up the stairs. No rustle of clothing, no tap of his boots, no sound at all. Higher, higher, he climbed.

Those rushing feet came closer and closer.

Then he could see the man, his legs rushing fast down the steps.

"Freeze!" Gunner roared. He wanted this man taken in alive. He wanted to know why he was targeting Sydney— or, more likely—why the guy had been *hired* to take the shot at her. Would the boss risk getting his hands dirty like this? Out in public, with a limited means of escape? Doubtful, but Gunner would make this man turn on his boss.

The footsteps didn't stop. Something heavy hit the stairs. A shot fired.

Ricocheted?

"I said *freeze!*" Gunner yelled. "Stand down! Stand—"

The man was running toward him. Gunner didn't see a rifle. The guy was sweating. His eyes were wild as he brought up his hands. Gunner saw the handgun gripped in the man's shaking fingers.

He's not going to stop. The guy was desperate to escape,

and he was about to shoot at Gunner. The man was ready to kill, in order to escape.

Gunner didn't hesitate. He pulled the trigger on his own weapon.

WHEN SHE HEARD the sound of the shots—two shots, fired closely together—Sydney started running toward the James Fire Building. Her heart was racing fast, adrenaline burning in her blood, and she *had* to get to Gunner.

Cops were in front of her. Slowing her down. She wanted to shove them aside—so she did. Then she headed into the building with her gun up, ready to do anything she had to do in order to help Gunner.

She found him on the stairs crouched over a body.

Sydney didn't lower her weapon. Her gaze swept over Gunner. *No blood. No blood. No blood.* The mantra repeated in her head until she could breathe normally again.

"He wouldn't drop his weapon." Gunner's voice. Flat. She lifted her left hand, curled it over his shoulder.

The cops were there, fanning around the body. Gunner's shot had been lethal, right to the heart.

The man's eyes were closed. His body lay sprawled and twisted on the stairs.

"There's a rifle, sir," one of the cops said.

Sydney lifted her head. She saw the young, uniformed cop pointing up the stairs.

Gunner rose. "He ditched it when he came down the stairs. I heard him toss it. Then he...he pulled his backup weapon."

Gunner hadn't been given a choice. She understood, just as she understood that it was never easy to take a life.

Whether Gunner was following mission orders and taking out a threat through his scope or fighting an up close enemy, it wasn't easy.

Never easy.

"Gunner?" she whispered, wanting him to look at her.

His head turned toward her. His eyelashes flickered. She knew Gunner wouldn't show emotion here. She'd seen him do this before. He shut down after a kill. Withdrew.

That was the way Gunner worked.

"I wanted to take him in alive," Gunner said softly. "I wanted to find out *why,* to find out who'd sent him."

Because Gunner must think this was a hired killer, just like the mercenary who'd targeted the EOD agents before. She glanced back at the man. Early thirties, blond hair slicked with sweat. She didn't recognize his face, had never seen him before.

The EOD would find out everything they could about him. They'd run down his fingerprints. Analyze the scene.

Her gaze flickered over him. There was a tattoo on the inside of the man's wrist. A striking snake. They'd track that tattoo, too. They'd find out who this man was and why he'd been shooting at them.

Gunner still held his gun in his right hand. Sydney tucked her own gun into the waistband of her jeans, then she reached for his weapon. "It's over now."

But Gunner shook his head. "No, I'm afraid it's just getting started."

THERE WAS SO much blood on his hands. Gunner knew he'd never be able to wash all of that blood away.

He was in the EOD office. He'd been questioned, cleared, briefed. The cops had handed their investigation over to federal agents—FBI personnel who would report their findings back to the EOD.

"Gunner?"

He turned to see Sydney standing in the doorway behind him. There was worry on her delicate features.

"Are you okay?" Sydney wanted to know.

He wasn't the one with a bullet in his heart. He should have tried for a nonfatal shot, but the man had been aiming his own weapon right at Gunner's head. There hadn't been time to do anything but fire. "I just killed our lead."

She frowned, then shut the door. Then she was coming closer to him. "You just saved my life, that's what you did."

He didn't speak.

"Why do you have such a hard time," she asked him, tilting her head back to better study him, "ever seeing yourself as a hero?"

"I do my job, Syd. That doesn't make me a hero."

"It does to me." She reached for his hands. The ones that had killed so easily before and, he knew, would again. He'd always been good at killing. "When I look at you, I see the man who saved my life today. The man who has saved me dozens of times in the field. You've saved so many. So *don't*—" now an order snapped in her words "—ever see yourself as anything less, understand me?"

She stared up at him, her bright eyes telling him that he was good. That he was worth something.

The woman was going to tear him apart.

A knock sounded at the door then. Sydney still held his hands. She didn't let go.

When the door opened and Slade stood there, Gunner wished she'd let go. He saw the flash of pain in Slade's eyes, but his brother quickly schooled his expression.

"I heard what happened." Slade's color was better. Not the pale mask of death that he'd looked like when he first came back to the U.S. "I wanted to make sure you were both okay."

Slade had been given clearance to come into the EOD office. Mercer wanted private updates with him, so Slade had access to some of the floors there.

Gunner carefully studied his brother. Did he know this man now? Had he really known him before? "I'm okay."

Slade's lips twisted. "Of course you are. Killing has always been easy for you." Slade's words uncomfortably echoed Gunner's own thoughts. "Aim and fire…" He laughed lightly. "Bet the guy never even saw you coming."

Gunner stiffened.

"Killing isn't easy for anyone," Sydney said, voice stilted. "A life is a life."

"Yeah, but some trash just needs to be taken out every now and then, right? And this bozo who targeted you…" His gaze focused on Sydney's face. "I'm glad he's gone. I don't—I don't want you in danger."

Sydney pulled away from Gunner. Actually, she put her body between Gunner and Slade. Gunner was struck by the fact that…she'd always been between him and his brother. From the first moment he'd seen her and—wanted his brother's girl.

She's not his any longer.

"You heard about the fire, too?" Sydney asked.

Slade nodded grimly. "What can I do? I want to help." He waited a beat, stepped forward, then added, "I *need* to help."

"We're not sure what's happening yet," Sydney told him, voice cautious. "Slade, we don't want you putting yourself in danger. You just got out of the veterans' facility. You need to recover more. You need—"

"I need to get my life back." The faint lines near his mouth deepened. "I'm not the kind of guy to sit on the sidelines. After two years, I *need* to get back in action. I want to be normal again. I want to be me." His voice roughed. "Let me help, both of you. I want to help."

Gunner could see the struggle on his brother's face, but he also didn't want to put Slade back in harm's way. Slade wasn't in shape to handle any dangerous missions, no way.

Slade straightened his shoulders. "I can help here, okay? In the EOD office. I can do grunt work, I can read through files. I can do *something*."

"Maybe you can," Gunner agreed, because he didn't want to hurt his brother's pride. Hadn't he already done enough to him? "We'll talk to Mercer and see what can happen."

"Good." Relief flashed in Slade's eyes, then his gaze dipped to Sydney once more. "I'm so sorry." A rasp had entered his voice. "Sorrier than I can ever say. I never, ever should have hit you."

She stared back at him. "You weren't yourself." Her words were flat.

"No, no, I wasn't." He came closer to her, caught her hands.

This time, Gunner was the one to tense.

"I'll prove to you that I'm better," Slade whispered. "I will."

Then he seemed to realize that he was holding her hands. He blinked, shook his head and backed away. "I'll go find Mercer. I want to talk to him first, plead my case, you know?"

He could try. Gunner wasn't sure that Mercer would allow the guy to do much, not with all the secure intel in the facility. But Gunner would talk to Mercer, too, and see if there was something very low-risk that Slade could do, something to help make Slade feel as though he was helping them.

Slade hurried out of the room. Gunner saw that Sydney had tilted her head, and her gaze was still on the door, even though Slade was gone.

Was she realizing that the man she'd known *was* fighting to return? It was too late for going back now, too late for them both.

"Sydney…" He exhaled slowly. "About Slade—"

She turned toward him. "Did you ever find out why Slade didn't make the EOD team?"

He blinked. That was the last question he'd expected from her.

"He seems to want to be here so badly, but he told me… he told me that he withdrew his agent application."

"That's what he told me, too."

A furrow had appeared between her eyes. "That's when he started taking all those charter trips. He said he was trying to save up extra money for the marriage."

The marriage.

"But after he disappeared, there was no money in his bank account."

He knew that. He'd helped Sydney pay for the funeral. But he didn't like where she was going with these questions. "What are you thinking?"

She bit her lower lip, then shook her head. The smile she gave him didn't reach her eyes. "Nothing. I'm just worrying over nothing." She backed up a step. "The techs are waiting for me."

"Don't leave the building without me," he told her, his worry breaking through.

Sydney gave him a little salute. "Wouldn't dream of it, sir."

Then she was gone, and he was left with a faint suspicion swirling in his own mind. At the time, he'd wondered why Slade's bank accounts had been cleared out. Cleared so that only dollars remained, when Slade had been doing charters for almost a year.

His money had vanished.

Gunner had pushed aside the mystery two years ago, but now he was wondering…just where had all of that cash gone?

SLADE TOOK A deep breath, then knocked on the door that led to Bruce Mercer's office. Well, the outer office, anyway. Because when he opened the door, he saw the hard stare of Mercer's assistant, Judith Rogers. Judith looked barely twenty-five, but he'd learned that the woman had the tenacity of a bulldog. He'd tried to get to Mercer before, and she'd blocked him more than once.

When she saw him, her auburn brows rose. "Do you have an appointment?" Judith demanded.

Great. He barely managed to keep his expression polite. Judith annoyed the hell out of him. "No, but he's going to want to see me."

"I doubt it." Crisp. "Mr. Mercer is a very busy man."

"Yeah, well, I think Mr. Mercer would like to know if he has a killer in his midst, don't you?" He tossed that out deliberately, knowing that Judith wouldn't be able to ignore those words. "Of course, if you just want to stand back and let an agent die…"

She stood instantly, all five foot nothing of her. Then she pointed at him. "Stay here." Her high heels clicked as she headed for Mercer's door. She was inside for—he counted—two minutes, and then she came back and told him, "Go in, he's waiting for you."

He didn't let his grin break free. He was good at controlling his expression. At showing only what he wanted folks to see. People were so easily fooled.

So easily.

He entered the main office and closed the door. He made sure to hesitate as if he were uncertain.

You're going down, Gunner. His brother had been downstairs, with his hands all over Sydney.

Right in front of me.

"Slade." Mercer sat behind his big, fancy desk. One of

his eyebrows had climbed. "Ms. Rogers told me that you had some information to give me."

Slade glanced over his shoulder, as if he were trying to make sure that no one could hear him. Then he nodded quickly.

"Have a seat." Mercer waved his hand toward the chair in front of him.

Slade limped toward the seat, making sure to drag his leg a bit, conscious of Mercer's assessing gaze as it fell on him.

"You're looking better."

"I am better." He'd been fine all along. That rehab had been a *joke*. He blew out a hard breath. "I heard about the attacks on Sydney."

"Did you." But the words weren't really a question.

Again, he nodded quickly. "I want to help." He let his hands tightly curl over the armrests on his chair. "Give me a job to do, give me *something*."

Mercer shook his head. "There's no way you're going into the field. You have no security clearance any longer— or the training needed—for a job like that." The man wasn't pulling punches. "And physically, mentally, you're far from ready for any mission."

That's what you think. But he didn't let the rage slip out. "Give me a job here. I heard the techs talking—they think someone tried to break into the system. I can watch surveillance video, I can read files, I can do *something*."

Mercer just stared back at him. "I thought you were here to talk to me about one of my agents being a threat."

Slade flinched.

"Do you have intel to provide to me?"

Slade looked down at the floor. "I want to help so I can prove it's *not* him."

Silence.

He forced himself to look up and, sure enough, Mercer

was still watching him with that too-assessing gaze. "Give me a name," Mercer ordered.

"He didn't leave me to die." Slade forced the words out in a rush. "I was wrong. It was the drugs talking. He couldn't have left me to die."

Mercer leaned forward. "You're talking about Gunner?"

"Yes." A rasp. "He didn't leave me to die, and he didn't try to hurt Sydney."

"Why does it sound like you're attempting to convince yourself of that?"

Slade glanced at the floor, took a deep breath, then looked back up at Mercer. "Because when we were teenagers, there was this…this girl that Gunner liked. Sarah Bell. Sweet little Sarah Bell." He could still see her in his mind. "She kind of looked like Sydney. Same light blond hair, same green eyes."

"Why are you telling me this story?" Mercer snapped.

He jerked to attention. "Sarah Bell…she broke up with Gunner. Said he was too rough for her, too wild. Then a week later, Sarah died."

He could still see all the flowers that had been at her funeral. Sarah had been particularly fond of roses. He'd put a dozen on her grave.

"Her whole family died," he whispered. "A fire broke out in their house while they were asleep. Someone had disabled their smoke detector, then poured gasoline all over the first level of their home. The fire started and they…" He swallowed the lump in his throat. "The newspapers said that the family never had a chance. They didn't wake up at all."

"Did the police find the arsonist?"

He shook his head.

"And you think that relates to this case because…?"

Did he have to draw the guy a damn map? "Because Sarah was with Gunner, and she left him. He told me, he *told* me that he wasn't going to let her go. She was his, and no one would ever take her from him." His breath rasped out. "Now he thinks that Sydney is his..." He let the sentence trail away.

Silence. The kind that stretched too long; then, finally, Mercer said, "I thought you said you wanted to prove it's not Gunner. Sounds to me like you're making a case for the arsonist *being* him."

"No, I—" He raked a hand over his face. "Maybe the drugs are still in my system. I'm being paranoid. I mean... the fires aren't even the same M.O., right? I'm sure the fire at Sydney's house wasn't set by gasoline and the detectors weren't disabled—"

"None of the alarms went off at Sydney's house, and while the arson investigation is ongoing, preliminary indications are that gasoline was the accelerant used."

He sagged in the chair. "But Gunner got her out? He was the hero last night, right? Not the bad guy. *Not* the arsonist."

Mercer's gaze gave nothing away.

"It can't be him," Slade whispered.

"If you're so sure that it's not him, then why are you in my office? Why did you tell Ms. Rogers that you had intel to give me?"

His hands dug deeper into the armrests. "Because... what if it *is* him? Our father...did Gunner tell you that he wound up in a mental ward? That's where he died. He'd gone crazy, and attacked his latest girlfriend—tried to kill her." His voice sounded hollow to his own ears. "We never saw him much growing up, but Gunner and I both always wondered...just how much like him were we?" He held Mercer's gaze. "How much?"

Chapter Eight

Sydney stared at the computer screen before her, absolutely sure that there had to be some kind of mistake.

For six hours, she'd been working with the other techs. They'd gone back through the system, tracking their hacker. Gone through every system link they could find.

They'd narrowed down the security breach. It had happened three days ago, at 0300 hours. Long before anyone *should* have been in the office.

The Guerrero case file had been accessed, her personnel file had been accessed and Gunner's file had been accessed. But according to the results she was seeing, their hacker had looked at Gunner's file for only two seconds. That wasn't long enough to learn any details. Just long enough to lead a cyber trail for them to follow. Long enough to show that someone had pulled the file.

Pulled it, but not scanned any information?

If their hacker wanted intel on Gunner, why not look longer? The hacker had been given access to her file for three minutes. He'd viewed all the Guerrero files for five minutes.

And it wasn't that the hacker had been interrupted. According to the report she was generating, he'd viewed Gunner's file first.

"Why?" Sydney whispered as she stared at the screen. He hadn't gotten any data from Gunner's file, so he'd gone there to what…lead a false trail? Gunner wasn't the target, just her?

"Sydney, we found the pass code that was used to get into the system," Hal West told her as he slid his chair toward hers. Hal was the lead systems administrator for the EOD.

She glanced up at him. A pass code would be needed to open the system, but their hacker had put a virus in place after he'd gotten access, and that pass code signature had been all but erased.

All but…

"It's an old code, one that was initiated over two years ago." Hal's face looked strained. Considering that she knew the guy had been working the computers for most of the night—while she'd been escaping from the blaze—that strain was to be expected. "The agent we originally assigned the code to was given a new access number a year ago." He shook his head. "Someone screwed up. When he got a new code, all privileges associated with the previous access should have been revoked. Someone didn't terminate the code authorization and—"

"Hal!" she snapped out. "Which agent had that code?"

"Uh…right," he said as his bleary blue gaze cut away from her and back to the nearby computer monitor. "Gunner Ortez."

She shook her head, an instinctive denial. "Gunner wasn't here when the files were accessed." She didn't even know why she said the words. Just—*not Gunner*.

But Hal was tapping on his keyboard and nodding. "He wasn't, or at least, the system says he didn't gain entry until 0500, but…that's his code."

"Then someone has access to our archived codes. We need a complete wipe on the system. Even if you *think* those codes are clear, we're purging them." Her heart was beating faster. It could be a setup. She'd sure seen setups before. Poor Cale. Evidence had been planted left and right to frame him. She knew better than to jump hungrily at the first bone that was tossed her way.

But maybe their hacker didn't know about the case with Cale. Maybe he didn't realize the lesson that all of the Shadow Agents had learned then.

And maybe he didn't fully realize...*we don't turn on our own.*

She hunched her shoulders and started tapping on her keyboard. This was an inside job, she didn't doubt that, but it wasn't Gunner. It wasn't Logan. It wasn't Cale. She trusted the other Shadow Agents with her life.

But she wouldn't overlook any possibility. Logan had assigned her to gather intel, so she would. She'd start by going back through the personnel and access files of every agent and support staff member who'd entered the EOD in the past six months.

She wasn't going to stop until she found more than just a red flag. She'd find hard evidence.

GUNNER STARED AT the charred remains of Sydney's house. Only a shell remained, blackened, gutted. When he thought of Sydney in that fire, fear knifed into him.

"Good thing you were here."

He glanced over to see Logan heading toward him. When Gunner had arrived moments before, Logan had been talking to the arson investigators.

Gunner remembered the brush of the fire on his skin as he ran up the stairs. "Yeah. Very good thing." If he hadn't been there...

"They actually found one of her smoke detectors. Fried, warped, but..." Logan glanced toward the house. "They managed to pry it open. The battery was missing."

What?

"It's definitely arson, of course. The chief says the point of origin was downstairs—actually, he says there were three points of origin. The guy wanted to make sure the house burned fast."

"He wanted to kill Sydney." Gunner's rage darkened the world for a moment.

From the corner of his eye, he saw Logan give a grim nod. "Yes, he did. The perp used gasoline as the accelerant. Disabled the alarms, waited until she went to bed…" He glanced over his shoulder at the woods that lined her property. "Probably waited out here, watching her, and when he thought he had the perfect moment to attack, he went to work."

The SOB.

"Why were you out here?" Logan's question was quiet, tense. "I mean, you and Sydney seemed to be staying away from each other at first, and now—"

I won't stay away from her again. He'd only come out there to do some on-site investigating. She was nestled inside the EOD office. With all the agents there, with Cale pulling extra guard duty, she should be safe.

Gunner rolled his shoulders, trying to push some of the tension from his body. "I came last night because Slade wanted to talk to her. I came out here to try to convince her to go see him."

Logan's eyebrows climbed. "You think that's a good idea?" He turned to fully face Gunner. "It's just you and me, man. So cut the bull. I've *seen* the way you watch her. What are you thinking? That you'll just step aside so he can have a shot with her again?"

Had he thought that? Or had he just felt so much guilt that he'd wanted to make amends? *I didn't know he was alive.* But for two years, Slade had suffered. Two years.

"You've been a captive, too, Gunner. The things they did

to you…" Logan shook his head. "Most men never would have come back from that."

Logan had seen him, after he'd crawled from that jungle. With his body stitched everywhere, looking like Frankenstein's monster.

"You've been through your own hell," Logan continued. "Don't you think you deserve some happiness, too?"

His hands clenched. "I wanted Sydney to have what—who—she wanted."

"And you think that's your brother? Uh, you might want to check that again. You're the one she's always watching. The way you watch her? With that too-intent gaze? Buddy, she watches you with the same stare."

"She's pregnant." The words slipped from him. Not deliberate, or, maybe they were. Because he wanted to tell someone. He had to share the news with someone, and Logan had always been a good friend.

Logan's eyes widened. "Yours?"

The question had him clenching his fingers into fists and taking a step forward. Maybe *not* such a friend for long.

Logan's hands flew up. "Of course it's yours! I meant, hell, I'm just stunned, okay? A baby… You and Sydney." He shook his head, and a broad smile split his lips. "That baby is going to wrap you around her finger!"

Yes, he was pretty sure that she would.

"A baby," Logan whispered, and his eyes widened. He glanced back at the house. "Oh, hell, man, you probably felt like your whole world was burning down last night."

"It was." Gunner didn't tell him that he hadn't known about the baby then. When he'd looked up and seen the flames, and known that Sydney was inside, yes, it had felt just as if his world was burning. Because it had been.

"We're gonna find him," Logan promised. "You know we will. With our resources…"

The EOD's resources were limitless. But even the EOD couldn't fight Mother Nature.

"A storm's coming in," Gunner said as his gaze rose to the thickening clouds above them. "That could wash away a lot of evidence." His gaze focused on the line of trees. If the guy had been out there, waiting, he might have left tracks behind. Gunner was very, very good at following tracks. "I'm going to see what I can find."

Logan nodded. "I kept the techs back because I figured you'd want first shot. Didn't want them messing up the scene."

Logan knew exactly how he liked to work.

"You lead the way," Logan continued, "and they'll be there to back you up." Then Logan clapped him on the shoulder. "Congratulations, man, you're going to make a great dad to that lucky kid."

Gunner tensed. "I…hope so."

Logan frowned at him. Before Logan could say more, Gunner headed toward the trees. He'd already scouted the area before, looking for the perfect vantage point that the attacker would have used. A spot that would provide him with good cover, but one that wouldn't put him too far away from the scene. The arsonist would have needed to get to the house quickly, and then be able to rush back and hide when the flames blazed.

Gunner wondered how long the man had stayed there. Had he watched as Gunner ran inside?

He eased through the light covering of brush at the edge of the woods. He made sure not to snap any branches. He didn't want to create any evidence confusion. His grandfather had taught him and Slade how to slip in and out of any place, without leaving any traces behind.

So far, he wasn't finding any evidence. No footprints

on the ground. No broken leaves or branches. The attacker had been careful.

But if he'd been watching for any length of time, he would have needed to find one spot. One perfect spot to sit and wait and watch. No matter how careful the man had been when he got in the woods, he would have left a sign at his waiting spot. Turned-down grass. A cigarette butt. Something. Most folks couldn't just wait for a long time in total stillness.

Gunner could. Most couldn't.

When they'd practiced with their grandfather, going out past the reservation and into the woods that surrounded the land there, Slade had always hated standing still. He'd taken to grabbing a piece of pine straw and braiding the pieces together, over and over, because Slade had needed something to keep his hands busy.

Some watchers smoked to help pass the time. A bad idea, because the prey could catch the scent of cigarettes in the air.

Some chewed gum. Some carried a toothpick.

Slade had twined the straw around his hand, an absent gesture, as he waited—and told Gunner what a stupid idea it was to follow their grandfather into the woods.

Gunner stilled and glanced back toward the house. This was the spot he would have chosen if he wanted to watch Sydney's home—to watch and not be seen. If he crouched lower, he'd be totally covered by the trees before him, but if he wanted to see, then he just shifted a bit to the left.

He had a perfect view of what had been Sydney's upstairs window.

He glanced down at the grass around him. It had bent, just a bit, enough to tell him that his instincts were right. The watcher had been here.

Gunner swept the ground with his gaze, looking for some

kind of path. He'd been on the road last night, and there hadn't been any other car on this dead-end street. That meant the watcher had stashed his vehicle some other place. Gunner knew that a highway waited, about four miles back through the woods. The guy would have needed to make a route back to that highway.

Gunner just had to find it.

The watcher was good. Gunner would give him that. It took him fifteen minutes of searching before he found the first broken branch. Sure, that branch could have been broken by a wild animal, but…

There was another snapped branch about ten feet away. Then another three feet.

The man had been in a rush to leave.

It was next to that snapped branch that Gunner stopped, frowning. He bent and picked up the braided pine straw that had been left behind.

He stared down at the straw, not wanting to believe what he was seeing. This threading…

He knew this threading.

When they'd been younger, Slade had tossed away pieces of straw like this dozens of times. His brother had twisted the straw, twined it around his hand, and—

"Gunner!"

He stiffened at Logan's call and his fingers tightened around the braided pine straw.

"Did you find anything?" Logan was closing in.

Gunner lowered his hand, squared his shoulders and turned to face the other man.

GUNNER FOUND SYDNEY typing frantically on the keyboard, her fingers flying. Her shoulders were hunched forward, and the light from the computer's monitor clearly showed the scowl on her face.

Even though the door was open, he rapped lightly. Hal, the admin working right beside Sydney, glanced over at him. When he saw Gunner, the guy's eyes doubled in size. "A-Agent Ortez."

"Hal, can I have a minute alone with Sydney?"

Hal jumped to his feet. "Sure thing." He gave Gunner a very wide berth as he hurried from the room.

Sydney just shook her head and kept typing.

Gunner frowned thoughtfully after the other man. "What's with him?"

"You intimidate him," Sydney said as she kept typing. "The way you intimidate most people you meet." She exhaled and finally pushed away from the computer and her chair spun so she could face him. She stared at him, giving him a considering look. "I think it's the eyes. The way they say, 'Yes, I've looked into hell a few times.'"

He blinked at her.

She smiled at him. "But I'm rather fond of your eyes."

No way were his cheeks flushing right now. Okay, perhaps they were, and he was very grateful for the olive skin that had to hide most of that flush.

Then her smile slipped away. "What did you find out at my house?"

He wasn't real eager to start sharing that, so he said, "What have you found out here?"

"Here?" Her lips tightened. "Here I've found out that it looks like someone used your old access code to gain entrance into the system."

"Mine?"

"Yes. Your personnel file was accessed, too, but only for a few seconds, not nearly as long as my file and the Guerrero file were."

His muscles locked. "Someone's setting me up."

She nodded. "That would be my thought." She pushed

out of the chair and closed the distance between them. "Now tell me what *you* found at my house." Pain flickered in her eyes. "Was anything left?"

"No, Syd, I'm sorry."

Her chin lifted, the way it always did when she was trying to pull her strength together. "That place…it was my retreat while I was in D.C. My *home* has always been in Baton Rouge. I'll get over this," she said with a firm nod. "I will."

He believed her, but there was still more to tell. "I tracked through the woods, looking for a sign of the arsonist."

"And?"

"I might have a lead."

She sighed. "Don't play this game. Tell me what you've got or I'll just go straight to Logan."

"I think it could be Slade." Harsh words. Words that he hadn't wanted to say, but she needed to be aware of the danger that could be right beside them both.

Her eyes widened. Not doubling in size as Hal's had, but still showing her surprise. "What?"

This was where he got to tell her that a few pieces of straw were making him suspect his brother. Flimsy evidence that hadn't exactly convinced Logan. "He was trained to leave no trail, just like I was. He's good, but…"

"Not as good as you," she finished quietly.

"He could never just sit still. He always had to do something to keep his hands occupied. He'd take pine straw, twist it, braid it." Gunner almost thought of the twisted straw as his brother's signature. Whenever they'd been kids, and he'd found the straw in the woods, he'd known that Slade had been there. "I found some of that braided straw in the woods near your house."

"But he had a guard on him. You told me—"

"Logan's checking with the guard to make sure that Slade didn't slip away." Once Logan had questioned the guard, then they'd have a better idea of where they stood. Right now Gunner just had a dark suspicion boiling in his gut.

"You really think Slade would try to kill me?"

Slade *had* attacked her once. The sight of the bruising on her jaw had enraged him. If Slade thought that Gunner was taking Sydney away from him, well, Gunner wasn't sure just how his brother would react.

The man he'd been years before...*no,* that guy wouldn't do something like this. But the guy who'd came out of the jungle, addicted to *muerte,* he just might.

"What about the man who took the shot at me? Do you think he's somehow linked to Slade? To the hacking?"

"I don't know." All he had were his instincts, screaming at him. "There isn't enough evidence yet to know what's happening." And the fact that she was turning up evidence to implicate him? That was even worse for the situation. "I just want you on guard. I don't want you ever alone with him."

She stared up at him. "My personnel file...whoever accessed it knows about the pregnancy."

The pregnancy could have been enough to push Slade over the edge. Gunner could see Slade hacking in to Sydney's file, wanting to learn everything about her, but there was no reason for Slade to hack in to the Guerrero file, *if* he even knew how to hack. "When was that access code of mine used last?"

"It's one that went obsolete—or should have gone obsolete—over two years ago."

When Slade had still been around.

The phone on Gunner's hip vibrated, right at the same time that Sydney's vibrated, too. Gunner pulled out his phone and read the text. "Tina?" he asked Sydney, sure she'd just gotten the same message from the doctor.

Sydney gave a nod, then quickly signed off on the computer, securing the machine.

Tina's text had said that she had blood test results that she needed to share with them, ASAP. She wanted them in the med room.

He knew that she'd been assisting with the autopsy on the man he'd shot at the James Fire Building. Tina didn't normally handle autopsies, but Mercer had ordered her in on this one because he wanted one of his close staff members with eyes in that morgue. And when Mercer gave an order, few folks ever refused.

Sydney was silent as they entered the elevator. Gunner felt too conscious of her every move. He wanted to talk to her about last night, but since he'd just dropped the bombshell of his suspicions on her, he wasn't quite sure how to lead into that.

He wasn't the guy with the smooth lines and easy conversation. He never had been. He actually found it hard to talk to people outside of his team. The rest of the world just didn't seem to understand him.

Especially women.

When he'd been a teen, there had been one girl he liked, a little blonde with green eyes. But when she'd talked to him, he'd pretty much wound up replying in monosyllables, and she'd started to date his brother instead.

What had her name been? He wasn't sure.

The elevator dinged. The doors slid open. Sydney walked out, and Gunner realized he hadn't said a word to her that whole time. Smooth. Gritting his teeth, he followed her into the med room.

Tina was waiting there with Mercer. Mercer had his arms crossed over his chest as he leaned back against a filing cabinet.

"Dr. Jamison has found some interesting results for us,"

Mercer murmured. Gunner noticed that the man's assessing stare drifted to him, then returned to Tina.

"It's the blood work." Tina pushed a report toward him and Sydney. "I found *muerte* in the man's system."

Muerte. "The same drug my brother was on?" His gaze snapped to Mercer. "I thought you said the drug hadn't made it to the U.S."

"That's what the DEA told me. Looks like they could be wrong about that."

Sydney whistled as she studied the reports. "These are some extremely high levels. We're lucky he didn't shoot up the whole block."

"The whole block wasn't his target," Mercer said quietly. "You were."

Sydney's fingers tightened around the report. "Do we know who he is?"

Tina nodded. "I got a hit on his fingerprints. Ken Bridges. He's ex-army, dishonorably discharged for conduct unbecoming." She cleared her throat. "He, um, almost beat a man to death while he was on a recon mission. The man was a civilian, completely unrelated to the mission."

"What had Ken been doing since the army?" Gunner asked.

"Looks like whatever he could get paid to do."

A gun for hire. Figured.

"The DEA's getting pulled in on this one," Mercer said. "They're going to investigate Ken, break apart his life and follow the trail they find back to the *muerte*."

The *muerte* trail already led to Slade. So he had to ask, "Are you questioning my brother?"

"Any intel that Slade can provide to us about the men who held him and addicted him will be used by the DEA."

Gunner gave a hard shake of his head. "That's not what I'm asking." He'd been blunt with Sydney and with Logan.

He'd be no less with Mercer. "Are you going to interrogate him? To see if he's linked to this guy?"

Mercer's head tilted as he studied Gunner. "Your brother has been either under guard or in a rehab facility for the majority of his time in the U.S. How is he supposed to have hooked up with a hired gun?"

"This guy's ex-army, right? Maybe he hooked up with him *in* rehab. Maybe there was someone there who gave him Bridges's number. If Bridges was addicted, then he'd probably know guys in that same rehab unit." It made sense. Mercer had to see that.

"If there's a link between them," Sydney said, "we can find it."

He had no doubt.

Tina was staring at them all with wide eyes.

"You think your brother is doing this? You really think he could be the one targeting Sydney?" Mercer asked as he uncrossed his arms.

"I don't want to suspect him."

"Why not?" Mercer asked softly. "He sure suspects you."

That was the last thing Gunner had expected to hear. He snapped to attention. "Sir?"

But Mercer was pointing toward the door. "Let's finish the rest of this conversation upstairs, Gunner. Dr. Jamison, good work. Sydney—"

"I want to be a part of that upstairs conversation," she said, voice tensing with a demand.

The ghost of a smile curved Mercer's thin lips. In his mid-fifties, Mercer still had the tough edge of a man half his age. "Since it's your life, I rather suspected you'd request just that."

Then Mercer walked toward the door.

Gunner glanced at Sydney, wondering what the hell she

had to be thinking about this turn of events. His brother thought he was the killer?

And I think it's him.

But the real question was…who did Sydney trust? Which brother did she think was there to protect her, and which was there to kill her?

Chapter Nine

They didn't go to Mercer's office. They went into an interrogation room, and that fact put Sydney on edge.

She glanced toward the two-way mirror. Was someone watching them? What in the world was going on?

As far as she was concerned, there was no way that Gunner was a suspect, and Mercer had better stop treating him that way.

"Gunner, you understand that I have to explore every avenue in this case." No emotion broke through Mercer's words. "You've been a fine agent here, and I have nothing but respect for the work that you've done."

Sydney couldn't stand it. "So why are we in *interrogation?*"

Mercer glanced over at her. He and Gunner were both seated. She was pacing like mad. "Because procedure has to be followed, and I don't want this situation coming back to bite me later," Mercer told her quietly.

She stopped pacing.

"So let's get through this as quickly as we can." Mercer looked back at Gunner. "Do you know a woman named Sarah Bell?"

Sydney frowned. The name meant nothing to her.

"Sarah." Gunner seemed to be testing the name. Then he nodded. "I knew her, a long time ago."

The door opened then, and Mercer's assistant, Judith, hurried into the room. She handed Mercer a file. "Thank you," he told her, inclining his head.

As Judith left, Sydney was pretty sure the other woman flashed her a look of pity. Of pity? What was up with that?

"How long ago?" Mercer asked.

"I was eighteen. She was...I think sixteen at the time? Sarah Bell...she was killed in a fire."

"Yes, she was."

Mercer opened the file and pushed some grainy black-and-white photographs toward Gunner. "I pulled the arson reports on her fire. The M.O. that the arsonist used, it's the same as the one that was used at Sydney's place."

Sydney grabbed the nearest chair and sat down—hard. Then she strained to see those photographs. The charred remains of the house had her swallowing a few times. Then she saw the newspaper reports that had been printed off and included in that manila file.

Family Perishes in Blaze.

"Sarah Bell and her parents all died in the fire," Mercer said. "Unfortunately, the arsonist was never apprehended."

Gunner leaned forward. "You think I had something to do with this?"

"Your grandfather passed away a week before that fire. His passing...when he was the only one to ever provide stability to your life...it had to leave you feeling lost."

"I wasn't lost." Flat. "I had my brother to take care of. He needed me."

"He needed you, but you *wanted* Sarah Bell?"

Now another picture was pushed forward. This one appeared to have been taken from a yearbook. A young girl with curly blond hair and sparkling green eyes. In the picture, she smiled, flashing dimples.

"I never dated Sarah Bell."

"Are you sure about that?" Mercer pressed. "Because your brother said you were sweet on her back then."

Gunner started to respond, then stopped.

The tension in the room ratcheted up. *He had cared for Sarah.*

"She was a nice girl," he said. "She never seemed to care that my clothes were old or that I had to work two jobs around my school schedule. Sarah…she was good to everyone."

"I heard she wasn't so good to you."

"That's what Slade said?" Gunner asked. Sydney saw a muscle flex along his jaw.

A nod from Mercer. "He said she rejected you, and you didn't handle that rejection so well."

Gunner laughed then, but the sound made goose bumps rise on Sydney's arms. "Slade was the one who dated her, not me."

"How'd that make you feel?" Mercer's gaze bored into him. "Angry? Enraged? A girl who should be with you… but she wound up with your brother."

Gunner shook his head.

But Mercer wasn't done. "Then it happened again, didn't it? Another girl you wanted…" He cast a fast glance toward Sydney. "But she wound up with your brother."

Enough.

Sydney jumped to her feet. The chair slammed back behind her, and it hit the floor. "Stop accusing him, okay? Gunner didn't do this!"

"But his access code was used." Mercer's voice was still without emotion. "Hal told me what he discovered today."

"He discovered a setup, *that's* what he discovered," Sydney snapped. "You can't actually believe that Gunner could be responsible for this—"

"I have to explore all possibilities," Mercer said again. "Every avenue."

Sydney huffed out an angry breath. "Why would he access the Guerrero file? He has no reason to do that."

"*He's* not the one talking right now," Mercer pointed out.

For an instant, Sydney was tempted to go across that table, boss or no boss. He wasn't just going to sit there and accuse Gunner. Not while she—

Gunner's fingers wrapped around her wrist. "Easy."

He must have realized just how close she was to lunging. But the last thing Sydney was feeling was *easy* at that moment.

"Pull up your security cameras," Gunner told Mercer. She wondered how he could sound so calm. "You'll see I wasn't even at the facility during the time of the breach."

"Funny thing about that…the cameras weren't working then." Mercer's lips thinned. "This facility is supposedly one of the most secure locations in the world, and our damn security cameras blacked out. You know what that tells me? It says we were hit by a professional, one with covert skills that would let him get in and out of a building without being noticed." His fingers drummed on the table. "It also tells me that we're definitely looking at an inside job. Someone knew all of our weaknesses. Someone studied them. And that person or persons exploited them."

Sydney frowned. Hal hadn't mentioned that the security cameras stopped working during the breach. He was the one who should've had an uplink to those videos. If they went off-line, he should have been alerted immediately. "Did you question Hal?"

Mercer nodded. "Who do you think I talked to first? The man was shaking so hard he could barely answer any of my questions."

And he'd been so nervous when Gunner came into the

room. She'd just written off that nervousness because Gunner truly did make most people tense up, but what if it had been more?

Hal was the one who'd found the evidence linking Gunner to the hacking.

Hal was the one who *should* have been alerted to the camera failure.

"If anyone knew how to get past the security system," she whispered, "it would be Hal."

Mercer shook his head. "His key card wasn't used for entry that night. Hal wasn't here—"

Sydney laughed, but the sound held no humor. She was still standing and definitely didn't feel like sitting. "Hal knows the system in this building from the inside out. If he wanted to slip in, he could."

Was she throwing Hal under the bus? At this point, Sydney wasn't sure. She just knew…Gunner hadn't done this. "I want to look at Hal's computer."

Or rather the roomful of computers that he actually had.

"Sydney…" Mercer began.

"I want to check his data. He said the authorization code linked back to Gunner. Well, that code should have been deleted years ago. By Hal. I want to see his computers. I want to find out just what searches he used to find that intel." Her heart was beating too fast, but Gunner didn't seem to be defending himself. *Why not?* So someone had to prove his innocence.

She wasn't wrong about Gunner. She wouldn't be wrong. There was no way that he'd tried to kill her.

No way.

Mercer was studying her with his hard gaze. Sydney held her breath, waiting, then… His head inclined toward her. "Go search the computers."

Yes. She nearly ran for the door. This was what she

needed. What she had to do. Gunner was clear. Or he would be, once she was done.

Because she wouldn't lose faith in the one man who'd pulled her from the darkness. He'd helped her before. She'd help him now.

SILENCE FILLED THE room after the door shut behind Sydney.

Gunner knew his body was too tense, but he wasn't exactly in the mood to relax.

"She has a lot of faith in you," Mercer finally said, voice considering.

Yes, she did. Enough faith to humble him.

"You didn't seem to have as much faith in her."

Gunner's eyes narrowed.

"I mean, you were so sure that she'd go back to Slade, right? You were the one who backed away."

"Listening to gossip, are you?"

"I listen to everything. In this business, you have to." Mercer sighed. "I don't like this."

"You think I do?"

"I think you're barely holding on to your control. You're so worried about Sydney that you can't even think straight." Mercer stabbed a finger toward him. "Get your head in the game, Gunner. Stop letting your emotions rule you."

He'd never let emotions rule him. Not until—

Sydney.

"If the evidence against you keeps piling up, I'll have to act."

Those words sounded like a warning.

"My gut tells me you're clear. I *know* you, and I don't want to be wrong about you."

"You aren't." Neither was Sydney.

"Then find my perp. Bring me evidence that I can use to nail him to the wall."

Gunner unclenched his jaw. "I want Cale Lane reassigned. Get him to start guarding Slade."

He trusted Cale. No way would Slade slip by him.

"Already done," Mercer murmured. Then he rose. The legs of his chair slid back with a screech. "Protect her."

With his life.

"Sydney reminds me…" Mercer began, but then his words trailed away. Sadness flickered in his eyes, and the lines on his face deepened. The man looked as though he was skirting sixty, but Gunner had no idea at all what Mercer's personal life was like. Did he have a wife? A family?

Mercer cleared his throat. "She reminds me of a woman I knew a long time ago. I lost her."

"I'm sorry."

"You'll be sorrier if you lose her, trust me." Then he headed from the door. "There are some things that even soldiers can't recover from."

If he lost Sydney, the baby…no, he'd never recover.

Good thing he wasn't planning on losing them.

SYDNEY SWIPED HER key card over the access panel, and when the lights flashed green, she pushed her way inside Hal's inner sanctum. The Hub, as he called it.

Hal wasn't there. Good. He should have gone home an hour ago. Time for her to get working and see exactly what was happening with his system.

She eased into his chair, started typing and immediately, the screen froze on her.

Hal had installed extra protection on his machine.

Good for him. Except…she'd been there when he'd installed that protection. He hadn't even bothered to glance over his shoulder to see if she was watching while he typed in his code.

She'd been watching.

And she *never* forgot a code.

Her fingers tapped quickly over the keyboard. She knew how to get around this system. Hal never gave her enough credit.

Then she was pulling up the searches he'd used in the mainframe, and yes, sure enough, the access code had linked to Gunner. Damn it.

But she kept searching. Looking for the security video feed from the night of the breach—a feed that should have been there.

Her eyes narrowed on the screen as she read the system file for the time of 0300 on the date of the breach. There were no reported errors with the monitoring system. No reported errors at all because...

Her fingers typed faster.

Because Hal had shut off the system thirty minutes before. She could see the override, right there on the screen. He *was* in on—

"I figured you would be the one to come and look at the security logs." The door behind her closed with a soft *click*.

Sydney tensed. She'd been so intent on the monitor that she hadn't even realized that Hal had come into the room.

But as she looked up into the monitor, she could see his reflection. He was walking toward her, and he had a weapon in his hand.

A gun.

He wouldn't have gotten past the security check-in downstairs with that weapon. But they had a weapons room on the second floor. As if it would have been hard for Hal to help himself to some equipment. After all, he controlled the access to most of the rooms in that building.

She inhaled a steadying breath. She didn't have a gun, but that didn't mean she was defenseless. She was the one trained for combat. Not Hal and his nervous hands. He might think that he had the advantage, but he'd soon realize the error of his ways.

"You were supposed to die, though," Hal said. "So it wasn't going to matter. The shooter was going to take you out. You'd be dead, so you wouldn't come in here and find out about me."

"Why?" She turned and looked at him. A deliberate move on her part. For someone like Hal, someone not used to doling out death, looking into the face of his victim would be hard.

Staring into her eyes, then killing her...even harder.

Her fingers curled around the pen she'd taken from his desk.

"I didn't want to," Hal whispered, and sure enough, his hands were shaking. "I didn't have a choice. He was going to hurt my family." His eyes teared. "They're all I have... he *knew* things about them. Too much. I had to do it."

"You had to turn off the cameras?" She wanted to keep him talking. Needed to.

Hal nodded.

"And you gave him the access code?"

"Y-yes."

The shaking of that gun was making her nervous. Her body was tense, ready to attack, and she planned to lunge at him soon, but she had to time her move just right. The last thing she wanted was a bullet hitting her or the baby.

The baby.

"Do you know I'm pregnant?" she whispered. "Please, Hal, don't hurt the baby." She meant that plea. The baby— the one she hadn't even felt moving inside her yet—mattered more than anything to her.

Hal hesitated. "Baby?" The gun began to lower.

It was the moment she needed. Sydney leaped out of her chair. With one hand, she grabbed Hal's right wrist—

his right hand still clasped the gun—and she shoved that wrist out wide, making sure he wouldn't have a shot at her. Then, with her other hand, she brought up her pen, aiming for his now exposed inner arm. She drove the pen into his arm because she knew that his reflex action at that attack would be to drop the weapon.

The gun hit the floor. Just as she'd anticipated. But it discharged on impact, and the shot echoed around her.

Instantly she could hear the scream of alarms. No way would a gunshot be missed in a place like this.

Then, as Hal was howling, she brought up her elbow and slammed it into his nose. She heard the snap and saw the spurt of blood from his nose. Hal backed away from her, crouching and...crying?

Sydney kicked the gun across the room. It skittered toward the entrance. She kept her hands loose at her sides, ready to attack again if necessary.

But Hal wasn't putting up much of a fight. He was trying to stop the blood that was flowing from his nose and saying—

"I'm sorry, I'm sorry, I'm sorry..."

"You're sorry?" Sydney demanded. The alarm was hurting her ears. "You pulled a gun on me. You leaked classified information. You need to be a whole lot more than just sorry."

He stood, or tried to stand, but his body kept trembling. His hand went to his side.

Over his shoulder, she caught the movement of the door as it opened.

"I want a name," Sydney demanded through gritted teeth. "I want a full description of the guy. I want to know exactly who paid you off."

Hal shook his head. "I—I can't—"

"Do you know what happens to people found guilty of

treason? Do you have any idea just how long you'll be in jail?" Not to mention the slew of other charges that would be coming against him.

He shook his head again harder this time. "I can't... can't go to jail."

Maybe you should have thought about that before you sold out the EOD and me.

"Give me a name. If you cooperate, then——"

"I *can't!*" And his left hand came up. His fingers were wrapped around a box cutter. He had been a busy man. "*Muerte,* I——"

A shot rang out.

Sydney was staring right into Hal's gaze, and she saw his eyes widen in shock. Then his body was crumpling as he fell to the floor. She rushed toward him. *No, no, no!* He couldn't die. He knew the identity of the man who'd infiltrated the EOD.

She put her hands on either side of his head, tried to make him look at her. "Hal?"

His eyes were wide open with shock and pain.

She moved closer, forcing him to see her. "Hal, give me a name."

"S-sorry..."

"Don't be sorry." There wasn't time for sorry. "Help me, Hal. Make this right. Give me a name."

But Hal wasn't going to give her anything. As she stared at him, all of the life vanished from his eyes.

"Hal?"

He was gone.

"Sydney?"

She looked up. Slade stood just a few feet away, a gun in his hand. Hal's gun. The gun she'd kicked across the room so Hal couldn't use it again.

"I—I saw him coming at you, I thought he had a knife…."

The box cutter could have done as much damage as a knife, but she would have been able to knock it out of Hal's hand. She knew plenty of techniques to disarm him.

"I couldn't let him hurt you," Slade whispered. His eyes—filled with horror—were on Hal's still body. "I just reacted. I just…shot."

Footsteps pounded in the hallway. She could hear them through the open door. Then Gunner was there, bursting into the room. "Sydney!"

He saw Slade with the gun. He lunged for his brother.

"Gunner!" Sydney called out.

Slade didn't fight him. Gunner yanked the gun away from Slade and shoved the smaller man up against the nearest wall. Then Gunner turned that gun on his brother. "What the hell are you doing?"

Sydney rose. "Saving me."

Mercer was there, too, breath heaving from his lungs. She saw Cale and a few other agents.

All too late to change what had happened.

She straightened her shoulders. "Hal attacked me. Slade came in and…he thought he was saving me."

Gunner glanced back at her. His eyes widened as his gaze swept over her. He put the gun down on a table, and then he was across the room in an instant, his hands running over her arms. "Is the blood yours?" There was a tight, desperate quality in his words that she'd never heard before.

Sydney shook her head. "All Hal's."

Gunner's hand was resting over her stomach now.

"I'm *okay.*" They both were. She looked to the right. Mercer had crouched next to Hal, but the others were watching her and Gunner. Silent, tense.

Gunner locked his jaw, gave a grim nod and slowly dropped his hand.

She heard a ragged gasp and her gaze met Slade's. He'd seen Gunner's hand on her stomach. Seen the fear and worry on Gunner's face.

He knows.

Slade's head tilted down. His hands clenched into fists.

Tears stung her eyes. Things should never have been this twisted.

"Why the hell did Hal go after you?" Cale asked.

"Because I knew what he'd done. I found it…" She pointed toward the computer. "Hal's the one who turned off the security feed. Probably so we wouldn't realize that he was the one here that night, doing the hacking. He used Gunner's old code. Hal set him up."

Mercer's fingers were on Hal's neck, looking for a pulse. He wasn't going to find one.

He must have realized that same fact because Mercer swore and glanced up at her. "Did he tell you *why?*"

Mercer wasn't the kind of man to take kindly to betrayals. But then, who was? Only with Mercer, she knew the retribution for betraying him usually involved death or imprisonment.

"He said…he said he didn't have a choice. That his family was threatened." But if she looked into his bank accounts, would she discover that he'd been paid off? Not just threats, but an enticing wad of cash to help him escape from the EOD and start fresh somewhere else?

There was always a price that had to be paid for a betrayal.

"Muerte," she whispered.

Cale's gaze cut to Slade. Slade shook his head.

"That was the last thing Hal said to me."

"Maybe he was afraid of death," one of the other agents muttered.

No, she didn't think he'd been talking about death so much as the drug. With the drug showing up in the shooter's blood, with that being the last word that Hal had spoken, the dots were connecting in a very deadly way.

"It's in the U.S." Mercer stood. He had blood on his fancy suit. "The bastards have it here, and the DEA doesn't even realize it." He waved his hands. "I want this room clear. Don't touch anything, hear me? I'm getting a crime scene analysis team sent in from the FBI. They owe me, and the feds are about to start paying up."

Sydney eased toward Slade. He looked up at her, his face pale.

"I heard the gunshot," he whispered. "I was in the hall-way. I didn't…I didn't even know you were the one in here. The door was ajar…I just slipped in."

And he'd seen her and Hal in a standoff.

"When I saw the weapon in his hand…" Slade swallowed. "I just fired. I killed him."

Gunner was at her back. Silent.

Slade's gaze dropped to her stomach. He swallowed. "There… Is there something you want to tell me?"

No, she couldn't tell him. Not now. Not in front of all the others. But Slade had just killed to protect her, so she had to say something. "Thank you," she whispered, and wrapped her arms around him, giving him a hug.

His hands closed around her. She felt the light touch of his lips on her head. "I'd never let anything happen to you."

She pulled back, stared into his eyes.

"Never."

She took a step away from him.

"Slade…" Gunner began.

Slade flinched. "I know I'm about to get busted for firing a weapon in here, okay? Mercer's going to rip into me—"

"You were here when I wasn't. I just..." Gunner leveled his stare at the other man. "I'm thankful."

But there was an edge in Gunner's voice. One that gave her pause. Maybe because...

She didn't quite believe what he was saying.

There wasn't any more time for talking or questions then. As Mercer herded them out, he separated her from the rest of the group and led her to his office.

She knew her own interrogation was about to begin.

She'd wanted to prove that Gunner was innocent, but she hadn't wanted anyone to die.

Two deaths in the past twenty-four hours.

What would happen next? Because Sydney was sure the nightmare wasn't over. Not by a long shot.

SHE WAS PREGNANT.

Slade walked down the hallway, trying to keep his movements slow and easy, even as rage built inside him.

Sydney was pregnant. He'd seen the way Gunner touched her stomach, heard his brother's desperate whisper.

Cale was walking behind him doing guard duty. Slade had just saved Sydney, been the hero, and they were still guarding him.

Gunner had looked as though he would choke when he realized Slade had been the one to save the day.

Too late this time, brother. For once, someone else got to be the hero.

Cale's hand wrapped around Slade's shoulder. "Mercer wants to talk to you."

Of course he did. Mercer would want to grill him some more when he should want to pin a medal on his chest.

But Gunner was the one with the medals, and he…he was the one left to rot.

Slade nodded. "Right," he said timidly. He thought the tremble in his voice was a good touch. Made him look as if he was still shaken after the shooting.

He'd planned to kill Hal that day, one way or another. He'd known the guy was a weak link, and he'd intended to eliminate him at the first opportunity. Only he'd wanted Hal's death to be linked to Gunner. More evidence and suspicion mounted on big brother.

No matter. At least Sydney was back to thinking he was the good guy. He could definitely manage to use that to his advantage.

As for putting more suspicion on Gunner? Well, he already knew exactly what he'd do on that score. And after the next attack, Sydney would be convinced that her lover was trying to kill her.

Chapter Ten

"Sydney!" She turned at Gunner's call. She'd been heading for the elevator. It was far past midnight, and she just needed to crash.

"Are you ready to leave?" he asked her.

More than ready. She'd been heading upstairs to find him, but now they could just head out to the parking garage together.

"I had your car brought in," he told her as they slid into the elevator.

"Thanks." She knew her smile had to be tired.

Gunner frowned at her, and then he leaned forward and pressed the emergency stop button on the elevator's control panel.

"Uh, Gunner?" The elevator had stopped.

He pulled her into his arms, kissed her. The kiss was wild, hot, desperate.

His hands were tight around her, his body so hard and strong. He kissed her as if she were some kind of lifeline for him. As if he needed her to survive.

Only fair, since she needed him so very badly.

Gunner lifted his mouth a few inches from hers and growled, "I thought you'd been shot. I thought Slade had shot *you*."

But no, Slade had been the one to save her.

"There was blood on you…"

She'd switched into some backup clothes that she kept at the EOD. Those bloodstained clothes had caused nausea to roll in her belly.

"I think you scared a good ten years off my life." His arms were still around her.

Sydney stared up at him. "I didn't think anything scared you." Gunner was the tough guy. The one who could stare death in the face and never back down.

"That was before you." He kissed her again. Still as desperate. "I need you to be safe."

She needed him to be safe, too.

His gaze searched hers; then he slowly eased back. "Better get us moving," he murmured, "or Mercer will send out a search team."

Because security was on full alert at the EOD office.

She gave him another smile and waited as the elevator resumed moving.

Gunner's fingers—broad, warm—curled around her shoulders, and he began to massage her as they headed down to the parking garage.

Heaven.

But that paradise came to an end all too soon. The elevator's doors opened. The garage was well lit, with security cameras positioned every few feet. She saw her little car waiting right next to Gunner's truck.

"You can ride with me," Gunner said. "I had your car brought in, just like you asked, but there's no need for—"

"I want to take my car," Sydney said, cutting through his words. "With everything that's happening, I want to make sure that I can stay mobile on my own." If she had to clear out quickly, she wanted the security of knowing that her own ride was waiting for her.

Gunner's jaw locked, and she knew he didn't like her

answer. "I will be right behind you," he told her. "I'll follow you back to our place." He caught her hand, pressed a kiss to her fingers. "Be careful."

Our place. No, it wasn't, not yet. But maybe they could talk about their place soon. About starting a home for the family they would have.

Sydney tried a faint smile for him. "I'm a federal agent. I can do careful, no problem."

He didn't smile back. The worry was there, shadowing his gaze.

She slipped into the car. Gunner closed the driver's-side door and watched her through the window.

He hadn't talked about marriage. Hadn't really talked about their future at all other than to say he wanted to be there for the child.

Did Gunner want a future with her?

She cranked the ignition. He kept watching her as she eased away from the parking spot; then he turned and headed for his truck.

She wanted a future with him. Baseball games and barbecues and Christmases spent around a tree. She wanted to wake up next to Gunner every day, and go to sleep next to him each night.

If only he wanted the same thing.

Her phone rang, surprising her. She had it hooked in to her car's system so she just had to press one button on her console to connect with the phone system. Frowning, she took the call. "Sydney."

"Where are you?" Slade's voice. Rasping.

Frowning, she drove toward the guard booth. She saw Myles, the night shift guard, and she flashed her ID at him. He nodded, then typed in the code to raise the gate.

"I'm...uh...just leaving the office," she said. Hadn't Slade gone home hours ago?

"Sydney, *be careful*."

Her fingers tightened around the wheel. "What's going on?" She began to ease away from the nondescript EOD building.

"Don't trust him. I know you think you can, but…*don't*."

Gunner. She swallowed. "Slade, why are you saying these things?"

"Because I saw the way he was with her."

Her? Did he mean Sarah Bell?

"You don't really know him. Not like I do."

"I—I thought you and Gunner were getting along—"

His rough laugh cut across her words. "Keep your enemies close…" he murmured.

She glanced in her rearview mirror. Saw Gunner's truck following her. The flash of his headlights lit up her car.

"Gunner isn't your enemy."

"He's yours."

Her foot pressed down on the brake as she slowed to a stop. The intersection was clear, so she started to accelerate again. "Gunner isn't my enemy." He was many things, but not that. Never that.

"You're blinded by him, just as she was." He sounded sad now. "Can't you see him for what he is? I don't want him to hurt you."

"He won't!"

"He was afraid that you'd go back to me. He's trying to play the hero—"

His words cut out on her. Bad connection. "I can't hear—"

"Maybe he didn't want you to die in the fire. Maybe he wanted to save you" —static crackled across his words— "so you'd be grateful. Then he took out the shooter before he could talk. Gunner got you out of the way *before* the bullet fired—"

She was straining to hear his words.

She lifted her foot to brake as she came up on a curve.

"—he knew the bullet was coming. Playing hero again."

Her jaw locked. "Gunner isn't playing anything. Look, I can't talk now. It's late and—"

Her brakes weren't working.

The car wasn't slowing as it headed into that curve.

Sydney pushed down on the brake again.

Nothing.

She held tight to the wheel and took the curve. She came out with the vehicle pushing too fast. There was another intersection up ahead. A red light shining. She pumped her brakes, trying to get them to work. "I can't stop."

"What? Of course you can stop trusting him, you can—"

No. She pumped again. The brake wasn't working. The pedal was going all the way down to the floor and doing nothing. The light was still red for her. Other cars were whizzing right through the intersection. She was going down a hill. Faster, faster. "*I can't stop! The brakes aren't working!*"

The red light flashed to green. Her breath rushed out and her car flew through the intersection. But she had to stop soon. She had to find a place to stop.

Another red light loomed ahead.

Change.

Change.

"Sydney!" Slade's frantic voice.

The light wasn't changing.

Another car was going through the intersection.

She spun the wheel hard to the right. The passenger side of her vehicle hit the other car, scraping up against the side, and that crash sent her vehicle careening back, back—

Toward Gunner's truck.

She turned her head. Saw him coming right toward her. Bright lights.

She braced for the impact.

"SYDNEY!" SLADE YELLED FRANTICALLY.

She wasn't talking to him now, but he could hear the scream of metal.

He spun around. Cale was running toward him.

"What's happening?" Cale demanded.

They were in the lobby of the EOD building. Mercer had finally finished grilling him. "I wanted to catch her before she left," he whispered. "I had to warn her—"

Cale grabbed his arms. "What's happening?"

"Sydney." The phone was still clutched in his fingers. "Her brakes stopped working. I could hear...I could hear her screaming."

Cale's eyes widened, and he whirled away. He started shouting orders, calling for a track on Sydney.

But it was too late.

Slade glanced down at his phone. The line had gone dead.

GUNNER SLAMMED ON his brakes. The scent of burned rubber filled his nostrils as he jumped from his truck. The accident he'd just seen had his heart thundering in his chest.

"Sydney!" He ran toward her. Moments before, he'd seen her frightened face in the glow of his headlights.

Her car had raced forward—then smashed into a light pole.

His shaking fingers curled around the door handle, and he yanked the door open. A cloud of white greeted him. The air bag. He shoved it back. "Baby?"

A groan slipped from her.

He started to breathe again.

"Gunner?"

Carefully, oh, so carefully, he unhooked her seat belt and eased her from the car. The other driver was out of his vehicle now. Yelling about fools who shouldn't be on the road.

Gunner lifted Sydney up against his chest. She felt small and fragile. Breakable. She seemed so fierce most of the time that he forgot just how vulnerable she could be.

He leveled a killing stare on the man who was yelling instead of checking to see if Sydney was hurt. The guy stopped midholler and backed up a few steps. "Call for help," Gunner snarled.

The guy nodded frantically and pulled out his phone.

Gunner carried Sydney away from the road. More cars had stopped now. Bystanders were trickling toward them.

He put her down on the nearby grass. Brushed back her hair. There wasn't enough light for him to see her face clearly. "Are you all right?"

She nodded. "The brakes didn't work," she whispered. "I couldn't stop."

Fear and fury battled within him. Another attempt on her life. This time, he'd been helpless.

"An ambulance is coming!" a voice called out. It sounded like the guy who'd been yelling minutes before.

Gunner slid his hands over Sydney's body, looking for any signs of injury. No broken bones. No cuts. But she winced when he touched her left shoulder. The seat belt would have cut into her there.

When he stopped his exam, she immediately wrapped her hands around her stomach. "I couldn't stop," she repeated again.

And he'd been helpless.

This ends now.

He pulled her against his chest and held her until he heard the wail of the ambulance.

When the EMTs rushed toward him, Gunner said, "She's pregnant. Just...please, make sure she's all right."

As she was settled into the ambulance, he finally looked around.

He saw that others had joined the crowd. Cale was there, with Slade.

Slade's haggard face told Gunner that he'd heard his words. The time for secrets was over.

"Meet me at the hospital," Gunner called out to Cale.

The other agent nodded.

Gunner wasn't letting that ambulance leave without him. He climbed inside and caught Sydney's hand.

"Gunner," Sydney whispered. "My stomach's cramping."

Tears stung his eyes. He held her hand tighter even as he bent and pressed a kiss to her lips. "It's going to be all right." The ambulance lurched forward, and Gunner began to pray.

SYDNEY WAS ON a special exam table. She was too early in her pregnancy for the doctor to hear the baby's heartbeat, so an emergency ultrasound had been ordered.

Gunner paced beside her, his expression even more fierce than normal.

The cramping had stopped, but the fear? Oh, yes, that was still there. She didn't want anything happening to the baby inside her.

Not my baby.

"Gunner, I'm scared." She could tell him. He was her best friend. Had been, even before they'd become lovers.

He stopped pacing and immediately came to her side. "Don't be. This baby is fine." His fingers twined with hers.

She wondered if he knew that she could see the fear in his gaze. Usually he was much better at masking his emotions.

Usually she was, too.

She stared down at her stomach, covered now by a green exam gown.

"I love you." Gunner's words were rough and rumbling, and at first, she thought she'd imagined them.

Because she'd wanted to hear them for so long.

Sydney shook her head, an instinctive move. He hadn't—

"I want you to marry me."

Now her gaze flew to his. "Gunner?"

His lips hitched up into a half smile. "This isn't the right place, is it? Not the right time. But I've never been *that* guy, Syd. The guy with the smooth lines and the perfect moves. I am the guy who loves you, though. The guy who'd give his life for you. Who'd do *anything* for you."

He wanted to marry her. Was this about the baby? Or—

"I want you. I love *you*." That half smile vanished. "Sometimes I think I started falling for you the first time I met you, but you were so far out of my reach then." He glanced down at their intertwined fingers. His hold tightened. "I still feel like you are. You deserve better than me, but I swear, if you give me the chance, I'll do everything I can to make you happy."

A knock sounded at the door; then, a few seconds later, a doctor and nurse were bustling inside.

The ultrasound technician was there, getting everything set up. She lowered Sydney's bed, angling it.

Sydney stared at Gunner. He was waiting for her answer.

Maybe Gunner had always been waiting, and she hadn't seen it. She'd noticed his silence, his watchful ways, but she hadn't realized what any of that meant.

Then she thought about their lives. The way he was always coming to her house in D.C. for dinner. The way he never forgot her birthday or the way he made sure that she never spent Christmas alone.

"Sydney?" Gunner asked.

"Yes," she told him, because if he wanted to build a future with her, she was more than ready to build one with him.

Gunner's face changed then. It lit up as she'd never seen it before. He didn't simply look dangerous or sexy just now…the man was gorgeous.

The monitor flickered on next to her. The ultrasound technician went to work. Sydney forced herself to concentrate on that monitor. She was afraid to look, but she had to do this.

"You're early on," the doctor said, "so what we're looking for is the sack…*well, well*…"

The doctor moved, blocking her view of the monitor. No, no, that couldn't be good. She squeezed Gunner's hand, probably cutting off his circulation.

But the doctor just smiled at her. "Some mild cramping early in pregnancy can be perfectly normal. The baby is fine." He nodded once, then said, "From the looks of things, they both are." Then he backed up and pointed to the screen.

As he moved his fingers and started talking, showing them the two tiny lives that were their babies, Sydney couldn't even hear his words. A dull roar had filled her ears.

Not one baby. Two?

She glanced back over at Gunner. She'd never seen a smile so wide.

And he'd asked to marry her, before he even knew about the baby's fate. He'd wanted *her*.

"Now, you're going to need to be careful. Carrying twins will mean that your body is doing twice the work."

Careful—not exactly part of life for the EOD.

"She'll stay safe," Gunner vowed, and she knew he meant the words.

Good, because she wasn't going to play the killer's game anymore. In that instant when she'd seen Gunner's headlights coming at her, she'd known that her chances for survival were running out.

No more games.

No more attacks.

The doctor finished up. Sydney dressed and Gunner went to stand guard outside her room. Even though she was afraid and had death stalking her, a bubble of happiness kept growing inside her.

Twins. Gunner. Marriage.

If she could just get the killer off her back, she'd have everything she'd ever wanted.

She pushed open the door.

"I'm sorry, Gunner, but you have to come with me."

Logan's words froze her.

"The hell I am!" Gunner snapped. He jerked away from Logan. "I'm not leaving Sydney's side. I'm not—"

"A witness saw you tampering with her brakes."

The words filled Sydney's ears.

She stilled. That bubble of happiness wasn't feeling so light anymore.

"And Sydney's neighbor had sent a lady out to house-sit while she and her husband were out of town. The house sitter *was* there that night, and she reported seeing your truck, just sitting out in the street, waiting, right before the fire started at Sydney's home."

Sydney shook her head. That bubble burst. "Gunner?"

He spun toward her. "It's *not* true. It's a setup!"

The nearby hospital staff started to ease back.

Sydney searched Gunner's face. Then looked at Logan. "Why are you doing this?"

"Because your life matters. I don't know what kind of game he's playing…" His jaw locked. "But it's ending."

Cale and Slade waited behind them, both watching with tense faces.

Sydney could only shake her head. "Gunner isn't the one playing this game. He's been saving me."

Slade stepped forward. "That's what he wanted you to think! He's not a hero. He never was."

Gunner's face seemed to have turned to stone.

"I won't believe this!" No, she wouldn't. "I trust Gunner." More than she trusted anyone else.

"Mercer wants him back at the office. *Now.*" Logan's voice was grim. "I'm sorry, but I have no choice here. Gunner's been termed a threat, and I have to take him in."

"Then I'm coming, too."

But Slade stepped in her path. "Why won't you see him for what he is? He's playing you."

Someone was playing her, all right.

"You can't have this much blind trust in him!" Slade's voice rose. "You're smarter than this!"

Yes, she was. The rest of the EOD should be, too.

She caught Logan's gaze. Read the message that her shock had almost blinded her to before.

Then she gave a quick nod. "I—I'm coming." But she let the faintest quiver slide into the words.

Gunner's eyes widened.

Slade's lips curved.

She realized that she'd just used the same quiver in her voice that Slade had used in his words a few times.

Maybe they were both good actors.

They were about to see who was better.

She wasn't letting Gunner go down for these attacks. No way.

"I think...I remembered hearing my captors talk about the *American,*" Slade whispered as he rubbed his chin. "I told Cale on the way here."

He'd just remembered? Wasn't that convenient?

And bull.

"I think Gunner's been working with them all along, using his ties to the EOD to bring the drugs into the country."

"Enough." Logan's fierce voice. "We say nothing else until we're back in the office."

But Slade thought he'd said plenty. Enough to have her turning her back on Gunner?

The man didn't know her at all.

Only fair, since she'd just realized that she never knew him, either.

"SYDNEY CAN'T KEEP being in the line of fire." Gunner leveled his stare at Mercer. "She needs to be taken out of the equation *now.*"

"Sydney's a woman with a very strong mind. Is that what she wants?" Mercer demanded.

Gunner flattened his hands on Mercer's desk and leaned toward him. "Sydney's not being risked anymore. Someone is using her to get at me." And he knew just who that person was.

Did Slade really think he was so smart? That no one saw through his lies?

Even being blood wasn't going to protect him.

"Haul his butt in here," Gunner demanded. "Lock him up. Keep him away from her." *And me. Before I tear him apart.*

"The house sitter did see you at Sydney's—"

"Really? Then where the hell was this person when the house was burning? Because no one came running out— no one tried to do a damn thing."

"She said she was scared. That she kept the doors bolted. She was just a kid, barely over sixteen." Mercer assessed him. "Why were you waiting outside Sydney's house?"

"Because I was getting up the damn courage to go and talk to her!"

Mercer raised a doubting eyebrow.

"And the witness who saw you tampering with her brakes?"

"I think the witness is already dead." Brutal, but true. "After he told you what he saw, he was dead. Because his words were a flat lie, and the real killer here isn't going to let him keep breathing."

Frowning now, Mercer reached for his phone. Gunner's teeth ground together as he listened to Mercer on the call. The big boss was demanding that the witness to the tampering be brought in, only...

Mercer glanced back at him. "He convulsed in holding, just a few moments ago. Tina's on scene. Says it looks like the guy overdosed."

"Get Tina to do the blood work," Gunner said as his mind whirled. "Because I'm betting you'll find *muerte* in his system."

Mercer gave the order, then hung up the phone.

"That's why he was making all those charter flights," Gunner muttered as he rose to his full height. "They were drug runs. He was making connections down there. Setting everything up." He raked a hand through his hair. "His accounts were cleaned out because he didn't plan on coming back to the U.S. He was leaving everyone—"

Leaving Sydney.

"Then he got into trouble down there." As if there wouldn't be enemies in the drug cartels. "He wanted us to bail him out." Only he and Sydney had almost died in the process.

Somehow Slade had survived. Thrived.

"He wasn't their captive." No, Gunner didn't think that had been the case at all.

The door opened behind him. A quick glance showed Logan coming into the room.

Logan, whose whisper-thin voice had ordered him to "Play along" at the hospital because he wasn't turning his back on him. The EOD stuck together.

Always.

"He was working us, the whole time. Slade wanted us down there so he could have an in at the EOD." So he could search their files. Make contacts to distribute the *muerte*. They'd thought he was an addict.

When he was the drug lord.

"Are you sure about all of this?" Logan shook his head. "We don't have proof, man. Every piece of evidence is pointing to you. We can't even bring in the FBI because they'd want to lock you up, not him."

"Because he's smarter than we realized. He's been working us all along."

"We need more evidence." Mercer stood behind his desk. "If Slade is behind the *muerte* spread, we have to bring him down and stop his whole cartel."

"Let him come at me," Gunner demanded. "Give him a straight shot at me. He hates me." That had to be obvious to them all. Otherwise, why plant all the evidence against him? "I can get you what you need."

But Mercer shook his head. "No, you can't." Definite. "You don't share with a man you hate. You share your secrets with those you love."

Sydney.

"He's tried to *kill* her," Gunner said, gritting his teeth. "I'm not risking her—"

"It's Sydney's life. She gets to decide the risk. Not anyone else."

"And she's carrying my babies," Gunner snapped right back. "So that means I get to—"

"Uh, babies?" Logan murmured, and coughed. "As in more than one?"

Gunner gave a grim nod.

"Hot damn," Logan said.

"So you see why I'm *not* risking the woman I love."

"You just—" Logan sputtered. "You just admitted to loving her? Who are you? Where's the real Gunner?"

Gunner ignored him. "She won't come in the line of fire. Use me. Set me up as bait, but not her. Not...*her.*"

"I think that's my call." Sydney's voice. Sydney—pushing back a side door in Mercer's office.

Gunner shook his head. "Where the hell does that door even lead?" he muttered. Every time he'd been in there, that room had been blocked.

"In case any of our other staff members have been compromised," Mercer said as his gaze cut to Sydney, "I took the liberty of having Sydney come in the...uh...private entrance. I didn't want to advertise her presence with us."

He knew that Sydney had worked closely with Mercer on a few other cases. It appeared she was privy to more than a few of the man's secrets, too.

"You heard it all?" Mercer asked her.

Sydney nodded. Her gaze stayed on Gunner. "Slade isn't going to come clean with you."

"And he's been trying to kill you!" All while wearing that fake mask of concern. He'd been playing them from the first.

Gunner had known for sure when he spun around in the hospital and met his brother's gaze. The tragic concern there... Slade had worn that same expression at Sarah Bell's funeral. But an hour after the funeral, Gunner had caught the guy making out with another girl.

So much for his grief.

"Am I supposed to die, too?" Those had been Slade's

words, and the memory of them had stabbed into Gunner, sharp like a knife, as he stood in that hospital corridor.

"Slade didn't withdraw his application to the EOD," Sydney said.

Gunner shook his head, trying to banish that memory.

"I found his original file—"

"And I remember rejecting him," Mercer added, voice like a bear's growl. "I never forget men I think can be a threat."

Sydney moved closer to Gunner. "He was turned away from the EOD. I found his drug test. He didn't pass it then. He was on an unknown drug at the time, one that our labs couldn't identify, but it raised red flags."

"That's why we rejected him and stopped using him on freelance work," Mercer added.

Sydney's hand touched lightly against Gunner's arm. "I got Tina to compare his old drug test with the result that we had on the *muerte*...he was on *muerte* back then."

"Bring him in here," Gunner said, his heart feeling as if it were encased in ice. How had this happened? His brother. "We can show him the tests, make him talk—"

Mercer shook his head. "You don't think I've already run at him, again and again? This guy isn't going to break for me." Before Gunner could speak, Mercer added, "Or for you."

"That's where I come in." Sydney's smile was a little sad. "If he thinks that I believe him, if he thinks that I've lost faith in you, then he will come to me."

"More likely, he'll *kill* you!"

"Not with you, Cale and Logan watching my back." She seemed so calm. How did she seem so calm? He was about to go crazy. "I know you'll keep me safe." So certain.

"This won't work." He wasn't talking to the others. They didn't matter. Just her. "He'll kill you. He won't talk."

"He asked me to run away with him before that last trip to Peru two years ago. Before his plane crashed."

Gunner was too conscious of the pounding of his heart. Too loud.

"I didn't go with him because…things were getting difficult between us, so I told him that I needed more time. He told me that he wanted to offer me a brand-new life. One that I wouldn't be able to imagine." Her shoulders rolled. "He wanted to bring me into the new world that he was creating. Into the new *life* that he was starting for himself."

A life as a drug cartel leader?

"Do you know why they call the drug *muerte?*" Logan asked.

Gunner shook his head.

"I did some digging with a contact at the DEA. The drug is named after the guy who's spreading it through South America…a man who reportedly rose from the dead to take over one of the biggest cartels in Peru."

Slade. Rising from the dead…

"If Slade truly wanted to kill me," Sydney said, "all he had to do was walk up to me and put a bullet in my heart."

Gunner's hands fisted.

"Instead, he's been playing with me. Punishing me. Punishing you. Hell, maybe he's even been testing us, to see how far we'll go in order to survive." Her lips thinned. "I won't be tested again. Mercer is setting up my house in Baton Rouge. We're getting out of D.C. Making him think that I'm turning my back on you and on the EOD. Making him think that I only want—"

"—him," Gunner finished for her.

"And if I'm right on this, he'll come after me. He'll think we're alone, and I *will* get him to tell me the truth."

"Or what—die trying?"

Her hand lifted. Her fingers feathered over his cheek.

"That's where you come in, Gunner. It's your job to keep me alive. To keep all of us alive."

He couldn't get enough air into his lungs. "There's another way...."

"No, there isn't. I'm the only one who he might trust here. I'm the one who can get to him. I'm the one who can end this." Her hand dropped, and he immediately missed the warmth of her touch. "You can have me in your sights every moment," she whispered. "If you think I'm threatened, if you think I'm in danger—"

"Then I will *end* him."

Her breath expelled in a relieved rush. "Then you're in?"

"You aren't giving me a choice." He glared at them all. Promised Mercer and Logan all kinds of hell if this turned south. "And there's no way I'm letting you leave town without me."

She threw her arms around him and squeezed the breath right out of him. "I love you, Gunner." A whispered confession that he knew no one else heard.

But it was a confession that he'd never forget.

Chapter Eleven

Sydney had tears trekking down her cheeks as Gunner was loaded into the back of the black SUV. Men in suits were on either side of him. His hands were cuffed.

"Sydney?" Slade's voice.

She turned and saw him walking up, with Cale by his side. Slade's steps were slow as he approached her, the limp seeming to give him more trouble today.

She knew that Slade had been in the interrogation room. She'd been in hell.

It was easy to keep the tears coming. Maybe it was the hormones or maybe she'd always been a better actress than she'd thought. Either way… "Gunner's being taken in by the feds. They have so much evidence on him…" Her voice trailed away. "I thought I knew him."

Slade came to her and wrapped his arms around her.

She shoved him back. "Don't touch me!" Now, that part wasn't acting. "I can't stand— I can't trust anyone. I—I thought I could…"

Pain flashed across Slade's face. "You can trust me, sweetheart. You always could. I've never stopped loving you."

She blinked up at him, trying to get the tears off her lashes. "After what I did to you?"

What she'd done? *Nothing.* Lived her life, tried to help him.

He'd been lying to her for years.

"Always," he whispered as he lifted his hand and wiped away her tears.

She'd just told him not to touch her.

Her jaw ached, and she tried to ease the clenching of her teeth. "I have to get out of here." She let her gaze cut to Cale. She shuddered, and glanced back at Slade. "I need to get away, to think."

"Where will you go?" he whispered.

A sad smile curved her lips. "To the only home I have left."

Now he knew just where she'd be.

Would he follow her?

She turned away from him, but not before she caught the curling of his lips.

Yes, he'd follow.

Then come and get me.

SLADE WATCHED THE black SUV pull away from the curb, triumph filling him. His brother had been taken into custody. The agents had followed all the bread crumbs that he'd left behind, and everyone there had turned on Gunner.

His brother was alone.

Sydney was sliding into a cab now. She looked so pale. So lost. So...perfect.

"It is safe for her to be alone?" Slade asked, keeping his voice raspy. He'd also done a pretty good job of keeping up his limp, as if that injury really bothered him anymore.

Cale stepped to the edge of the sidewalk. "Now that we have Gunner, she'll be safe. She...she turned in her resignation when she found out the truth. Sydney doesn't want to be part of the EOD anymore."

The cab eased into the flow of traffic.

His Sydney. Going home.

He knew exactly where her home was. Since her place near EOD headquarters had been torched, she'd return to the only safe haven that she had—in Louisiana.

Now would be the perfect time to get to Sydney. She'd be alone, isolated in Baton Rouge as she hadn't been with Gunner dodging her steps in D.C.

Her guard would be lowered. No more EOD agents trailing underfoot.

Just Sydney.

Just me.

"This is where we say goodbye," Cale told him.

Slade turned toward him. "No more guard duty?"

"You were the one who was right all along. You'll be getting a full apology from the EOD, and compensation, of course."

Of course.

Cale offered his hand. "I wish things could have been different."

Slade took his hand. Shook it. "Maybe they will be now." Everything could be different.

He'd once planned to take Sydney away, to start a new life with her. Sure, he couldn't tell her about what he'd really done down in South America, but why should she ever have to learn that truth?

Maybe it would be the time for them to start fresh. To start over.

Cale walked away.

Slade began to whistle.

And if Sydney didn't want him…if she refused the offer that he made to her, then, while she was all alone in the swamps that she foolishly loved so much, he'd kill her.

Her mistake to leave all the protection around her. Sydney had always thought she was so smart and tough.

When, all along, he'd been the one pulling the puppet strings.

He walked down the sidewalk, still whistling and planning for his reunion in Baton Rouge.

THE HOUSE WAS too quiet. Sydney stood in her living room, far too aware of the silence that surrounded her. She was back in Baton Rouge, back in the house that she'd loved so much, for so long.

The place seemed to be filled with memories of Gunner.

She turned toward the large window in her den. If Slade showed up—*when, not if*—she was supposed to keep him in front of that window. Because this position would give Gunner a perfect shot at the other man.

Exhaling slowly, she looked out of that window. The edge of the swamp and twisting cypress trees stared back at her. She saw no sign of Gunner, but she could feel him.

Watching.

Protecting.

Cale was out there, as well. Stationed at another watch point and staring down his scope, too. They had the main windows under watch so that they could see into the house.

She'd taken care of making sure they could *hear* what was happening inside the house. A bit of surveillance equipment, carefully hidden, and they were linked into the audio feed. They'd hear anything that would be said tonight.

Logan would also *see* what went down, since he was in the surveillance van hidden in her garage, and he was watching every single thing that happened on the monitors in there.

Their intel had already told them that Slade had hopped a plane out of D.C. He was coming after her; it was just a matter of time.

Sydney kept staring out of that window.

When she'd first come home, she'd felt Gunner all around her. Remembered the way they'd made love in that house. She could even have sworn that the sheets in her room still carried his scent.

She'd seen the memory of him at the kitchen table—Gunner staring at her with his dark gaze, watching her so hungrily.

He was everywhere.

Did he understand how completely he fit into her life?

Headlights appeared in the darkness. Her heart beat a little faster.

Almost showtime.

Almost.

She put her hand on the glass. *I'll be safe, Gunner.*

Then she turned away.

GUNNER WATCHED SYDNEY put her hand on the glass pane. His own hand was curled around the weapon in his hand. He could see her lovely face so perfectly through the scope.

"Target is on scene," Logan said in his earpiece.

Just as they'd planned. So far, everything was going just according to Sydney and Mercer's plan.

They'd wanted to pull Slade out of D.C., to make him think that he was safe, that no eyes were on him.

Insects chirped around Gunner, and the swamp behind him stretched for miles.

The place was secluded, all right, and Slade would no doubt think it was the perfect spot for him to approach Sydney.

He'd be wrong.

But I still don't like this.

No way did he want Sydney alone in the room with his brother. Slade had become twisted, whether from the drugs or something else, and Gunner knew there were no limits to what the man might do.

Gunner wouldn't feel safe until Sydney was in his arms again.

"I have a visual." This came from Cale. "Target is leaving the vehicle and approaching the house."

Now they would see just what secrets Sydney would learn, and just how very far his brother had fallen.

"WE'RE OKAY," SYDNEY whispered as she belted her fluffy, terry-cloth robe. The robe was huge, but that was the point, right? To disguise what she was wearing underneath it.

A bulletproof vest.

Gunner had been adamant on that point. He wanted their babies protected. She did, too. She just had to make sure that Slade didn't see any sign of that vest.

The doorbell pealed. She glanced at the clock. Just a little after midnight. Her hand quickly ran through her hair, tousling it so that it would look as if she'd gotten out of bed. Then she waited a few moments, not wanting to rush to the door too quickly.

The doorbell pealed again.

With quick steps, she made her way to the door. She glanced through the peephole. Saw Slade's face under her porch light. Her hand flipped the lock and she opened the door. "Slade! What are you doing here?" Sydney thought she did a pretty good job of projecting surprise into her voice.

He smiled at her, the smile that had once made her think he was such a charming guy. The smile she now understood was a lie.

"I couldn't let you be all by yourself, sweetheart. Not when you were so broken up." He stepped over the threshold. She eased back, carefully putting distance between them. "You might think everyone has let you down, but I haven't."

Yes, you have.

He shut the door behind him, locked it. When he moved, she saw the slight bulge under his jacket. He'd come to comfort her, but he'd also brought a weapon?

He came to kill me.

Her breath felt cold in her lungs. She'd thought that he'd try to keep charming her first. Sydney hadn't believed that he'd go straight for the kill.

She backed up another few steps. He followed her, falling into line with her picture window. Perfect positioning.

"It's after midnight," she told him as she pretended to try to smooth her hair. "You shouldn't be here now."

"I needed to see you." His gaze raked over her robe. He frowned. "And you wanted to see me, or else you wouldn't have let me in the door."

Her head moved in a faint nod. "I needed to...I needed to talk with you. About Gunner. I didn't know that—"

"—he was a monster?" His gaze came back to her face. "Now you do. Now you know you were with the right brother in the beginning."

The right brother has you in his sights now.

She locked her jaw. "I didn't think that I could be so blind." She'd arranged things deliberately in the den. Her hand waved toward her computer. The screen was off now, but papers were scattered across the desk, making it look as if she'd been hard at work earlier in the night. "So I started digging on my own. The powers-that-be at the EOD might be satisfied with the way this scene played out, but I'm not."

Because she was looking so carefully for it, Sydney caught the faint hardening of Slade's eyes.

"The EOD did its job."

But Sydney shook her head. "I'm not sure of that. Gunner

was swearing to me that he was innocent, that he'd never hurt me, never do all of those things…"

"He's a liar, sweetheart." He stepped closer to her. Her gaze slid down to his legs, then rose.

She held her ground this time. She wanted to make sure they both stood in front of that window. With the lights on in the den, they would be shown perfectly. *Perfect targets.*

"I'm sorry, but you were wrong about him."

Another hard shake of her head. "I—I can't be wrong." Then she lifted her chin. "I went back, pulled all the records that I could find on the fire at Sarah Bell's house."

A long sigh broke from him. "Why put so much faith in him? You're only hurting yourself." His hand lifted. Trailed over her cheek. "Let me help you heal."

She hated his touch. "I found an old article online. Gunner's football team…they won the state championship that same weekend. The weekend of the fire at the Bell home."

His nostrils flared. "So?"

"So the state championship game was held in a city four hours away. Gunner was with his team the whole time. They went on a bus together. They came back on a bus together… He didn't start that fire."

His hand fell away.

She shoved her fingers into the heavy pockets on her robe. She had her own weapon stashed in one of those pockets.

"I did more checking," she whispered.

He spun away from her and paced toward the window. "On damn Gunner? Always…*Gunner.*"

"No. On you."

His shoulders stiffened. With it being just the two of them, he wasn't working nearly as hard to conceal his reactions. Maybe because he didn't care.

He'd also lost his limp.

"Sydney…" He sighed out her name. "I came down here to comfort you so we could be together again. I know you've always loved me."

"I did love you. Once." That feeling was nothing like what she felt for Gunner.

He was still staring out of the window, and presenting such a fine target. "Before Gunner," he growled.

"Before you started to change," she whispered back.

SLADE'S FACE FILLED Gunner's scope. The rage there, the hate, was frightening to see.

But Sydney wouldn't see it. She couldn't. Slade wasn't looking at her. He was just staring out into the darkness.

Planning his attack.

Gunner's left hand pressed against his transmitter. "He's going to make a move soon. Be ready." That much fury couldn't be held in check for long.

They were wired into the audio feed that Sydney had set up, so they were hearing every word that she said. She was baiting Slade, pushing him.

That pushing was working.

Gunner hadn't been at a state championship game the weekend that Sarah Bell died. The game had been two weekends after the fire. But it looked as though Slade didn't remember that.

A flaw in his plan.

Then Sydney started talking again, and Gunner felt sweat trickle down the side of his face.

"YOU MADE SO many trips down to South America before—before—"

"Before Gunner left me for dead?" He turned toward her, his face expressionless. "Let's not forget that part. Gunner and *you* both left me."

"I wondered about all of those charter trips. Especially when I discovered that every account you had was empty. Cleaned out."

His lips curved. The sight was chilling.

"You'd become angry before that last trip, too. I remember the fights we had. You accused me—"

"—of cheating?" he finished. He glanced down at his hands. Both hands had fisted. "I thought you might be sleeping with Gunner back then. I saw the way he looked at you, and the way you looked at him."

"I wasn't—"

"Not then. But now?" His eyebrows climbed. "You're going to try telling me that the baby you're carrying isn't his?"

"It is." *They* are. "And that's why I had to keep digging. I couldn't give up on him. *I couldn't.*"

"You should have." So soft.

She kept talking. "It was when I was digging, trying to find where all your money went to…that was when I discovered that you'd set up extra accounts in the Caymans."

He laughed. "You and your damn computers. You could always find out too much on them." He reached into his jacket and pulled out his weapon. "Like I said, you *should* have stopped."

GUNNER'S FINGER TIGHTENED around the trigger.

"Hold!" This was Logan's order, growled through the transmitter. "She's still got him talking. We need to learn as much as we can."

They needed to make sure that not a single bullet so much as grazed her skin.

"Hold, Gunner. That's a direct order."

He wasn't following orders now. He was protecting the woman he loved.

Slade hadn't aimed the gun at her yet. It was still by his side. The second that gun started to rise…

Gunner would fire. Brother or no brother.

"I FOUND OUT you were never the man I thought you were. Even before your plane went down…back then, you were drug running, weren't you?"

He laughed, and completely dropped the mask that he'd been wearing. The twisted fury and hate was there for her to see, burning so hot. "Yeah, I was. I was earning more money than I'd ever made in my life. Those jerks at the EOD had turned me away. Said I was too unstable. Screw that! I was the best they could've had, and they wouldn't even give me a chance."

Her hand tightened around the weapon that was still concealed in her oversize robe pocket. "So you took your own chance?"

"I took the jobs that came to me. I made connections… money…so much money." He rolled his shoulders. "You don't know what it's like to have nothing. *I do.* I grew up with nothing. Dirt-poor on a reservation in the middle of nowhere. No father. No mother. I wasn't even raised by my blood. The grandfather that Gunner talks about so much? *Not mine.*"

"But he took you in," Sydney said. "He helped—"

"My father signed custody of me over to him. Said I'd be with *family.* I didn't want to be with them. I didn't want Gunner's castoffs. Didn't want to always be in his shadow."

There was pain there, breaking through the fury.

"I swore I'd do anything I had to do in order to get out of that place. I wouldn't be poor again. No one would look down on me." His smile flashed—not the charming one, But the cold grin of a killer. "Do you have any idea how much money I have? How much power?"

"No…" *Tell me.*

"I am *muerte.* I found it on one of my runs. I knew I could take over down there. When you and Gunner came for me the first time—"

When they'd all nearly died.

"I was fighting for power then. Your entrance, your backup…it was appreciated." The grin kept chilling her. "Of course, it would have helped more if you hadn't abandoned me."

"You were dead!"

"Actually, yes, I was."

Her breath burned in her lungs as surprise rolled through her.

"But thanks to the *muerte,* I came back."

"I don't understand."

"My men dragged a doctor to me—some relief worker they found. He brought me back, I don't even know how… injections, luck. Hell, maybe the devil just didn't want me. The doc even said that the *muerte* might have saved me, that it was working in my body, stopping the blood loss."

"What happened to the doctor?"

"When I recovered, I slit his throat."

Brutal. But she knew that was exactly who—what— Slade was. A brutal killer. "And you became the cartel ruler down there?"

"I am *muerte.*"

"Why?" She breathed out the word as if she was frightened. And she was. The man before her was a walking nightmare. "Why did you want the EOD to come and rescue you? You were free and clear. We thought you were dead. Why—"

"Because I was ready to expand. I knew that you'd taken out Guerrero recently…."

The Mexican arms dealer. Now everything was connecting. Her heart thudded into her chest. "He had links to the drug trade. That's why you accessed his file at the EOD, you wanted to know—"

"I wanted to know what assets of his I could still use in Mexico, and what assets I needed to eliminate."

"You mean kill."

"Yes." A shrug. "I knew it would be easy enough to get that intel from inside the EOD."

"So you worked us all...you threatened Hal—"

Another cold laugh. "I paid him. There was no threat. Of course, I never intended for him to live long enough to collect his cash."

"And the shooter? The man who fired at me—"

"I connected with him while in rehab." The gun was held loosely in his hand at his side. She was tense, her gaze drifting to the gun far too often, but he acted as if he wasn't even aware he'd pulled out the weapon. "You can meet the most useful contacts in the oddest places."

"You hooked the guy up with *muerte*."

"In return, he agreed to take a shot at you. I *did* tell him to miss, by the way. That was just a scare shot."

"And at my house? The fire—"

His smile vanished. "I was supposed to be the one to save you."

"Were you supposed to save Sarah, too?" Whispered.

"No, I wanted her to burn."

She had never known him at *all*. "What about when we were in Peru—that shot on the beach? That was you, wasn't it?"

"Guilty."

How had he gotten the gun then? Had he arranged for one of his men to meet him?

"Figured it was never too early...to start driving a wedge between you and Gunner." He glanced down at the weapon.

His sigh seemed a little sad. "Now, I'm afraid, you are going to have to die."

She shook her head. "Slade, no, don't do this!"

"But I don't have a choice. As soon as I heard what you had to say…that you'd found evidence, your fate was set." He was still staring at the gun. "You won't stay quiet, and I can't take the chance of you ruining things for me. I've got big plans. I'll use the assets of Guerrero's that will work for me. I'll bring my trade right up the border…I'll have so much money and power that no one will ever be able to touch me." His gaze came back to her. "But you have to die first."

He was going to do it.

She backed away, easing toward the couch so that she could drop and have some sort of cover. "You still have a chance," she told him. "Don't—"

"You're the only one who knows the truth about me."

He watched her with the unflinching gaze of a snake, ready to strike.

Sydney shook her head. "No." Then she dropped her own mask. Let the fear slide away and let her own fury burst free. "The EOD knows, too. Logan, Cale and Gunner? They've been listening to every single word that you said. And guess what? You're in their sights now."

Eyes widening in shock, he swung back toward the window. Sydney dived behind the couch.

"No!" Slade screamed.

"Yes," Gunner whispered.

Slade whirled from the window and lifted his gun toward the couch.

Gunner's finger squeezed the trigger. The bullet flew through the window, shattering the glass, and slammed into Slade.

One shot.

The man staggered, then tried to aim again.

Gunner fired once more.

Even as that second bullet found its target, Gunner saw Logan burst into the den. Logan raced toward Slade as the man slumped to the floor.

Over.

Because he'd just put two bullets into his own brother.

"CLEAR!" LOGAN YELLED.

Sydney rose from behind the couch. Slade was on the floor, with Logan over him. There was blood, a lot of it, and she hurried toward the men.

Slade's eyes were open. He was glaring up at Logan, even as Logan held his gaze and his gun right on the other man. "You're being taken in," Logan told him. "We've got your confession recorded. You're not getting away."

Slade clenched his teeth. "I…I'm not going in! I won't—"

"You don't have a choice," Logan growled. Then he talked into his transmitter. "We need that ambulance. Send the EMTs through." He leaned over Slade. "The wounds aren't fatal. You'll stand trial for what you've done. *Muerte* won't survive—"

"You think…I'll…roll on the cartels? They'd *kill* me…"

The front door flew open. Sydney glanced up. Gunner was there, racing toward her.

He grabbed her in his arms and held her tight. She could feel the thunder of his heartbeat against her chest. "You're making me lose too many years of my life," he muttered.

Not anymore. The nightmare was over. He was clear. Slade was contained. It was *over.*

An ambulance's siren roared outside.

"The big hero…" Slade groaned. "You think this…is how you stop…me?"

Gunner lifted his head but didn't ease his hold on Sydney. "You're my brother." He shook his head. "How the hell did you wind up like this? I was there for you when we were growing up, keeping you safe, making sure—"

"Sure that I was in your shadow." Slade heaved up. Blood pulsed from his wounds. "No…more."

Gunner's body was as hard as a rock against hers. She could only imagine the pain that he had to feel. His own brother had been setting him up, willing to let Gunner spend his life in jail.

The siren kept wailing outside. The EMTs had been kept close, as a precaution, and in moments, they were rushing inside her house.

Logan eased back a step so that they could get to their patient. Logan had already taken Slade's gun and bagged it for evidence.

But when the EMT reached for Slade, Slade's body started convulsing. His eyes rolled back in his head. He jerked and twisted. The EMT swore and leaned over him.

That was the moment when Slade yanked out the backup weapon from the holster on his ankle. He moved so fast—so very fast—and had that weapon at the EMT's head in seconds.

Everyone froze.

Everyone…except Slade and his hostage.

Even as the blood darkened his shirt, he rose to his feet. Slade yanked the young EMT up, keeping the man in front of him. "Drop your guns," Slade ordered, "or I will put a bullet into his head right now."

Gunner stepped in front of Sydney, shielding her with his body. He didn't drop his weapon.

"Drop it, *hero*," Slade snarled. "Or watch him die."

"P-please…" the man begged.

She couldn't see his face, but she could hear his fear. The tension in the room weighed down on them all. She heard the shuffle of footsteps. Slade and his hostage, backing up a bit.

Backing up…and that retreat would put them right in front of her broken picture window.

Was Cale still positioned on the other side of the house? Or had he moved? She hadn't been hooked in to their transmissions, and she didn't know if he'd been repositioned when Gunner rushed inside.

Her palms were sweating, her heart racing too fast.

"I'm not going to…jail…" Slade said. "And sorry, brother, but you're not getting…the girl…."

Her hands grabbed for Gunner because she knew Slade was about to take the shot. "No!" Sydney screamed.

The blast of gunfire shook the room.

But Gunner didn't fall.

"Syd…ney…"

Slade's voice.

Gunner rushed forward, and she saw that Slade had been hit again, only this time, this time she knew the wound was fatal. Slade's skin was ashen, his eyes barely staying open. The EMT had lurched away from him, and Gunner had caught his brother's body just as Slade fell.

Sydney glanced toward the window. Another bullet hole had broken the glass.

Cale.

Protecting his team.

"Slade?"

She glanced back at Gunner's voice. He was curled over Slade's body holding his brother's hand.

Slade seemed to be trying to stare up at him.

Two brothers.

"Can we…go in the woods…?" Slade's voice. Weak with pain, sounding lost. "I want to go…with you…Gun…"

She saw Gunner's throat move as he swallowed.

"Is…Grandpa comin'?"

Slade didn't sound like a man anymore. More like a lost child. Maybe in those last moments, he was.

"Grandfather's already waiting for you," Gunner said, his own voice rumbling. "Go on to the woods. Stay with him. I'll join you later."

"P-promise…?" Slade's breath rushed out. His chest stilled.

Gunner's hand clenched around his. "I promise."

Sydney wrapped her arms around Gunner and held him as tightly as she could.

THE GRAVE WOULDN'T be empty this time. Gunner stood, silent, during the service as his brother was put to rest. Sydney was by his side, her small hand cradled in his. Logan was on his right. The friend who'd never doubted him. The friend who'd always be there.

Jasper Adams had come to the service, too. The ex-EOD agent waited across from Gunner. Jasper's wife, Veronica—Cale's sister—had her arm curled around his waist.

And Cale…he watched the proceedings just as silently as Gunner.

When Gunner had taken his shots, he'd tried to keep his brother alive.

When Cale had fired, there had been no choice. To save Gunner, he'd had to take the kill shot.

But Cale still looked at him with guilt in his eyes. He shouldn't do that. Gunner would have to talk to him soon, have to make the other man realize—

I understand.

The service ended. The small group walked away, all but Gunner and Sydney. They lingered for a moment. He looked at the flowers. Thought about his brother. "I want to remember him the way he was, back when we were kids."

Going for hikes in the woods.

Once, Slade had loved those hikes as much as Gunner had.

Once.

"Then remember him that way," Sydney whispered. "Remember him happy. Remember the good parts."

He glanced over at her. Sweet Sydney. His saving grace.

"Remember the love, and push everything else away."

He bent toward her and rested his forehead against hers. "I love you." He'd told her before, but he needed to say the words again. He wanted to say them, over and over.

Her soft hand slid over his jaw. "And I love you."

A gift. One he'd always treasure, just the way he treasured her.

His head lifted. He cast one last look toward his brother's casket.

Remember the love. Push everything else away.

"Enjoy your walk in the woods, brother. One day, maybe I'll see you again."

Until then, he'd be walking with Sydney. With the children they had on the way. He'd remember the love, he'd show those children so much love...

And with Sydney, he knew they'd be happy. He'd prove that he could be a good father. A father his children would be proud to have.

They turned away from the grave. The sunlight was so bright. It chased away the shadows, and it showed him the hope that waited. With Sydney. With his friends.

With the life that would be. All he had to do was just reach out and take that life. Just reach out...

He turned Sydney in his arms, held tight to her and kissed her.

And he knew he'd found his perfect home.

Epilogue

Getting called into the big boss's office couldn't be a good thing. Cale squared his shoulders and swung open the door that would take him into Mercer's inner sanctum.

Mercer glanced up, no expression on his face, and waved Cale toward him. "Have a seat."

Right. Nodding quickly, Cale took the offered seat.

Mercer's fingers drummed on his desk. "It seems that you're working out quite well as a member of the Shadow Agents."

"Sir, they're a good team." Good people. But taking that shot, taking out Gunner's brother…that shot was going to haunt him.

Every death did.

"And you're a good asset to that team. Cool under fire, determined and willing to do whatever's necessary for the mission."

Cale stiffened. He didn't like that "whatever's necessary" part.

"So I think you're going to be the perfect man for a very special assignment."

Cale leaned forward.

"It's an assignment that has the *highest* priority at the EOD." Intensity deepened Mercer's voice. "I want a man on this case, a guy I can trust one hundred percent." He stopped drumming his fingers and pointed at Cale. "Are you that man?"

"Yes, sir."

"You'd better be," Mercer muttered. "Son, you'd damn well better be...because if you fail on this mission, if *anything* goes wrong, I will make you regret it the rest of your life."

Cale managed to keep his expression neutral, with a whole lot of effort.

"Are we clear?"

Cale nodded.

"Good." Mercer flashed a smile that Cale was sure had made plenty of men shudder in fear. "Then get your bags packed, because you're going to Rio."

THE DOOR CLOSED behind Cale Lane. An interesting man. A dangerous man.

A man who'd better be the right choice for this mission.

Mercer opened his drawer. Carefully he pulled out the file for this case. He flipped through the dossiers, then paused when he saw her picture.

Cale had *better* be the right choice.

Because if this mission went wrong, if *anything* happened to his daughter...

"I will make you regret it the rest of your life." Cale had no idea just what hell he'd bring down on him.

Because Mercer never made threats.

Just promises.

*   *   *   *   *

Her kiss was a tender expression of gratitude…

But Preston's reaction to it was fierce and swift. He pulled her close and deepened the kiss. She didn't resist. Giving in to temptation, she melted into him.

With each heartbeat, his touch became rougher, his kiss burned hotter. Then to her complete surprise, he eased his hold.

Abby looked into his eyes and saw the iron-willed control he held over himself.

"I'm sorry," she said. "You didn't start this, and I can see you don't want to…"

"I don't *want* to?" He laughed, a dark, edgy sound. "I want you, Abby. I care about you more than I should. But you need to be protected—even from me."

"You want me…" she said slowly, savoring the words. "Then show me."

FALCON'S RUN

BY
AIMÉE THURLO

MILLS &
BOON

First published in Great Britain 2013
by Mills & Boon, an imprint of Harlequin (UK) Limited,
Eton House, 18-24 Paradise Road, Richmond, Surrey TW9 1SR

© Aimée and David Thurlo 2013

ISBN: 978 0 263 90368 3
ebook ISBN: 978 1 472 00735 3

46-0813

Harlequin (UK) policy is to use papers that are natural, renewable and recyclable products and made from wood grown in sustainable forests. The logging and manufacturing processes conform to the legal environmental regulations of the country of origin.

Printed and bound in Spain
by Blackprint CPI, Barcelona

Aimée Thurlo is a bestselling author. She's the winner of a Career Achievement Award from *RT Book Reviews,* a New Mexico Book Award in contemporary fiction and a Willa Cather Award in the same category. Her novels have been published in twenty countries worldwide.

Aimée was born in Havana, Cuba, and lives with her husband of thirty-nine years in Corrales, New Mexico. Her husband, David, was raised on a Navajo Indian reservation.

With special thanks to Doug Baum
and Dr Steve Komadina, who shared with me
so much of their time and expertise about camels.

Chapter One

Armed with her favorite guilty pleasure—a caramel vanilla cappuccino—Abby Langdon left Sunny Perk in the distance and navigated the long gravel road that led to her ranch. Later, she'd put on a pot of coffee, but for now, her fix was complete.

Already she was anticipating the hard work and long day ahead. Sitting Tall Ranch and its special mission had always been her dream come true. Young victims of illness, poverty and abuse came to her ranch daily for a respite from their challenges. Her guests had witnessed the worst life could hand out, but Sitting Tall Ranch was the haven where they could forget their troubles and just be kids.

Abby slowed as she neared the abandoned pickup parked alongside the road. She'd seen it earlier when she'd left the ranch. Somebody had probably run out of gas then gotten a ride.

Abby drove through the gates, parked and headed to her office, a separate *casita* behind the main house. She was holding her to-go cup in one hand and reaching for her keys with the other when she heard a familiar voice to her left.

"Abby! Wait up!"

Ten-year-old Bobby Neskahi, hands down her favorite guest, was struggling up the sidewalk. Juvenile rheumatoid arthritis had damaged most of his joints and left him to rely on braces, but whatever had caused the panicked look on his face was urging him to move fast.

He stopped in front of her, catching his breath. "Carl's hurt! He's not moving."

"Where is he?" Her heart suddenly beat overtime. Carl Woods was her caretaker, animal handler and all-around right-hand man on the ranch.

"He's inside Tracker and Missy's turnout area. He's on the ground, and he didn't move or answer when I called him." Bobby grabbed her hand. "He might be dead. I couldn't see him breathing. Come on! You gotta help!"

Abby touched Bobby firmly on the shoulder, then handed him her keys. "Bobby, I need you to go into my office, call 911 on the desk phone, then stay here until the police arrive. You'll have to show them the way. I'll go check on Carl."

Bobby nodded and Abby took off running toward the stalls.

Jogging around the corner of the barn, Abby nearly collided with a wheelbarrow stacked with bales of alfalfa hay. Stopping just in time, she began inching between the wheelbarrow and the fence. Out of the corner of her eye she caught a glimpse of movement.

As she turned to look, a large figure leaped up from behind the stack and forced an empty feed bag over her head.

"Hey!" Sputtering from the debris in her eyes and mouth, she fought to pull the bag off.

Strong arms grabbed her wrists, yanked them down to her sides, then lifted her off the ground.

Abby tried to kick her captor, but he just grunted, hauled her several steps, then flung her violently onto the ground.

DARK, ANGRY CLOUDS were building over Copper Canyon. "Storm's heading our way." Hot from exertion despite the cool, early hour, Detective Preston Bowman had already shrugged off his shirt as he continued working alongside his brother, repairing gaps in the fence line. Their late foster father's place belonged to all of them now.

As the wind from the downdrafts intensified, Preston could feel the force of the approaching storm. The sky continued to darken quickly, turning the new day into near twilight.

Kyle, taller than his brother by one inch and just as muscular, wiped his eyes with a dirty hand. "Rain I like. Sandstorms, not so much, bro."

Preston was tired, though he'd never admit it. His sore muscles were a constant reminder of why he'd chosen city life instead. As a cop, Preston was more used to wielding a gun rather than a shovel, axe or sledgehammer. Even though he was six feet tall and in excellent shape—police work demanded it—he was ready for a break.

Kyle reached for his shirt. "I'd forgotten what it feels like to be sandblasted."

"Have you decided if you're going to be coming home for good?" Preston grabbed his own shirt and ducked inside the toolshed.

"Not yet," Kyle said, joining him in the small shelter. "I have some things to work out first." He shook his head and shrugged. "Can't say anything else—classified."

Preston nodded silently. He didn't have to know the details to realize whatever it was had hit Kyle like a hard kick to his gut. Despite that, he knew his brother would find a way to deal with it.

Inside each of his five brothers was a fighter who never gave up. They'd all been tested at an early age, long before they'd even known how to protect themselves from life's hard knocks.

Their stories were all different but shared the same core. They'd been wards of the state, abandoned by people who were supposed to have protected and loved them. Survival instincts had become second nature to each of them early on.

When life did its best to bring them to their knees, they got up and kept fighting. It was what they did best. The difference was now they had each other's backs. Though none of them were bound by blood, their pasts had forged unbreakable ties among them.

A flash of lightning was followed immediately by an ear-splitting crack of thunder that shook the ground. Hearing a horse's panicked whinny, Kyle shot out of the shed and ran toward the corral. "Red!"

The large mahogany horse with the dark mane was bucking wildly, racing around the corral and tossing his head.

"Red's used to his own stall inside Gene's barn. He doesn't like it here," Kyle said.

Preston took the horse by its halter, led him to the side of the house and stood there with him. "He'll settle down now that he's here with us, sheltered from the wind," he said. "How come Red's here? Did Gene loan him to you for a few days?"

"No. He's donating him to Sitting Tall Ranch. The owner, Abby Langdon, was looking for a gentle mount for kids with special needs. Red's steady as they come—except around thunder. If he's inside a barn, he's okay, but not if he's outside. Since I'd planned on keeping him here for a day or two so I could go riding, I checked the weather ahead of time. It was supposed to be okay, just a little cloudy, but this front's a day early."

As they stood waiting for the storm to pass, Preston kept his arm over the horse's neck. The animal seemed to be handling things better now.

"Have you opened the envelope *Hosteen* Silver left for you yet?" Preston asked, referring to their foster father.

"No, not yet. He knew things before they happened and that always spooked me. There's also something else I need to take into account now. After Daniel, Gene and Paul opened theirs, they ended up getting married within months. I'm thinking that I'll hold on to mine for another decade or so," he said and flashed his brother a quick grin.

Preston laughed. "Just so you know, they're not all letters that foretell upcoming events. Mine's a sketch." Preston reached for his wallet and took out a folded piece of paper. "I made a copy to keep with me until I figured it out."

"Nice. The old man was a good artist, though he seldom had time for that," Kyle said, studying it. "That's obviously Copper Canyon and there's Falcon. It looks just like the fetish he gave you when you turned sixteen."

"I've carried that carving with me every day since," Preston said, lifting the leather cord that hung around his neck. A small leather pouch hung from it. "Falcon's a faithful spiritual guide. I think he helps me see what others miss. That's a great asset in police work."

"In the sketch, Falcon's swooping down on that owl and defending something… a nest or maybe its mate? The background's mostly in shadow and hard to make out. Can you see it any better in the original?"

"No, not even enlarged."

"What's that drifting down?" Kyle asked, pointing. "A gray feather?"

"Feather, yes, but in the original, it's blue."

"*Hosteen* Silver used to say that blue jays, or piñon jays as he called them, stood for peace and happiness," Kyle said. "So was he saying that you'll be so busy fighting you'll miss out on happiness?"

"Your guess is as good as mine," Preston answered.

Kyle shook his head. "Everything about that man was mysterious. Even his name. *Hosteen* means mister. Silver was a nickname given to him because of his long silver hair."

Noting the wind had calmed down and things were returning to normal, Preston started leading the horse back to the corral. Just then a big barn owl flew out of the pine tree beside him. The bird swooped past him with a faint rustle of feathers, then turned sharply and angled up toward the cliff, disappearing into the background of rocks and brush.

Preston led the horse away quickly, grateful that Red had seemed oblivious to the owl and was now back to his usual calm self. His one fear—thunder—had subsided.

"The worst is over," Preston said.

"Not by a long shot, bro. *You're* the falcon in the drawing, and that was an owl we both saw swooping down out of that pine. For you, it's just starting."

Before he could reply, Preston's phone rang. He turned the reins over to his brother, gesturing for him to put the horse away, and answered the call.

Mere minutes later he met Kyle, who was standing by the department's SUV. Preston had changed shirts and was ready to go. "I need to race over to Hartley. I'm the closest cop and some kid just reported what he thinks is a dead body at Sitting Tall Ranch."

"Watch your back, bro. Looks like things are already in motion."

Preston slipped inside the SUV, then glanced out the window, his face hard, his gaze deadly. "Whatever's coming will find me ready and waiting."

Chapter Two

As Abby fell, her head hit something hard. Dizzying flashes of light exploded before her eyes, and for a moment she lay dazed and unable to move.

Her attacker grabbed her under her arms, dragged her several feet, then dropped her to the ground again. Disoriented, she waited for several long moments, hearing the fading sound of heavy footsteps.

Slowly regaining her wits, Abby sat up, tugged the bag off her head and looked around, trying to get her bearings and cope with the dull ache radiating from her head. She was in the stall prepared for the new horse, Big Red, who was due to arrive in a day or so. Both upper and lower stall doors were closed, but light still filtered in.

Abby listened for a moment, looking around. She was alone, and with the exception of the sound of horses moving about in the nearby stalls, snorting and anxious to be fed, she could hear nothing unusual.

Still cautious, she pushed the door. It was latched from the outside and wouldn't budge, and both sections of the Dutch door had been connected with outside barrel bolts, so she couldn't go under or over by opening just one. Peeking through the narrow gap, she saw where the metal latch had been lowered into the catch. Somehow she'd need to raise the big pin about an inch.

Abby peered around her, hoping to find a piece of baling wire she could work between the door and jamb. Unfortunately, she also had a safety rule requiring that no baling wire or metal objects be left on the ground where an animal could get tangled or cut up.

Poking through the hay debris, she noticed that one of the heavy wire tines of the metal feeder bolted to the wall had broken away from the weld at the bottom and could be twisted loose. That was what she needed. Thirty seconds later she managed to work the latch free, and the door swung open.

Abby hurried outside. Nobody was around. The horses in the pen ahead were moving about nervously, and when she drew closer, she saw Carl lying facedown on the ground by the feeder.

Hank, one of their two resident camels, was in the adjoining turnout. When he saw her, he roared loudly, the distressed sound reminding her of Chewbacca in *Star Wars*.

"Carl?" Abby scaled the fence and ran over. As she bent down for a closer look, she saw that the back of his head was a wet mass of tissue and blood. No one could have survived that kind of head injury. Outrage and sorrow gripped her.

Abby was struggling for breath when she heard a car door slam in the distance. Wondering if the attacker could have been the driver of the pickup parked on the road, Abby raced uphill. If she could read the license plate, she'd be able to give the police something solid to go on.

Once at the top, Abby saw the pickup and rushed out onto the road for a closer look. That was a mistake. The driver spun the truck around and accelerated, coming straight at her.

Abby stared at the darkened windshield, frozen in terror. The driver's face was lost to her, but his intent to kill her was clear.

Just then a dark SUV with flashing lights came racing over the hill—a response to Bobby's 911.

The SUV swerved left, cut around her, then slid to a stop between her and the oncoming truck.

The pickup quickly returned to its lane, then sped past the SUV and continued over the hill.

An officer wearing a dark Hartley police jacket stepped out of the SUV. As Abby went to thank him, her knees buckled.

He was there in an instant, his arms secure around her waist and holding her gently against him. "Hang on, ma'am. I'll call an ambulance. Your head's injured."

"No, I'm fine," she said quickly, stepping back to stand on her own. She touched the emerging bump on her forehead. At least she wasn't bleeding.

Abby looked up at him, straight into the darkest eyes she'd ever seen. His steady gaze was like the man himself—strong and hard—a rock to lean on. "You just saved my life."

"I'm Detective Preston Bowman of the Hartley P.D. You're safe now," he said, his voice calm and reassuring.

For a moment she felt tempted to step right back into his arms and rest against his hard chest. To forget…

She drew in a sharp breath. "I'm Abby Langdon. You need to come down to the ranch right away. Something's happened to Carl Woods, my head trainer," she said, telling him everything in a short burst.

"Let's go," he said, hurrying back to his SUV with her. "Hop in."

"This whole thing…it feels like a nightmare…but it's real," she whispered, closing the passenger-side door.

"All I caught was glare off the glass. Did you see the driver's face or his license plate?" he asked, easing down the hill, then making the turn into the long driveway.

"No, but it wasn't for lack of trying," she said.

"All right then. I called it in as soon as he took off. We'll see what happens now. I've heard of what you do here, Abby. Now tell me more about your animal handler."

"He's…" Her voice broke and she brushed away a tear. If she started crying now, would she ever stop? She took a deep breath and held it together.

He pulled up in front of the logs anchored in place to serve as a parking barrier. "Just point me in the right direction. This is a police matter and I'll handle it."

His steady voice and calm confidence made it easier for her to trust him. He'd stepped into an unpredictable situation and had taken charge effortlessly, as if it was second nature to him. Something assured her that Detective Bowman was very good at his job.

They climbed out of the SUV, and she led him quickly to the turnout area alongside the barn. As they approached, she saw that Bobby had left her office and was now standing just outside the welded pipe enclosure where Carl lay.

"I need to get Bobby away from there," she said quickly. "He's too young to deal with things like this and he's seen too much already."

"Bobby's your son?" he asked, noting that the boy was Navajo.

"No, he's always my first guest of the day. He's also one of my regular helpers," she said. "He found Carl and made the 911 call. Is it okay if I go take care of him?"

"Yeah. This is no place for a kid. Find a place where he can stay, just make sure he doesn't leave the property. He may have seen or heard something that could help us."

As Abby hurried to the boy, she could see Carl's body in her periphery. A silent scream rose inside her, filling her mind and nearly obliterating her ability to think.

"He's…dead, isn't he?" Bobby whispered.

He seemed remarkably controlled considering the circumstances. But she'd seen that same look on other faces before and recognized it for what it was. Many would mistake it for indifference, but fear, the kind that clung with razor-sharp tentacles to your soul, often mimicked bravery. She remembered seeing it in her twin sister's eyes as treatment after treatment had failed to cure her.

Taking a deep breath and forcing herself to focus on the present, Abby turned her head and saw Detective Bowman had ducked through the gap in the welded pipe fence. He had latex gloves on and was now crouched next to Carl's body. After checking for Carl's pulse, he looked up and shook his head, affirming what she already knew.

Abby focused on Bobby. "We need to leave. Other officers and medical people will be here soon and will need us to point the way back here."

Bobby didn't move, his gaze still locked on Carl. "Do you think Missy or Tracker kicked him?" he asked in a thin voice.

She hadn't even considered that possibility until now. "I can't imagine either of those horses hurting anyone. They're the calmest animals I've ever known. I've never seen either of them spook, not under any circumstances," she said, taking an unsteady breath. Somehow her voice had remained steady but her hands were shaking badly. Not wanting Bobby to see that, she jammed them into her pockets. "Carl was their trainer and the animals knew and liked him. They never even flinched or pulled away when he cleaned their hooves. There's no way they hurt him."

"Then who did this?"

Abby drew in another unsteady breath. "I don't know, Bobby. That's what Detective Bowman is here to find out." She tried to urge Bobby along, but he refused to move.

"I'm going to miss Carl, Abby. He was my friend and I don't have that many. The kids at the foster home play a lot of football and baseball, but I can't. Carl liked the same kind of games I do. We'd pretend we were spies and do a lot of cool stuff." A tear trickled down one cheek, but he brushed it away instantly.

She wanted to give him a hug, but she knew Bobby would think she was babying him and would hate that. "It's okay to be sad. I am, too, Bobby."

He nodded but didn't answer her directly, avoiding the subject altogether. "The detective's Navajo, like me. Did you notice? He has to work around the body and that's dangerous, but he knows how to protect himself so he'll stay safe," he said. "See that leather bag on the cord around his neck? That's not jewelry, and he's not just trying to look Indian. That bag protects him."

"From what? I don't understand," Abby said.

"Spirits stick around and like making trouble for people. Mrs. Nez—she cooks for us back at the foster home—told me that," he said.

Abby hesitated, unsure what to say. "Carl would never hurt either one of us, not when he was alive or now that he's passed on," she said. "Bobby, you may not need a hug, but I do." She bent down and held him. As she did, Abby felt the tremor that shook his small body.

After a moment she stepped away and Bobby refused to look at her, almost as if embarrassed. "Tell the detective that I followed the rule of three, okay?"

"The what?"

"He'll know," he said. "We better go. The sirens are coming closer."

She nodded. "You're right. We'll need to stay out of everyone's way."

They walked back up the path away from the barn and the enclosures. Abby set a slow pace, but not so much that Bobby would think she was deferring to him. Bobby faced many difficulties daily, but he had a lot of pride, something that helped him endure.

Hearing Hank the camel roar loudly, Abby halted. "Bobby, go ahead without me. Make sure the other officers and emergency people know where to find the detective. I need to get the horses out of the turnout area and move Hank to another pen so the police can work in peace."

"Okay, but if you get scared or something, shout out or whistle. I'll hear you."

"Thanks," Abby said and smiled. Bobby was as loyal as could be. It was one of the many reasons she was so fond of him.

Abby jogged back to where she'd left the detective. Though the horses were clearly upset by the stranger in their enclosure, they were still acting in a predictable manner. Both stood as far away from Detective Bowman as possible, at the innermost corner of the enclosure, watching him, their ears pinned back.

"Detective, let me put halters on the horses and lead them to another pen. They'll be out of your way then."

"No, stay put. This is a crime scene," he said. "I see a hoof pick over there and a coffee can with some traces of grain. I'll dump that out then check their hooves, scrape off any dirt and debris into the can and then bring them out to you."

Preston looked around for a rope and halter but, finding neither within arm's reach, decided to forego using them. He bent down and checked each of Missy's hooves. Using the pick, he collected dirt and what could be blood and hair. Once finished, he grabbed the mare by the mane and led her over to Abby, who immediately opened the small turnout gate.

"You know horses," Abby said.

"Yeah. It was part of life where I grew up."

Abby grabbed Missy's mane as he'd done and led her out to another corral. By the time she returned, Detective Bowman was waiting with Tracker.

Abby grabbed the horse but as her gaze strayed to Carl, a lump formed at her throat. How could this have happened? Nothing made sense to her anymore.

"Was he a close friend?" Preston asked, as if sensing the turmoil inside her.

"We weren't close, but I considered him a friend. He was a good, loyal employee and a man who'd believed in my dream for Sitting Tall Ranch." She wanted to keep her voice steady, so she paused for a moment. "Do you know how...he died?" she added in a strained whisper.

"Not yet, but I'll find out. You can count on that."

Detective Bowman walked away from her and crouched by Carl's body once again. This time he looked around slowly, taking in the setting, not the victim. Although the gesture had seemed almost casual, she had a feeling he didn't miss much. Then, surprisingly, he looked back at her. His gaze was penetrating...and unsettling. She wanted to look away but somehow couldn't quite manage it.

To her, he represented the unknown...and that scared her. Would he be an ally, or would his appearance mark the last days of Sitting Tall Ranch? She'd made her mistakes—well-meaning ones, but if they came out now... Determined to guard her secrets, she moved away.

"We'll be blocking off several areas with yellow tape," he called out while taking photos with a small camera. "It may take a day or two before we're ready to take the tape down, so be prepared."

She tried not to give in to the unadulterated panic rising inside her. This wasn't just about Carl, not anymore. If the ranch became synonymous with danger, no parent would want their kids here. She'd lose her funding and have to shut down.

Sitting Tall Ranch was a place of healing and hope. There was no other place like it in the area. What they offered kids was something worth fighting for, and she intended to do whatever was necessary to keep the ranch's doors open.

"I'm going to need access to the animals," she said as Hank

let out another loud bellow. "Please try to keep that in mind when you put up the tape."

"No problem. I've got you covered."

"And please," she said softly, "work quickly. We need donations to survive, and with the economy, those have become harder and harder to get."

"You need closure, too, and finding answers is what I do best," he said. "Trust me."

She looked at him and blinked. She normally hated it when anyone said that. The words were usually empty and, if anything, meant she should do exactly the opposite. Yet there was something about Detective Bowman that assured her he was as good as his word.

Hearing another vehicle approaching, he turned his head to look, then glanced back at her. "Here comes Joanna Medina, the medical investigator," he said. "I'll need to speak to you and the boy as soon as I can, and when I do I'll let you know what we've found."

"Okay, thanks," she said. "I'm going to move Hank, the camel that's being so vocal right now. After that I'll be in my office, the *casita* behind the main house."

"One more thing," he called out to her. "The kid, Bobby, he didn't move or touch the body, right?"

"No, I think he would have been afraid to. He told me to tell you he'd followed the rule of three. He said you'd know what that meant."

Preston nodded. "Don't touch them, don't look at them, get away from them."

"The ghosts of the dead—that's the source of worry, right?" she asked.

"Not exactly," he said, meeting her outside the corral. "The *chindi* is the evil side of a man that remains earthbound waiting for a chance to create problems for the living. Our traditionalists believe that contact with the dead or their possessions is a sure way to draw it to you."

"You're an officer, so you're not…a traditionalist?"

"I'm a detective who does his job," he said, waving at a woman wearing a lab coat and carrying a heavy-looking medical case. "I have to get to work now. I'll come find you once we're through here and we can talk about what you saw before I got here."

As he strode away, a cold shudder ripped through Abby. She'd known anger, worry, love and ultimately loss. Yet she could count on one hand the times she'd experienced pure, unadulterated fear. Now as she watched the detective meet the medical examiner, she felt its icy-cold touch clawing into her again.

Carl was dead, and someone had attacked her here twice. No matter how hard she wished it wasn't so, the truth was that the ranch was no longer a safe haven.

Trying not to look back at Carl's body as she passed by, Abby returned to the pen that held Hank. Sensing that she was upset, the tall, gawky but somehow elegant animal nuzzled against her.

"Come on, old friend." She placed a halter on him, opened the gate and led him away.

As she walked, tears gathered but she blinked them away. She wouldn't fall apart now. She'd do what had to be done. Carl had shared her dream. He'd loved what they did here at the ranch daily: giving kids a chance to be kids again. He would have expected her to fight to keep it alive.

One way or another she'd see to it that Sitting Tall Ranch weathered the approaching storm.

Chapter Three

Preston considered the information he'd already gathered while the medical examiner worked. At first glance it had looked like an accident, a trampling death, but there were some inconsistencies. The wound to the back of the victim's skull showed no trace of sand, something sure to have been left by a horse's hoof, especially in this churned-up stall.

There also weren't any deep impressions or hoof marks near the body that would indicate the vic had been trampled. In fact, the only fresh prints near the body appeared to be from the vic's own boots.

He'd seen plenty of cowboys injured by horses at rodeos, but the way Carl's body lay seemed posed somehow. A cowboy kicked by a horse usually landed askew, not neatly on his face with arms laid out flat by his side. The fact that someone else had been on the premises and had attacked Abby, then tried to run her down, supported the likelihood of foul play.

That's when he'd taken another look at the ground by the body and discovered that someone had methodically obliterated the footprints along a strip of ground leading to and from the enclosure's gate. It had been skillfully done, but Preston was an experienced tracker and had spotted the signs.

Dr. Joanna Medina glanced up from the body. She was in her late fifties, with short silver hair and blue eyes that looked world weary and a little sad.

"You were right. This wasn't an accident. The wound on his head appears to have come from a blunt object. There's a second bruise on his chest, too. It's elongated, as if made by a stick or shovel." Joanna stood and handed him a clear plastic evidence bag. "Here's everything I found in the vic's pockets."

"Do you have a time of death for me?"

"All the markers tell me he died last night between nine and midnight."

As she prepared the body for transport, Preston, still wearing gloves to avoid fingerprint contamination, studied the vic's possessions. There was a small notepad with feeding schedules, a ranch staff ID and a wallet with five bucks but no driver's license. Because there was no metro bus service and only one cab company around, it was unusual for locals not to have a license. He'd ask Abby about it.

As he walked back, Preston glanced over at the parking area and saw that the ranch's staff was starting to arrive. They all wore dark blue T-shirts with a special logo. Yet the animal handler was wearing a plaid shirt.

The door to Abby's office was partially open, and as he approached he felt a touch of cool air coming from inside. Preston stepped into the room, and Abby, who'd been sitting on the sofa next to the Navajo boy, came to meet him.

Now that he finally had a chance to take a closer, leisurely look at her, he realized that Abby Langdon was a stunner, with shoulder-length honey-brown hair and big hazel eyes. The loose clothing she wore didn't hide the fact that she had curves in all the right places.

"Did you figure out what happened?" Abby asked.

He shook his head. "It's much too soon for that, but I've got some more questions for you." Even as he spoke, he saw her expression turn from hopeful to disappointed. He softened his tone. "We'll get to the bottom of it, but these things take time. All I can tell you is that it wasn't an accident."

The color drained from her face. "This couldn't have had anything to do with our ranch. It has to be random...craziness."

"What do you know about the deceased?" he asked.

Her eyes widened. "You think Carl provoked this somehow? But that just can't be. He was a gentle man. He caught spiders and relocated rather than killed them."

"Relax. I'm just gathering information," he said.

She took a deep breath and nodded. "Sorry."

He saw her lips tremble but she quickly brought herself under control and turned her head to smile at Bobby.

Preston liked her. It was a purely instinctive reaction, but he trusted his gut. Just past those beautiful hazel eyes and that shaky smile beat the heart of a warrior. Yet hers was a gentle toughness.

The boy rose to his feet and came over. "I'm Bobby Neskahi," he said. Honoring Navajo ways, he didn't offer to shake hands. "I knew...him," he said, avoiding the name of the deceased, also according to Navajo custom. "Probably better than almost anyone," he added.

Preston wondered if the kid had been raised a traditionalist or was simply showing him the proper cultural respect.

"I'm *Diné*," Bobby said.

"We both are," Preston said, trying not to smile. *Diné* meant The People and signified those of the Navajo tribe.

Bobby moved back to the couch, and as he walked, Preston realized that the kid was no stranger to pain.

"Can we talk alone—Navajo to Navajo?" Bobby asked.

"Of course," Preston said, then looked at Abby.

"I'm not sure that's a good idea," she said, giving Preston a wary look.

"We'll keep it informal, not official." At her hesitation, he met her gaze. Looking someone in the eye was considered rude inside the Navajo Nation, but he'd learned over the years that those outside the tribe found it a sign of honesty, not disrespect. Though it hadn't come naturally to him, over time he'd adapted to the custom.

"Okay, but I'm staying right outside."

As Abby left, Preston sat down on the couch and gestured with a nod for Bobby to do the same. "Abby told me that you were the one who found the body this morning," Preston said.

He nodded and swallowed hard. "Yeah, but I stuck to the rule of three."

"I know," Preston said. "So tell me, Bobby, how well did you know the ranch's animal trainer?"

"Do you want me to avoid using his name or not?" Bobby asked. "I wasn't raised on the Rez but I don't want you to think I don't know any better."

"It's safe to use his name. I'm a police officer, so I'm a modernist."

"Mrs. Nez has been teaching me about our ways. She says modernists are like apples—red on the outside and white on the inside."

Preston laughed. It was an old saying, and he had a feeling Bobby was testing him. "I've heard it all, kid." He gazed into Bobby's hard brown eyes and for a moment saw a glimpse of himself at that age. He'd been so afraid to show vulnerability. The world was seldom kind to those perceived as weak. That was a lesson he'd learned in foster care quickly enough, and he had a feeling it was even more so for Bobby.

"Abby's trying to be brave, but on the inside she's scared. This isn't her fault, so you need to fix it."

"Fix it how?"

"Catch the bad guy before she freaks out. I can help. Carl and I were buds."

"Okay. Let's start at the beginning. First of all, what were you doing here so early in the morning?" Preston asked.

"I always come in super early because my foster father—

Mr. Jack is what we call him—drops me off on his way to work. He has his own janitorial company, and some of the places he cleans want everything done before they open for business."

"Okay, the answers that. So what do you usually do when you get here?"

"I say hi to Abby, then go help Carl feed the animals. He starts work even earlier than my foster dad."

"Tell me what you saw this morning," Preston pressed.

"I was going past the pens when I saw him just lying there on the ground. I saw the blood on his clothes and got scared so I went to get Abby." He paused, then looked up at Preston. "The horses weren't anywhere near him."

"Tell me more about Carl," Preston said.

"Carl was really old, like sixty. What I liked most about him was that he treated me just like he did everyone else," Bobby said, then looked away and wiped a tear from his face with a swipe of his hands. "He never gave me that 'poor kid' look. To him I was just me." He stared at his right leg, which was encased in a brace.

Bobby became quiet and Preston didn't interrupt the silence.

"Carl didn't have a lot of friends, kinda like me at the foster home." Bobby looked up at Preston and met his gaze. "He talked to the rest of the staff and all, but they weren't really his friends. He only had one other friend besides me and Abby. Rod Garner, Lightning Rod, who used to be in the NBA. Carl liked going over there and playing one-on-one with Lightning. Mr. Garner's got a huge basketball court—six goals. I've never been there, but Carl told me about it."

Preston nodded, beginning to understand Bobby more. "So what else did you two talk about?"

"Stuff," he said with a shrug. "We were always solving puzzles and riddles like real spies, you know? That was fun.

Carl liked games where you had to use your head, not your thumbs, and hated games where you had to trust your luck."

"You mean like gambling?"

"Yeah, like that. I tried to give him a buck once so he'd buy me a scratcher, but he wouldn't do it. I said I'd split the money if I won, but he still said no. Told me gambling was like throwing your money away and I was too smart to fall for stuff like that."

"He was telling you the truth. The odds always favor the game, not the gambler. Lottery, scratchers, casinos—they're all the same except for the odds."

"Don't you think that sometimes you just have to take a chance?" he said.

Preston didn't answer. "What would you have done with the money had you won?" he asked, trying to get a better handle on Bobby.

"Give it to Abby," he said without any hesitation. "She needs the money to keep the ranch and help kids like me. I wish she could find a rich guy to marry—someone who could help run the ranch and pay the bills. Do you know any rich guys?"

Preston heard coughing—more like choking—and Abby walked in a heartbeat later. From all indications, she'd been listening.

"Michelle's here, Bobby. She can give you a ride back home."

"Not now. Let me stay and help. You'll need to look in Carl's office, and if I go with you I can tell if anything's missing or been moved around."

Abby looked at Preston. "Bobby's got a photographic memory—really," she said.

"Not just that. I rule when it comes to puzzles and problem solving, too." He looked at Preston. "You don't believe me? Okay. I'll prove it." He gave Preston a once-over. "Betcha you spent some time outside working earlier this morning."

Preston smiled slowly. "How do you know that?"

"Your boots are real dusty but the dust is darker than the ground around here. You also have some red horse hair on you and we don't have any red horses. You were probably chopping wood or weeds or working real hard without gloves, 'cause the palms of your hands are all scuffed up. Maybe rope burns?" Bobby offered.

Preston smiled slowly. "Good observations. You might be another Sherlock Holmes someday, kid."

"Maybe. So can I stay?" he said, looking over at Abby. "Please?"

"Okay, but I need to speak to the detective alone right now. Go help Michelle feed the llamas."

"Sure." He turned to Preston. "We're counting on you, okay?" he said, then walked slowly out the door, closing it behind him. Abby waited several seconds before speaking. "I was eavesdropping because I didn't think it was a good idea for Bobby to speak to you alone. You don't know a thing about that boy."

"That was the purpose of talking to him."

"I still think you should have had an adult present."

"He found the body, but he's not a suspect," Preston said. "You seem to have heard pretty much everything we talked about, so why are you worried?"

"You don't understand. Bobby sometimes comes across as a tough kid and in a lot of ways he is, but he's been betrayed and abandoned by people all his life. Carl was one of the few adults he trusted. Now he's gone, too. Can you imagine what he's going through? You have to cut him some slack and be careful what kind of questions you ask him. It's important that he continue to remember Carl in a good way."

What touched Preston most was her protectiveness. When

he'd been Bobby's age, he, too, would have gone to the wall for anyone who'd cared enough to defend him.

"I have no intention of doing anything that would hurt Bobby. I'll be careful around him, but I'm here to do a job. That means digging for the truth even if it turns out to be something you don't want to hear."

"All right. The truth doesn't frighten me. How can I help you find answers?"

"Let's start with some straight talk."

Chapter Four

Abby watched Detective Bowman as he checked his notes. He was handsome in a tough, streetwise way. Somewhere along the way he'd shrugged out of his police-issue jacket and was now wearing a navy shirt with the sleeves rolled up.

He looked muscular, like a man used to hard, physical work. His shoulders were wide, and his chest was as broad and strong as she remembered from this morning. She suppressed a sigh. He wasn't a pretty boy. His nose was a little crooked, like he'd broken it at one time, but that just heightened his appeal.

Detective Preston Bowman was fascinating to watch. Even as he wrote in his notebook she could sense a restless energy about him.

As he shifted, her gaze fell to the badge clipped to his belt and, on the other side, his handgun. That reminder was all she needed to rein in her thoughts. He was a law enforcement professional here to do a job, and this was no time for distractions.

"Carl didn't have a vehicle, so I'm assuming he had a bicycle or drove one of the ranch's trucks?" he asked.

As he looked at her, she felt the power of his gaze all through her. Detective Bowman was all male, with cool eyes that didn't miss much and left her feeling slightly off balance.

"What is that, Detective—a trick question? You've undoubtedly already run his name through the MVD and know that Carl didn't have a driver's license. If he needed to go someplace, he either hitched a ride with one of our volunteers or rode his bicycle, which is in his office in the barn."

Preston held her gaze a moment longer, but she forced herself not to even blink.

"You paid him by check?"

"Yeah, but he preferred cash. He didn't have a bank account," she said.

He looked at her, surprised. "And that didn't seem odd to you?"

"Carl was one of a kind," she said with a sad smile. "He also didn't have a credit card or a cell phone. In this day and age, that's hard to believe, but it's true."

"No prepaid cell phone either?"

"I can't say for sure, but I really doubt it. It just wasn't his style." As much as she wanted to trust him, she knew they weren't really on the same side. He was here only to investigate the crime. Her priority was protecting the ranch and, more importantly, the work they did here.

"After we're done and the scene is released, do you plan to reopen right away?"

"I haven't decided yet," she said, then as her voice wavered, she swallowed hard. "Without knowing why someone came after me, I can't guarantee anyone's safety. Just being around me could endanger the kids and I can't let that happen."

"I can't give you any real assurances, but based on the evidence, the guy who jumped you didn't want you dead. He had his chance. My guess is that he only wanted to scare you."

"Do you think it was the same person who killed Carl?"

"Not likely. Woods died last night, between nine and midnight approximately. That means his killer would have had to stick around for six to nine hours."

"But *two* violent incidents that close together? That's a huge coincidence, don't you think? We've never had any trouble here," she said. "Let's assume the killer did stick around. What do you think he did all that time?"

"Searching for something? You tell me. This is your ranch, so your guess will probably be better than mine."

Hearing a knock on the door, she excused herself and went to answer it. A tall, wiry, redheaded man in a Western shirt and jeans came in.

"Stan," she said.

The man took her hand for a moment. "Abby, I'm so sorry. Carl was a good man."

She gestured toward Preston. "This is Detective Bowman from the Hartley police," she said. "He's investigating Carl's death." The words sounded odd even in her own ears. "Detective, this is Stan Cooper, my accountant and business advisor."

"You can add ranch volunteer to that list, too," he said, brushing alfalfa leaves off his shirt instead of offering to shake hands. "I just brought in a trailer loaded with hay, saw the police and learned what happened."

"I'm still trying to come to terms with everything," Abby said.

"I know this is hard on you, Abby, but you've got a more immediate problem. Some kids with special needs have just arrived, and right behind them is a camera crew from the local cable TV station."

She rubbed her forehead with her fingertips and closed her eyes for a second, trying to push back a migraine. "I made a lot of calls already this morning, but I couldn't reach everyone, particularly the ones who were already on their way."

"That's okay. Put it out of your mind. Right now you're going to have to go out there and make a statement to the press," Stan said. "You need to make sure everyone understands that the ranch will have to remain closed for the time being. Explain that your priority is cooperating with the police so this unfortunate incident can be cleared up. Don't let them draw you into long discussions. Keep it short and simple."

She nodded. "I'll handle it."

"After the initial interview, don't talk to the press again," Stan said. "Stay low profile. That's my professional and personal advice. The longer this story remains front-page news, the worse off the ranch will be. Something like this could scare away current and future benefactors."

Abby moved to the window and looked outside. "I really don't want to turn those kids away now that they're here. They really look forward to spending time at the ranch and I hate disappointing them."

Preston followed her gaze. "Is it just those three kids?"

"Yes. I got hold of the others due in today and told them I'd reschedule."

"If you could keep them well away from the crime scene area, you could still let them ride the horses and pet the other animals," Preston said.

"Absolutely not," Stan said quickly. "Abby, think about it. The media is already out there taking photos. If you say that the ranch will have to be closed for now, people will see that as your way of putting the kids' safety first. Yet if you say that's what you're going to do and then invite those kids in, you'll lose credibility. The public will see images of kids riding horses and petting camels right next to half a dozen police cars and lots of yellow crime scene tape. Your donors are going to run for cover."

"I'll figure this out, Stan. Stop worrying," Abby said firmly.

As she stepped out of the office, she had no idea what she was going to say. Then, making a spur-of-the-moment decision, Abby went to meet the kids. After briefly explaining the situation to the adults who'd brought them, she focused on the children.

"I know you've all been looking forward to this, but the police have important work they need to finish." Abby glanced at Lilly, a small seven-year-old girl who'd been to the ranch once before. Her illness was terminal and, with her, each day counted. The other two, both boys, were new to Standing Tall Ranch.

"So we have to go back?" Lilly asked, her expression so downcast it tugged at Abby.

"I'll tell you what. There can be no horseback riding this time, but how would you like to come say hello to Hank and Eli, our camels?" She saw their faces brighten.

"I'm Jason," the tallest boy said, balancing well on two prosthetic legs. "I'm eight and I've never even seen a camel. Can we pet them?"

"I'd like that too," the other boy said. "I'm Carlos."

Abby recognized him from his file. Carlos was a victim of abuse and still had trust issues.

"Are they friendly?" Carlos added.

"Absolutely. We'll pick up some treats for them as we go over to their pens."

Out of the corner of her eye, Abby saw a camera crew hurrying over to her, but the detective moved quickly to intercept them.

A wave of relief swept over her and she smiled. She liked that man already. Beneath the stern cop exterior was a gentle heart. She'd make sure to thank him later.

PRESTON IDENTIFIED HIMSELF to the reporters. He knew a few already, like Marsha Robertson. She was an area reporter for the number one network affiliate in the state, which was based in Albuquerque.

He gave them all a quick rundown. "That's all I have for you at this time."

"A source tells me the owner was also attacked," Marsha

said, "perhaps by the killer. How can you be sure that those kids are safe?"

"There are a dozen or more police officers here. They're safe, just as you are."

"Right now, sure, but later…then what? Once the crime scene is released and the officers all leave, will Sitting Tall Ranch open up and return to business as usual?"

"That's a question you'll have to ask the owner."

"And that would be me," Abby said, walking up with Bobby at her side.

"The safety of the children always comes first, so the ranch will be closed until we can find out exactly what happened. I've made an exception for those kids because they were already here. Our riding instructor, Michelle Okerman, will stay with them while I speak to you, and if you'll glance over from time to time, you'll see the difference just being around the animals makes to these children."

Abby paused and looked directly at each reporter there. "This ranch is a nonprofit whose sole purpose is to brighten the lives of kids who might otherwise have very little to smile about. One of our guests today is in the last stages of a serious illness and deserves extra consideration. That's why I decided to let Sitting Tall Ranch rise above its present circumstances and come through on promises made."

Preston saw that Abby's answer had hit just the right tone with the reporters. He had a feeling more donations would soon come in. In fact, he intended to send her a check himself.

As the reporters moved away, Stan approached and said, "Well played."

"I didn't *play,* Stan. I told them the truth."

"Yes, well, now concentrate on staying low profile till this blows over."

"And that'll be soon, right?" Bobby asked, looking up at

Preston. "The CSI unit will get DNA from something, or trace evidence, and then you'll go arrest the bad guy."

"I wish it were that simple, but it's not. Right now we're gathering evidence, and then we'll be interviewing a lot of people. Once we have a suspect, we'll move in and arrest him or her." Seeing Officer Michaels signal him, Preston excused himself momentarily.

"What's up?" he asked Michaels as he walked over to the barn.

"We processed, photographed and logged in the evidence. When will you be ready for us to process the vic's residence, the bunkhouse?"

"Hang on. I want a chance to look around there first. Did you or Gabe interview the staff?"

"Everyone who's on-site now, yes. That includes the riding instructor, Michelle Okerman. She teaches the kids about balance and paying attention. Basically, she walks next to the mounts and helps them each step of the way. Monroe Jenkins, the police chief's son, is here this morning, too. He volunteers a lot in the summer and does whatever needs to be done. Ilse Sheridan is also here. She's Lightning Rod Garner's personal assistant and volunteers her time to help train the horses. The last time any of them claim to have seen the vic was yesterday afternoon."

"Thanks. I'll let you know when you can process the bunkhouse. In the meantime, walk through the grounds and check out each of the other structures. We don't know where else the intruder went. And verify that there's a bicycle inside the barn office."

Michaels nodded. "Got it. We've already set up a search pattern."

When Preston returned to where Abby was standing, Bobby was speaking to Michelle. The boy was favoring his right leg and swaying slightly from side to side.

Abby followed his line of vision. "He's conning her," she whispered with a tiny smile. "Michelle was hoping to divert Bobby by asking him to talk to the kids, but he knows where the action's going to be. He'd rather stick with us."

"That kid's in pain. I don't think he's faking it," Preston said.

"His disability is real, but he's learned to use it. Don't ever underestimate him. Bobby's highly intelligent and knows how to manipulate adults to get out of whatever he doesn't want to do."

Preston didn't comment, still unconvinced.

"Jack Yarrow, his foster parent, prefers dropping him off here first thing in the morning because Bobby makes his wife nervous. He can read her like a book and tells her what she's about to do next, which creeps her out big-time."

"He's incredibly observant," he said with a smile.

"It's all part of a game he plays. Bobby can't let go of the hope that he and his biological father will be together again someday. After his dad gave him up, Bobby made up the story that his dad's in the CIA and had to leave to protect him. He told it so many times, he actually began to believe it. He reads everything he can about spy craft and pretends he's training so he can join his dad someday."

"He's protecting himself from a truth that hurts too much to accept," Preston said, remembering his days in foster care.

"The problem is that this game he plays often gets him into trouble. When he's told not to do something, he pretends he's a spy on a secret mission and finds a way to do it anyway," she said. "I'm willing to bet that most of the time he doesn't get caught."

"He may be a handful, but he's got a lot going for him," Preston said, chuckling. "Kids who've been bounced around often need something or someone to believe in. Bobby had a hard time finding that, so he created it. In my mind that deserves a high five."

Just then Bobby came up. "When will you be checking out Carl's office?"

"I'm going over to the bunkhouse now," Preston said. "I'll check the office after that."

"Great. I can help you at both places. I've been at the bunkhouse lots of times too," he said.

Abby gave him a surprised look. "You have?"

"Sure, after Carl finished his chores, he and I would play games. We both loved anagrams and riddles, and sometimes we'd make up our own codes and send each other secret messages."

"On a computer?" Preston asked.

"No," Bobby said. "Just on paper. He was *good,* too. We'd try to make the codes impossible to break, like real spies would, but he'd win most of the time."

"What happened when you won?" Preston asked, following his gut.

Bobby smiled. "I'd get to feed the camels."

"Alone?" Abby asked, her voice rising.

"No, Carl would always stay with me, watching, but I'd be the one who did it," he said, a touch of pride in his voice.

"Sounds like the camels are your favorites," Preston said.

"Yeah, Hank and Eli are cool. They remember stuff. There's one guy who swatted Eli just to get him out of the way once, and Eli never forgot. After that, he'd set the guy up by acting real calm, then biting at him the second he got close."

"Are you talking about Joe Brown?" Abby asked.

Bobby nodded.

"I caught him manhandling one of the horses and fired him on the spot," she told Preston.

"I'm going to need to interview everyone who might have had some grievance against the victim or the ranch. Can you get me a list of all current and past employees, say, going back six months?" Preston said.

"No problem," Abby said.

As they headed toward the bunkhouse, Bobby slipped in smoothly between Preston and Abby. Preston noted it silently, wondering if the boy had a crush on Abby. Or maybe there was more at play. Considering Bobby's past, it was possible the kid didn't trust cops.

"So Carl had the use of the bunkhouse rent free?" Preston verified as they neared the small building about the size of a one-car garage or a startup home on the Rez.

"It was part of the package since I couldn't pay him what he was worth. Carl agreed to fix up the interior for me, too, as long as I purchased the supplies," she said. "When I first bought Sitting Tall Ranch, the property had been unoccupied for years. Everything had been neglected and most of the buildings were practically unlivable."

He looked around. The barn and storage sheds had fresh coats of paint, the corrals had up-to-date welded pipe fencing and the areas were well maintained. There wasn't a weed in sight.

"You've done a good job. The place shows the care you give it."

"That's what you do with a dream," she said softly, then unlocked the bunkhouse door.

Chapter Five

Preston put on a fresh pair of gloves as he stepped inside. "Come in with me, but *don't* touch anything," he told them. "And be careful where you step. If there's something on the floor, leave it there."

Preston remained in the doorway a few seconds longer and just looked around. He'd expected a utilitarian place designed to fit the needs of its one resident, and he'd been right on target. The interior held the stamp of the working man who'd lived here.

An easy chair made of blue vinyl and patched with duct tape in several places was backed against one wall. A small table a few feet in front of it held an old TV with rabbit ears and the digital converter box needed to translate the signal.

There were pencil and black ink sketches on the wall and the supplies needed for more—stiff white paper, charcoal sticks, markers and pencils—on the shelf of a nearby empty bookcase.

"He loved to draw," Bobby said, standing at the doorway with Preston, "but he threw out most of his stuff. If he wasn't happy with the way it came out, it went straight into the trash."

Abby nodded. "I tried to salvage a charcoal sketch he'd thrown out once, but he wouldn't let me keep it. When I gave it back to him, he just tore it up. He made me another one, though, and I hung it in the main house, my home."

Preston led the way into the room, then saw Bobby staring at the bookshelf. "Something missing?" he asked the boy.

"Yeah, his coffee can is gone," Bobby said.

"He kept coffee on the bookshelf?" Preston looked around for a coffeemaker but didn't see one.

"He drank coffee like crazy, but it was all instant," Bobby said. "The coffee can was his bank—that's what he called it. It was old, like from twenty years ago, and all dented. He said that he used to buy that brand when he was a lot younger and having it around brought back good memories." Bobby paused, swallowed hard, then in a heavy voice added, "He told me about it being his bank because we were friends and he trusted me."

Abby stepped closer to Bobby and said, "How about we wait outside for you, Detective?"

Bobby shook his head. "No, I'm okay. I just miss him, that's all. Let me stay and help."

Preston heard Abby sigh and saw her nod.

"Anything else that looks out of place, Bobby? Walk around and take a good look, but remember, don't touch anything," Preston said.

Abby stayed right beside Bobby as they took the lead. Preston followed, his gaze on Abby. She was leggy and had a great figure, but what appealed to him most had little to do with her looks.

She was obviously a woman whose feelings ran deep. She cared a lot for Bobby and the rest of the kids who came to the ranch. He made a mental note to find out more about her, and not just because she was part of the case he was working.

They passed through a narrow hall and an open door and entered Carl's bedroom. Inside they found an unmade bed, one wooden chair, an old oak desk and a small three-drawer chest. On top of the desk were several lottery tickets, two scratchers, tickets from a slot machine and a couple of chips from the casino.

"You sure he didn't gamble?" Preston asked Bobby.

"I never saw stuff like that here before. There's no way those were his. He thought gambling was stupid. Someone must have put them there," Bobby said. Then he pointed to the coffee can on top of the chest of drawers. "He didn't keep the can there either. It was always out front, on that shelf."

Preston lifted the lid, but there was no cash inside, only two more lottery tickets.

"Think hard, Bobby. Did you ever see the cash that was supposedly inside the can?"

"I never looked inside it—that would have been rude. But he wouldn't have lied to me," Bobby said.

Abby smiled at Bobby, then looked at Preston. "I can tell you this much—Carl was always careful with his money. He had to be. He never wasted a dollar."

"Yeah, Detective Bowman," Bobby said. "I'm just a kid, but I know serious gamblers. That's all they talk about—winning, betting, the odds."

"Did you learn that from your parents?" Preston asked.

"No, no way. My mom died when I was three or four, and my dad, well, he gave me up 'cause he's a spy and can't afford to have a kid hanging around. He travels all over the world," Bobby said proudly. "I know about gamblers because my last foster dad had the habit. All those guys ever talk about is hitting the big time."

"Carl wouldn't even take part in the dollar World Series pool or the weekly football winners the staff had," Abby said.

"And why would anyone keep losing tickets?" Bobby said, pointing to the desk. "People throw that stuff out once they find out they lost." He paused, then added quickly, "They *are* losing tickets, right?"

Preston glanced down. "I'll have to check the numbers, but

the scratchers are no good." He entered the numbers into his notebook, then put it into his pocket.

"You need to get your lab guys in here and fingerprint this entire place! Like on TV. Especially those tickets. Once you find who put them there, you'll be able to close the case. Right?" Bobby asked, his voice rising with excitement.

"We'll need more than that, Bobby, but we'll start by taking prints," Preston said. "There's a uniformed officer outside named Michaels. Can you find him for me?"

"Sure!" Bobby turned around, lost his balance for a second and fell against Preston.

Preston helped steady him.

"Let go. I'm fine," Bobby muttered.

As Bobby ambled off in a rush to go, his side-to-side gait was barely noticeable.

Preston took a step and instantly noticed that his jacket pocket felt lighter. It didn't take him long to put things together. Bobby hadn't accidentally lost his balance at all. He'd had a specific goal in mind.

Preston nearly laughed out loud. He wouldn't say anything right now, but he'd settle this with the kid later.

"Did you see that? Bobby left with scarcely a trace of a limp," Abby said. "When he's excited or distracted, he isn't so aware of the things that are wrong with his body. I first noticed that when my twin sister got sick, and that's what eventually led me to open Sitting Tall Ranch. Here kids have something fun to do and think about. We lift their spirits and, believe it or not, that's a big part of the battle."

"What happened to your sister?" he asked.

She shook her head and looked away, her eyes misty. "Another time."

Sensing that she regretted having spoken so freely, he dropped it for now. "I haven't seen any mail around here anywhere," he said, focusing back on work. "Did Carl have a post office box?"

"Not that I know of," Abby said.

"No bank account, no bills... Something's not right," he said, thinking out loud.

"I paid his utility bills," she said. "I know it sounds like a really sweet deal, but Carl could have worked at any ranch in the county for far more than what I could pay him. He was the best animal trainer I've ever seen."

"Exactly what kind of training did he do for you?"

"He made sure the horses were worked daily and that they'd respond to cues without any problems. He also worked with the llamas and made sure they'd be steady and reliable around the kids. We also use the camels for promos and fundraisers. Hank, in particular, can be terribly stubborn, and if he gets mad, he'll just refuse to cooperate. Away from the ranch that can be a problem, but when Carl went along, they were always on their best behavior."

As Officer Michaels came into the bunkhouse, Preston went to meet him. "Have the team process this place and collect fingerprints. I have reason to suspect the killer was here."

"Got it. And in answer to the bike question, there's an old five-speed in the barn office."

"Thanks," Preston said, then looked over at Abby.

"That's Carl's," she confirmed.

After Michaels left, Preston placed the casino tickets and other gambling pieces in an evidence bag, then signed and dated it. "I'll follow up on this personally."

"Can you let me know what you find out?" Abby asked.

"Not right away. This is a police matter now, but I will say this—I have a reputation for closing my cases. I never give up till the job's done."

"We have that in common."

"You built this place from scratch. Is that right?"

"Yeah, and it didn't happen overnight. The only reason I succeeded was because I refused to take my eyes off the goal."

"That's the way I work, too."

"So what's next?"

"I'll go through this place with the crime scene team. I find it hard to believe the victim was so out of touch with modern-day society—no phone, no bank account and so on. My gut tells me that he was hiding something. Maybe we'll find some answers here in the bunkhouse."

As the crime scene team moved in, Preston met them at the door. "Keep a lookout for any paper trail—mail, bills, receipts, social, anything. There's got to be more to this guy than we've seen so far."

Preston remained with the crime scene unit and worked alongside them for another hour. After finding nothing, he went back to the ranch's office. The hopeful look on Abby's face speared through him.

"Did you find something helpful?" she asked.

"No. I'm sorry. Sometimes progress on a case doesn't come quickly or easily."

"I'd never say this in front of Bobby, but I'm terrified the man who killed Carl will come back for me," she whispered, standing by the window and watching Bobby speak to the kids. "Is it safe for any of us here now?"

He wanted to hold her like he'd done before and calm her, but the badge at his belt kept him where he was. "Miss Langdon, we'll have patrol officers close by tonight," he said, using a professional tone of voice, something experience told him would give her the added confidence she needed. "If there's any problem at all, dial 911. You'll have help almost immediately."

"Thank you," she said then with a shaky smile, added, "And call me Abby, please. You saved my life."

"Abby it is then," he said. "Call me Preston."

"Preston," she repeated, as if savoring the name.

Calling her by her first name made good sense. He had to establish rapport with a witness and victim. But deep down he knew his motives weren't strictly aboveboard and professional.

He liked Abby and that could be a problem. He wouldn't have given a strictly physical attraction a second thought—one night or two of hot sex, then move on. But he wanted to be personally involved this time—to help her even the odds and to protect her as if she belonged to him somehow. Maybe it had something to do with how she'd felt in his arms—her scent.

Trouble. That's all that could come of this. Enough.

Before he could say anything else there was a knock on the semi-opened door. It was Gabe Sanchez, an officer from the crime scene unit.

"We're wrapping up here for now," he said. "Anything else you need from me?"

"Process the prints as soon as you can," Preston said, going to meet him. "I'll be heading to the casino next to follow up on those receipts and chips."

"Without a warrant? Better come on strong, put your bad cop on and hope it's enough."

"We'll see how far I get," he said with a shrug.

After Gabe left, Preston went back into the room where Abby waited.

"I gather you're expecting trouble with the casino staff. If you are, maybe I can help."

"What's your connection with that place?"

"Lightning Rod Garner, the former NBA star, is one of the ranch's biggest supporters. He's also one of the casino's main shareholders. Do you know him?"

"Only by reputation. He's had a few run-ins with the police," Preston said with a scowl. "Temper, mostly."

She smiled hesitantly. "I know he can be hard to deal with, particularly if he doesn't consider you a friend, but deep down, he's a good man. Let me take you over and introduce you. That should help."

"I'll keep your offer in mind, but right now I'd like you to check your files and give me the name of Carl's next of kin."

It had been no more than a flash in her eyes, but his link to Falcon helped him see what was necessary. More attuned to Abby now, he sensed worry and nervousness—classic signs that she was holding something back.

"If he had any relatives, he never spoke about them, nor did he list them in his employment application." Then, in a gentle voice, she added, "He was a solitary man but not an unhappy one. He enjoyed his job and life here at the ranch."

Falcon's gaze didn't miss much. Abby was hiding something from him, and one way or another he was going to find out what that was.

"Carl Woods seems to be surrounded by mystery, but it won't stay that way for long. No matter how deeply buried, secrets are never safe from me."

Her eyes widened and as he held her gaze, he saw the unmistakable glimmer of fear.

Chapter Six

Abby handed Carl's employee file to Preston. "That's all the information I have."

Before he could comment, Bobby came in. "My foster mom's here. I have a doctor's appointment this afternoon. I'll be back just as soon as I can, okay?"

"No, Bobby, stay at home until I call you," Abby said. "We have to keep the ranch closed for now. It may not be safe for you here."

"But—" Bobby stopped speaking abruptly, looked at the floor, then back up at her. "Can I talk to you for just a minute—alone?" he added.

Leaving Preston behind, Abby met with Bobby in the kitchen area. "Okay, what's up?"

"You haven't been around cops much, Abby, and I want you to know that you can't always trust them. They might pretend to be your friend, but they're not."

"You think Detective Bowman is like that?"

"Probably. When one of the kids at the foster home is hassled by the cops, the officers always come to talk to the rest of us. They try to trick us into telling them stuff so they can put the one they're after in jail."

"Maybe the problem isn't the cops but what the kids did to get the attention of the police."

"Abby, you're a good person, but don't trust him. He thinks you're keeping secrets from him."

"What makes you say that?" she asked quickly.

A horn blared outside. "Mrs. Yarrow doesn't like waiting. I better go."

Abby watched Bobby hurry to the door, but before he could step outside, Preston stopped him.

"Before you leave, Bobby, how about giving me back my notebook?"

Bobby smiled. "Hey, yeah. You dropped it back at Carl's place. Guess I forgot to give it back."

Abby watched the exchange. "He picked your pocket, didn't he?" she asked as soon as Bobby was gone.

Preston smiled but didn't answer.

"Don't be angry with him. I know it was wrong, but he was trying to protect me. In his experience, cops haven't always been the good guys," she said. "He's afraid you might hurt me or the ranch and probably wanted to slow you down."

"He's a great little pickpocket—I'll give him that," Preston said. "It took me a couple of seconds to notice what he'd done."

"Are you going to press charges?"

"Nah, I got it back, and I can't fault him for wanting to protect a friend."

"He doesn't have many of those. There's not a lot of common ground between him and the other boys at the foster home, so they tend to give him a hard time."

"Kids often target anyone who's different from them," Preston said. "That can be especially bad at a foster home because you're in such close quarters."

"You've dealt with kids from foster homes before?"

"You might say that—I was one," he said.

"You grew up in foster care?" she asked.

"Yeah. I had a tough time of it until *Hosteen* Silver, a medicine man from our tribe, decided to foster me. I met my five brothers there at his home," he said and smiled, remembering. "It took time for us to become a family, but we're all close now."

"Bobby would love a chance like that. He wants to know about his tribe, but the only real contact he has is the cook at the foster home, Mrs. Nez."

"*Hosteen* Silver was a remarkable man. He gave my brothers and me the confidence we needed to leave the past behind us and take charge of our lives."

"The kids who come here are all facing tough times. They're not in charge of anything—not their bodies or their lives. Helping them forget their troubles for a while strengthens them so they can continue their fight."

He paused for a moment. "You love this ranch and are committed to the work you do. I get that," he said at last, "but by holding back you're not helping anyone, least of all yourself."

Before she could answer, Michelle came rushing in. "We've got a problem. Stan was helping out by cleaning the camels' pen but somehow he ended up in the corner. Now every time he tries to go past Hank, the animal threatens to bite him."

"I better get over there. Without Carl, this falls to me," she told Preston. "I think Hank must have misinterpreted something Stan did. Camels are practically famous for holding grudges."

"I'll go with you. Maybe I can help," he said.

They reached the large enclosure a few minutes later. Stan was against the fence opposite the gate wiping a green wet mixture off his shirt. "Hank's in a bad, bad mood today. He spit at me."

"Actually, they don't spit. They throw up on you." She gave him a sheepish smile. "That doesn't help much, does it?"

"No," Stan said, scowling. "Now I'm grossed out."

"We'll get you out, then Michelle and I will finish up here," Abby said, then glanced back at Preston. She was going to explain to him that Hank loved women and children, but when she turned, she saw Hank nuzzling Preston like an old friend.

Her mouth fell open.

Stan stared. "How did you do that?" he asked, quickly moving out of the pen.

"It goes back to something my foster father taught me," Preston said calmly. "All things—including animals and people—are connected. I approached the camel enclosure with a Song of Blessing, what we call a *Hozonji.* I honored the link between us and the camel responded by doing the same. It's all about showing respect and demanding the same in return."

Abby wondered if he was trying to send her a message. Was he telling her to respect his profession and trust him to solve the case? His eyes held hers with an intensity that left her feeling bare…and exposed somehow.

Hank stretched his rubbery lips, trying to kiss Preston.

Abby laughed. "They're really gentle creatures. They're calmer than horses but they're more…emotional," she said after a beat. "How would you feel about volunteering here sometime?"

"After the case is closed, I'll do my best to fit some hours into my schedule."

"Good."

Preston glanced at his watch. "I need to go now and check out a few things. Make sure no one goes into the areas that are cordoned off."

"All right. Do you know how long it'll be before the yellow tape can be taken down?"

"I'm not sure. Some details need to be handled first. I'll let you know as soon as possible."

Abby walked back to the parking lot with him. "Carl's killer took the life of a very good man. He's done enough damage. Don't let him harm my ranch, too. Find answers quickly, Preston, please."

"We want the same thing, but you're holding out on me, Abby, and that's slowing me down. Eventually, I'll uncover whatever it is you're keeping back. Save us both some time and come clean."

He stopped walking and looked directly at her without so much as a blink. She shifted uncomfortably. There was an intensity about Preston that left her feeling off balance. She wasn't in control—he was. The message was clear.

"I know nothing that can help you find the killer," she said.

"Let me be the judge."

She stared at the ground. Maybe he did deserve to know, but some secrets weren't hers to tell. Finally looking up, she shook her head.

"If you want me to catch the killer quickly, Abby, don't stand in my way."

Before she could answer, he strode away from her with the long, confident steps of a man used to being in charge.

She watched him for a moment longer. He was all steady strength and power kept in reserve. For a second her thoughts drifted and she wondered what it would be like to lay in his arms, to touch and caress him until passion overcame all reason. It was the man beyond that iron will, the one hidden by the badge, who she wanted to see most of all.

Realizing the turn of her thoughts, she sighed. She was truly losing her mind.

Glancing around, she forced her thoughts back on the ranch. She couldn't do anything more for Carl, but the ranch needed her now. Seeing Stan and Michelle outside the barn pointing up at the weathered roof, she knew what had to be done next.

Making an impromptu decision, she headed to her truck. Maybe she couldn't help Preston catch Carl's killer, but she knew how to raise badly needed cash. Her first order of business—pay Rod Garner a visit.

Chapter Seven

As Preston drove west in the direction of the casino, he thought about Abby's offer to talk to Garner. If he hadn't been the kind who went by the book, he might have taken her up on it. The casino visit was bound to be a train wreck. He and Jennifer Graham, the head of security there, had a history. They'd dated for a while, and things hadn't ended well. She'd wanted more—he'd wanted less.

Maybe he *was* going in the wrong direction. He pulled off the road, waited for a break in traffic, then turned around. All things considered, he might be better off talking to Rod Garner first. Garner and Carl had supposedly been friends, so that gave him some leverage. With a little luck, Garner would help the investigation along by giving him fresh insights into the victim.

If things went smoothly, he'd also try to persuade Garner to pull some strings for him at the casino. He had to convince Jennifer to give the department access to surveillance videos. Verifying that Carl had been there on certain dates and finding out who he'd come into contact with might help establish a motive and suggest a suspect. Of course, it was all speculation at this point, and he sure as heck didn't have enough for a court order.

He was headed to Garner's estate when his cell phone rang. "I need your report, Sergeant," Preston heard Police Chief

Jenkins say as soon as he answered. "Miss Langdon and Sitting Tall Ranch are important to our community. They've put us on the map in a very good way. My own son works there as a volunteer."

Preston updated him on what he had so far. "I'm en route to Rod Garner's residence, sir. Garner was one of Carl Woods's friends, apparently."

"Interesting—a ranch hand and a millionaire former NBA star."

"Not what you'd expect, sir, but I've learned that Garner is also one of the ranch's benefactors. I think he'll cooperate with the investigation."

"Getting him on our side makes sense, Bowman. Garner's got a lot of fans, and if he gets the word out that he wants this resolved, we might get the cooperation of people who wouldn't ordinarily come within a mile of a cop."

"Yeah, that's my take, too. Unfortunately Garner also has a reputation as a troublemaker, so I'll have to tread carefully."

"Whatever it takes. Keep me updated," the chief said, then ended the call.

As Preston pulled into the long, tree-lined driveway of the former basketball star's home, he saw a familiar pickup at the far end. Sitting Tall's logo was emblazoned on one of the doors.

Reaching the parking area, Preston glanced around and saw Abby heading down the cobblestone walk toward the front entrance.

He parked beside her pickup and called out to her.

Abby turned her head, smiled and walked back to meet him.

"We must have just missed each other on the highway. I didn't expect to run into you here," he said, glad to see her anyway.

"I'm here to ask for a donation. We need a new roof on

the barn. There's no way it'll withstand the gusts and down-
pours we get during monsoon season," she said. "Rod's always helped us when we're in a bind, and I'm hoping he'll
come through for us again."

"Do you deal with him directly or talk to his assistant,
Ilse Sheridan?"

"I speak to Rod. He trusts me and he likes being involved
with the ranch. He believes in my dream."

"It's not a dream anymore," Preston said. "It's a reality."

"Some of it is, but there's so much more I'd like to do," she
said, falling into step beside him. "I'd love to build special
quarters that could accommodate a few overnight guests. A
day at the ranch can really tire out some of the kids, and trans-
portation can be an issue. If they could spend the night…"

Although she was still speaking, Preston's attention was
momentarily diverted by two vehicles coming up the drive.
The first was a small pickup with a dented fender. The bed
of the truck was filled with gardening supplies. The driver,
wearing a ball cap low on his head, pulled up and parked
across the parking lot opposite to where they were standing.

As the driver climbed out, Preston noted that the floor of
the cab was littered with beer bottles. If that was one of the
estate's landscape people, Garner needed to take a closer look
at the help.

The second vehicle, a long white limo, entered the lot and
soon came to a stop in front of the walk. Like everyone else
in town, Preston recognized Lightning Rod Garner's ride.
Garner, who'd lost his license after his third DWI, had hired
a local man as his full-time chauffeur. That level of luxury
was almost unheard of in this part of the state except for wed-
dings, funerals and homecoming dances.

As the limo driver came around to open the door for Garner, the man from the pickup quickened his pace and headed
toward the big car. His stride was unsteady, like a man who'd

had one too many, and he seemed oblivious to everything except Garner.

Preston caught a glimpse of what the man was holding just inside the sleeve of his jacket.

"Abby, move behind the engine block of your car *now*."

"What—"

"Do it."

As Preston moved to intercept the guy in the cap, the man's focus remained on Garner, who was just stepping out of the car.

Preston took advantage of the situation and moved forward quickly, drawing his weapon. Once he was within ten feet, the man finally turned his head and spotted him.

"Police officer! Put down the gun and lay flat on the ground. Now!"

The man swung his weapon around. Preston could have taken the shot at point-blank range but instead chopped down hard using his own pistol. He caught the man's wrist and knocked the gun out of his hand.

The guy yelped, then lunged for Preston's weapon.

Preston's hard left jab caught the guy in the jaw and the suspect staggered sideways and fell.

Preston moved in, forcing the suspect's face down into the gravel, then cuffed him.

"What the hell's going on?" Garner asked, rushing over.

"Stay back and call 911," Preston said.

AFTER TWO PATROL officers arrived to transport the assailant to the police station, Abby, Preston and Garner met in his home office. The wood-paneled room was huge and well appointed, and Preston took it all in slowly, thinking the house at Copper Canyon would probably fit in this space. Even the high ceiling, which incorporated a domed skylight, was composed of thick wooden beams and rich wood panels. The only place he'd ever seen an office like this was on TV.

Preston took a seat on a huge black leather sofa, and a leggy short-haired blonde wearing an expensive-looking tailored tan pantsuit appeared out of thin air and offered him a scotch.

"No, thanks. I'm on duty."

"I'll take one, Ilse. Bring me that special bottle I've been saving," Rod said. He looked at Preston. "Don't mind me, but I usually don't have people trying to gun me down. Wanting to kick my butt, yeah, but coming after me with a gun, no."

"Did you recognize the man who came for you?" Preston asked, watching out of the corner of his eye as the attractive blonde poured the scotch.

"Never seen him that I can recall," Rod said, taking the scotch and downing it with one swallow.

"His name is Phil Gorman. Does that ring a bell?"

Garner looked down at his empty glass as he shook his head. "Ilse, look up the name and see if he's ever done any work here."

"So you've never had any personal dealings with Gorman?" Preston insisted.

"Hey, dude, I see and talk to a lot of people, but I don't always remember them. Maybe I've seen him, maybe not, but he's no one I deal with regularly. That kind of contact I remember."

"Okay, fair enough," Preston said.

"Did he say why he came after me?" Rod leaned back on the plush leather chair and stretched out his legs. It was an action that made him seem even taller than his six-foot-eight frame and required a lot of room, which fortunately he had.

"Yeah. He blames you and the casino for his business troubles. I don't have details yet," Preston said.

"Another guy who can't man up and take responsibility

for himself. They're always looking for someone to blame," Rod muttered.

"I'm not so sure he's telling us the real story. I think there may be a lot more to the hit," Preston said. "First, Carl's murdered, then someone goes after Abby, now this."

"Someone attacked you?" Rod sat up and looked at Abby quickly. "You okay?"

"Yeah, it was scary, but I came through it," she said.

"Detective, you see a connection between everything that's happened?" Rod asked.

Preston nodded. "The one thing you and Abby have in common is Carl. There's a link somewhere, and I'm going to find it."

"Carl and I liked playing one-on-one on the basketball slab here on the estate. Afterward, we'd down a few cold ones. That's the extent of our friendship," he said. "As for this shooter today, I'm thinking that maybe he followed *you* here."

"Me? What makes you think that? He was moving right for you," Preston said.

"This kind of thing doesn't happen to me, dude. People in this community like me," he said. "I keep thinking of a TV show I saw last night, a suicide-by-cop thing. The guy's life was going down the toilet, but he didn't have the guts to kill himself. He set it up by taking a hostage and waving around a gun so the cops would have to shoot him."

"That's what you think happened here?"

"Yeah, he pulled his gun and aimed at me, but then you screwed up his plan by not taking him out. Are you sure his gun was even loaded?"

"It was," Preston said. He started to point out that no one had followed him to the estate either when Abby rose to her feet, her eyes sparking with anger.

"I know you don't like cops, and you're having a tough time saying thank you," she said, resting her arms on the edge of

Rod's desk, leaning forward and looking directly at the big man. "But the detective saved your life and you're sounding like an ungrateful horse's butt. You owe him. Now get over it, and say thank you."

Rod cracked a slow smile. "A horse's butt?"

"You heard me," she said, not backing down.

Rod shrugged and extended his hand. "Sorry, dude. You came through for me so thanks. I get anxious around cops. Knee-jerk reaction from my days back in Jersey. I think it's an allergy," he said with the wide smile that was as much a part of his trademark as his outrageous personality.

"I'm glad I was in a position to help." Preston shook his hand.

"We're going to have to work together so things can get back to normal at the ranch," Abby said. "I need to open our doors again as soon as possible."

"How can I help?" Rod asked.

"You can cooperate with the detective…and if it's not too much to ask for right now, we could sure use a donation to our barn roof fund. With the economy still so weak—"

He held up a hand, interrupting her. "Ilse!" he bellowed.

The woman came back in instantly.

"Cut a check for a barn roof."

"Amount?" she asked, looking at Abby.

Abby gave her the estimate, then quickly added, "I know that's high, so whatever amount Rod can afford will help."

"Give her the entire amount," Rod said.

"Thank you so much!"

"Abby, when Stretch Jackson's kid was diagnosed with cancer, you and the ranch helped give that little girl something to smile about. You let her ride the camels and that was all she talked about till she passed away. I told you back then that I wouldn't forget. So whatever you need, come to me. If I can't get it, I'll help you raise the cash."

"Your support means the world to us, Rod. Thanks again."

"Now tell me how I can help your investigation," Rod said.

"I need to fill in some of the blanks in Carl's life," Preston said. "You knew him, so maybe you could tell me about Carl's gambling habits and who he met when he went to the casino."

"Dawg, you're way off the mark. Carl was no gambler. He'd only go to the casino when the ranch was working a promo there or when he was promised a free meal. After playing one-to-one here, we'd clean up, cool down, then head over there for dinner."

"How often did you two get together?" Preston asked.

"Two, sometimes three times a week. I'm six foot eight so it was nearly impossible for me to find anyone willing to play pick-up ball. Then I met Carl. Nothing intimidated the guy. He was only six foot two, but he was fast and lean. He'd played basketball in high school and loved the game."

"So how long have you two been friends?" Preston asked.

"About two years. I'd seen him trying to rig up a goal on a light pole over by the bunkhouse, so I told him to forget it and come over here. I've got goals indoors and out. He and I hit it off from the start. We'd play hard outdoors, like back in the 'hood, then when the weather was bad, in my gym."

"What else can you tell me about Carl? Did he worry about anything in particular? Did he tend to look over his shoulder a lot, like someone who knew he was a target? Anything that comes to mind might help."

"Dude, we didn't get into that touchy-feely stuff. We played basketball. The guy had good moves on the court—I can tell you that—plus an old-school hook shot that was accurate and hard to block."

"When you went to the casino, was he more comfortable playing the slots than the game tables?" It was an old interrogation technique. You stated something as a fact, then waited for the response.

"B-man, aren't you listening?" he said, coming up with a nickname for Preston. "Carl didn't gamble. He watched me play a few hands of poker one time, but he wasn't interested, even when I offered to cover him. As for the slots, he told me that it was a game for suckers."

"So besides basketball, what else did Carl like to do?"

"Sketching and painting. He told me he'd lived hard and fast all his life, and it was time for him to slow down. He also loved working with animals."

"Rod, here's the thing. I found some slot machine tickets at the bunkhouse. If Carl didn't put them there, they might have been left by his killer," Preston said. "The quickest way for me to rule out Carl and maybe identify a possible suspect is to check surveillance tapes at the casino. Problem is, I don't have a court order, and there's no way I can get one based on what I have. Can you help me cut a few corners by speaking to their head of security? It'll speed up the investigation."

Rod shook his head slowly. "I can't help you there, B-man. Had you asked me a few weeks ago, maybe. I owned quite a few shares in the casino, but I had to sell them to cover some bad investments. I can talk to some of their people, but my word doesn't carry any weight there now."

Though she'd been pretty quiet till now, Abby spoke. "Until this case is closed, I can't reopen the ranch, and our reputation will continue to take a hit. By helping Detective Bowman, you'd be helping us, too."

Rod expelled his breath in a hiss. "Okay, I'll see what I can do, but I ain't promising anything. You hear?"

"Loud and clear." Preston stood and Rod shook his hand. "One more thing. Gorman is being booked right now, but I'd like both of you to go to the station with me and make an official statement."

"I'll follow you there," Abby said.

"I'll get my attorney first, then meet you there," Rod said. "Me and the police...not a good combination."

Preston bit back a smile.

Abby followed Preston outside. "Carl really cared about the ranch and he worked hard. Whenever I needed something done, he took care of it without a question. You're investigating the murder as if it's Carl's fault somehow, but he was one of the good guys."

"Even a good person can have secrets." He said it mostly to see what her reaction would be.

Abby averted her gaze and, promising to meet him at the station, walked away quickly.

"You're hiding something, pretty lady, and that's a bad idea," he murmured, his words nothing more than a whisper in the wind.

Chapter Eight

After giving her statement, Abby waited alone in Preston's office. Restless, she paced the small, windowless room, trying to learn more about him. There were no personal photos on his desk and the only thing on the wall was a commendation for bravery. It was framed but hung in a section of the wall that was partially hidden each time the door was open, as it was now.

All she really knew about Preston was what she'd learned from doing an online search using her cell phone. Last year, he'd stopped a robbery in progress. He'd been at the bank on personal business at the time and had subdued and handcuffed the armed suspect before anyone was hurt.

Preston appeared to be as dedicated to his job as she was to her ranch. He was cool under pressure and accomplished whatever he set out to do, but there was another side to him, too. She'd seen glimpses of it in the way he'd treated Bobby and the gentle strength he'd shown her when he'd held her after that man had tried to run her down. Intuition told her that beyond the badge lay a man of passion whose feelings ran deep and strong.

She shook her head, exasperated with herself, and tried to think clearly. She'd been nearly hysterical, about to be run over, and under the circumstances any overreaction to a place of safety was understandable.

Preston came in just then, and the total absence of emotion on his face warned her that something bad was coming.

"Please sit down," he said coldly. "The clerk will bring in your statement shortly. You can read it over, make any corrections, then sign it."

"Then I can leave?" She wasn't sure why she'd asked that, except maybe to make sure she would be free to go.

"We need to discuss something first."

Here it was. Somehow, even before he spoke, she knew he'd found out.

"The crime scene investigators have processed the evidence, and a few important facts about Carl have come up."

Abby said nothing. She wasn't sure how much he knew, and she figured she'd be better off not speaking at all.

Preston remained quiet, allowing the seconds to stretch out.

Abby squirmed. The total silence between them was completely disconcerting. She stared at her lap, then with effort made herself look directly at him. "Some secrets are meant to be shared, but others deserve respect."

"Your logic doesn't apply to a murder investigation."

"This is the first time I've ever dealt with a murder, so you'll have to forgive me if I don't know the rules," she shot back, then cringed when he didn't react at all.

"You knew Carl had a criminal record."

It wasn't a question. She exhaled loudly. "Yes. His real name is...was...Carl Sinclair, not Woods."

"Did you think we wouldn't find out?"

"No, quite the opposite. I knew you would, and that's why I waited," she said. "When Carl came to me asking for a job, he told me the truth about himself. He'd grown up in Hartley, then moved to Denver, San Francisco and other cities, where he made a living as an art thief. Eventually he got caught and served his time. He swore he was clean now and asked that

I let him prove himself. I ran a background check, like I do with everyone who works at the ranch, and the investigator verified Carl's story. After that, I knew I could trust Carl. As badly as he'd wanted a second chance, he didn't come to me under false pretenses."

"He served time for burglary—four years to be exact."

"I know. He learned to work with horses while in prison, but then you know all that already. What you probably don't know is how good he was with animals. They responded to him in a way that was nothing short of amazing. You may have found out about Carl's past, but you know very little about the man he became. Carl worked hard to make the most out of the chance I gave him. That's why I'd like people to remember Carl Woods, the man he was at the time of his death, not Carl Sinclair, the man he'd been a long time ago. Can you keep all this private?"

"I'll try, but information like this has a way of getting out."

"People won't understand," she said with a tired sigh. "I don't care what they think about me. I know I did the right thing hiring him. I'm just afraid that it'll hurt the ranch."

"Some will use Carl's past against you, but don't underestimate the public. Many will side with your decision to give Carl a chance," he said. "Giving folks a hand up is what you do every day at the ranch, Abby. Look at Bobby. The world sees a handicapped Navajo kid, but you don't accept that definition, so Bobby doesn't either. What you did for him was force him to redefine normal."

"He did that on his own. Bobby's super smart."

The clerk came into the room with Abby's statement and placed it on Preston's desk.

He was quiet until the woman left, then met Abby's gaze and held it. "Remember one thing, Abby. You want answers and so do I. No more secrets. Don't make my job harder than it already is."

Abby read her statement and then signed it. "If you don't need me anymore I should get back to the ranch. I have to take care of the animals, then hit the sack. I'll have to be up early for a staff meeting. I want them to hear about Carl from me first, not pick up some distorted gossip around town."

Preston stood when Abby did, ready to walk her to the door, when he saw Rod Garner striding down the hall toward his office.

"Did you find out anything new about the guy who came after me?" Rod asked, stepping into the room.

Preston nodded. "It turns out the casino hired away the cook at his restaurant, the Night Owl Café. Business started to suffer and Gorman couldn't find another chef good enough to keep his regular customers. He went out of business and blames you because he found out that you recommended his former cook to the casino."

"I remember the café," Rod said, nodding slowly. "The chef there was very good. Since the meals at the casino were just average, I told the restaurant manager about the guy. I had no idea what happened after that."

"Gorman has other problems, too, including substance abuse, so it was just a matter of time. One of the reasons his chef quit was because he wasn't getting a regular paycheck. Gorman was on a downward spiral. He'll at least have a chance to get clean in jail. They have a rehab program now," Preston added. "On the surface it doesn't look like there's a connection to Carl."

"But you're still not convinced?" Rod asked.

"Let's just say I'm keeping an open mind," Preston said.

As Abby walked away down the hall, she received a call from Michelle, who was at the ranch.

"I thought you'd want to know that we've received the horse Gene Redhouse donated. Kyle Goodluck, Detective Bowman's brother, just dropped him off."

"We have a stall in the barn prepared for Red, so put him in there and let him get settled. Could you come in early tomorrow? We need to hold a meeting. Tell the volunteers who are there tonight to come, too, if they can. I'll call the rest of our regulars once I get back."

As Abby headed to her truck, she thought about tomorrow's meeting. Would they continue to respect her judgment or lose faith in her, thinking she was unrealistic and a hopeless optimist? Yet, it was precisely her ability to believe in people and herself that had helped make the ranch a reality.

As she thought of her staff, Abby turned and walked back to the station. She could use some support. Moments later, she found Preston still in his office at his computer.

"I'd like to ask you a favor," she said as she knocked on the open door.

He waved at her to have a seat. "Sure. What's on your mind?"

"Would you come to the ranch tomorrow morning, say, seven? I'd like you to tell the staff about Carl—that he'd paid his dues and hadn't been in trouble since. As a cop, that'll carry more weight coming from you," she said and explained why she was concerned. "To believe in the ranch, they need to trust me."

He met her gaze and held it. For a moment it felt as if he were looking straight into her soul. Did he feel the magic building between them? Did he know the way he affected her?

After what seemed like an eternity, he nodded. "All right."

Hearing a commotion outside, he stood. "Come on, I'll walk you out. It sounds like one of our uniforms is bringing in someone who has had too much to drink."

She fell into step beside him as they crossed the parking lot. "My work has some very sad moments but, by and large, it's about making things better. Things stay upbeat most of the time," she said. "Your work has got to be so much harder than mine. How do you deal with the pressure that comes with being a homicide cop?"

"To me, it's all about preserving the balance between good and evil. As a Navajo, I believe that everything has two sides. Evil needs good to define it, and good is needed to keep evil in check. I'm here to make sure harmony is restored."

As they reached her truck, she glanced over at him. Preston stood tall, his wide shoulders thrown back. Everything about him was solid and unwavering. No matter how tough the circumstances, he was the kind of man who could be relied on.

There was just something about him that inspired confidence and as she looked at him, she knew the future of her ranch was in good hands.

PRESTON SET OUT to Abby's first thing the following morning. He was nearly there when Gabe Sanchez from the crime scene unit called.

"You're at it early," Preston said.

"Figured you'd want answers as soon as possible."

"You got that right."

"I've got preliminaries for you," Gabe said. "There were traces of the vic's blood and hair on the blade of a shovel we found near the barn, but the absence of blood in the horse pen tends to indicate that he wasn't killed there. He was struck somewhere else, then moved to that corral afterward."

"Yeah, that matches up with the fact that someone went to a lot of trouble to hide his or her footprints."

"We also checked the gambling tokens and tickets you found. The prints were smudged, but the few identifying characteristics we found didn't match the vic's."

"Interesting. Looks like the killer may have planted those. It's possible Carl may have been killed around the bunkhouse, judging from the time of death, then moved to the pen to mislead the investigation. The extra blood could have been scooped up and buried somewhere else," Preston said. "It's time for me to take a closer look at the staff. This may have been an inside job."

As Preston hung up, he considered the possibility that Abby had an enemy in her ranks. The killer could be someone she trusted, and that was bound to make things tougher. Her fierce loyalty to her staff, judging by the way she'd kept Carl's secret, might blind her to danger.

Abby was more vulnerable than she realized. As a homicide cop, he worked long hours and spent a lot of time alone, but his brothers were there for him, day or night, and just a phone call away. From what he'd seen, Abby had no close friends or family.

Preston prided himself on being a tough cop, as hard as any on the force, and that was because he never brought emotions into the picture. As he pulled into Sitting Tall Ranch and saw Abby stop to pet a horse, something told him that was all about to change.

WHILE THE STAFF gathered for the meeting, which had been delayed ten minutes, Preston saw his brother Kyle standing just inside the office door.

Preston took him aside. "Did you decide to volunteer here?"

"Yeah. I came by this morning to check on Red and offer my services. I figured you could use an additional pair of eyes and ears here. I've already introduced myself to some of the volunteers and met an accountant named Stan Cooper. Turns out Stan didn't care for Carl at all. He said the man worked hard, but there was something about him he never trusted."

"Interesting," Preston said.

Just then Abby stepped to the front of the room. Preston and Kyle stayed back, keeping an eye on the others gathered there.

"We all have private lives," Abby said, telling them about Carl's past. "Carl told me who he really was and asked for a chance to prove himself. I gave him one and he never let me down."

As Preston stepped forward all eyes turned to him. "Ms. Langdon is right about Carl. From everything I've been able to find out, the man had cleaned up his act. It's important to remember, too, that he was the victim of a crime, not the perpetrator."

After Preston finished speaking, a photo of Carl appeared on the small TV screen in the corner of the room. The sound had been muted, but Michelle, who'd obviously glanced over, pointed. "Hey, look! What's that all about?"

Abby turned up the volume, stepped back and listened to Marsha Robertson's news segment.

"Though well liked and respected at Sitting Tall Ranch, where he took care of the animals, it appears that Carl Woods, aka Carl Sinclair, had a hidden past. Our source has verified that he was a convicted art thief who served a four-year prison sentence. There's speculation that Sinclair may have been keeping other secrets which might have led to his murder."

"How did they find out so soon?" Abby asked, looking back at Preston.

"I was afraid this would happen," he said. "I saw Marsha Robertson at the station earlier. She has sources everywhere."

Abby sat down on the corner of her desk and faced the gathering. "Although this is bound to make things worse, you should all know that the backlash against the ranch started even before that news segment. I checked my email first thing this morning and found out that the 4-H kids who volunteer here won't be returning for a while. Their parents and the 4-H sponsors are insisting they stay away until this matter is resolved. That means we'll have to set up new feeding schedules and split up the work among the rest of us."

Preston nodded, pleased with her reaction. Though kicked while down, she'd gotten right back up. She was a fighter. All she needed was a hand, and he intended to do all he could to help her.

Chapter Nine

After the staff meeting was over, Michelle came up to Abby. "Can I talk to you privately for a moment?"

Somehow this sounded like more bad news. Ignoring the knot in her stomach, Abby smiled. "Sure. What's up?"

"I've had some cash flow problems lately and I'm behind on some of my bills. Miller's Horse Farm won't let me use their facilities until I get caught up, so I'd like to make you a trade. I'll add fifteen volunteer hours to my regular work schedule here if you'll let me use one of the arenas for my weekly riding classes. I'll work around the ranch's schedule, of course."

"I could use the help, so it sounds doable," she said, "but there's something I need to know. How come you're in trouble financially? What happened?"

"It's nothing bad, Abby, so don't worry. I just got in over my head when I bought a new horse trailer. Now the payments are eating me alive."

Abby smiled. "Okay. I was that way, too, when I started buying tack for the animals."

As they walked outside, Abby heard the sound of a big engine in the parking lot. A tow truck was backing up to the ranch's pickup, and two men were standing by the driver's-side door, which was open.

"Hey! Get away from my truck!" Abby yelled, then broke into a run.

Abby heard footsteps behind her. Turning her head for a second she saw Preston almost catching up to her. Michelle was right behind him.

"What's going on?" Preston asked, matching her speed.

"Those men are trying to steal my truck!"

He slowed to a walk as they approached the tow truck. "These guys are from a repo company, Abby. You behind on your payments?"

"No chance," Abby said. "Stan handles all those details for me and he would have told me if there was a problem."

"Hang back and let me check things out for you. These guys are trouble. I've been called to deal with them before," Preston said.

Kyle came up beside him. "Got your back, bro."

Preston went to the men by the tow truck. "Before you hook anything up, let me see your paperwork."

"Butt out, Indian. The lady's a freeloader. She's missed three loan payments in a row, and we're duly authorized to take the truck." He waved a manila folder full of papers.

"That's just not true," Abby said, her hands on her hips. "If there had been a problem, the bank would have notified the ranch. You've got the wrong address and the wrong truck."

"Save the story, lady. We've heard it all," the big guy said. The other two men came around to stand beside him. One was holding a length of tow chain.

"I'm telling you the truth—and you're not taking my truck," Abby said, stepping up to the man. "There's been some kind of mistake. Let me talk to the bank. I'm sure I can clear this up in five minutes." She reached out for the folder, but he pulled it away.

"Too late. We're taking the pickup. Next time make your

payments," he said, then laughed and threw the folder full of papers at her.

"I'm a police officer," Preston said, instantly getting into the man's face.

The two other men stepped forward. One tried to grab Preston by the arm, but Kyle hurled himself at the guy, tackling him to the ground.

As they fought, the other guy took a swing at Preston. Blocking the punch, Preston grabbed the man's extended arm and bent it inward at the elbow until the guy fell to his knees in agony.

The big guy took advantage of the situation and grabbed Abby, holding her arms by the wrists far enough away so she couldn't kick him. Abby tried to twist free, but he tightened his hold.

"Back off, you two," he snapped. "Let go of my crew."

Preston held his hands up and stepped back, then suddenly shoved the guy he'd been fighting in the chest with the palm of his hand, knocking him straight into the leader. As the two collided, Abby twisted free and the big man fell to the ground.

Kyle still had the third guy pinned, but the one Preston had shoved whirled around, throwing a roundhouse punch. Preston ducked, kneed the man in the groin and drew his weapon before the leader could react.

"You're all under arrest," Preston snapped. "Down on your knees."

"We are within our rights taking this truck," the leader said, putting his hands in the air.

"We'll have to verify that. But whatever the case, you've assaulted a police officer and a civilian, a woman half your size. You're facing charges, so don't push your luck."

"There are two patrol officers on the way," Abby said, holding up her cell phone, signaling she'd dialed 911.

Preston and Kyle, intending to turn the trio over to the uniformed cops when they arrived, escorted the men to the front gate. The suspect in handcuffs led the way while the other two, hands locked behind their heads, followed.

"Consider carrying extra sets of cuffs while you're working this case, bro," Kyle said.

"I'll keep that in mind."

After the men were taken to the station, Preston went to Abby's office. She was just hanging up the phone. "I spoke to Stan. He said it was a glitch in the software. He's got an automatic payment set up, but he thinks it may have gone into someone else's account. He'll get things straightened out in the next hour or so."

"Abby, what were you thinking?" Preston demanded. "You shouldn't have argued with that guy. He outweighed you by at least one hundred pounds."

"I knew you'd be there to back me up. You asked me to trust you, remember?" she asked. "So I did."

"She's got your number," Kyle said, chuckling.

PRESTON stood alone with Kyle in the nearly empty bull pen at the station. It was close to noon now and Abby was still giving her statement to the clerk.

"So what's the deal with you and Abby Langdon? Are you seriously interested in her?" Kyle asked.

"No interest other than professional. She needs a hand and I'm in a position to help. Nothing more."

"Why don't I believe you?"

Preston started to answer when Abby came up to him. "May I speak to you for a moment?"

"Sure," he said, then glanced back at Kyle. "Thanks for the help, bro."

"No problem," Kyle said and strode off.

"All the paperwork is done and I've signed my statement,"

Abby said as they walked down the hall toward Preston's office.

"Good. You won't be seeing those guys again anytime soon. They'll be spending the night in jail, then they'll be facing a judge tomorrow."

"That's one less worry for me tonight," she said.

"What's bothering you?"

"I've been wondering if it's really safe for me to stay at the ranch alone at night. If I'm sound asleep, I may not hear a problem until it's too late. The killer is still out there."

The worried smile she gave him tore at his guts.

"I'm not a coward," she added quickly.

"I know you're not. You're just dealing with something that's part of my world, not yours."

"I've faced tough situations before but never anything like this." She shook her head. "How do I handle it?"

"Step back and don't let things overwhelm you. I'll find the killer. That's what I do best."

Seeing her shudder, he had to fight the urge to pull her into his arms. They were at the station and acting on that urge was a bad idea. What he could do was keep her company for a little longer.

"I'm going to grab a hamburger across the street," he said. "Join me?"

She glanced at her watch and shook her head. "I'd like to, but I've got to go back. I have to meet with Stan and go over the quarterly reports." She paused, then smiled. "But here's what I can do. Why don't you meet me this evening for dinner? I make one mean green chile cheeseburger and it'll be my way of saying thanks for being there for me today."

"Just doing my job," he said.

"No, you've gone above and beyond."

As she looked up and he saw himself reflected in the softness of her eyes, heat flashed through him, hot and strong.

"Okay, I'll tell you what. I'll come early, help you with the livestock, then we'll eat," he said, trying to get his mind back on the right track. He didn't need physical distractions like this. Entanglements had never turned out well for him, probably because he didn't trust the emotions that went along with them.

"Can I recruit your help fixing dinner, too?"

He laughed. "Hey, I think I'm getting a raw deal there."

"Nah, I just want you to help me make sure there are no leftovers," she said with a smile.

"Then I'm your man." As he spoke, he knew instantly that it had been a poor choice of words. Something flashed in her eyes and the attraction between them surged to a new level. What the hell was he getting into?

Chapter Ten

The rest of the day had gone by quickly. Stan had straightened things with the bank and had made out their proposed quarterly budget. If donations didn't hold steady, things promised to get tough.

Now, working side by side with Preston, Abby was in a far better mood. They'd finished refilling the horses' water troughs and were walking back to the main house, her home, as darkness finally descended over the ranch.

"You look tired," he said.

"I am, but physical work helps me unwind. When I'm tired I also tend not to worry so much. I'm a great one for waking up at three in the morning and stewing over a million what-ifs."

"Trying to head off problems is a good strategy, but endless worrying is not."

"I know, but sometimes I just can't help it."

It was honest and to the point, like she was. "Do you ever regret dedicating so much of your life to this place?"

She took a deep breath. "Sometimes I wonder what my life would have been like if I'd made more traditional choices. As it is, I rarely date, and my private life is practically nonexistent, but the ranch does give me something in return. I have a very special family here. The children's faces change often, but what we share at the ranch connects us forever."

"Dedication—to anything—always carries a price," he

said. "A lot of women have come and gone in my life, but the truth is, I'm married to police work."

She smiled. The similarities between them only heightened her attraction to him. It was all very unsettling—but undeniably exciting. "Doing what we're meant to do is satisfying, but it can also be lonely at times."

"Maybe so, but I've got family nearby. Most of my brothers live in this area. What about your family?"

"After my sister passed away, Mom and Dad were heartbroken. They both died within a year, one right after the other," she said. After a long pause, she continued. "Watching someone you love die a little each day breaks your heart in a way that never quite heals. Sandy was my fraternal twin and a part of us was connected. For a long time after her death, I was lost. Nothing made sense to me. If everything could be taken from you at any given moment, why bother doing anything at all? I'm not sure if there is a hell, but that's as close to it as I've ever found."

"So how did this ranch come about?"

"When Sandy started going downhill, the thing she wanted to do most of all was go horseback riding. She loved horses, but we didn't own any. I tried finding someone who'd let her ride, but people were worried about liability if something went wrong. I finally got a local rancher to agree and the difference that outing made in Sandy was amazing. For a few hours she got to do something *she* wanted. She died in peace a few weeks after that." She swallowed hard. "Wherever she is, I'm sure she's on a horse," she added with a sad smile.

Her sorrow stabbed through him. He remembered what it was like when he'd found himself alone so many years back. Goodbye could be the cruelest words of all time, especially coming from the most important person in your life.

Although he wanted to pull her into his arms and comfort her, she moved back and shook her head.

"I'm fine. Memories can hurt, but we go on," she said in a slightly steadier tone. "I'll always miss her, but it's thanks to her that this ranch was founded. Her spirit lives on here."

He reached for her hand and gave it a gentle squeeze. "Did the idea for the ranch come to you right away?"

"Not immediately, no, but as time wore on, I saw that a ranch like this one would be the perfect way to honor her life. We may not be able to change our final destination, but we can make the most out of the time we've got," she said, stopping to give the horses a few carrots. "My dream was to create an extraordinary ranch for kids facing major challenges." She looked at him and smiled sheepishly. "The problem was that I was nineteen at the time and had no money."

"So you got donations and sold your idea to a bank?"

"Eventually, yes, but first I needed capital of my own," she said. "I opened up an employment agency that provided skilled workers for small or large construction projects anywhere in the state. My business grew quickly, and three years later I sold it. I made enough of a profit to buy this ranch, but I still needed investors who could share my vision. Helping Sitting Tall Ranch become what it is today took time and a lot of effort." She looked around her and smiled. "Mostly, it was about never taking no for an answer."

As she moved away from the horse pen, a camel roared, spooking the horses.

"That's Hank. Something or someone he doesn't know or like is moving around over by his enclosure."

He started to reach for his gun, but she shook her head. "It might just be a stray dog. Hank's more vocal and territorial than your typical camel. He lets everyone know if he sees something that's out of place or different somehow."

"That's a really loud call. Did he do that the night Carl died?" Preston asked.

She blinked. "He might have, but although we didn't get any rain, we had some pretty loud thunder that night."

"I'm going to check it out."

"I'm going with you," she said.

"Stay behind me then," he said, heading back to the camel pen.

Both camels were at the far end of their welded pipe enclosure, less than fifty feet from the bunkhouse.

Abby nudged Preston and gestured to a small beam of light just outside the rear of the bunkhouse.

"I'll handle it," he whispered, reaching for his gun. "Stay back."

As he crept forward, Abby caught a glimpse of the intruder's face. "Wait, Preston. That's one of the high school kids who volunteers here."

Abby immediately strode toward the teen, who was standing in the open and illuminated by the full moon overhead. "Norman, what on earth are you doing here skulking around like this? And who's that with you?" she added, seeing a shadow a few feet away.

"It's me, Abby. Don't be angry," another familiar voice said.

"Meet Norman and Jenny Rager," she told Preston, then focused back on the pair. "Tell me what you're doing here?"

"It was so much money! And we would have split it with you," Norman said. "Honest!"

"You've lost me," Abby said.

"*The Inquisitor,* the statewide tabloid, is offering two hundred bucks for a photo of the bunkhouse and the stall where the body was found."

"It wasn't just for the money, Abby," Jenny said. "People are saying that Carl was just another crook with a good line and you fell for his story. We figured that if everyone could see where he lived, how simple his life was, they'd realize Carl was just a regular hardworking guy."

"And we didn't break in," Norman added quickly. "The gate was open and we parked in the parking area. You weren't around, so we came back here."

"You're still trespassing," Preston said sharply.

"I'm going to let this go," Abby said with a sigh. "But if either of you pull something like this again, I'll press charges. Clear?"

"Clear!" Norman said, then hurried back with his sister Jenny toward the parking lot.

"If that 'bloid is offering money for photos, this could get ugly," Preston said.

"I'll make some calls tomorrow morning and see if I can get them to stop. I know some people."

By the time the kids had left and they were back at the ranch house, Abby was exhausted. "Come in. I promised you dinner, and by now you're probably starving."

"Yeah, but you're beat. I can see it on your face. Let me take a rain check."

"Are you sure?"

"Yeah. I can head back to the station and check out a few things."

"Like the tabloid photo offer?"

He nodded. "But I think that's just routine for the tabloid. Anytime there's a local story like this they like to sensationalize it. That's how they sell papers," he said. "One more thing before I leave, Abby. Consider installing security cameras."

"I don't know about that," she said slowly. "If I do, it might worry people even more. I'd be publicly acknowledging that I believe the ranch is no longer safe. Keep in mind that my battle will be fought—and won or lost—in the court of public opinion. A move like that could work against me."

He nodded slowly. "There's one thing you need to consider—the fact that you never heard Hank roar the night Carl was killed could mean it was an inside job."

"No. I know my people. No one who works for me could have done something like that. It's more likely that the killer came in from a different direction and avoided Hank's enclosure altogether."

Preston held her gaze. "I know you want to believe that, but you have to stay open to the possibility. Until we know for sure, stay alert and don't lower your guard," he said. "Will you be hiring someone to take Carl's place?"

"Not right away," she said. "It takes forever to find someone who's willing to work very long hours for a flat rate in exchange for living quarters."

"I'll help you spread the word. Maybe someone at the station will have a retired relative or know of someone who's good with animals, like an old cowboy."

"Thanks. I appreciate that." Before she could say anything more, they heard Hank's ponderous groan. "Again?"

"Maybe someone besides Norman and Jenny got the same idea. Wait here," Preston said, holding up his hand.

As he ran off, she remained behind for a moment, then changed her mind. Though Preston was a well-trained police officer, everyone could use a hand now and then. Years of moving eighty-pound hay bales had given her incredible strength to put into a right hook. Or she could give an attacker a boot kick in the shins, if it came to that.

Chapter Eleven

Preston saw a shadowy figure creeping around the barn. All the animals seemed agitated. Judging from the shape and the way the suspect moved, the person was male and was wearing a dark-colored hoodie. In the bright moonlight he could see that the tall, broad-shouldered man was spray painting graffiti on the side of the barn.

"Police! Don't move!" Preston called out.

The man took off instantly, running at full speed. Preston was fast, but by the time he reached the road, the man was racing away on a motorcycle. He was too far away for Preston to get a plate ID or even the make of the machine.

Preston called it in. "I won't catch him now," he said as Abby caught up to him. "I should have waited until I got closer before I said anything. He's heading back to the highway, so tracking him now is not a possibility."

She shone her flashlight on the side of the barn. "What's that supposed to mean?" The drawing depicted a stick figure inside a circle with a diagonal line across it. "I don't understand. What's he saying? No stick figures? No art? Wait—no people, no kids?"

"Probably," Preston said and took photos of it with his cell phone. "Unless you have some paint solvent, you should cover this over before anyone arrives tomorrow morning. Don't give the tagger the satisfaction of having others see his work."

"I have a gallon of barn-red paint left over for touch-ups. It'll cover in one coat and won't take long."

By the time she came back out with paint, tools and a battery-powered lantern, Preston had taken off his jacket and bolo tie and placed them over the top rail of the fence.

She smiled, set down the paint can and a cardboard box, then turned on the lantern. "You're not dressed for this. I'll take care of it. Once I get the paint all stirred and in the tray, I'll just need a few minutes. I've got a big roller and years of experience painting exterior walls."

"So do I, so count me in. You get the paint mixed while I take off my shirt." He saw her stealing quick glances as he hung his shirt next to his jacket. The first time it was curiosity. After that, it was because she liked what she saw. Biting back a smile, he got to work.

Though she tried not to get caught looking at him, she couldn't help sneaking a few glances at Preston. His strong shoulders and bronzed arms rippled with muscles as he moved the roller in diagonal and vertical strokes, applying the paint.

As he bent down to replenish the roller, she checked out his lower half and had to bite back a sigh. He was a living, breathing temptation.

"Like what you see?" he asked without even looking back.

"How did you know—" She pressed her lips together and glanced away. "Wow. Walked right into that, didn't I?"

He laughed, then turned around to face her. "No harm in looking," he said, then allowed his gaze to take her in from top to bottom slowly.

Heat, the kind that teased and tantalized, spread all through her, but she managed to hold back a shiver of pleasure. He'd seen way too much already in her expression.

They finished painting quickly, then washed the tray and roller in a big utility sink inside the barn.

"Okay, we're done here. Let's head back to the house. The least I can do to say thank-you is microwave us a frozen pizza."

He removed the latex gloves she'd provided, then before reaching for his shirt, noticed a paint smudge on his chest and tried to rub it off with his hand.

"Let me get that," Abby said, moistening a hand towel with water.

She came up to him. "Hold still for a sec. The paint's water-based, but now's the time to wipe it off."

As she stood close, she became aware of everything about him. The heat from his body enveloped her, sparking her senses. Her hand began to tremble as she wiped the paint away.

"No need to be nervous," he said, wrapping his arms around her waist and pulling her against him.

As she looked up into his eyes, she saw the fire there and her breath caught in her throat. She should have stepped away, but everything feminine in her demanded she stay. Abby wrapped her arms around him and shivered as he nuzzled her neck, leaving a trail of moist kisses there.

She pressed herself against him, wanting more, and as she drew in a breath, his mouth closed over hers. The kiss was slow and deep, then grew more demanding with each passing second.

He drew back, taking a breath, but she brought his lips back to hers, unwilling to have it end so soon.

He lowered his hand to her bottom and pressed her against him, letting her feel his hardness.

Knowing she was desired heightened her pleasure but soon it became too hot. Fighting herself, she took an unsteady step back.

He released his hold on her but stood his ground, his chest heaving, his eyes still gleaming with a dark fire. "Sorry."

"No, don't be. It was…wonderful. But we had to stop."

One-night stands, however tempting, weren't for her. After the passion cooled, they only made her feel emotionally drained and more alone than ever.

"Come on," she said, picking up her flashlight, which had been resting on the fence post. "With everything's that happened, we're too wired to rest. Let's have dinner."

"I was hoping for dessert first," he said with a crooked grin.

She laughed. "Will you settle for three-cheese pizza and some beer?"

He raised his eyebrows in surprise. "You didn't strike me as the kind who'd have beer in the fridge."

"Busted," she said, chuckling. "I've had the same six-pack in there since our staff's last monthly get-together. It's one Saturday a month and very informal. Basically, we grill hamburgers and everyone brings something—potluck style."

Once they'd reached the main house she led him into the living room. The old ranch house was decorated southwestern style with a leather couch, two chairs and a wool area rug over brick flooring. The walls held various "before and after" shots of the ranch.

He accepted the cold beer she handed him—a local brew.

Abby took a box of pizza out of the freezer and placed the contents onto the bottom of the box atop the silver heating surface. "I can add some green chile to it so it's a New Mexican pizza. You game?"

"Always," he said.

As their eyes met, she felt a prickle of excitement. Preston was all about self-control and restraint, a police officer through and through, but when he'd held her, she'd caught a glimpse of the rough, powerful man he kept tightly leashed.

She bit back a sigh and looked away. She had to get her thoughts back onto safer channels. Why was she making such a fuss over a kiss or two? This just wasn't like her.

"The living room's nice, but it doesn't say much about you or your style. Is that intentional?"

She started the microwave, then glanced back at him. "You're right and, yes, it's intentional."

He waited and didn't interrupt the silence.

"To build a dream, you have to be able to weather a lot of disappointments. That requires some separation between the dream and the dreamer." The microwave dinged and she pulled out the pizza. "I sometimes bring donors into my living room and entertain there. The rest of the house is just for me—a place where I can retreat from the worries of every day. My favorite room is one I converted into a small library. It's filled with romance and fantasy novels."

"I would have said those two are the same," he answered with a grin as they ate. "Isn't fantasizing part of romance?"

She laughed. "You tell me," she said, meeting his gaze and holding it.

She'd only meant it as a playful, subtle challenge, but when he didn't look away, she felt a stirring inside her, a yearning for what simply wasn't meant to be.

"Another beer?" she asked, going to the fridge just to put some distance between them.

"No, I'm good."

By the time she joined him at the table, she felt more in control. "You clearly know your way around women, Preston, and when you want company it's a safe bet that there's no shortage of volunteers. But I think you should know that I can't handle casual flings. I'm just not built that way," she said as they finished eating.

He leaned forward and tucked a loose strand of hair behind her ear.

He never said a word, yet that one fleeting touch sent shock waves all through her. She stood and took their plates to the sink. More than anything, she wished she could jump back into his arms and kiss him again. She'd almost forgotten what it was like to feel desired and so deliciously and powerfully feminine.

As she gazed out her kitchen window at the barn, she took a deep breath, composing herself. She had to stay focused on the ranch and keep the terrible thing that had happened from harming it.

"Carl's death was a devastating blow, but now the ranch is becoming a target, too. I realize that tagging and those dumb emails are just minor annoyances in comparison to what's already happened, but when is this going to stop?"

"Wait—what emails?"

"It's nothing, just nuisance letters."

"Show me what you're talking about."

"They started showing up in my inbox a few hours after we found Carl's body. I've deleted most of them, but by now there's bound to be some more there."

"Let me take a look."

She walked to the hallway, then stopped and glanced back at him. "I don't have a laptop, so we'll have to go into my home office. That's where I keep my personal PC."

"The part of your house you don't like people to see," he said with a nod. "Don't worry. I'll keep your secrets." His slow smile was full of mischief. "Let's see…you're a hoarder? You have a collection of overdue library books stacked ceiling high. They're in rows, with just a narrow aisle in the middle."

She laughed. "You're a bonehead."

"A what?"

"Forget it. Follow me," she said. Although she knew Preston was just trying to set her at ease, she wished she hadn't had to bring him back here. He knew too much about her already.

Abby stepped inside her home office and went directly to her desk. As she sat down, she saw him still standing at the door and gaping at the room.

"Well, say something."

"I've never seen so much pink in my life."

She saw his gaze drop to the area rug. It was nearly room size and hot pink with pale pink flowers. As he took a few more steps into the room, he looked at the daybed. It was covered with a pale pink throw. The end tables were white and held glass lamps etched with pink roses.

"It was just for me, so I decorated in a way that would remind me that—" She stopped talking and glanced away.

"I know," he said in a surprisingly gentle voice. "Sometimes we need a reminder that we're more than the person we let the world see."

"Yes, exactly." Putting things together and seeing the bigger picture was what he did as a detective, but knowing how easily he could read her was a surprise. "Everyone sees me as a tomboy, always in jeans and, more often than not, covered in hay. But part of me likes girly things—like pink." She shrugged. "That's the side no one sees. Do you have a hidden side, too?"

He nodded but didn't elaborate. "Your computer?" he said, getting back to business.

She typed in several commands, then waved toward the screen. "There you go. That's a new email but it's just like the others."

"How many have you received so far?" he asked.

"Six, maybe eight. I haven't really kept count."

"All by the same sender?" he asked.

"Yeah, 'Crazyman.' He's insisting that I close the ranch before a kid's murdered." She shuddered. "Listen to this one."

Preston leaned over her shoulder as she read Crazyman's latest email out loud.

"'In prison Sinclair was known as Shadowman because no one, not even the law, knew much about his past. His secrets will now haunt you and your ranch. Shut down and get out before someone else dies.'"

Abby swallowed hard. "And look at the top. He sent a copy to the local TV channel. He's trying to destroy this ranch and bury it under a ton of bad publicity, but why?"

"What he doesn't realize is that he's just given us a new lead. Crazyman knows something about Carl Sinclair's past that we didn't—until now. I'm going to do whatever's necessary to find him, but to track him down I'll need a copy of your files."

"No problem. I'll get what you need," she said, reaching for a flash drive. "I hope you catch this creep. I don't care who he is. No one's running me out of here."

"Leaving wouldn't be such a bad idea, Abby, at least temporarily. Take yourself out of danger until we can close this case."

"Do you think I'm not tempted?" She blinked back tears of frustration. "But if I do I'm just another person who can't walk her talk. I tell the kids to hang on and never give up, to believe that things will get better. Yet if I can't stand my ground now, who am I to speak to them of courage? I'll be admitting that fear has the power to derail everything in its path."

Silence stretched out between them.

"That's a good reason to stay," he said at last. "Navajos believe that good is necessary to keep evil in check. As a detective, that's what I try to do—restore the balance. You're doing that, too, by standing up to someone who's trying to bully you."

"It's not an easy choice but I have to make my stand here."

"Then I'll fight beside you," he said. "But think hard about getting surveillance cameras—not for the long run, just for now. They can be hidden from view, or disguised, so no one except you would have to know they're there."

"That all sounds expensive, and our budget's already

strained to the limit. Do you know anyone who might be willing to donate the service, maybe as a tax write-off?"

"As a matter of fact, I do. How about Level One Security?"

Her eyes grew wide. "They're one of the top companies in the state. They even protect government buildings. Do you think there's a chance I could talk them into it?"

"Oh yeah. I know the owner. He's overbearing and a pain in the butt, but deep down—I mean *really* deep down—he's a great guy," he said and grinned. "Daniel Hawk, the owner, is my brother, and another brother of mine and his wife are his partners."

"Great! Then I have the inside track. Can we gang up on Daniel?"

He laughed. "That's the spirit. I'll try to bring him over tomorrow. Okay?"

"Absolutely...and thanks."

"See that? I'm not so bad, even if I'm not wild about pink."

"You're wild enough at the right times." She'd meant it as a mischievous compliment, but his response took her breath away. His eyes darkened instantly and the storm raging there made her weak at the knees.

"I have to get back to the station. I want to drop the flash drive off at the lab so the tech can work on it. He keeps odd hours and I'm betting he's still there."

She led the way back up the hall to the front of the house. "My life here at the ranch has never been easy, but there's no place I'd rather be—even now," she said, standing by the front door.

"Dedication is almost a bad word these days, but not in my book. Nothing worthwhile ever comes easy, Abby." He lingered a moment longer. "But fight the right battles."

His gentleness soothed her even as it made her yearn for more. Yet that side of him vanished the instant he stepped outside.

Preston took in the area with the cold, practiced eye of a cop. "Trust no one, Abby."

"Except you?"

He held her gaze and brushed his roughened palm against the side of her face. "No, not even me."

Chapter Twelve

Preston had gotten practically no sleep last night because he kept thinking about Abby. She was in danger. Every instinct he'd developed over the years as a cop assured him of that.

More than ever, he needed to keep things strictly professional with her. Yet every time he closed his eyes he remembered how soft she'd felt against him and how good she'd tasted.

He glanced at the clock on his nightstand. It was five-thirty. With a curse, he tossed aside the covers and stood. Naked, he parted the curtains and gazed into the woods area behind his house.

He liked being a bachelor and the freedom that came with it. The only neighbors he had here were the wildlife. After several break-ins at his old apartment, he'd purposely bought a place that was hard to find. Here, if someone came after him, he wouldn't endanger anyone else. A cop made enemies. That was just the way it was.

It was also another reason why he had to keep his hands off Abby. She deserved more than he could offer. She was a woman who played for keeps and he wasn't the type to make commitments.

As a homicide cop he faced danger every day. He enjoyed the challenges and risks that came with the job, but some things—like love—were just too big a gamble.

Trusting in those kinds of relationships went against what life had taught him. Everything had two sides, including love. It could satisfy and fulfill for a while, but it also had the power to destroy whatever it touched.

But there was something about Abby that made him want to take a chance. He'd never met anyone like her. Not many people outside his family understood his dedication to law enforcement. Abby not only knew where he was coming from, but she also had a passion of her own to pursue.

He licked his dry lips and for a moment could almost taste her there. He grew hard despite his attempt to hold on to common sense. What the heck was wrong with him? He knew plenty of women who'd be happy with whatever conditions he cared to set. Abby was off-limits.

He stepped into the shower, hoping to cool his blood, and soon discovered that the water heater had shut down sometime during the night. The water was ice cold. Maybe it was an omen. Cursing, he moved fast.

By the time he finished getting dressed, coffee was brewed, thanks to the timer set last night. Dark and strong, just the way he liked it. He took the cup to his desk and checked his work emails. He'd filed his report last night and asked the IT tech to track Abby's emails ASAP. The guy had been working on it when Preston finally left the station. Though he hadn't expected the results this early, the answer was already there in his inbox.

It was six-thirty now. That meant Daniel and Gene, both early risers, would be awake. Kyle, probably not. With a devilish grin, he telephoned Kyle first.

He heard his brother's groggy voice as he answered the call. "What the—"

"It's Preston. I need your special skills."

"Dude, this early?" he growled. "My special skill right now is sleeping. Unless someone's dying, can it wait till, say, nine?"

"No," Preston said. "I need you to go to Señor Java, that coffee shop on West Central. Abby Langdon's been receiving some threatening emails, and I just learned that they originated from that location. The sender used a fake email address and they were sent via Wi-Fi. That's as far as our guys at the station could track it."

"So, why don't you go talk to the staff?"

"No can do. The owner hates cops and knows most of us, but she won't know you. Since there's no last name to connect us, you should be okay, but here's the deal. If the owner finds out you're working with us, she'll bounce you right out on your butt."

"She?" Kyle asked, sounding more interested now.

"Yeah, she. Jade Solis is one hot babe but hard as flint."

"Just the way I like them," Kyle said.

"Since when have you ever been choosy, bro?" Preston said with a laugh. "Just see if you can get me a lead. The last two emails were sent yesterday, one before 8:00 a.m. and the other after 6:00 p.m."

"Like before and after an eight-to-five job. Got it. I'll get what you need and check in with you later."

"Watch yourself."

"She have an in-house boyfriend?"

"Nah, but Jade won a national mixed martial arts competition last year. In high school, she was the only girl on the wrestling team. She doesn't need anyone to back her up. She's the entire package all by herself."

"Glad I have health insurance," he said, laughing. "Guess you're gonna owe me one."

"Just watch your step. I don't want to have to bring you flowers at the hospital."

"Nah, I'm a lover, not a fighter."

Preston hung up and laughed out loud. He'd known this was the kind of assignment Kyle would never turn down.

Next, he called Daniel and explained what he needed. "Sitting Tall Ranch is in bad need of a good security system that includes hidden cameras. It's a short-term thing and it's got to be pro bono."

"I've heard of Abby Langdon's troubles and know what's going on. I've got some surplus equipment just sitting on the shelf that I can configure for her, but first I'll need to look at the layout of her place," Daniel said.

"Don't let anyone know what you're doing. I have a strong suspicion that the perp works there in one capacity or another."

"How soon do you want to move on this?" Daniel asked.

"I can meet you at Sitting Tall Ranch this morning and you can have a look around, but actually putting up cameras will have to wait till no one's there."

"Not a problem. I'll have to check the cameras I have on hand and see which ones meet her needs. Each job requires something different, and I've got several models on hand. So how soon do you want to meet?" Daniel said.

"Thirty-five minutes?"

"We can be there in thirty. I'll bring Gene with me. He stayed over last night. Had some business in town, then a flat tire and by then it was too late to drive back up to his ranch."

"Not buying it, bro. Lori probably kicked his sorry butt out," he joked, knowing from the difference in sound quality that Daniel had put him on speaker.

"Now you're the expert on women?" Gene called out. "Dude, when's the last time you dated a woman long enough to remember her last name?"

"No woman with a brain would put up with him," Daniel said. "After a few hours listening to him talk shop, she'll break out in tears, make up some excuse about her sick friend, then run for the door."

"Nice. Okay, guys, time to go to work—you know, what real men do to earn a living."

"Yeah, yeah," Daniel said. "See you when we get there."

AFTER BEING INTRODUCED to Daniel and Gene, Abby excused herself. "I've got to meet with Stan and crunch some numbers. It won't take long. Walk around and make yourselves at home," she said.

Preston accompanied Daniel, who was taking snapshots and jotting down notes. Gene had gone ahead to check on Big Red.

"She'll need at least two cameras covering her home, two outside in the barn and bunkhouse area and a few special ones inside," Daniel said. "They'll have to work with infrared, too."

As they finished the walk-through, Abby hurried up to them. "Sorry. I'm running behind this morning," she said, "but I sure do appreciate you coming out, Daniel. Any help you can give me will be appreciated."

"The way I see it, you'll need several cameras in key places. Those will relay everything to an off-site location, and if anything looks odd or the system malfunctions the police will be called in immediately."

"That sounds terrific, but I'm not sure it's fair to you. Having people constantly monitoring cameras will run into serious money. Since it's pro bono, maybe you could just put up a couple of cameras and record activity during off hours."

Daniel shook his head. "My tactics are proactive. I don't do things halfway," he said. "You do excellent work and my company's happy to help you out."

Gene arrived just then. "Big Red loves his new home, Abby. Nice to know he's in good hands," he said, then glanced at his brother, a mischievous twinkle in his eye. "Dan's always been slow to join the party, but I'm glad he's found a way to contribute to Sitting Tall Ranch."

Seeing Daniel's eyes narrow as he glared at his brother, she smiled. "I'm very happy to accept whatever help you give us." She fished a set of keys out of her jeans pocket and handed it to Daniel. "These will give you access to every lock on the ranch and to my house. Just return them when you're done installing the cameras…or is that something you turn over to your staff?"

"Usually my people do this, but not this time."

"Thanks so much, Daniel. Now, if you'll excuse me, I have a few more animals waiting for breakfast and water troughs to top off. I'll be back in five or ten minutes."

"I'll help out with the water. Be right back, guys," Preston said, and he smiled at Abby as they walked away.

PRESTON CAME BACK five minutes later, alone. Abby had stopped to groom a mare in a pen about a hundred feet away.

Daniel grinned from ear to ear and Gene patted Preston on the shoulder. "How about that—you two taking care of the animals—together."

"Yup, that's the way it starts. I hope she doesn't break your heart, bro. She's beautiful and sexy. In other words, *way* out of your league," Gene said, watching Abby place a halter on a horse, who obligingly lowered his head for her. "That's a sweet ride."

"Watch your mouth, or I'll close it for you right now," Preston said.

"I was talking about the horse but, hey, if you want to fight, don't worry, I'll take a dive. Don't want you to get beat up in front of your lady," Gene said.

"She's not my lady," Preston said, his voice practically a snarl.

"Enough, guys. Here she comes, and she picked up a guest along the way, and not just the horse. Play nice in front of the kid," Daniel said, cocking his head toward Abby, who was walking toward them with Bobby and the mare on a lead rope between them.

"This is Bobby Neskahi," Abby said a moment later, introducing the boy, then looking at Preston. "He just told me something you need to hear, Preston," she said, then looked at Bobby and nodded. "Go ahead."

"I didn't think of it sooner or I would have said something," Bobby said.

"What is it, son?" Preston asked.

"I told you that Carl didn't have friends here except me and Abby, but I'd forgotten something. Carl had one friend he didn't want anyone to know about—even me. The guy was only here once that I know about. It was in the evening and when Carl saw me coming up the walk to the bunkhouse he almost shoved the guy out the back door. I don't think Carl wanted me to see the guy's face."

"When was this?"

Bobby thought about it. "Before school let out. More than a month ago, I guess."

"What makes you think they were friends?" Preston asked.

"I heard Carl tell him that their days doing time were behind them and they needed to move on. Then he hugged him, like they were buds."

"So, Bobby, you never saw his face?" Preston asked.

"Not then, no, but I went around the bunkhouse and pretended to be petting the llamas. The guy walked right past me like I wasn't even there, just another kid, you know?"

"Bobby, you'll never be 'just' another anything," he said and smiled. "What made you remember now?"

"Abby asked me if I knew a tagger who wore a hoodie because she'd had trouble with one yesterday," Bobby said. "The only person I could think of was Carl's friend. He'd worn a dark blue hoodie, but it wasn't covering his head at the time."

Preston glanced at Abby. "Any objections if I show Bobby some mug shots?"

"It's not my call," Abby said.

"I'll clear it with his foster parents," Preston said.

Preston watched Abby walk off with the boy, and by the time he glanced back at his brothers, both were grinning.

Irritated, Preston glanced away and dialed. Sometimes family could be a real pain in the butt.

Chapter Thirteen

Narrowing down a list of Carl's cellmates didn't take long, and showing their photos to Bobby went even faster.

As his foster mother came inside Abby's office to pick him up, Bobby looked at Preston. "Do you want me to go with you when you pay the guy a visit, just to make sure it's the same person and all that?"

"That's not necessary," Preston said, shaking his head.

"Bobby, you have physical therapy today and we're going. That's the end of it," Kay Yarrow said.

"You heard her," Abby said. "We'll see you tomorrow."

Seeing Bobby look so dejected tugged at Preston. "Can I have a quick word with him before he goes?"

Kay Yarrow nodded.

Preston took the boy into the next room. "I know you want to look out for Abby, so I've got a special job for you. Whenever you're here at the ranch, keep your eyes open and call me if you see anything that doesn't seem right—anything at all, okay?" He handed Bobby his card.

"Seriously?"

Seeing the look of hope in Bobby's eyes reminded Preston of his own past. He knew what Bobby was going through. Until *Hosteen* Silver had come along, he'd lived in one foster home after another—a disposable kid—wanting desperately to belong somewhere and believing it would never happen.

Bobby had made a place for himself here at the ranch and was afraid that it was about to go away, leaving him alone again.

"You love Abby and this ranch, so I can't think of anyone who'd do a better job of keeping an eye on things."

"I would have done it anyway, you know?" Bobby looked up at Preston.

"I know," Preston said. "But it's official now. Get going."

"I hate physical therapy. It never really gets me anywhere, not with stuff that counts. No matter what I do, I'll never be able to play—" He shook his head, then shrugged.

"Play what?"

"It's dumb, I know. I just wish I could play baseball, or at least catch or hit a ball, but I suck. Everyone else just laughs."

"Then let's make a deal. You keep your eyes open, and I'll teach you to catch and hit a baseball."

Preston heard Kay clear her throat. "Time to go now—seriously," he added.

Bobby left with a smile on his face and Abby noticed it immediately. "Those physical therapy sessions are really tough on him. The exercises can be painful, and sometimes it's hard to see progress," she said. "What on earth did you say to cheer him up like that?"

"Just guy talk," he said. "I offered to teach him how to play ball."

"He's been wanting that for a long time. I tried, but I can't pitch or throw, let alone hit a ball. I wasn't much help."

"Then I'll teach both of you," he said. Then he showed her the mug shot of the man Bobby had identified. "Do you know this man?"

Abby studied the photo. "What's his name? He looks vaguely familiar, but I can't place him."

"Edwin Bain," he said.

Abby's forehead furrowed. "It's that scar above his left eyebrow…" After a moment she looked back up at Preston. "I've seen him, but his name isn't Edwin, or even Ed. If I'm right, that's Greg…no wait, Gary something. His hair is lighter and longer, and his face is fuller, too."

"How sure are you that it's the same guy?"

"He looks older now than in that picture, but I'm pretty sure it's him. He calls that his lucky scar," she said, pointing, "because a half inch lower and he might have lost his eye. I must have embarrassed him when I asked about it because the next time I saw him he'd let his hair grow out even more, covering it up."

"And you met him where?"

"Last time I saw him, he was working at Barton's Feed Store."

"Looks like that's where I'm going next."

"Maybe I should go to help point him out. That's an old photo, and the scar's hidden."

He thought about it a few seconds. "Okay, stay behind me. Once you confirm he's the guy you have in mind, I'll take it from there."

Soon they were on their way in Preston's SUV. Abby glanced around. "This fits you."

"What? The SUV?"

"Yeah," she said, and with a tiny grin, added, "It's powerful, stealthy and unmarked."

He took a deep breath. "I'm not unmarked."

"Tattoo?"

He smiled.

"Aw come on—how about a hint, like what and where?"

He remained silent.

"Not even a tiny clue?"

"Nope."

He stared at the road and tried to stay focused, but the light fragrance she wore was making him crazy. It was a gentle scent, like lavender in the spring, and difficult to ignore, just like she was.

"What do you plan to say to Carl's cellmate—if that's him?"

"I need to find out everything he knows about Carl. The murder may be linked to an enemy Carl made back in prison."

"You think someone followed him to the ranch after all these years? Carl served four years and had been out six months before I hired him. That was two years ago."

"Some people have long memories," he said, glancing in the rearview mirror. "Hang on." He made a sharp turn onto a side street without signaling.

"What the—"

"Just checking to see if my hunch was right. A white car was following us. It was staying well back, but it was there."

She turned around in her seat. "Are you sure it's gone?"

"Yeah. It kept going straight."

Preston made several more turns, took an alternate route, then finally pulled up next to Barton's Feed Store and parked. The lot held only three cars at the moment, but the small, locally owned feed store made a slow, steady business.

Because the main building was small, Barton's stored stock tanks and feeders outside behind chain-link fences. Two men were working there, trying to rearrange the pallets to maximize space. The tarps that would be placed over them to protect the merchandise lay nearby on the ground.

"Gary works in the back at the loading dock. He usually helps me load the bales into my truck."

"Let's go there first, then," Preston said.

Knowing ex-cons could spot a cop miles away, Preston forced himself to walk at a leisurely pace. He didn't want Gary, aka Ed, to make a run for it if he was involved.

Once they came around the corner of the building, Abby

spotted the man. "There, on top of that stack of hay bales," she said, pointing.

The man stood about eight feet above them.

"Hey, Miss Langdon," he said, seeing her. "How many bales do you need today?"

"Can you give me a few minutes of your time first?" she asked. As he started to come down, Abby added, "My friend would like to ask you some questions."

He was halfway down the stack when he saw Preston standing there, looking up.

"I'm Detective Bowman. Relax. I just have a few questions for you."

Gary kicked at a bale of hay, knocking it off the stack and down toward Preston, then tried to slide off the back of the pile.

Preston, who'd managed to jump aside just in time, ducked around and grabbed Gary's leg before he reached the ground.

Gary tried to twist free but fell on his back from three bales up. Preston pinned the man in place with his knee, twisting his arm behind his back to keep him there.

"You've got no right—" Gary said.

"Buddy, you just assaulted a police officer."

"I stepped wrong on a bale of hay while climbing down, lost my balance and the bale fell next to you. It was an accident."

"Tell that to your parole officer."

"Look, I freaked out when you said 'detective.' Cut me some slack, will you? It took me four months to find this job."

Preston jerked the guy to his feet.

"What's going on?" a man's voice suddenly boomed behind them.

"Mr. Barton, it's okay," Gary said. "One of the bales slipped off the stack, that's all. I was apologizing for the accident."

Tim Barton glanced at Preston, noting the badge on his belt. "Is that what happened, Officer?"

"There's no problem here," Preston said. "I only need to ask your employee some questions about a friend of his. It won't take long."

Barton looked at Abby. "Word's out about what happened at the ranch. Now I hear parents are afraid to let their kids volunteer there until the killer's caught. I think you're getting a raw deal, so the next fifty bales are on me."

"Thanks!" Abby went up to Barton. "Let's go back inside. I need to place an order."

"Can you use a few bags of grain, too?"

"Yes, that would be terrific!" she said and walked off with the owner.

Preston bit back a smile. There was just something about Abby and her dream that brought out the best in people.

He looked back at Gary—Ed Bain—his expression turning hard. Good, for some reason, also attracted evil. "If you know something, you might as well spill it now. Your job may be hanging in the balance."

"I went to visit Carl after I got paroled. I was hoping he would talk to the ranch's owner and help me land a job, but he wouldn't even hear me out. He had a good thing going and didn't want to screw it up, I guess."

"Tell me about Carl. What was he into? Drugs, something else?"

"Carl? You've got to be kidding. The only thing he was really into was art, and these days he was perfectly happy doing his own charcoal sketches. He was good, too. When I first heard that he got offed, I figured he'd gotten himself involved with some art dealer who wanted him to forge some drawings for him."

"Did you have a solid reason to believe that?" Preston asked.

"Just what I knew about him. He was always sketching, doing stuff that was usually better than what you'd see in art galleries. I once asked him why he didn't put some of his work up on the internet and make a few extra bucks, but he said he wasn't interested. Maybe he was trying to avoid the attention. I always had the feeling that he was hiding from someone or something, and that's why he was living under the radar— no phone, no car, no nothing," he said. "That's all I know."

"If you think of anything else, call me," Preston said and handed him his card. "And don't leave town."

Preston walked across the yard and saw a face he recognized: Marsha Robertson, the TV reporter. She was sitting inside her white sedan and looking directly at him.

Preston walked over and leaned in the driver's side. "What brings you here?"

"Probably the same thing as you. Looking for leads into Carl Sinclair's death and trying to find out how it all ties in to the ranch."

"There is no tie to the ranch other than the crime happened there." He stood up straight. "You were following me before. Don't do it again. If you do, I'll arrest you for interfering with an ongoing police investigation. Clear?"

"You win this round, Detective Bowman."

Preston stood back as Marsha drove off. Moments later, Abby came up. "Was that the reporter?"

"Yeah, she was the one who was tailing us. I tried to warn her off," he said, then shrugged. "It won't do any good though. She's after a story, so nothing I say is really going to make her back away."

"I'll deal with whatever trouble she creates as it happens. Right now I really should get back to the ranch."

"Has something happened?"

"I want to talk to Bobby. The Yarrows are planning to take all the boys up to their cabin in the mountains this coming weekend, but Bobby hates it there. He wants permission to stay at the ranch until they return," she said. "Bobby has a tough time because he can't go hiking without slowing everyone down, and that creates problems with the other boys. They give him a hard time. Bobby always ends up being left behind."

"You're going to let him stay?"

She nodded. "I told Kay I'd put him up, and do everything I can to make sure he's safe. He'll help with the animals and there's always room—and a need for an extra pair of hands willing to work."

"And you like having him around."

She nodded and smiled. "Yeah, I do. I love Bobby. He's a great kid."

"He'd do just about anything for you."

"That's exactly the same way I feel about him."

"Have you ever considered fostering him?" Preston asked. In his day, strangers would often invite foster kids to their homes for special events, like holiday parties. Things had changed a lot in the past twenty years, but people still drew the line when it came to getting involved full-time. They had lives of their own.

"There are a lot of rules when it comes to fostering, and they're there for good reasons," she said. "The truth is, Bobby needs more than I can give him. Unlike the dad he barely knew, Bobby needs a male role model who'll see him as differently abled, as opposed to disabled."

"I hear you," he said with a thoughtful nod. "I've never been physically challenged, but I know how tough things can be for disposable kids."

"*Disposable* kids?" she asked, looking at him in surprise as they got into the SUV.

"That's what we called ourselves back then." He saw the look of sympathy in her eyes and turned away. He'd hated it back then and it was no different now. "It was a way of re-minding ourselves that we had to learn to deal."

"How did you end up in foster care, Preston?" she asked softly. "Do you mind if I ask?"

Silence stretched between them as Preston drove toward the ranch. His situation wasn't exactly a secret. He'd give her the facts and let it go at that. "My mom had an issue with drugs. One day she didn't come home. I had a cleaning job at the hardware store, so I had enough cash to get by for a while. After a month, social workers showed up on my doorstep and I was placed in a foster home," he said, his tone letting her know that he didn't need, nor want, sympathy.

She got the message and offered neither.

"I think what bothers Bobby most is that, although it's a tribe-approved home, he's the only Navajo there right now. Child Services is trying to find him a Navajo family, but only a limited number of foster homes are licensed by the tribe. Since Bobby needs specialized care that's more readily available here in Hartley, they've kept him with the Yarrows. It's a good compromise, but he's had problems getting along with the other kids."

"I remember my first foster home. I was the only Navajo there, too, and I took some grief, but each one of those kids was hurting. Most of them believed they hadn't measured up somehow, and that's why they'd been placed in the system. Others coped by convincing themselves that their parents would be back for them soon. Bobby's story about his father being a spy is more imaginative than most, but it's not unusual."

"Did you make up a story for yourself?"

"No. I knew my mother wouldn't be coming back. She had other…priorities."

"How old were you?"

"Twelve."

Abby reached for his hand. "What she did made you a stronger man. I can't imagine anyone I'd like in my corner more than you."

Her words took him by surprise. Most people offered pity. Yet the way Abby was looking at him made him feel invincible, like one of the legendary warriors of his tribe.

"I'm sure that Bobby senses that you two are alike in some ways. That's why he trusts you," she said.

He shook his head. "No, I don't think it's trust. Bobby sees me as a necessary evil. If he cooperates with me, maybe I can solve the case a little faster. Then things will get back to normal for you and him. With Bobby, trust has to be earned."

"Is that the way it is with you?"

"Yeah. In that way I'm no different than Bobby."

He remembered the bad times like they were yesterday. When a person who's supposed to love you no matter what bails, everything changes. The hurt fades eventually, but distrust remains, a scar that'll always be there.

As they pulled up in front of the ranch, Abby asked Preston to stop by the mailbox. After retrieving her mail, she hopped back into the SUV.

"Thanks. You saved me having to walk back," she said, then suddenly stopped sorting through the stack.

"Is something wrong?" he asked.

"This letter has no stamp on it," she said, holding it up for him to see. "I'm hoping it's a donation. Sometimes people will leave a check, or cash, for us in the mailbox." She tore open the envelope, then stiffened.

"It's not a donation," she said in a taut voice. "This is from the same person who's been emailing me."

"Crazyman?"

"Yeah. He wants Sitting Tall Ranch closed for good."

Chapter Fourteen

She couldn't keep her hands from shaking, so Abby kept the letter on her lap as she read it out loud. "'Your first mistake brought death. How many more will pay if you keep the ranch open?'"

Her voice wavered on the last line and she swallowed hard.

"Don't let him get to you. That's what he wants."

"I'm responsible for hiring Carl, and if you're right, danger followed him here. Am I now endangering everyone else connected to the ranch just so I can keep things going?"

"There's no reason to believe that, and you're already taking all the precautions you can. Except for Bobby, who you're keeping close, you don't have kids coming in right now. You're only doing what has to be done, like taking care of the livestock."

"I trusted Carl, and look what's happened. If I'm that bad a judge of character, maybe I'm not fit to run the ranch," she whispered, voicing her greatest fear.

Though her voice had been barely audible, he still managed to hear her.

"You're letting him twist your thinking," he said. "I'll tell you what. Let's get down to basics. You trust me, right?"

"Of course."

"See that? You're an excellent judge of character," he said. She smiled.

As Preston parked in front of the ranch's office, Abby saw Bobby standing on the sidewalk, waiting. "I have to know whether Carl was doing anything illegal here, Preston. For my own sake and that of the ranch."

"I'll find out," he said. "Right now I'd like to talk to some of your volunteers. I see a few faces I haven't spoken to before."

"Some of the younger kids have flexible schedules that depend on whether they've got exams or other school activities. During the summer, they pretty much come and go all the time. A handful of our adults are also on drop-by status. It sounds a little crazy, but everything gets done."

"All right. Looks like we've each got work to do," he said, gesturing toward Bobby.

"Feel free to talk to anyone you want and wander around. I'm going to see what's up with Bobby," Abby said and picked up the mail.

"Leave the one from Crazyman in the SUV. The chances of getting prints from it are remote, but you never know."

As Preston walked off, Abby went to meet Bobby. She had the mail clutched so tightly in her hand she bent the edges, a detail Bobby didn't miss.

He shot Preston a dirty look.

Catching it, Abby eased her grip and forced herself to smile. "Bobby, you're back early. Something wrong?"

"No, PT was cancelled. Air-conditioning went out. Looks like you're the person with something wrong," he added.

"What do you mean?" Abby saw that Bobby was watching Preston, who was out of earshot.

"He said he could help, but he hasn't. That's why something's bothering you. Right?"

"I got some bad news, but it has nothing to do with Preston. He's doing his best."

"Wait—he wants you to call him by his first name? It's a trick," he added quickly. "They only make friends with you when they want something. That's what happened last year when one of my foster brothers got arrested. The cop was real nice to us, then he came to get Rodney."

Abby sighed. Bobby wasn't a normal ten-year-old, but it saddened her to see just how cynical he'd become already. "Detective Bowman's not like that."

"You *like* him?"

"Yes, of course. He's working hard to find answers, and when he does, I can open up the ranch again."

"Yeah—but you *like* him?" he asked, giving the word a deeper meaning by emphasizing it.

"Maybe," she said, understanding what he meant. "I really don't know him all that well yet."

"He likes you."

"What makes you say that?" she asked, curious.

"I see the way he looks at you."

She laughed. "He looks at me when he talks to me. So do most people, Bobby."

He shook his head. "No. When you're *not* looking. He likes you," he repeated.

"Bobby, you're imagining things. Now let's get to work. We need to groom the camels, and you're good with Hank. You can get him to *koosh,* to lie down, so we can reach his back."

Bobby smiled. "I like Hank."

"Yeah, I know. He likes you, too. I don't let just anyone groom him, you know."

Bobby practically beamed. As they walked, he looked away from her and in a whisper, said, "I like the detective, too."

"Was it that hard to admit?"

He shrugged. "He said he'd teach me to play ball. I hope he keeps his word."

"Wait and see, then you'll know."

After they'd brushed Hank, Abby saw Preston trying to

talk to one of her volunteers, a college-aged girl. She kept turning her back on him as she worked.

"Looks like the detective needs my help," Bobby said.

"He does, does he?" Abby replied with a tiny smile.

"Yeah, he's not getting anywhere. Cassie won't even look at him. He's making her nervous. If I go with him, maybe people won't feel like he's about to arrest them or something."

"Maybe so, but you should probably ask him if he wants your help first. If he says not now, then come back."

"Okay."

As Bobby walked off, she saw Ilse Sheridan leading Big Red into one of the big enclosures. Abby went to meet her.

"You're early today. Thanks for giving us some extra time, Ilse."

"Glad to help out. Rod wanted me to drop off some donations he got for you from his NBA buddies. With the new rumor that's going around, he was afraid donors would be few and far between, at least for a while."

"I don't understand. What rumor?"

"You haven't heard?" Ilse stared at her in surprise. "It's just gossip, but it'll have an effect."

"Go on," Abby said.

"Some people are saying you need to be audited to prove that donations are really going to the ranch. Carl was a convicted thief, so they're wondering what else was going on here."

She felt the blood drain from her face, but dismay soon turned to anger. "That's beneath contempt. My finances are an open book." Seeing Stan by the ranch's office door, Abby waved, signaling him to wait for her. "I'm going to stop that nonsense in its tracks."

PRESTON SAW ABBY storm away from Ilse Sheridan. Curious, he figured he'd go talk to Ilse next. Officers Jerry Michaels and Gabe Sanchez had collected statements from those present the day Carl's body had been found. Now he needed to account for the whereabouts of the rest of the workers here and see if they had an alibi that covered the vic's time of death.

As he approached Ilse, Preston caught a glimpse of Bobby out of the corner of his eye. The kid was hanging back, but Preston knew he was listening to everything that was going on.

"Ilse Sheridan?" he said. "Remember me?"

"Detective Bowman," she said with a nod. "How may I help you?"

"I'd like you to answer a few questions for me."

"I'd be happy to," she said.

"Do you normally volunteer here this time of day?"

She shook her head. "No, not usually. I made an exception today because Mr. Garner asked me to come by and drop off some donations he'd collected on behalf of the ranch."

"Where were you last Sunday between nine and midnight?"

"You don't honestly think I had—"

Preston held up one hand. "I'm asking everyone the same question. It's just procedure."

Ilse relaxed. "I came after work and stayed till around ten, maybe a bit after. I was exercising Tracker. I take him out for a run, then groom him and put him away for the night."

"Who else was still here when you left?"

She paused, considering it for several long moments. "That's hard to say for sure because this place is so big. Usually though, by ten everyone's gone. Abby gets up real early, too, so sometimes she's already gone to bed by that time. Offhand, I don't remember if her light was on or off when I left that night."

He noted the way Ilse kept glancing to her right, losing eye contact each time she spoke. Instinct and experience told him she was lying or uncomfortable about something.

He continued his questions but soon realized he wasn't getting anywhere. After he thanked her and moved on, Bobby came up to him.

"She didn't tell you everything. Remember when I told you I hear and see things 'cause people don't pay attention to me?" Seeing Preston nod, he continued. "Sometimes Ilse meets Monroe here. They like each other."

"You think they're trying to keep it a secret?"

"Yeah, 'cause when people are around, they barely speak to each other. I know what's going on because I saw them ducking into the toolshed Sunday night. I was still here because my foster dad was late picking me up. He had an extra job. Anyway, I went to the barn to give Tracker some carrots, heard some weird noises and looked through one of the gaps in the wall between the boards. They were in there, kissing and stuff. It was embarrassing."

"Did they see you?"

"Nah. They were too busy with each other. Besides, spies know how to sneak around. I've been practicing. I read what to do in Angus McAdams's book, *Spycraft*. I even bought my own copy."

"How long were you here last Sunday?"

"I left at about seven-thirty or eight."

Preston checked his notes. According to the statement he'd given Gabe Sanchez, Monroe had supposedly been at an Isotopes game in Albuquerque at that time. "You sure you saw them Sunday?"

"Yeah, the next morning...that's when I found Carl," he said in a whisper-thin voice.

Preston considered what he'd just learned. It was possible Ilse and Monroe had been here and maybe seen the killer or knew something they were leaving out to cover their relationship. The Isotopes story could have been a hasty attempt to give the police an unverifiable alibi.

"You think they did it," Bobby said.

It hadn't been a question and that surprised Preston. No one, not even his foster brothers, had ever been able to read him so easily.

"It doesn't matter what I think. I need evidence. Police work isn't about guessing—it's about facts," he said.

"Yeah, I suppose," Bobby said. "Do you think you can hurry up and work faster? This place is all Abby's got, and she's really worried she might lose it."

"I know."

"It can really hurt when you have something really important, then it's taken away, especially when it's not your fault."

Preston felt the tug in his gut. "Yeah. I learned that back when I was in foster care."

Bobby's eyes grew wider. "You were a foster kid? Why'd you become a cop?"

Preston laughed. "Okay, kid, you're going to have to explain that."

"Cops pretend to be your friend, then once they get what they want you never see them again."

Preston walked beside him, trying to figure out what had happened to Bobby. "Not all cops are like that, but it's a tough job. Sometimes it can make the rest of your life…difficult."

Bobby looked at Preston, then back down at the ground. "It's hard to believe anyone when all you get is excuses."

"Yeah, but here's something you can count on from me— I'm going to teach you to play ball."

"I'm not athletic—and it's not just 'cause I've got JRA. I can't catch even when the ball hits me in the hands."

"It's just a matter of timing and practice. I can teach you. And as far as throwing the ball goes, I taught my brother Rick, and that guy couldn't hit the side of a barn when we first started," he said and laughed.

"Did he have problems getting around?"

"Not like yours, but he was a total train wreck. He couldn't go through the house without knocking something over. He was clumsy and overweight back in high school. Now, he's six foot four and trimmed down to around two-twenty."

"Is he still clumsy?"

"That depends on who you ask," Preston said and smiled. He wished he could tell Bobby more about his brother. None of them, except Daniel who'd found out by accident, knew exactly what Rick did for the FBI. Some sort of undercover work—that's all he'd been able to put together. Rick would be home in another year, and Preston was looking forward to seeing him then.

Before Preston could say anything else, he heard tires on gravel and saw a truck pull to a dusty stop by the office. Ed Bain, from the feed store, got out and strode toward Abby.

Sensing trouble, Preston broke into a jog.

"This is your fault, you witch," Bain yelled, raising a fist as he closed in on her.

Preston stepped between them, blocking the man's advance. "Put your hands down."

Bain stopped, lowered his fists, then kicked out, aiming for Preston's groin.

Preston stepped sideways, dodging the kick, then grabbed the man's boot, twisting it like a corkscrew. The man yelled in agony, falling to the ground on his face.

Preston dropped down and grabbed Bain's arm, twisting his hand up toward his neck painfully.

Bain yelped, groping with his other hand to break the hold. Preston just applied more force, and Bain curled up, tears in his eyes.

"Stop resisting," Preston ordered.

Bain gave up, and Preston brought both of the man's wrists together and handcuffed him.

Still holding Bain's arm, Preston looked over at Abby. "You okay?"

"I'm fine," she managed to say in a shaky voice.

"You might as well call my parole officer," Bain spat out. "At least in prison I won't have to beg for food and a place to sleep."

"You have a job. What's your problem?" Abby asked him.

"The problem is you got me fired, you dumb—"

Preston tightened his grip. "Watch your mouth."

"Maybe you should bring him inside," Abby said, noting that all the volunteers were watching.

Preston read him his rights as he pushed him inside Abby's office.

"Yeah, yeah, I've heard it all before. Go ahead and take me in. The job at the feed store was all I could get around here. Now that it's history, so am I."

"Why were you fired?" Abby asked.

"After you left, I managed to smooth things with Barton, but then that reporter came back and started pushing me for answers about Carl. Barton said he didn't need that kind of publicity, so he fired me," Ed said.

"You're talking about Marsha Robertson?" Preston asked him.

"I don't know her name. She's the hot blonde on local TV. She said there's a burglary ring that has been breaking into area houses and she wanted to know if I knew anything about that. She also kept asking about Carl and what had happened between us. She then asked me 'why,' not 'if,' I'd killed Carl. That's the part Barton heard."

"Answer one question for me," Preston said. "Have you been sending Abby Langdon threatening letters? You might as well come clean. You're going to jail anyway."

"Letters? What the hell you talking about now?"

"The person who wrote these letters knew Carl's nickname—Shadowman."

"Dude, everyone in the pen knows each other by their nicknames, and it wasn't just me and him in there." He turned to Abby. "Do I look like the letter-writing type? When I have something to say, I get in your face."

Abby looked at him, then expelled her breath in a soft hiss. "Preston, let him go. He didn't actually hit me and I'm not going to press charges."

"You should," Preston said firmly.

"No. He wouldn't have lost his job if we hadn't led the reporter to him," she said and looked at Ed. "I'm going to ask Tim Barton to take you back."

"If he doesn't, can I work here? I'll do whatever you need. I know animals. Carl and I worked on the same program."

Abby shook his head. "I can't hire you, at least not now. This ranch is under siege. I'm fighting just to keep the animals and pay my bills," she said, "but give me a chance to talk to Tim. I think I can convince him if you agree not to lose your temper again—with anyone."

Seeing him nod, she stepped into the next room while Preston remained with Ed.

"She's not going to press charges. How about you?" Ed asked.

Preston pushed him against the wall and held him there. "If you *ever* lay a hand on her, it will be the last thing you ever do. You get me?"

"I didn't actually do—" Seeing the lethal glare Preston gave him, he stopped speaking and just nodded.

Ten minutes later Abby came back to the room. "Okay, you have your job back but if you give Tim any trouble—being late to work, not doing what you're told, arguing with a customer—you're out."

"I won't give him a reason," he said.

"Remember what I said." Preston's voice was barely a whisper as he removed the man's handcuffs.

Once Ed left, Preston glanced back at Abby. She was looking out the window, her arms wrapped tightly around herself. He'd never been impulsive, but this time something snapped inside him and he pulled her into his arms. "You're not in this alone, Abby. Your fight is my fight, too."

"No one's ever jumped in for me like that. I should have said thanks...."

The gentleness in her gaze, and the fear that lay beyond that, were too much for him. She needed tenderness, but when he lowered his mouth to hers and her lips flowered open, heat shot through him. His heart began to thunder and heat poured into his veins. She was sweet and soft, the very qualities that were missing from his world of cold, hard facts and logic.

He was demanding and rough, but she surrendered to him easily, giving as much as he wanted to take. Fire coursed through him as he ravaged her mouth. He'd never felt this greed—this overpowering need for someone else.

Yet what raged inside him was more than passion. The proof was there when he moved away from her. "Abby...."

Those big, beautiful hazel eyes stayed on him until he couldn't stand it anymore. "I have to go work on the case. I'll be in touch later."

He strode outside to his SUV, his body aching, his blood on fire. Cursing himself, he got behind the wheel. To help Abby, he'd have to keep his priorities straight and focus on the investigation.

As he tried to get the memory of their kiss out of his mind, he remembered the way she'd looked at him. The longing in her eyes would haunt his dreams long after tonight.

Chapter Fifteen

Preston loved police work. It was at the heart of everything he was and had ever wanted to be. Yet sometimes it was necessary to cut a few corners.

"Call Daniel," he said to the cell phone resting beside him on the seat of his SUV.

"Hey, bro," Daniel greeted over the speaker. "What's going on?"

"I'd like you to get me everything you can on Ilse Sheridan, Stanley Cooper, Michelle Okerman and Monroe Jenkins, my boss's son," he said. Due to his government security contracts Daniel had high-level clearance and could get into databases that would take him a folder of paperwork to access. "I need you to keep it off the record, too."

"Don't I always?"

"One more thing. I want you to see what you can get me on a ward of the state, a child named Robert or Bobby Neskahi. I want to find out about his parents."

"That's a lot tougher. Most of those files are sealed by the Office of Children, Youth and Families or the courts. Are you stopping by later?"

"Yeah. I'm hoping together we can find some answers. Someone's working real hard to close down Sitting Tall Ranch, and I need to find out how it all connects to the murder."

"What are your instincts telling you, bro?"

"That there's way more to this case than I'm seeing, and Sitting Tall Ranch is right in the middle of everything."

PRESTON DROVE TO Stan Cooper's office next. He'd wanted to talk to the accountant away from the ranch. In his own office, the man would be more relaxed and focused, something that would work to Preston's advantage.

He found the place quickly and went inside. While Stan finished a conference call, his leggy blonde assistant offered him a cup of coffee. She was easy on the eyes and flashy but not his type. More like Rick's or Kyle's. Of course, any female was Kyle's type. He smiled at the thought.

Several moments later, he was ushered into the small but well-appointed office. Several black-and-white charcoal sketches hung on the wall, all depicting southwest landscapes and animals. Old black-and-white panoramic photos of Navajo Dam dating back to the sixties were there, too.

"I like the photos," Preston said.

"I spent a lot of my time up in that area as a kid," Stan said, shaking Preston's hand. "So what brings you here, Detective?" he asked, a worried frown on his face.

"I'm digging hard into the case. Since you play a big part at the ranch as accountant, advisor and volunteer, I thought you'd be able to answer a few questions for me."

"That'll depend on the questions," he said. "I can't give you current specifics of Abby's financial situation, but the ranch is a nonprofit so some of those records are public."

Preston took a seat and leaned back in the chair. It was soft leather and probably cost a small fortune, but it was definitely comfortable. "My primary interest is Carl Sinclair's murder."

"Terrible business," Stan said, sitting behind his desk. "Is there a chance it was a random thing? Someone got caught trespassing and Carl stepped in?"

"It's too soon for me to come to any conclusions," Preston

said. "I came looking for your take on the people who work and volunteer at the ranch. I'd ask Abby, but she tends to see the best in everyone…"

"And that clouds reality," he said, finishing Preston's unspoken thought. "Don't think I haven't spoken to her about that, but Abby's…well, Abby. She does things her way, and her idealism sometimes trumps her common sense."

"You see things more objectively, so keeping that in mind, let's start with Ilse Sheridan and Monroe Jenkins."

He barked a laugh. "You heard about that, did you?" He shrugged dismissively. "Ilse's only playing with him. In my opinion she enjoys the attention of a man fifteen years younger than she is. The fact the kid's the police chief's son just adds spice to the mix. There's nothing serious going on there, but you might not want to tell that to Monroe."

"I understand Ilse and Monroe were both close to Carl." He knew no such thing, but sometimes it helped to intimate that he knew more than he did. People tended to speak more freely then.

Stan looked puzzled for a minute, then smiled. "Wait— you're talking about the nights Monroe and Carl got together to play chess? Ilse wasn't involved in that. Carl had been depressed about something and Monroe picked up on it. Since he knew Carl liked chess, he decided to bring a board and talk him into playing a few games."

"Did it help?"

"I don't know. Carl was hard to read. The guy was a mass of contradictions, too. He never had much to say and he never asked anyone for help, but if you needed his, he was always there to lend a hand. Let me give you an example. Monroe was having problems at school, and his dad was all over his case. When Carl found out, he helped Monroe study for his tests, and the kid passed with flying colors. Carl also helped me." He rolled up his sleeve to show Preston his silver-and-turquoise watch. "I love this thing. It was given to me by my father. One day at the ranch, I lost it. We searched everywhere. Nada. Zip. I figured it was gone for good."

"You wear that to the ranch?" Preston asked, eyebrows raised.

"Not usually, no, but that day I was in a hurry and forgot. The catch must have caught on something, and it came off. I was really pissed at myself and tried not to think about it," he said. "The next morning, Carl called. He'd found it down between two bales of hay where I'd been working. I offered Carl a reward, but he wouldn't hear of it."

"He could have easily sold that watch and no one would have been the wiser," Preston said, thinking out loud.

"Yeah, which is why I wanted you to hear about that. Carl was a complicated man. I can't say I trusted him completely, but I think he really appreciated the chance Abby gave him. In my opinion, he wouldn't have willingly messed that up for the world."

Preston took notes, then looked up. "As a businessman, what's your opinion about the ranch's financial situation? Can Sitting Tall Ranch weather the hard times ahead?"

Stan leaned back in his leather chair, a grim look on his face. "It's going to be hard for Abby to keep things running considering her current cash flow problems, but she has an option. If she wants out, I can always make some things happen for her."

"What do you mean?"

"I'm part of an area investment group and we've made her a good offer for the ranch. She stands to make a profit and though it won't be substantial, she'd have enough to relocate to another, smaller ranch."

"What did she say about that?" Preston asked.

"She refused to even consider the deal. She doesn't want to start over. To her, Sitting Tall Ranch is in the perfect location and she's determined to stay and fight, though I've warned her that she could end up losing everything. There's more working against her than the current criminal investigation."

"Like what?"

"My investment group is small but well connected, and although this is nothing but rumor at this point, word reached us that there's a large corporation interested in the land next to her ranch."

"What kind of corporation?" Preston asked.

"J&R Sports Paradise. Attorneys connected to them have been checking zoning requirements, asking for copies of traffic studies and checking utility services. I understand that they want to build one of their full-scale franchises here. That'll include an indoor and outdoor gun range, archery and even a motocross. All that activity next door to the ranch is bound to make the animals less stable and the parents of high-risk kids extremely nervous."

"So what was your investment group planning to do with Abby's land?"

"We've studied that company and know how it works. Once it buys the primary property, it'll target adjacent ones. Then the company will acquire allies in the local government and business community with the promise of more jobs and tax revenues, then move to rezone and even devalue adjacent properties. Our investment group can make sure we're in position to sell at the best possible price before politics force our hand."

"Abby can do the same."

"No, she doesn't have the resources to play that game. Closing this ranch and opening a new one is an expensive proposition. First, she'll have to find a suitable property, then there's the logistics of zoning, obtaining exotic animal permits and finding new donors. She'd also have the cost of housing the animals until she finds a new place. She could sell them, but it took her years to find the right ones. They're all temperament tested and were donations from patrons who wouldn't necessarily be there next time."

"Those are valid concerns. I can see why she'd prefer to fight it out here," Preston said.

"Personally, I think her reluctance goes deeper than that. To her, it's personal, not just business. She's put her heart into that ranch and can't bear the thought of walking away."

Preston exhaled softly. He wondered what part Bobby played in that. She loved that boy, and if she moved, she'd have to leave him behind.

"Thanks for your time, Stan," Preston said, standing up.

Preston left the office and drove directly to Daniel's place. His primary job was to find the killer, and it was possible this other threat to the ranch might have played a role in what had happened. He needed more information.

Preston arrived at Daniel's office on Hartley's west side forty minutes later. He stopped at the gate and seconds later was buzzed in.

Daniel's office was a large rectangular warehouse in the middle of a three-acre compound enclosed by a tall chain-link fence.

Daniel greeted him at the door of the main building. "Figured you'd show up around lunch, so I bought extra. Kyle's eyeing your plate now, so you better hurry."

Preston took a whiff as he stepped inside. "Mrs. Pinto's Navajo Tacos." As he entered the kitchen area of the big, open room, he saw Kyle lifting the lid on the only take-out dish that was still untouched. "Hands off, or I'll have to shoot you."

Kyle laughed. "Can't blame a guy for trying."

As Preston sat down, he glanced over at Daniel. "Anything yet on the background search?"

"Grab your plate and let's get to work," he said, leading the way to the main computer area. They pulled up chairs around the big, table-size flat monitor.

Sweeping his fingers across the display, Daniel transferred the information onto a large, split screen, wall-mounted monitor.

"So far they're all coming out clean. Ilse Sheridan has an MBA from State. She started out at an Ivy League school, but transferred after disciplinary issues that weren't specified. She's worked for Garner for three years, ever since he retired. Near as I can figure, she has no life. She relocates every time he buys a new house—his last one was in Santa Fe. Monroe Jenkins lives at home and is going to community college. Basically he's a B student and clean. So no dirt on the chief's son."

Preston nodded and swallowed his frustration along with a big helping of cheese, meat and tortilla.

"Since I couldn't find much on the other names, I decided to dig deeper into Carl Sinclair's past," Daniel said, removing the previous images and displaying Carl's prison photo and criminal record. "I even called in a favor or two and got one of the correction officers to give me some background. He said that at one point, the head of one of the prison gangs, a bad dude by the name of John Dietz, lost his good luck charm. He assumed someone had stolen it and ended up putting a few inmates in the prison infirmary. As it turned out Dietz had left it in his pants pocket. Carl, on laundry duty, found it and returned it to him. Carl was under Dietz's protection after that. No one messed with him."

"Sounds like Carl had some survival skills," Preston said.

"In prison, yeah, but he lasted less than three years after his release," Kyle said.

"Maybe I need to focus on his career as a thief. According to the reports I've read, everything said to have been stolen by him was eventually recovered, but there's another possibility I haven't been able to check out," Preston said. "What if Carl took paintings that were never reported missing because the victims of those thefts didn't have legal ownership?"

"Unreported crimes? Black market stuff? That's an interesting angle, but it sounds almost impossible to follow up on," Daniel said.

"Yeah, I know." Preston glanced at Kyle. "So what did you get from Jade at the coffee bar? Anything?"

"Well, I got her to talk to me, but I don't have anything you can use. She remembers a guy who comes in early in the morning and after work to sip coffee and use the Wi-Fi, but she said that's her busiest time of day. All she could tell me about him is that he's my size and wears a baseball cap low on his head and shades."

"Inside?" Preston asked.

"Yeah, I asked her that same question. She says that her paying customers can wear whatever they want. If they cause trouble, she takes care of it. Otherwise, as long as they place an order and mind their own business, she leaves them alone," Kyle said. "I'm having dinner with her tonight, so I'll let you know if she remembered anything else."

"You're having dinner with Jade?" Preston asked, surprised.

"Yeah."

Preston expelled his breath in a hiss, then turned his attention back to Dan. "Now I've got to figure out if Carl was somehow involved in the rash of burglaries we've been having all over town."

Daniel shook his head. "No chance. I've already checked into that for you. The nights the last two break-ins took place, Carl was at a fundraiser at the casino that showcased the camels. Celebrity and corporate bigwigs were offered a camel ride into the desert at one grand a pop. They raised twenty thousand that night, but that included a huge chunk from Rod Garner, who bought out half the rides. Getting those camels was one of the smartest things Abby ever did. They've allowed the ranch to stay in the black even through tough times."

Preston paced the room restlessly. "As Navajos we're taught that everything is part of a larger pattern, even good and evil. Falcon lets me see what others miss, but these events are impossible to piece together."

"That's because key elements are still coming to the surface," Kyle said.

"Someone's trying to scare Abby away from the ranch. That's a given. The rest is murky. There's a corporation interested in her land, but it would use their business connections and economic muscle—all legal. Why risk breaking the law by trying to scare her out?"

"*That's* what's really bothering you, bro," Daniel said. "This is your beat, and knowing that someone's threatening a woman right under your nose is making you crazy."

"It's more than that," Kyle said quietly, looking at Preston. "You really like this woman, don't you?"

"Okay, you've got me. I like her, probably more than I should," he admitted grudgingly. "Abby touches a lot of lives and makes a difference. I respect that. For instance, there's a kid who hangs around there, a Navajo boy named Bobby Neskahi. He's in foster care. Right now the ranch is his real lifeline."

"Speaking of Bobby, you asked me to check up on him," Daniel said. "I got some background, but it's all unofficial. I couldn't access anything that's under Child Services, and I didn't feel right hacking into those files."

"I can respect that," Preston said. "Show me what you have."

Daniel manipulated files and commands on the display surface and sent a new screen onto the wall monitor. "Bobby's mother died when he was three. He continued to live with his dad, but the man had a serious gambling problem—and one enemy too many. Neskahi Senior was shot in a fight after a private card game and had to be hospitalized. Bobby lived at home, by himself, for weeks because tribal services had no record of him. His dad finally called Child Services and gave up custody. It took a fight and a half to get the kid to go with them. He was sure his dad was coming back."

Bobby's stories about his dad the spy now made a lot more sense. Bobby had desperately needed to hold on to something that explained why he hadn't mattered enough to make his dad want to stick around.

"The woman on her own, a foster kid, that's almost *your* story," Kyle said.

Preston looked at Kyle, the only one of his brothers who'd come close to being able to read him, and nodded. "I understand both of them. Abby's committed to an ideal and Bobby's...trying to survive."

"Son of a gun," Daniel said. "Sounds like you're falling in love."

"No, I'm not the family type," Preston growled. "I like living solo and coming and going when I please. I'm married to my job."

"That'll soon come to an end," Daniel said with a grin. "The tough cop's getting soft."

"Wanna test that out?" Preston stood and faced Daniel. "Take off your weapon and come over here to the carpet. Let's see what you've got, bro."

Once they were away from the computer table, Preston tried to turn him around and pin his arms behind him, like he would a suspect. Daniel knew his moves, though, and stepped to the side, sweeping Preston's legs out from under him and sending him crashing to the carpet.

Preston was quick and grabbed Daniel's foot as it came by, knocking him down, too. They were rolling around try-

ing to pin each other when Kyle stopped laughing and whistled loudly.

"Cool it, guys. You've got a call, Preston. It's Abby."

Preston jumped to his feet and took the phone.

"Bobby spotted someone sneaking around the ranch," she
said. "The man's staying out of view so I can't see him right
now, but it looks like he's searching for something."

"Where are you now?"

"In my house with Bobby. Can you come over?"

"I'm on my way, and I'll call a patrol unit. You two make
sure the doors are locked and *stay inside*."

Preston ended the call, then requested a police unit as he
picked up his weapon and keys from the counter.

"Abby's got a prowler. I'm going over there," Preston said,
heading for the door.

"We've got your back," Daniel said, Kyle already a step
behind him.

"We may get there before the patrol car arrives," Preston
called out to his brothers. "I want the dirtbag in working order.
Other than that, it's whoever gets to him first."

Chapter Sixteen

Driving over in two vehicles, they took the truck bypass around Hartley and made it in twenty minutes. After verifying via phone that Abby and Bobby were okay, Preston coasted into the parking lot, engine turned off to avoid making noise. As Abby had said, no vehicles except hers were on the grounds and he could see no one in the immediate area. The volunteers wouldn't arrive until later, during feeding time, and with no kids on the premises, Michelle wasn't on the grounds either.

Preston's brothers had parked along the road. They were going to come onto the ranch via the west flank of the basically rectangular property. Preston moved in silently, using the buildings to screen his approach. They'd all agreed to give the suspect some room and see if they could figure out exactly what he was after before moving in.

Preston soon spotted a figure in the shadow of the barn. He watched as the person, a man, judging from his size and stride, slipped around the near corner and headed to Abby's hay truck, which was parked across from the barn.

"He's by the hay truck," Preston whispered into his phone to Daniel and Kyle.

Using the barn itself to screen him, Preston cut across the yard and reached the shadows where the man had stood only seconds earlier. Another fifty feet and he'd be close enough to recognize a face—if the person turned around.

When the man fished something out of his jacket pocket, Preston's muscles tightened. A small bottle with a rag hanging from it could be only one thing—a homemade fire bomb.

Preston stepped out of the shadow of the barn and called out. "Police officer! Place the bomb on the ground, then step away from it and get down on your knees."

The man, his face still hidden by the hoodie and sunglasses, set the bottle on the ground. Then, instead of doing as he'd been ordered, the guy cut around the truck and bolted north, racing down the row of outdoor enclosures.

Daniel broke radio silence. "We see him. Kyle and I will cut him off before he reaches the far end."

Preston remained in pursuit, narrowing the distance. Far ahead, he could see Daniel and Kyle climbing a corral fence at the north end. The intruder was caught in the middle.

Just then the man stopped, opened a stall gate and started yelling. The two horses inside spooked and ran out at full speed. Preston had to leap onto the fence and dive over the rails as the animals raced past him, snorting and bucking.

The suspect had reached the camels by then and threw open their gate. He started yelling again, but this time the animals held their heads up high into the air and just stared at him. The guy grabbed a lead rope draped over the fence and hit one, yelling as he did. Both camels thundered past him, racing toward Kyle and Daniel at the far end.

Going down the line, he spooked the animals in two more enclosures. Preston had to jump over the fence and into a turnout area to avoid being trampled again, and when he looked back, the intruder had disappeared.

As Kyle and Daniel worked their way up the fence line slowly, the animals began to calm down. Preston met his brother about halfway, talking softly as he passed each wild-eyed animal.

"Are you okay?" Daniel asked. "Those first two horses almost ran you down."

"Yeah, I'm just pissed off." Preston turned to look back at the ranch house and saw a uniformed officer coming up with Abby right behind him.

"I heard the animals going nuts. What happened?" She looked around and inhaled sharply. "Where are the rest of them?"

"The intruder opened the gates, then spooked them half to death. He used the confusion to get away," Preston said.

"I've got to get all of the animals back into their pens. They'll come to me, but if they're worked up and scared, they may be hard for anyone else to catch. I don't know if the gate out front is open or closed either, with all the coming and going. I need to keep them from wandering out onto the road and causing an accident or getting hurt."

"Where's Bobby now?" Preston asked.

"He's safe back at the house. The doors are locked," she said. "I've already called his foster mom and she'll be picking him up shortly."

"Give me your keys," he said. "Then call and tell Bobby that a uniformed officer is coming to meet him."

Preston looked at the officer and gave him the house keys. As the officer went to check on Bobby, Preston glanced at his brothers. "Stick around, guys."

"Sure thing. We'll search outside the grounds and herd any animals headed toward the highway back in this direction," Kyle said.

"The camels probably didn't go far," she answered. "They're a bit barn sour and don't like to leave a familiar place. Let me get some lead ropes, halters and treats to lure them in."

Once they reached the driveway, Preston studied the tracks. "The horses headed north, but the camels went west."

"We'll round up the horses," Daniel said. "We know how to handle them."

Abby gave them several halters and lead ropes, and they split up.

"I'm pretty sure I know where Hank and Eli went," she said. As they walked down the road in the opposite direction of the highway, she pointed straight ahead. "I walk them down that arroyo sometimes, and they feed on the brush. Once we spot them I'll get Hank. You take Eli."

"How will I be able to tell them apart?" Preston asked, noting the camel tracks led in the direction of the arroyo, as Abby had predicted.

"Eli's quieter. Hanks more vocal and likely to kick if he's angry or agitated. Considering a camel can kick in four directions, those feet are quite a weapon."

They left the highway and started walking up the wide ten-foot-deep wash, which was dry and sandy on the bottom at the moment. The camel tracks led down the meandering channel to a sharp right-hand curve.

Daniel called in a short time later and Preston put him on speaker. "We've gathered up three of the horses and can see two others back at the ranch, behind the barn. Guess they never got out."

"That's great," Abby said. "Which ones got out completely?"

"Well, one's Big Red and he knows me. I grabbed his mane, and I'm leading him in. The other two are following, and Kyle's back there with them. They're the oldest ones, I think."

"That'll be Missy and Tracker. They're very gentle and will just follow along," she said, loud enough for her voice to carry.

Before Daniel could answer, she heard a familiar squeak from around the curve.

"That sounds like a dog toy but out here?" Preston said.

She smiled and shook her head. "That's actually Hank's alarm call. I need to let him know it's me."

They hurried to the curve in the arroyo channel, and about a hundred feet ahead they could see the camels. Preston stopped as Abby moved closer to them.

"Hank, I've got treats," Abby called out. "Come on. Butterscotch ones! Time to go home." She stopped and waited.

Both camels came toward them, ambling down the sand-layered arroyo.

"That's a good boy," she said and held out the treats. "Let's go home, boys," she said, haltering both and giving Eli's lead rope to Preston.

"I feel like Lawrence of Arabia," he muttered.

"They're great here in the desert. Low maintenance compared to a horse and a lot gentler. Takes a lot to rile a camel, but once you do, they don't forget."

It took another hour to get all the animals back into their stalls and check to make sure none were injured.

"Since we've got the place to ourselves right now," Daniel told Abby, "I'd like to set up a couple of cameras. They won't feed into our monitors back at the office, but they'll record. The others can be put up later, but I think we need something for right now."

"That's fine," she said.

As Kyle and Daniel drove off in Kyle's pickup, Abby glanced back at the house. "Bobby's still inside the house and I bet he's scared, even with the officer there."

"Let me go," Preston said. "I'll release the patrolman and talk things over with Bobby until his foster parents pick him up. The boy did a real good job today, spotting the intruder like that."

As Preston headed back, Abby slipped into the camel pen to remove their halters. Feeling really down, she leaned against Hank, fighting the tears forming in her eyes. What was happening? Up to now, Sitting Tall Ranch had been a dream come true. She'd led an almost perfect life, giving kids time away from their challenges and becoming part of a community she'd learned to love. Now she couldn't even keep her own animals safe!

Hank made a soft gurgling noise, as if to comfort her. "I'm okay, Hank. I'm glad you are, too."

Abby went to the barn and hung the halters in the remodeled stall that served as their tack room. Hearing a sound behind her, she spun around, her heart at her throat. That's when she saw it was only Charley, the donkey, poking his head over the door of his stall.

Abby took a breath, but instead of calming down, she began to tremble, and no matter how hard she tried, she couldn't seem to stop. Leaning against the door of the tack room, she slid downward until she was in a sitting position, her arms around herself. She rocked herself silently for a moment or two, scarcely aware of what she was doing.

Abby wasn't sure how long she'd stayed there, but when she heard Preston calling her name, she wiped her face quickly and stood. "I'm over here, in the tack room."

Preston walked up, took one look at her and pulled her into his arms. "Today was a win, Abby. Sure, he got away, but we kept him from doing any harm."

"I usually don't fall to pieces like this, Preston, but I just don't know how to deal with what's happening."

"I do. Let me handle it."

"But I'm running out of time. I put everything I have into this ranch, and I can't lose it now. If I do, then Sandy..." She buried her head against his shoulder and said nothing more.

"What about Sandy?"

"One of the many things this ranch does is keep Sandy's memory alive for me," she whispered. "It was my way of affirming that her death brought about at least one good thing. If I lose it…"

"You won't lose the memory of your sister or of anyone you love. That's inside you, safe and sound," Preston said. "No matter what happens to this ranch tomorrow, next week or in thirty years, Abby, you've already won. You took your dream, made it real and shared it with a lot of kids."

"But I might not be able to hold on to Sitting Tall Ranch and that possibility terrifies me. It would be like losing a piece of my heart. I've tried to be strong, but…"

"Everyone can use a helping hand from time to time. That doesn't make you weak. It makes you human." He walked with her to the house, keeping her close to his side. "In fact, I've got a great idea. Let me move into the bunkhouse until the case is closed."

"No, the ranch is too dangerous now. I have to stay, but not you."

"I can handle danger. I'm a police officer and that's what I do," he said. "Falcon will be right there to help me, too."

"Is he one of your brothers?" she asked.

Preston smiled. "In a way," he said, going back into the house with her. "Falcon is my spiritual brother." He reached into his shirt and lifted the leather cord around his neck. A small pouch hung from it. He opened it and took out a black fetish carved out of jet. "This is Falcon, *Hosteen* Silver's gift to me. Its magic will protect you, too," he said, holding it in the palm of his hand.

"Tell me more about Falcon." She took the delicately carved bird, studied it for a moment, then returned it to him.

Abby watched him place it back carefully in the pouch as she waited. She wanted to know everything about this man who was so gentle with her, yet could become such a fierce protector the instant danger closed in.

"All but one of us—Paul—got the fetish on our sixteenth

birthday," he said, taking a seat on the sofa. "For me, my foster father chose Falcon because when my brothers fought, I'd be the one who stepped in to break it up."

"That sounds like a dangerous thing to do," she said.

"Nah, we knew each other's moves too well," he said, chuckling. "Sometimes I'd take a misplaced hit, but we never went all out with family."

"How does Falcon fit in with the role of peacemaker?"

"Falcon is about harmony and the value of hard work. Since he hunts close to the ground, Falcon focuses his searches and sees what others might miss. He shares that gift with me and that's helped make me a good detective."

"I wonder if I could get a falcon fetish for myself. If I can see trouble coming, it might help me get through this."

Preston shook his head. "Falcon's not right for you, but I think I know what would be a good match. I'll bring it to you."

"I'd love that, but I should be giving *you* a thank-you gift, not the other way around. You're even willing to stay in the bunkhouse and I know that wouldn't be easy for you. Beliefs like the *chindi* are part of your culture. You may not believe in it, but you still respect it."

"Yeah, I do," he said with a nod, "but as a cop, I've learned to work around it." He brushed the side of her face with his palm. "I'm needed here."

"I do need you," she whispered, then stood on tiptoes and brushed a gentle kiss on his lips.

It had only been meant as a tender expression of gratitude but his reaction was fierce and swift. He grabbed a fistful of her hair and pulled her to him.

A delicious fire coursed through her when he parted her lips and deepened the kiss. She didn't resist. Giving in to temptation, she melted into him as he lay back on the couch and pulled her over him.

With each heartbeat, his touch became rougher and his

kiss burned hotter. Then to her complete surprise, he eased his hold and helped her sit up.

Bewildered, it took her a moment to gather her wits. Taking a shaky breath, she looked into his eyes and saw the iron-willed control he held over himself.

"I'm sorry," she said, straightening her clothing and moving away from him. "You didn't start this, and I can see you don't want to…"

"I don't *want* to?" He laughed, a dark, edgy sound that sent its vibrations all through her. "I won't take more because you're not ready for what I have to offer." He stood. "Abby, you're a good person. You live in a world of light and hope, but my world's rough and dirty. I can't give you anything except moments, and you deserve more than that."

"I haven't asked for promises. I need your strength and you want…my softness. Why is that wrong? I know you have feelings for me. I can feel it in here," she said, pointing to her heart.

"I'm trying to protect you," he said, his face tense, his mouth set, "but I'm just a man. Don't push me."

"It doesn't seem I can," she said in an unsteady voice. "Maybe if I dressed differently—more feminine, showing myself off more…"

"Abby, I'm trying to give you a break. I want you. I care about you more than I should. You need to be protected— even from me."

"You want me…" She said it slowly, savoring the words.

"How could you doubt it?"

"Then just let go. *Show* me what you feel."

Her words broke his control and he hauled her into his arms. He kissed her roughly, crushing her lips and drinking her in.

She gasped as he left her mouth and rained kisses down the

column of her throat. His hand tangled into her hair, urging her head back and exposing her to more of his kisses.

With rough hands he worked her blouse open easily, then with the expertise of a man who'd been with many women, undid her bra in one fluid motion.

When he pressed his mouth to the tip of her breast, her knees almost buckled, but he held her against him, letting his touch burn into her.

She loved the feel of his calloused hands on her. To be wanted by this man who was all passion and courage…nothing could be better than that. Somehow she found herself braced against the wall as he removed the rest of her clothing, kissing all the areas he exposed.

Preston found her hidden places, and she whimpered helplessly as sensations too powerful to resist washed over her. That burning…that need…

"I can't stand up anymore," she said in a ragged voice. "I'm going to fall."

"Hold on to my shoulders," he said, tasting her until she came apart.

In one wonderful moment of pure pleasure, her world shattered. Too weak to stand, she would have fallen if he hadn't risen to his feet and held her tightly against him.

After several moments, her breathing evened.

"That's what's in my heart," he murmured.

When she looked into his eyes, she saw the fire that still raged inside him. "Stop holding back. Let go," she whispered. "I need to feel you inside me, taking and giving me everything."

He had no words. He was past thinking. He kissed her hard, his heart thundering.

Feeling her tug at his clothing with trembling hands, he helped her, shrugging out of his shirt and then unbuckling his belt. Every time her fingertips brushed his skin he grew harder and moved closer to the edge.

He could have taken her right there, but this was Abby. He wanted more. For her. For him. "Easy…" he murmured. "Bed?"

"Down the hall, to the left."

"To the pink bedroom?"

"Yes."

He lifted her into his arms and carried Abby to her room.

He set her down gently on the bed, but before he could lie next to her, she held her hand out. "Wait. Can I just look at you?"

"If that's what you want," he said, sucking in a breath as her gaze seared over him.

"Your tattoo?"

His laugh was a husky growl. He turned around to reveal that over the base of his spine was the word *Naalzheehi*.

"It means hunter," he said. "My brother Rick and I went out one night with Conner, a Special Forces buddy of ours. We came up with secret tribal war names for each other, like the *Diné* warriors of old. Conner's uncle took care of the tattoos as part of a ritual."

"The hunter…but why place it there?" she asked with a bemused smile.

"A war name is a source of power that must remain secret from all except those you trust. The spine symbolizes a man's strength. It seemed fitting."

She held out her arms to him, inviting him onto the bed. "Tonight, you're not a hunter…you're just…mine."

He lay over her, but she pushed him back gently, kissing him with infinite tenderness. Her caresses nearly broke him. No woman had ever treated him with this sweet care.

Abby didn't just leave a trail of moist kisses down his body—she loved him with each caress. Her touch was exquisite torture, and as she explored his body, trying to please him, fire coursed through his veins.

"No more," he said, sucking in a breath. Taking her in his arms, he rolled over, positioning her beneath him.

As he slipped inside her softness, he heard her gasp. Somehow he forced himself to slow down, but when her fingers dug into his buttocks and she arched up, he was lost.

He clamped his hands over hers and held her as he took her and finished what was meant to be.

His breathing evened slowly. He wasn't sure how long he'd lain on top of her when he finally shifted and gathered her against him. Seeing the dreamy and contented look on her face, he smiled.

"You were right," she said.

"About what?"

"Pink, you don't like the color, but it didn't matter."

He laughed. "I had more important things on my mind."

"Will you stay, even if I fall asleep?"

"Yes. Just close your eyes and listen to my heartbeat." He brushed a kiss over her forehead and held her.

HE WOKE UP hours later and watched her sleep. As a disposable kid and a cop, he'd seen too much of life to believe anything called love could ever last. Sure, Abby needed him now, but after harmony was restored, there'd be no room in her life for a cop. All he could bring to the mix was darkness.

Some things were just not meant to be. He tightened his hold on her. Happiness was elusive, and that meant you needed to live moment by moment.

This was as good as it got. For tonight, she was his.

Chapter Seventeen

Abby woke up in Preston's arms. They'd made love, rested, then made love again. Now it was close to dawn and her life, with all its demands, would soon call to her.

She stirred slightly and gazed at him. Though she'd fallen in love with Preston, she knew his feelings for her were more...complicated. He'd made love to her with his body but had kept at least a part of his heart out of her reach. That was something that might never change.

Yet no matter what, he'd still cared enough for her to risk his job, something she knew meant everything to him. The knowledge filled her with a fierce sense of protectiveness and love.

He opened his eyes. "Checking me out—again?"

She laughed. "I'm worried about you."

He laughed. "You destroyed me last night, but I think I can still function."

"That's not what I meant," she said, poking him in the ribs. "Be serious."

"I was," he said, laughing.

"Your superiors will be angry."

"I wasn't planning to tell them," Preston said.

"What if they find out?"

"I'll say you needed protection, and I volunteered."

"I can talk to the mayor if you get into trouble. He's one

of our biggest donors and he loves the ranch." She sat up and met his gaze. "If you have a problem, I'll help you. I promise."

"Stop worrying." He checked his watch and gave her a quick kiss. "I need to stop by my place and get a clean change of clothes, then I'll have to go by the station. I'll get Kyle to come over while I'm gone. One of us will be here from now on."

"If your brother says no—"

He kissed her again. "My brother won't say no to me. We're there for each other. End of story."

He got up, pulled on his jeans, then fished out his cell phone from his shirt pocket and dialed Kyle. "I need you at the ranch," he said. "I want round-the-clock protection for Abby." He listened to Kyle's response, then hung up. "All set. He'll be here in thirty."

"I'll make some coffee," she said, then realizing she was naked, tugged at the sheet.

He laughed. "You're shy now?"

"It's daylight."

"And?" he pressed.

"My body's not perfect."

"It is to me," he said, pulling the sheet away from her. "Just perfect."

She laughed, still self-conscious as his gaze took her in slowly and thoroughly. "Detective, we both work for a living, so we better get going. Behave." She reached for her robe, then hurried to the kitchen. "Eggs? Toast?"

"No, just juice and coffee."

He came into the kitchen moments later, phone to his ear. "Coffee?" he mouthed.

She handed him a cup, and he continued speaking to whomever was on the other line.

"I'll be in to question him shortly."

Preston placed the phone back in his shirt pocket, came

closer and parted her robe so he could gaze at her. "As I said, beautiful."

She felt her knees go weak.

"I have to go," he said, giving her a slow, deep kiss. "Think of me."

With that, he was gone. Abby leaned back against the counter and took a breath. It was like standing in the middle of a tornado. Everything around her was falling apart, but in the center, for a moment, there was love.

ABBY WAS OUT feeding the animals less than fifteen minutes later. It was seven in the morning and already she was running behind. Usually by this time she would have had at least two volunteers present but, today, no one was around.

After mucking out the llama and donkey stalls and feeding the animals, she heard a truck pulling up near the barn. She glanced over and saw Michelle.

"Where do you want me to start?" Michelle asked, hurrying over to meet her.

"I've gotten the llamas and donkeys taken care of, except for topping off their water troughs. The camels and horses are still waiting their turn."

Michelle looked around. "Where are the volunteers? It's summer. Monroe and a handful of kids should have been here by now."

"I know, but I suspect word got out that we had problems again yesterday," she said, updating her.

"I haven't seen or read the news, but reporters monitor police channels so I'm willing to bet that's how the story got out." Michelle took a deep breath. "I've been meaning to ask you something, Abby. Are you planning to sell the ranch? I saw Stan looking around the place a few days ago, and he told me he was working up an offer for you."

"Stan did make me a fair offer, but I'm not selling, Michelle. I'm making my stand here. The ranch and I obviously have enemies, but we still have a lot of friends."

As she glanced back at the house she saw Kyle. He appeared to be casually looking at the animals, but she knew he was here ready to help in case of trouble. Taking comfort from the thought, she got back to work.

PRESTON SAT AT the breakfast counter and sipped a strong cup of coffee. He'd stopped by his house to get some more clothes, passed by the station and was now at his brother Daniel's place.

"Paul says he's going to cut his honeymoon short and help us out," Daniel said.

Preston shook his head. "He shouldn't do that. He's been through enough and deserves time off. Tell him to stay put next time you hear from him."

"I will, but he may not listen. Gene's sticking around, too. He's still in the shower, I think. We're with you, bro. I also spoke to Rick last night via a video connection. He really wanted to come, too, but he can't swing it. He did say that he plans to be home in a few months, and this time he's going to stay," Daniel said.

"We all know he's in the FBI, currently overseas, but do you realize that you're the only one who has any idea what he does?"

"Yeah, but it's not like he confided in me. I found out by accident."

"How the heck did you do that?" Preston asked.

Daniel shook his head. "Can't say. I got a few calls afterward though. Glad I had DOD clearance."

Gene walked into the room shirtless, barefooted and holding a mug of steaming coffee. "This coffee will wake up the dead. By the time I finish, I'll be ready to work. Where do you need me today?"

Preston smiled. That was the thing about being one of *Hosteen* Silver's foster sons. You never had to ask for backup. It was there the moment trouble appeared, sometimes before.

"I'd like to toss some ideas around first. I still don't have a handle on this case. Someone wants Abby to shut down the ranch, but there's nothing there that's particularly valuable and worth all the trouble. All I've got is an admitted purchase offer from her accountant who wants to resell the property to a corporation that may or may not be coming to the area," he said. "Basically, I've got zip."

"All this time you've been searching for evidence linked to the murder, but let's try a different angle," Daniel said. "Let's look at the ranch through the eyes of the intruder. He wasn't after Abby, so where was he heading? We need to walk around those areas and see what's there."

"Good idea," Gene said.

"Let's go to the ranch and take a closer look." Preston stood and checked that he had his phone and weapon in place. "Time to go." Confidence high, he walked to the door. When *Hosteen's* boys came together, nothing stood in their way for long. Abby didn't realize it yet, but the best of the best were on her side.

PRESTON ARRIVED AT the ranch minutes ahead of Daniel and Gene. As he stepped out of the SUV he saw Kyle standing in the shade by the barn and tying knots with a lead rope. It was all very casual, but Preston knew it was his brother's way of standing guard without seeming to do so.

Seeing Abby in one of the empty stalls, Preston went to join her. "You've only got three helpers today?" he asked, glancing at Bobby, Monroe and Michelle, who were grooming horses.

She nodded, brushing hay off her sleeves, then fastening her hair into a ponytail. "Monroe just showed up, but he'll have to leave soon. The bad publicity is killing me, Preston.

Rod said he's going to free Ilse's time so she can come help more often, but I'm barely holding my own right now."

"Things will turn around soon," he said, resisting the urge to take her hand and reassure her with his touch.

Seeing Daniel and Gene walking up the sidewalk, Abby greeted them with a smile. "What's going on, guys?"

"We're going to join forces and figure out why someone's targeting the ranch. One possibility is that there's something here someone considers a threat or wants so much they're willing to kill to get it. We're going to look around and see what we can find," Preston said.

Bobby came around the corner of a stack of hay bales and walked over to join Preston. "I'm back now, so I can help you. I'll notice if anything's been added or taken away recently."

"Good idea. It'll give us an extra set of eyes familiar with the place. Come on then," Preston said, leading the way inside the barn storage areas.

"What's behind that closed door?" Gene asked, pointing.

"Leather bridles, tack, saddles, things like that," Abby said.

Preston tried the door handle. "It's not locked," he said, looking at Abby.

"It's not meant to be. We keep the leather in that room to keep it clean. A lot of hay and dust flies around when we're mucking out the stalls, and I like things in top condition and clean when we saddle up for the kids."

Preston opened the door and Bobby, standing beside him, sucked in his breath.

"My bridles!" Abby said. "He's cut them to pieces, and look at the cinches. They're ruined! We need this tack so the kids can ride. It took years to accumulate all this. Why does this person hate me so much?"

"I don't think it's personal, Abby," Preston said. "This is about making you miserable so you'll leave."

"But why?"

"Once we have the motive, we'll probably be able to ID the suspect," Preston said.

"We didn't put any of the cameras inside the barn, but there's one outside," Daniel said. "Let's see who came in and out of this building." He went outside and, after a moment, brought back a flash drive and attached it to his tablet PC. Unfortunately, once the nighttime images appeared, the subjects on the screen were much harder to see.

"I want to link to my computer, so I can enhance the images, but the Wi-Fi here is too weak," Daniel said.

"Let's go back to the office to view this," she suggested.

As they walked back, Preston remained beside her, and although it was killing him, he didn't touch her. He had to keep his mind on the job.

"The infrared images aren't sharp, but these cameras were quick and easy to hook up, and we needed something right away," Daniel said. "The cameras I plan to install next will have higher resolution."

Once inside her office, Daniel immediately accessed the video, and they all gathered around to watch, even Bobby.

"Those are all my people going in and out of the barn. Even when we can't see faces, I recognize them from their general build or the way they walk."

They continued watching the feed. They saw the animals being fed, then as nighttime descended, no more people were about. Eventually, they spotted a lone figure, in shades of white, gray and green, moving toward the barn. He looked behind him once, then slipped inside.

"The tack room door won't show from this camera angle so we won't be able to tell if he went inside that area or not," Daniel said.

"Play it back," Preston said and looked at Abby. "Can you tell who that is?"

"No. I can barely see him and that loose hoodie hides his build."

"I know who it is," Bobby said.

They all looked at him.

"I can't see his face," he added quickly, "but look how he moves his shoulder in a circle, like he's trying to work out some kinks. That's Monroe. I'm sure of it. He hurt his rotator cuff chopping firewood on a camping trip and it still bugs him. I've seen him do that lots of times."

"Wait a sec, guys," Abby said. "Monroe's the police chief's son. He's one of my hardest-working volunteers and he's always the last to leave. Just because he went into the barn after hours doesn't mean he vandalized the tack. He'd have no reason to do something like that."

"Monroe was here when we arrived. You think he's still here?" Preston asked.

"Probably. If I'm around, he usually lets me know before he takes off," Abby said.

"I need to talk to him," Preston said, remembering that Ilse and Monroe had been meeting on the sly.

"There's no way Monroe's responsible for what happened," Abby said. "Let me go with you and we'll both talk to him."

"No, this is police business." He could see the worry and fear in her eyes. Abby needed to believe that people were basically good and that right always prevailed. He'd been that way once, too—naive, trying to see the best in everyone. That had died the day his mother abandoned him.

Reality was a hard teacher. As a cop, he dealt with the worst in human nature almost every day and sometimes the good guys lost. That darkness had taken its toll on him, and bringing it into Abby's life could destroy the woman he loved. He had to solve this case quickly, then move on.

Chapter Eighteen

As Preston approached, Monroe was emptying the wheelbarrow into the compost pile. "A word," Preston said.

Monroe set the handles down and turned to face him. "Something wrong?"

"Why don't you tell me?" Preston said, his voice deadly.

Monroe took a step back, refusing to look him in the eye. His face was turning red, but Preston couldn't tell if it was anger, fear or embarrassment at the thought of getting caught. It didn't matter.

"There's no place for you to go, kid. Don't even think of running," Preston growled, shifting to the side and trapping Monroe between him and the pipe fencing.

"You know, don't you?" Monroe whispered. "One word of this gets out and my dad will go nuclear. That's why I couldn't tell you."

"Go on," Preston said, wondering where this was all going.

"Ilse is ten years older than me, but that woman's *hot*. The night Carl was killed we were both here late. She and I...well, it's not really serious, but we'd been messing around. We'd meet here sometimes after everyone else was gone and Abby had turned in. That night in particular I really needed to talk to Ilse. I got engaged to someone else after some heavy-duty pressure from my parents, and I wanted to give Ilse the news myself—basically end it."

"She never mentioned being here," Preston said.

"We agreed never to tell anyone about that night or our meetings here. She was just keeping her word. Besides, neither one of us saw or heard anything that could help you find Carl's killer."

"Who else was around that night?"

Monroe shook his head. "We didn't see anyone. We went into the hay barn, then spread a tarp on the ground and…said goodbye. After an hour or so we both went home."

"You saw her leave?"

"She was getting into her car as I left."

Preston nodded slowly, his gaze still on the kid. "So why did you sneak back in here last night?"

Preston saw the kid turn a shade paler.

"How…"

"Don't waste my time," Preston snapped.

"I got a text from Ilse asking me to meet her. I was afraid she'd get angry and tell someone else about us if I didn't come, so I hurried over. She never showed up. That's when I checked the text message again and realized it was an old one I'd forgotten to delete." He brought out his cell. "I guess I was hoping I'd be a little harder to forget."

Preston almost burst out laughing. The kid had moved on, but he still wanted Ilse pining for him. "Guy, she's out of your league. Chalk it up as a pleasant experience and let it go."

"Yeah, I know," he said, "but it's harder than it sounds."

Daniel joined Preston as Monroe walked away. "I heard."

Preston chuckled softly. "That poor kid. He still has a thing for Ilse, but the chief and his wife are making him go in another direction. Smart people."

"So what now?"

"Install those other cameras here as soon as possible. In the meantime, I need to talk to Abby."

"Be careful," Daniel said in a quiet voice.

Preston stopped in midstride. "What do you mean?"

"You're hard as nails—the one brother who never lowers his guard—but you're different around this woman."

He thought of denying it but then changed his mind. "Yeah, maybe so, but it's not a forever thing. I just want to make sure she wins this fight."

"We'll be right there with you every step of the way."

"Glad you said that, bro, because there's something I need you to do for me."

PRESTON STOPPED BY the station for the second time that day to check in with the lab people. After getting some updates, he realized that what the case needed now was legwork.

As he walked back to his SUV, he checked his watch. He wanted to run one personal errand before getting back to work. Abby's courage had been continually tested and she'd held her own, but there was one more thing he could do to help her fight.

Preston drove into town and parked at the curb in front of a small store on Second Street called Southwest Treasures. Pablo Ortiz, a short, rotund man with gray hair and an easy smile, greeted him from behind the old-style oak-and-glass counter. The Zuni man had carved the fetishes he and his brothers all wore.

"What brings you here today?" he asked as Preston searched beneath the glass, studying the array of small fetishes there.

"I'm looking for White Wolf," he said.

"That's a special fetish. It'll only fit someone who's willing to protect her territory and her family at any cost," Ortiz said.

"*Hosteen* Silver told us about it. It was the one worn by the only woman he ever loved," Preston said.

"This morning I finished polishing one I carved from white turquoise, a stone as rare as White Wolf herself."

Pablo brought it out and showed Preston the intricate carving. It had delicate features and showed a standing wolf, ready for the hunt. Courage and passion were evident in its pose.

"This is perfect. I'll take it."

Ortiz placed the small fetish in a medicine pouch but not before sprinkling it with corn pollen. "This will feed its spirit and keep it strong."

"Thank you, uncle," he said, using the title out of respect.

It was almost dinnertime and he was on his way back to his SUV when his phone rang. It was Abby. He picked it up quickly.

"Everything okay?" he asked.

"Yes. Daniel set up another camera by the house that'll feed into his computer. He'd planned to hook it up somewhere else, then decided I needed it here more," she said.

"I'm glad he was able to do that."

"I also wanted you to know that I've asked Kyle to give Bobby a ride home."

"So you're alone?" he asked quickly.

"Not completely, no. Michelle is around. She took one of the horses out on a training ride, but she'll be back in a while," she said. "I just needed a little time to myself, Preston," she said calmly. "I'll be here at the house and can call 911 if necessary. One of the new cameras your brother put up also monitors the area around the house. I'll be fine."

"I get where you're coming from," he said after a beat, "but I wish you hadn't done that."

After hanging up, he looked at the medicine pouch. He'd respect her need to be alone and catch up with her later. His brother's camera would let them know almost instantly if anything went wrong.

ABBY LOOKED AROUND the living room, enjoying the stillness of the moment. Realizing that she'd become afraid to be by herself, she'd intuitively known that she had to face that fear as quickly as possible. With precautions in place, she was glad for a little time to think things through.

She'd just sat down on the couch when she heard a knock at her door. She sighed. This had to have been the shortest alone time in history.

"It's me—Michelle. Do you have a second?"

Abby opened the door and invited her inside. "Hi, Michelle. How did the ride go? Any problems?"

"No, not at all. Big Red's a great mount. That horse has a kind spirit and does his best to protect his rider."

"So what's bothering you?" she asked, noting that Michelle seemed ill at ease.

"I'm going to have to cut the hours I'm spending at the ranch and get a part-time job elsewhere. I was hoping to hold my riding classes here and pick up some extra money, but I don't have enough kids signing up."

"Because you're teaching here?"

"Maybe. I don't know. I've stopped trying to figure things out, I just deal with what's in front of me," she said.

"That's actually really good advice," Abby said, "but if what you want is a steadier paycheck, I may be able to help. With Carl gone, I'm going to need a new head wrangler, and the animals here love you. Will you take his place? The pay isn't great, but you'll have lodging."

Her expression lit up instantly. "That would be terrific."

"It may be a week or two before you can start, though. We'll need to clear out the bunkhouse and Carl's office and that'll mean going through everything there. The police may want to monitor that process, so I'll have to ask."

"I can wait, and if you need help with all that, just let me know."

Michelle started heading to the door, then stopped and turned around. "You've helped me out several times, Abby, and I'd like to do something for you in return. I know you trust Detective Bowman, and you may even be falling for him, but I've heard some things about him that you need to know."

"Like what?"

"The man's in love with his job. That always comes first." She smiled. "And I'm in love with this ranch."

"It's more complicated than that. Your life here at the ranch, under ordinary circumstances, is a peaceful one, and that's one of the many things you love about it. Detective Bowman's a cop. He probably chose that job because of the promise of danger and excitement," she said. "Abby, face it—you two are as compatible as snow and summer sunshine."

"That's why he won't be around after the case is closed," she said softly. "I've known that from the start."

"It's already too late for warnings, isn't it?"

"I'll be fine," she said, walking Michelle outside and back to her pickup. "See you tomorrow."

As Michelle drove off, Abby glanced up at one of the new cameras. It was well hidden, mounted high underneath a roof overhang, melding into the afternoon shadows but pointed at the house and its immediate surroundings.

She was walking back, lost in thought, when she saw one of the horses pacing, head down. Afraid that the horse might have the beginnings of colic, she hurried over to his pen. A closer look told her that the animal wasn't sick. Abby glanced around, trying to figure out what was bothering him, and caught a glimpse of a shadowy figure going around the barn.

Afraid for her animals, Abby looked up at the camera, pointed ahead, then quietly headed toward the figure, cell phone in hand. Daniel, or whoever was monitoring the feed, would now know she was on the move, and on the way she'd call 911.

Unless her animals were threatened, she intended to stay behind cover, but she wanted to get a look at the person who was causing so many problems for her. Hopefully, it would turn out to be a stranger, not a traitor associated with her ranch.

Abby followed him as he headed past the pens and toward the shed just beyond the barn. Realizing he wasn't after her animals, she decided to stay well back and stopped near the bales of straw they'd eventually use for bedding. When he passed by on his way back out, she'd be able to see his face and still remain hidden.

Minutes ticked by. Soon she heard a car pulling up, tires crunching on the gravel. She turned around to see who it was, but her shoulder struck a bale and the thump gave away her position.

Before she could move away, the intruder jumped her from behind and tackled her to the ground.

Abby fought back, kicking and trying to turn her head around to get a look at his face. As he pushed her back to the ground, he scraped her forehead.

Stunned, she turned her face away. It had to have been a watch or a ring. She'd felt the pain of hard metal.

Hearing approaching footsteps, Abby cried out. "Help! Over here!"

Her attacker jumped up and disappeared around the corner.

Abby sat up slowly, touching the dampness of blood on her forehead.

Preston ran up just then. "You're hurt," he said, seeing the trickle of blood running down her face.

"I'm fine. Go! Hurry! The guy ducked around the side of the barn."

"I'LL BE BACK." As Preston ran over, he saw the back door of the hay storage area swinging shut, but no one was around. He raced down the front of the stalls, passing the animals at a sprint. Suddenly he struck something with his foot, tripped and hurtled facedown onto the ground with a thud.

He scrambled back up, anticipating an ambush, then spotted the rake the suspect had obviously tossed into the path. He'd been checking the stalls as he passed and had missed the handle in the darkness.

Spinning around, he looked for the suspect. None of the animals appeared unduly alarmed, and there was no movement on the other side of the grounds. The runner was gone, and he had no idea which direction to search. Maybe the man had doubled back.

Preston raced back to the other end of the barn. He had to make sure Abby was still safe. He turned the far corner and saw her still sitting there, holding a tissue to the cut on her forehead.

Before she could protest he lifted her into his arms. "I'm carrying you back to the house."

Chapter Nineteen

Under the bright lights of her kitchen, Preston cleaned and inspected the long but shallow cut just above Abby's brow. "It's a head wound so it's going to bleed a while, but it's not deep," he said, dabbing it with a damp paper towel.

Abby saw that his hands were shaking. Preston had a gentle heart, though he seldom let anyone see that side of him.

"I'm fine," she said. "If I hadn't been distracted, I might have been able to give you a better description of his face. All I can tell you for sure is that he was wearing some kind of weird makeup—green and black—in splotches."

"They sell that stuff for bow hunters nowadays to break up their facial patterns, but this guy isn't hunting deer. He's afraid of being recognized," Preston said.

Seeing that the cut had stopped bleeding, he finally took a deep breath. "I have to go back there and take a look around. I want to know what he was after."

"He was headed to the shed by the barn, but I keep it locked. It's not that there's anything of great value in there. I just don't want the kids inside. I have ant poison and things like that in there."

"This confirms my theory," Preston said. "The suspect's after something he believes is here at the ranch. He wants to run you out because he needs the freedom to roam at will and look for whatever it is. It also explains why he stayed around so long after killing Carl that night."

"He was still searching. I wish I knew what he's after. I'd cheerfully hand it over to him if he'd leave me and the ranch alone."

Preston grabbed a powerful fluorescent lantern she kept on the table. "I'm going to borrow this and look through the interior of the shed and barn."

"I'm going with you. Two pairs of eyes are better than one."

"Not necessary. I have Falcon's gift, remember?"

"Okay, let me rephrase—six pairs of eyes are better than four," she said.

He smiled. "Okay, let's go."

It was soon clear that the intruder had never made it inside the shed. Preston spotted a few deep marks on the door that told him he'd tried to break in. He looked for prints, but the ones he found on the knob were too smudged.

"What I still don't understand is how Carl's connected to this. Carl really cared about this ranch and its mission. He worked harder than anyone else except me."

"My gut tells me we need to focus on who he was before he came here. No one can outrun their past, Abby," he said. "Sometimes we fool ourselves into thinking we can, but it's always there, waiting for us around every corner."

"New beginnings are possible."

"Spoken like a person who has never tried to outrun something," he said.

"You're wrong. My past is filled with painful memories I wish I could leave behind, Preston. I haven't led a perfect life. You've put me on a pedestal, but I don't belong there. I've made plenty of mistakes, some that I've come to regret, and I've taken chances when I shouldn't have," she said. "But here's the thing—life goes by fast and if you spend too much time weighing all those what-ifs, you'll miss out on what's there in front of you," she said, reaching for his hand.

"Taking what's there can carry a high price...later," Preston said in a quiet voice.

"I know."

He took her into his arms and kissed her gently. "A cop's life—"

"Is perfect for you," she said, interrupting him. "You don't have to say anything else."

PRESTON SLEPT LIGHTLY and remained in the front room of her house that night. Close to dawn he got up and went outside to take a look around. He moved silently, melding into the twilight shadows. Everything appeared peaceful, but he knew in his gut that was only temporary. A storm waited in the wings.

As he headed back to the house, he heard a vehicle, then saw Kyle pulling in. His brother came over and handed him one of two cardboard cups with lids.

"I was going to down both coffees, but you look like you need some just as much as I do," Kyle said.

"You've got that right. I was up most of the night going over Carl's case file. I've given up on the idea that Carl's murder was an unpremeditated attack by a local enemy of his," Preston said. "The more I dig into the vic's past, the more gaps I find in his history."

"Like what?"

"Carl claimed he worked solo, but there's no way he could have pulled off some of those heists by himself. The one in Denver especially caught my eye. No alarm was triggered, something only possible if two wires, in two separate locations, were cut at almost the same time. I called the investigating officer. He said that Carl had no known associates, and although he was certain Carl had worked with an accomplice, they were never able to get him to change his story."

"Maybe he partnered up with his fence or had an insider who helped him out," Kyle said.

"Taking it from there, what if that person knew Carl had held on to some of the merchandise instead of splitting the take? That would explain all the searches," Preston said.

"Yeah, and Carl's partner would have been ticked off about losing his share."

"Anger would also explain getting beat up as opposed to shot. The killer came wanting answers. Of course now that Carl's dead, his logical next step is finding what Carl did with the stuff."

"Makes sense," Kyle said.

"The problem is that it's all conjecture. I've got nothing except the murder of a thief and some unexplained searches."

"There's a lot of ground to cover on this ranch." Kyle took a breath and looked around. "It could be anywhere, even buried along the fence someplace."

Preston shook his head. "No. Concentrate on the man. Everything we know about Carl tells us he was careful and paid attention to the smallest details. He would have wanted to keep stolen paintings safe and someplace he could monitor them."

"Yeah, you're right, but where do we begin?"

"Let's go take a second look at the bunkhouse and Carl's office in the barn. Focus only on places where he might have hidden a valuable painting."

Preston and Kyle had begun looking in Carl's office when Abby came in.

"I'm glad you're taking one last look around," she said. "I've promised Michelle the job of head wrangler, and that means I'll have to clear out all of Carl's things." She looked at the charcoal sketch to her right. "I'm going to keep his southwest landscapes, though."

Preston studied the drawing closest to her. "I recognize that place, but it's not laid out right." He took a closer look. "That rock formation is on the road to Shiprock, on the right-hand side, and past Kirtland, but the sketch is reversed. We're actually viewing it from behind."

"Yeah, you're right," Kyle said. "Interesting perspective."

"Something else, too," Preston said. "I remember seeing a charcoal sketch similar to this one in Stan Cooper's office."

"I know the one you're talking about, but that's not one of Carl's," Abby said. "Stan's painting is by Burt Yancy, a well-known southwest artist. Maybe that's why Carl painted it this way, so it would have his own mark."

Preston nodded but didn't say anything at first. At long last he lifted it off the hook. "It's kinda heavy considering there's no glass and the frame's just cheap plastic," he said. "I'm going to take the sketch out of this and see if there's something special about the paper."

Preston undid the back and removed the plain cardboard backing. "It's ordinary drawing paper."

"He liked to sketch, but he wasn't rich," Abby said. "You buy that stuff by the tablet, I think."

Preston remained silent. He was sure there was something he wasn't seeing—yet.

He closed his eyes for a moment, like *Hosteen* Silver had taught him to do, and concentrated, calling on Falcon to help him.

A moment later he opened his eyes. Setting the sketch aside, he examined the backing for several seconds. "Carl slit this cardboard in half, then glued it back together around the outside. There's something sandwiched inside there."

Preston worked the two layers apart carefully and pulled out another painting, an oil depicting a rodeo scene. "This one's by Whit McCabe. I don't know much about art, but I've heard that name."

"He dates back to the early 1900s," Abby said. "We studied

him in school. 'Rodeo' isn't his most popular painting, but if it's authentic, I bet that painting would bring in six figures."

"Okay, so why wasn't this ever reported as stolen?" Preston asked, lost in thought. "Then again, maybe it was, and after the insurance was collected, the case faded into the background. Art's not my specialty."

"Daniel could do a fast background check on it," Kyle said, texting Daniel and sending him a photo of the painting. "There's got to be a sales record for anything that valuable."

"I have a feeling that this is what the intruder has been looking for all along and why he's been tearing this place apart," Preston said. "Carl hid it well. It was easy to overlook. We did, even after taking it out of the frame."

"Once the news about this painting spreads, the killer won't have reason to come back here and I won't have to worry anymore."

"Not necessarily. What if—" Kyle started to say more but then clamped his mouth shut when he saw Preston shake his head, then gesture for them to meet him outside.

"Ask Daniel to come over, Kyle," he said once they were out on the sidewalk. "I want to have this place swept for bugs. The killer, probably someone who spends time here, knew Carl had something he wanted. It's possible he kept his eyes—and ears—on Carl before making his move. I would have if I were in his shoes." He looked at Abby. "I'd like to have Carl's office, bunkhouse and even your place checked for electronic listening devices. Are you okay with that, Abby?"

She nodded. "If you find something, will you be able to track it back to the killer?"

"I hope so," Preston answered.

"Do you think there are other paintings still hidden here?" She glanced at Kyle, remembering what he'd started to say, then looked back at Preston.

"It's a possibility," Preston answered.

She swallowed hard and gestured to the pickup and small sedan just pulling into the parking lot. "That's Stan in the truck and Bobby in the sedan," she said. "I should go."

"Take care of whatever you need. I'll handle things here and let you know if anything new comes up."

ABBY WALKED AWAY from Preston quickly. She'd barely held it together, and she didn't want him to see her fall apart. If everything they'd said about Carl was right, then she was at least partially responsible for the trouble the ranch was in. After all, she'd hired him.

Abby took a deep steadying breath and forced a smile as she greeted Bobby and Stan.

"Stan, what brings you here so early?" He was wearing his suit and bolo tie, so she knew he hadn't come to volunteer tending the animals. "More bad news?"

"Yeah, Abby, I'm afraid so. I went over the accounts and we need to talk."

"All right," she said, wondering how many hits a person could take and still remain standing. As she glanced over at Bobby and saw his shaky smile, she knew the answer. She would never give up.

"Let's see what the bad news is and how we can turn it around," she said, leading the way to her office.

Bobby took her hand and smiled.

"Have you had breakfast, Bobby?" she asked, knowing he tended to skip it altogether if his foster father was in a rush to get going. That's why she kept cereal and milk in the office fridge.

He shook his head. "But it's okay. I'm not hungry."

"Go to the kitchen and pour yourself a bowl of cereal anyway while Stan and I talk."

As Bobby left, Abby offered Stan a seat on the chair across from her desk.

"I made all the payments this month and checked to make sure everything went through. After I finished, I took a closer look at your cash reserves. You're in trouble, Abby. Your operating funds are lower than they've been since opening day at Sitting Tall Ranch. Painting the buildings and buying hay for the rest of the year took a chunk out of your account."

"Donations slow down in the summer and pick up in the fall. That's the way it always is."

Stan shook his head. "It's more than that, and you know it. Word's out that J&R Sports Paradise is going to buy the empty acreage next to yours. The Double T ranch is already planning to add their land to that deal rather than get a lower offer later on. If those acquisitions go through and you won't take J&R's offer, things are going to get real tough."

"I know," she said.

"J&R will go to court to have this entire area rezoned, shutting you down. They have the resources and political clout to make that happen. Your best option is to preempt that by selling out now to my investment group. That's the only way you'll have enough money to relocate. Try to fight this in court, and even if you win, the legal costs will bleed this ranch dry. You could lose everything."

"That'll never happen," she said. "This ranch has friends, too. I intend to fight."

"At least raise enough money to lawyer up. Sell some of the animals, maybe the llamas and the camels. That could buy you some good legal representation when J&R starts to get ugly."

"Those animals were donations to this ranch. I can't do that."

"Yes, you can. It's business, and it'll help you raise some cash *and* cut down on your overhead. The camels, in particular, could bring in a decent sum. There are recreation parks and zoos that would appreciate camels with training."

She swallowed hard, but not trusting her voice, she remained silent.

"You need to save what you've got, Abby. Think about it, okay?"

She walked him to the door without saying a word. Everything had gone so wrong, so fast.

After Stan left, she closed the door behind him and slumped back against it. "Don't the good guys ever win anymore?" she whispered to the empty room.

"Sure they do," Bobby said, coming in.

She straightened up immediately. "Bobby, I thought you were having breakfast."

"I was, but you and Mr. Cooper weren't whispering, so I heard what he told you," he said. "I figured you needed a friend right now."

"Bobby, listen to me. You can't tell anyone what you heard, okay? I'm not sure what I'm going to do, but I'll make things work. When I first began talking to people and asking for funds, a lot of them refused to believe Sitting Tall Ranch could ever be more than a dream." With a smile and a shrug, she added, "Sometimes you just have to follow your heart."

"I won't say anything, Abby, but you really need a rich friend, someone who can help you keep this place alive."

She smiled at him and shook her head. "The ranch can always use donors, but I'll never pick friends based on how much money they have. That's not a good way to measure someone's real worth."

Bobby thought it over, then nodded.

"Why don't you go help Michelle with the animals?" she said, then added, "Lock the door on your way out."

"Okay, Abby," he said, and left.

PRESTON MET DANIEL over by the ranch's bunkhouse, but an ingrained caution kept him glancing back in the opposite direction. He saw Stan leave Abby's office first, then Bobby came out minutes later.

"Did you hear what I just said?" Daniel asked.

"Yeah, you want to know why I didn't call the department and ask them to sweep the place," Preston said, focusing on his brother. "The reason I didn't is because I'm trying to avoid leaks to the press. That would just complicate things right now."

"I hear you. My equipment's a generation ahead of the P.D.'s anyway," he said with a quick grin.

"Our budget these days is nearly nonexistent," Preston said. "Here comes Bobby. Watch what you say around him. He's a sharp kid."

Bobby approached Preston a moment later. "Can we talk?"

"Sure," Preston said, leading him away from Daniel.

"It's about Abby. She's in trouble."

"What's going on?" Preston asked quickly.

Bobby started to say something, then shook his head. "I can't say, I promised, but I overheard some stuff. Maybe she'll tell you."

"Okay, I'll go talk to her," Preston said.

"Good. I have to help Michelle right now. Looks like I'm the only volunteer who shows up early these days."

Preston told Daniel where he'd be, then went back to the ranch's office. The door was partially open, so he didn't bother to knock.

Abby wasn't in the main room, so he went to the kitchen. What he saw blasted a hole through his gut. Abby was sitting at the table and crying softly.

"Abby, what's wrong?" he asked, pulling her into his arms.

"No one's supposed to see me like this," she said. Taking a breath, she stepped back and quickly wiped the tears from her face. "Didn't Bobby close the door?" She smiled. "No, of course he didn't, the little sneak. He went looking for you, didn't he?"

"He's a smart kid and he's totally loyal to you, as I am. Now tell me what happened."

"So he didn't tell you?"

"He said he'd promised you that he wouldn't."

Abby nodded, then with a trace of reluctance, told him what Stan had said. "It scares me, Preston, but I'm not going to sell the animals or the ranch. If I can't fix things here, that failure will hang over me like a cloud, and that'll keep me from ever getting the backing I'll need to start over. I have to make my stand here." She took a deep breath, then let it out slowly. "Sometimes you just have to go for it and be willing to accept the consequences if things don't pan out."

"No matter what it takes, I won't stop until the killer's behind bars," he said, tilting her head up and meeting her eyes. "You've got my word."

"I'll do all I can to help you," she said, straightening her shoulders. "No more falling apart."

He wanted to hold her but knew that wasn't what she needed from him right now. "Abby, you've got courage, but you need a little help. Remember when we spoke about fetishes?"

She nodded. "You said Falcon was wrong for me, but you knew the right one."

He reached into his pocket and brought out the small leather pouch. "Open it."

As she held the tiny carved figure of White Wolf, he saw her expression change from weary determination to fascination. She'd opened her heart to him, and now the beliefs that had always given him strength were helping her.

Somewhere along the way he'd fallen hard for Abby, and the connection between them was as real as the White Wolf fetish she held in her hands. Leaving her would tear him apart, but when the time came, he'd do what had to be done. He wouldn't allow the darkness of his world to cast its shadow over hers.

"It's so beautiful," she said softly. "Tell me more about Wolf."

"White Wolf. This fetish is for those who think with their hearts. She's all about loyalty, protectiveness, caring and love. She bestows insight."

"What an incredible, precious gift."

"White Wolf is now your spiritual sister. When you feel hemmed in by circumstances beyond your control, clear your mind and think about White Wolf, then see what ideas come to you."

"I will." She wrapped her arms around his neck and kissed him gently. "I'll carry this with me always, and every time I look at it, you'll be there in my thoughts."

Before he could answer, they both heard a light knock on the door. Turning, they saw Daniel walk in.

"I've got some bad news," he said, motioning them toward the door.

Chapter Twenty

As soon as they left her office, Daniel held out a small device in the palm of his hand. "We found a half dozen of these in the bunkhouse and the office. They're cheap RF models but effective. They're easily available, too, if you know where to look."

"RF?" Abby asked.

"Radio frequency. These are listening devices that send conversations to a radio receiver within range," Preston said.

"So I've been bugged. Can the person on the other end still hear us?" she asked in an almost whisper.

"No. I've disabled these," Daniel said, "but you might have more in your office and in the house. I'd like to check."

Her eyes widened. "Please do!"

Daniel went through her office, then her house. After he was done, he joined them and showed them the four small listening devices he'd found. "The two in the ranch office were on or around your desk. The ones in your home were on your portable phones."

"This would explain how our moves were second-guessed from the very beginning. I thought it was the reporter's fault, but I may have been wrong about that," Preston said.

"Kyle also found out something interesting about the painting by Whit McCabe," Daniel said. "While I was sweeping the buildings, Kyle used my computer and did a search. 'The Rodeo' disappeared ten years ago from a private collector's gallery. That's before Carl went to prison. It was insured for six figures. Selling something high profile like that to a legitimate gallery or collector would have been impossible, of course, and on the black market it would have only commanded a fraction of its worth."

"So maybe Carl was biding his time, looking for just the right buyer," Preston said.

"That doesn't sound like Carl, but I'll tell you what does—and this is something you need to keep in mind," Abby said. "If someone was keeping tabs on Carl, he would have known. Carl was always on his guard. He was the only person Bobby never could sneak up on."

"Maybe he found the bugs but left them in place, deliberately misleading whoever was listening in. Inmates learn a lot of survival skills in prison, so that makes sense," Preston said. "But here's something else—he didn't run. That tells me he wasn't afraid for his life. Carl may have had something he felt would keep his ex-partner at bay—leverage of sorts. He wasn't concerned when his killer came calling because he was counting on something else to protect him—a bargaining chip, information that could lead to a bigger payoff or penalty."

"Then why didn't he use it to save his life?" Abby asked.

"Remember that Carl was beaten to death. Rage often overwhelms logic," Preston said.

"So we're now looking for something else he hid in the office?" Abby asked.

"Yes, but this time it wouldn't be something he needed to safeguard in the same way he did the painting. We're talking information of some kind—notes, a letter, something his partner would have really wanted or feared. And it's bound to be in a place that's meant to be overlooked."

"Can I help?" Bobby asked.

Abby jumped and turned around quickly. "Bobby, I'm going to have to put a bell around your neck."

Preston smiled. "I knew you were there."

"Yeah, I know," Bobby said. "I saw you glance out of the corner of your eye. Spies do that."

Preston smiled. "You're good spotting little details, Bobby, so come along with us."

Daniel and Kyle followed Preston and Bobby into the barn and stopped to look through the open door of Carl's small office. Visible were a filing cabinet, an old desk and chair, an ancient rotary phone and a few shelves with business papers. "You're the one who has the eyes for things like this, Preston," Daniel said.

Preston nodded. "I'd like to focus on the ordinary at first, like floorboards that aren't flush, trim that's loose, gaps between objects. Concentrate on potential hiding places."

As they all started searching, Preston got down on the floor and worked his way slowly toward the old wooden desk. He was looking for changes in elevation, but as he shifted to one side, the bottom of Carl's chair caught his eye. There was a tiny slit in the cushion.

"I've got something, but it might just be a sign of wear on an old chair." He studied the slit at the inside end of the cushion. The diagonal cut disappeared beneath the back of the chair.

With Daniel's help, Preston loosened the metal post that held the two parts in place and removed the back rest, which slid into a metal bracket. The slit, easily visible now, was longer than he'd realized. Part of it had been hidden by the mechanism.

Preston reached inside with a gloved hand. "I've got something." A moment later he pulled out a small spiral notebook.

"Cool," Bobby said.

"Do you recognize Carl's writing?" he asked Bobby as he opened the notebook.

Bobby nodded.

Preston took a closer look at what was written inside. The first section, a total of maybe five pages, was easy to read, but then the words stopped and gave way to what was clearly a number-based code. "Can you make this out?" he asked Daniel.

He looked at it and expelled his breath in a hiss. "I've got some decryption programs I can run it through," he said. "It's probably some number-for-letter substitution code."

"Can I see?" Bobby asked.

When Preston showed it to him, Bobby smiled. "He and I came up with this code. We'd leave notes for each other, spy-craft, you know? I told you that when I meet my dad some-day—"

Preston stopped him gently. "*How* do you decode this?"

"Simple. The letter A is 26 and B is 25, all the way down to Z, which is one. So Bobby would be 25-12-25-25-2. Get it?"

"I'll program the decryption and it can translate the numbers automatically for us," Daniel said. He tried to use his smart phone but after a moment looked up. "I'm not getting a connection from here."

"That's why Carl used the old-school landline," Abby said. "Let's go to my office. You'll have a reliable Wi-Fi connection there."

Five minutes later Daniel had decoded the first section. "Here's a quick rundown of what I've got so far. Right before the police caught up to him, Carl had a falling-out with his partner. The guy discovered that Carl hadn't been splitting the take fifty-fifty and was out for blood, so once Carl left prison, he changed his name and went into hiding. Carl figured that one day the guy would track him down, so he kept a few things in reserve in case he needed money to run."

"So Carl hadn't really turned his life around," Abby said softly.

"Yes and no," Daniel said. "He wasn't a thief anymore, but

he also needed to survive. That took priority over returning what he'd taken."

"So who *was* his partner?" Preston asked.

"The journal never mentions anyone, including Carl himself by name. I'm guessing that was his way of remaining anonymous in case it was found prematurely."

"It also protected Bobby, too, in the off chance he might have found it during one of the games they played," Abby said. "Carl knew Bobby had a good eye." She looked over at Bobby, who nodded solemnly.

"There's a second part here, too, but it uses a different code entirely," Daniel said. "I'm guessing that section will reveal which pieces of art Carl held on to and maybe where he stashed them. My computer's trying to decrypt it now, but it may take time, depending on how complex the code is."

"I bet I can figure it out," Bobby said. "I know how Carl's brain worked. He and I used to play spy all the time and make up all kinds of ciphers. We'd pretend that we were CIA field officers and needed help from our agents," Bobby said. In a sad voice, he added, "I'll miss him."

Preston looked at Bobby for a second, then making up his mind, added, "Bobby, give me your cell phone."

He pulled it out of his pocket and turned it over to Preston.

Preston found the camera app, then, taking the notebook from Daniel, took photos of the relevant pages. "I'm trusting you with this, Bobby, but I need your word you won't tell *anyone* that you're helping the police. That has to be top secret. Will you agree to the terms?"

Bobby nodded. "Yeah, and you can trust me. Just ask Abby."

"I don't have to, I trust *you*."

Bobby beamed him a smile. "I'll crack it, probably faster than the computer because it didn't know Carl. To really solve a puzzle or break a code you need to think like the person who made it up. That's what Angus McAdams said in his book *Spycraft*. Of course, that's not the author's real name. He had to keep his real identity hidden."

Preston glanced at Abby, Daniel and Bobby. "The existence of this journal has to stay between us for now. That way there'll be zero chance that the information will be leaked to the press. As long as Carl's partner doesn't know we have this, we have the advantage."

"But Carl didn't give us any names," Abby said. "We have no way of identifying this person."

"Carl obviously committed most of his thefts in Denver and on the West Coast, but he may have started his life of crime here in Hartley. What if he formed his partnership here at the very beginning? None of the other investigators have been able to find that person, but maybe they've been looking in the wrong place," Preston said. "The first thing we need to do is find out who Carl's associates were before he left for the big city and track their movements. Perhaps one of them has recently moved back here, from Denver or one of the other cities where Carl operated."

"You're looking for an old buddy of Carl's, maybe a criminal who never got caught?" Abby said.

Bobby looked at them. "You should talk to Mrs. Whitcomb. She came to our school to tell us about the old days. She's lived here forever, and Mr. Whitcomb was a famous lawman. He was the only sheriff around for like a hundred miles."

"Sadie Whitcomb—I know her," Abby said. "She doesn't have a lot of money, but once a month, like clockwork, she sends us a small check. I'm sure she'll help us." Abby smiled. "But I should warn you she's quite a character. Unless she knows you, she won't open her door. She'll just pretend she's not home. She's close to a hundred so you won't be able to use your badge to push her either."

"How's her memory?" Preston asked.

"For what happened two days ago, not so good, but forty years ago, that's like yesterday. She can remember details that'll amaze you. I invite her to the ranch from time to time so she can look around and have some fun. She's just amazing."

"Where does she live?"

"Down the same road as Meadow Park."

"The retirement community? That's about ten miles from here," Preston confirmed. "Let's go."

As they left the office and walked to his SUV, Preston glanced off in the direction of the barns. "Ilse sure gets around."

Abby saw Ilse laugh and then give Stan a quick kiss. "Don't see too much in that. Ilse likes men and she's single," she said and shrugged. "Deep down she's got a good heart. She volunteers here a lot."

Preston watched them for a second longer, then climbed into his SUV. "They look like old friends having fun."

"They probably are friends. Both of them spend a lot of time working here."

Preston followed Abby's directions to a small *casita* surrounded by fruit trees a quarter mile off the main highway. A chain-link fence bordered the property. The small front yard, probably a lawn at one time, was mostly gravel now. Two cats were watching them from a bench atop the small porch.

Abby led the way, but as they stepped onto the porch, Sadie opened the door. "I saw you pull up, Abby. Did you come for a donation? I read in the paper about all the troubles you've been having."

Sadie invited them to take a seat on the sofa and after hearing what they wanted, she nodded. "I can help you. I knew Carl Sinclair when he was just a kid, and even back then I can tell you he was always up to no good." She looked directly at Abby. "I'm so sorry that I never took a closer look at Carl Woods. If I had, I could have warned you, Abby."

"It wasn't your fault. I knew about his past, but I believed him when he told me he'd changed," Abby said.

"His kind doesn't change," she said, leaning back in her chair. "My husband, Jeremiah, was the county sheriff back then, and he kept a close eye on troublemakers like Carl."

"Did he ever actually arrest him?" Abby asked.

"No, he never could get anything on him or his buddy, another troublemaker Jeremiah couldn't abide. When several Whit McCabe paintings were stolen from a collector here in town, Jeremiah was sure Carl and his friend were responsible because Carl had worked for the man at one time. Jeremiah tried hard to find something to tie them to the theft but couldn't. Then the owner of the stolen paintings passed on, and his son wasn't interested in art. He settled for the insurance money and auctioned off the rest of his dad's collection. There weren't any other suspects, so I think the insurance company stopped looking after that."

"Did your husband ever mention Carl's partner by name?" Preston asked.

"All I remember is that Jeremiah called him 'The Liquidator.' From the bits and pieces he told me about, the man dealt in stolen property, but he also knew how to cover his tracks. He never flaunted his wealth, and when he wasn't traveling, he spent his time at a small cabin just this side of Navajo Dam," she said. "He died in a hunting accident a few years before my husband passed. Guess he didn't have any living relatives because no one ever claimed the body." She paused. "Come to think of it, his cabin is probably still up there above the lake. I suppose you could go take a look."

"Do you know where it is?" Preston asked.

"Only that it's northwest of Navajo Dam, off the main road. Jeremiah mentioned that you had to go past a cliff with two large rocks that looked like fangs at its base. There was a gully and a dirt road that led up the hill. You couldn't see the cabin from the highway, I recall him saying."

"I'm not sure if that's going to be enough to find the place," Abby said.

"I camped out in that area when I was in high school, and we drove up that highway a dozen or more times. Believe it or not, I know the cliff that she referred to. *Hosteen* Silver said they were *Tsé Íi'áhí,* like the two Churchrock Spires east of Gallup," Preston said.

"Spires, I get, but I don't speak Navajo, dear," Sadie said. "What does that word mean in English?"

"Sorry, ma'am. Loosely, it means 'standing rock,'" he said, turning to Abby and nodding. "If those rocks are still within sight of the road, we'll find them."

Chapter Twenty-One

The drive took them through the town of Bloomfield, then past the small community of Blanco. Preston kept glancing in the rearview mirror.

"Hang on," he said, then suddenly braked hard and took a sharp left down a farm road.

Abby hung on to the door handle to balance herself in her seat. "What are you doing? We're not even close to the dam!"

"There was a dark green vehicle back there. He was hanging way back, so I'm not really sure it was a tail, but I saw it after we left Sadie's." Preston stopped and looked back into the mirror again. "He's gone now."

"So what do we do now?"

"Wait five minutes, then continue our drive. Keep a watch for green vehicles parked by the highway, in case he's hoping to pick us up again," Preston said. "I couldn't really tell if it was a van or an SUV, but I am sure of the color."

Eventually they got back on the road, crossed the massive rock and earthen dam and entered the pine-covered hills above, leaving the big canyon behind. They drove along the highway just under the speed limit, not wanting to miss any of the landmarks. Preston took a wide curve, and off to their left he spotted the low sandstone cliff with the two rocks at the bottom.

"Tsé łí'áhí." Preston nodded in that direction. "Smaller than I remember, though."

"Pointy and like fangs," Abby said. "Sadie was right."

They continued around the long curve and as they rounded the bend, he saw a dark green SUV pulling off the shoulder and onto the highway. It passed by, heading in the opposite direction. The driver had his head turned away, and Preston couldn't get a clear look.

"Is that the same SUV you saw before?" she asked.

"I'm not sure," he said.

With no oncoming cars, he was able to do a one-eighty on the highway and parked along the shoulder where the SUV had been moments earlier. A three-wire cattle fence was in place on both sides of the road.

"The ground is soft, and it won't be an easy hike, but it looks like we have to walk from here," Preston said.

"Good thing I'm wearing boots," she said.

They'd hiked about twenty feet up the wash when Preston noticed something on the ground up ahead. "Footprints. Maybe the person in the van came this way, too."

"Call of nature?" Abby asked.

He sniffed the air and glanced around. "Naw, I smell… gasoline?" Up ahead he saw a thin curl of black smoke rising into the air just around the curve of the arroyo.

"Campfire?"

"Not with gasoline," he said and handed Abby his keys. "Go back and get the fire extinguisher out of my unit. Hurry."

As Preston raced up the slope, he noticed the increasingly strong smell of burning wood and gasoline. About a hundred feet up, the ground evened out and Preston saw an old, sturdy-looking log cabin about fifty feet ahead. Its roof was mostly intact, but one side of the cabin was on fire with flames shooting out about two feet into the air.

Preston looked around for something to use to fight the

fire and saw a gallon-size metal can on the ground, like from a cafeteria kitchen. He'd use that to scoop up wet sand from the wash and maybe slow down the fire until Abby returned.

The can reeked of gasoline; the container probably was left by the arsonist after he'd siphoned fuel from his SUV. Needing to work quickly before the fire ignited the surrounding forest, Preston used it to dig out some wet sand from the wash and throw that onto the base of the flames.

It seemed to help. Or maybe the logs were so wet from recent rains they didn't want to burn. He quickly scooped up more sand and threw it against the base of the flames. The fire died some, and the hole he was digging in the wash was now filling with water. There was hope.

Two minutes later, he saw Abby come over the rise, fire extinguisher in hand. "This is heavy," she yelled, running up.

"Let's trade," he said, holding out the can.

"After all my running uphill?" she said, pulling the safety pin on the extinguisher. "No way. Give me some room."

Within twenty seconds, Abby had put out the flames. "Shall I work it over some more?" she asked, coughing from the smoke of still-smoldering wood.

"I reached water level in the wash," Preston said. "Stand by. I'll flood it."

Five minutes later the wall, nearly soaked with muddy water, was still intact.

"We use cans like that to scoop out grain at the ranch. I don't suppose you'll be able to get fingerprints from it now, right?" she asked.

"I've obliterated them with the wet sand, water and my own prints, but I had to slow the fire down."

"You think the person in the SUV did this?"

"Almost certainly," Preston answered. "Did you happen to get a look at the driver's face?"

"No, I was looking around for the cabin," she said, then

glanced back at the small building. "Do you think we'll find any of the answers we need here?"

"You never know." Preston looked at the small porch. "The door is sturdy and there's a rusted padlock in place, protected by the hasp. Let me see if there's any sign of a break-in."

They circled the cabin, but the windows, boarded over, hadn't been broached and the structure itself looked intact.

"Did you happen to notice the tire ruts in the back?" Preston asked. "There's a road back here somewhere, but I'm guessing the guy in the SUV couldn't figure out where it was."

"So now that we're here, how do we get inside the cabin?"

Preston smiled. "I have some skills, but look away. It's better if you don't actually see what I'm about to do." He reached into his jacket pocket for the special lock picks he kept in case of an emergency.

Soon they were inside, looking around the two-room cabin. Dust and cobwebs covered everything. "No one's been inside for months—years maybe," he said.

"The dresser drawers have some men's clothing, but it's old and threadbare." Abby went to the bookcase next. The books, mostly paperbacks, were yellow and dried up. The newest book was from 1995.

Preston picked up a small picture frame from a simple wooden desk. "I think this is Carl," he said, looking at the faded photo.

Abby came over to take a closer look. "He looks much younger in this photo, of course, but it's him. From the way they're dressed and the haircuts, I think it was taken in the mid-sixties. I don't know the man with him. Do you?"

Preston shook his head. "Maybe the owner of the cabin? I'll run a special facial-recognition program and find out."

"What if he doesn't have a criminal record?"

"If he ever applied for a driver's license or had VA papers, my brother's computer will ID him. That's why I'm going to ask him to do it. He has fewer rules and regulations to worry about."

"Jealous?" she asked and smiled.

He met her gaze and held it. "Abby, you probably won't believe this but, no, I'm not jealous. I've always played things by the book."

"What's changed?"

"You're more important to me than any rule book," he said, then took her hand and brushed a kiss over her knuckles. "We're making progress on this case, Abby, so it won't be long before you have your life back."

She wanted to ask if he'd still be a part of it but remained silent. She had him here with her today. She wouldn't ask him for more than he could give.

THEY WERE BACK in Hartley, in Daniel's kitchen nook sipping hot coffee, when Dan called them across to his work area.

"It took longer than I expected, but I've got an ID for you. The man in the photo is Miles Gates," he said.

"The name's not familiar to me," Preston said.

"According to court records, thirty or so years ago Gates was the local go-to guy if you wanted high-end art stolen. He never did the job himself. He provided intel and support. Like Carl, he lived in the Four Corners area most of his life."

"The photo tells us that they were friends, or at least colleagues, but if he's passed on, the trail ends there," Abby said. "There's no one else in the photo."

Preston stood silently, staring at an indeterminate point across the room. "I need to find someone who's connected to those two men. Carl had no family, but maybe Gates did."

Preston sat by the computer and got to work. As the minutes ticked by, no one interrupted him.

"Stan Cooper," he said at last. "That's the link."

"Stan? If you think he has anything to do with the problems I've had or with Carl's death, you're way off the mark. When I first opened the ranch, bookkeeping was nearly my downfall. Stan stepped up and took over—pro bono. He also introduced me to people like Rod Garner. Both of those men have been crucial to the ranch's operations. Stan's one of the good guys."

Preston shook his head. "Stan's grandmother remarried late in life. She was Miles's wife. He'd told me before that he'd spent a lot of time in the area around Navajo Dam, but I didn't have enough to put things together then."

"You can't hold Stan responsible for something his relative did," Abby said.

"No, but Stan's the common denominator. Here's my theory. Stan either remembered Carl or did some checking up and somehow confirmed his identity. Then maybe he tried to shake Carl down and pressure him to give up the missing paintings. Something went wrong and it led to Carl's death."

"You have nothing, bro," Daniel said.

"Abby, tell me what you know about Stan and Ilse," Preston said.

"I'd never seen her fooling around with Stan until today."

Preston paced, lost in thought. "Here's something we hadn't considered. What if the thing she supposedly had with Monroe was only a smokescreen? She came on heavily to the kid the night Carl was killed, but it might have been a way to keep him busy while Stan dealt with Carl."

"You're seeing way too much in this," Abby said. "Ilse's a free spirit. I may not agree with the things she does, but she doesn't have to answer to anyone but herself. Her life's her own."

"I'm not convinced, but obviously I need to find a stronger connection between those two. That means I'm going to need to dig deeper into Ilse's past. She's more of an unknown."

"I ran a full background on her," Daniel said. "No warrants, no arrests. If there had been any flags whatsoever, I would have found them."

"Go further back, to her college days. Remember the disciplinary action?" Preston said.

"Her official record didn't specify any of the details, but I can hack into the college's computer."

"Do it."

Several minutes later Daniel looked up. "It's sketchy, but she apparently put a bug in the math instructor's office, then tried to blackmail her."

"Like the listening devices at the ranch?" Abby said. "But Ilse's college days are long behind her. So she sowed some wild oats back then, so what?"

"It establishes an M.O.," Preston said. "What if Ilse found out about Carl? Garner said Carl told him the truth about his past, so if Ilse had been listening in when he did, she would have known. It's possible she told Stan after that and they joined forces."

"Rod does careful background checks on everyone in his circle. His former assistant handled Ilse's, but Ilse would have been the one responsible for running a check on Stan. Maybe that's when she made the connection," Abby said.

Preston expelled his breath in a hiss. "It's all plausible, and even likely, but it's just a bedtime story unless we find proof."

"How do we do that?" Abby asked.

Preston remained quiet, then after a beat looked up. "We get creative and work fast."

Chapter Twenty-Two

"Here's the way I see it," Preston said. "We'll need to sweep Garner's office, but there's a problem. The minute I tell him why I want to do that, he might toss me out on my ear and handle the problem himself."

"I can help you there," Abby said. "If Ilse and Stan have been working against me, I need to know, and to hold up in court, the search would have to be done right. Rod loves the ranch so I'm sure I can persuade him to give us his permission."

"Obviously you'll have to do that when Ilse isn't there, so you have to time your request right," Daniel said. "And I shouldn't be part of this. You'll want Garner to stay calm and that'll work better if he's around people he knows."

"Let me call Rod now. I know how I have to handle this." Abby reached for her cell phone and a moment later Ilse put her through. "Rod, I need a huge favor. Do you have time for me today?" she asked a beat later.

"For you—always," he replied. "What can I do for you?"

"It's something I'd rather not talk about over the phone. Okay if I come over?"

"Sure, when should I expect you?"

"How about in twenty minutes, say, five-thirty? I know Ilse leaves around five. Is that too late?"

"Nah, just come over. You've got me curious now."

They were on their way in Preston's SUV a short time later. "It's really important that you don't discuss the case until *after* I sweep Garner's place," Preston said.

"No problem," Abby said with a nod. "Just follow my lead, and don't let it throw you if he loses his cool. The best way to respond is don't react in kind."

"I gather you've seen him at his worst?"

She nodded. "Rod's hot-tempered. I was there one time when Ilse forgot to book his tickets to an NBA game he wanted to attend. When he goes crazy like he did that day, he can be hard to deal with."

"Does he get violent?" Preston asked her.

"Not in the way you think. He doesn't attack anyone, but I've seen him hurl things across his office and smash stuff against the wall. He won't deliberately aim at anyone, but be ready to duck anyway."

Preston's jaw clenched.

She glanced at him. "I mean it—don't let it get you upset. Just stay calm."

"Got it."

WHEN THEY ARRIVED at Rod's home, they were shown in by the butler. The second they stepped into the den, Rod looked at Preston, then back at Abby. "Didn't know you were bringing the law. I'm not going to like this visit, am I?"

"I was hoping that you could show the detective your gym and basketball court. The department may do a special fundraiser for us," she said. "Maybe have the police versus the fire department or something like that."

"Sure, come on," Rod said, instantly in a brighter mood. "Count me in on whatever you plan to do, too. I'll be happy to help."

They left Rod's office and went outside, crossing the lawn to another building.

"Rod, before we go any further—I haven't been entirely honest with you," Abby said, stopping and turning to look at him.

Rod glared at Preston instead of Abby. "What kind of game do you have my girl playing?"

"No, listen," Abby insisted, forcing him to look back at her. "I'm trying to protect you."

Hearing the words made him react in exactly the way she'd hoped. "Little girl, whatcha talking about?" he asked with a grin.

"Ilse may not be the person you think she is," Abby said. "I really hope I'm wrong, but we've found some bugs in and around Carl's office and the bunkhouse. A few were in my house, too. Because of Ilse's past, we have reason to suspect she's responsible."

"You think Ilse's been spying on people—and on me?" Rod said, an edge of steel in his voice.

"Which is why we needed to get you outside. We don't know anything for sure, but isn't it worth finding out?" Abby asked him, making sure to keep her voice soft and calm.

"That's why you're here?" he asked, looking at Preston.

"I brought some special equipment that'll tell us for sure if your place is bugged."

"Let's go."

Abby recognized the angry gleam in Rod's eye and the set of his jaw as they walked toward Preston's SUV.

"Rod, are you okay?" she asked.

"Yeah, but Ilse and I are going to war if I find out she's been bugging my office. That's *not* cool," he said through clenched teeth.

ABBY AND ROD stood in the doorway, far back as Preston swept Garner's office with methodical precision. The first bug he found was right underneath the big man's desk. He held it up for them to see.

Before Rod could react, Abby pulled him out through French doors and onto the patio.

Rod instantly picked up a vase filled with flowers and threw it against the wall. Water trickled down the wall and flowers scattered all over the tile floor. Rod paced like a caged tiger. "She was going to sell me out, wasn't she?"

"Rod, easy. Anger won't solve anything."

"Oh yeah, it will. Next time she shows up she's going to find out why no one messes with me."

Preston came outside and held up three electronic monitoring devices in two separate packs. "They're not transmitting, so you can speak freely," he said. "Assuming she didn't also bug the patio."

Preston checked but found nothing.

"I owe you one, guy, and I always pay my debts, as Ilse is about to find out," Rod said.

"Play it smart by playing her. It'll get you a lot further," Preston said. "Ilse handled the background checks on people in your circle, right?"

"Yeah, man. A guy in my position has to be careful. Everybody's a user and a con artist these days. I had my people run a check on her, too, and she was clean."

"Yes, she was—back then. Now she's involved in something that's illegal. Any idea why? Does she have any money problems?"

"I have no idea," he said with a shrug, "but if you let me handle this my way, I guarantee I'll get answers."

Preston shook his head. "I believe Ilse may have played a part in Carl's murder and I need the kind of evidence that'll stand up in court. The best thing you can do right now is give me permission to search her work area. Are you okay with that?"

"Sure. Do whatever you need. Nail her hide to the wall," Rod said.

Abby kept Rod outside as Preston began to search. "Are you sure you're going to be okay? Is it possible she managed to get something that might be embarrassing to you?"

He laughed. "Honey, these days I lead a downright boring life. During my days playing pro ball, well, that was a different story."

"Do you remember where you were when Carl first told you who he was?" Preston asked him, coming back out.

"Yeah, my office, having iced tea. We'd just played some pick-up ball out on my court." He pressed his lips tightly. "Ilse set him up, didn't she?" he said in a low growl.

"We don't know anything for sure yet, but that's the way it looks to me," Preston said. "Let me check around some more."

After about twenty minutes Preston called them into Ilse's office. "I found two unused burn phones, one taped beneath a drawer, an RF receiver disguised as an MP3 player and earphones. She was monitoring your conversations both on the phone and off. Ilse is in this up to her neck."

"Arrest her," Rod said, storming around the office. "I'll press charges. And I'll sue her, too. I want life as she knows it to be *over*. Carl was a friend of mine. If she set him up, she pays," he said, striding around the room. "That man trusted *me* and that trust was violated here in my own home. No way she's getting away with that."

He picked up Ilse's coffee cup and threw it on the floor, shattering it into a dozen pieces. "I'm pitching her out to the curb with the rest of the trash." He kicked away Ilse's desk chair, and it flew across the room and bounced off the wainscoting.

"Seeing her behind bars is your best revenge, but you need to play *her,* remember? Stay cool, and don't tip our hand,"

Preston said. "Once I gather more evidence I'll take her down."

Rod stopped pacing and looked Preston in the eye. "Okay, I've got that out of my system. What do you need?"

"Information. Does Ilse have a car?"

"Not her own, no. The SUV she drives belongs to Garner Inc.," Rod said. "What are you after?"

"I'd like to track her whereabouts the night of Carl's murder," Preston said.

"Easy. The SUV's got a GPS," he said. "I'll get you the chip. It'll tell you everywhere the SUV's been, along with the dates and times. It's *my* wheels, so you don't have to worry about a warrant. You've got my permission to access anything you need."

"I'll give you a receipt for it, and once we've copied the data, you can have it back."

"Let's go. The SUV she drives is the green one that's parked in front of the garage. It'll only take me a few minutes to pull the chip. I do this every year for my accountant— tax deductions, you know."

Preston looked at his watch. "Is there a chance Ilse will need the SUV and catch on?"

He glanced out the back window. "Ilse lives in that *casita,*" he said, pointing. "The glow through the curtains is from her 40-inch TV. That tells us that she's viewing her favorite TV show, which she records on her DVR. She watches it religiously as soon as her workday is over. For the next hour or so, she'll stay put."

Five minutes later, memory card in hand, Preston went back to his SUV and called the station. After speaking to the IT tech, he uploaded the GPS data via his MDT. Before long, he had the information he needed in a clear printout.

Preston went back to the house and met with Abby and Rod. "Ilse was up by Navajo Dam," he told Abby but didn't fill in the details for Rod. "More important, she went to the bus station a few hours after Carl's death."

"No way Ilse would travel by bus. That chick's high maintenance. She rents a car if she goes out of town on private business."

"Well, considering she's still around and didn't take any trips, I suspect she stored something in one of the lockers there," Preston said.

"Okay, B-man, what's next? Can you get a warrant and search the lockers?" Rod asked.

"No, just the ones she's using, and we'd have to specify what we're looking for. Since we don't know the answers to either of those questions, we can't make a move. Right now all I can get her for is misdemeanor invasion of privacy. To get her for anything more, we need to handle it differently. First, I'll need to put all the bugs I found in your office back where they were."

"Say again?"

"You heard me," Preston said. "We don't want to tip her off. What we need to do is set her up by having her overhear a staged conversation. I'll make sure it rattles her enough to force her into making a mistake."

"I don't know about that," Rod said. "Ilse doesn't rattle easily. That's one of the reasons I hired her. Even when I lose my cool, she barely blinks."

"Speaking of that, make sure you replace that broken cup in her office, and maybe the vase on the patio. When she comes back here, it has to look as if nothing out of the ordinary happened."

"You bet," Rod said. "How long do you need to set everything up?"

"Till morning. When does she get to her desk?"

"Eight-thirty," Rod said. "Unless something special is coming up, Ilse keeps regular hours."

"We'll set things in motion then. Just play along with whatever I say."

"You've got it."

After leaving Garner's estate, Preston drove toward Daniel's place, where he arranged to meet his brothers.

They arrived fifteen minutes later. Preston waited as the heavy metal gate opened so he could drive through. "This is going to be an all-nighter, Abby. You sure you want in? I can take you home right now."

"Michelle is going to be with the animals, so I'm staying. Everything I value is on the line." Even as she said it, she realized how true that was. And there was more than her beloved ranch at risk. Standing with her in the thick of things was the man she'd learned to love.

THEY'D ALL CATNAPPED a few hours on the sofas in Daniel's sitting area, but it was close to daylight by the time they went over the details one last time.

"Everyone know what to do?" Preston's gaze took them all in, one at a time—Abby, Daniel, Kyle and Gene. Once everyone nodded, they stood.

"Let's grab something to eat, then get back to the ranch," Preston said. "From this moment on, we keep things as routine as possible."

ABBY SPENT THE next two hours tending the animals. She was getting ready to return to Rod's place when she saw Bobby's foster dad pull up.

"In all the confusion, I totally forgot that I'd promised Bobby he could stay here this weekend!" she said, thumping her forehead with the heel of her hand.

Preston shook his head. "Don't make a big deal out of it. Kyle should be here any minute. He can watch over Bobby while he's guarding the ranch." He gestured toward the gate as he finished speaking. "There he is now."

Preston hurried to meet Kyle. "Hey, bro, one more favor."

"Dude, what'll you ever do without me once I'm gone?"

"I'll try to bear up," Preston said, biting back a grin. "Now listen up. We need you to watch over Bobby while you're here. In another thirty minutes, if it goes according to plan, things are going to get heavy."

"You hope," Kyle said.

"My plans don't fail," Preston said.

Preston then called the station and verified that a patrolman was in position and keeping an eye on the guest house inside Garner's estate. The officer was to report in if Ilse returned there any time during the day.

Then Preston joined Abby. "Ready?"

"Whenever you are."

As they got under way, Abby listened as Preston went over their plans one more time. If Preston was right, and Ilse and Stan were behind Carl's murder, the case would be solved soon. After that Preston would go back to his life and get involved in another case, and what they'd shared would soon become just another memory. She swallowed hard at the bittersweet prospects ahead.

"Hopefully this will all be over for you soon, and you'll be able to pick up your life right where you left off."

She shook her head. "I can never go back to the way things were. I've learned too much about myself. The ranch will always be at the center of my life, but I don't want it to be my entire world. I want...more."

He nodded slowly. "You deserve the best of everything, Abby."

"After the case is closed, will you still come to visit?" She hadn't meant to voice it out loud, but now that she had, she didn't regret it. She needed to hear his answer.

"I wish the answer could be yes, but I'm not the man you need beside you, Abby." He tightened his grip on the wheel until his knuckles turned white. "Our worlds would collide and eventually destroy one or both of us. A cop's work is filled with long shadows, the kind that follow a man after he quits for the day. You need to focus on hope and optimism. That's the heart of everything Sitting Tall Ranch does."

"Shadows have always been part of my life, Preston, and I've never hidden from them. I face them, then try to push them back, at least temporarily, for the kids." She paused. "The real problem between us is that you don't trust love and, without that, no relationship can survive."

He looked at her for a moment. "I admit there's some truth to that—" Before he could go on, he got a text message from Rod. "Here we go. Ilse's at work now," Preston said, reading it. "Time for us to get things rolling. You ready?"

"Absolutely," she said.

As eager as she was for closure, she knew that saying goodbye to Preston would follow, and nothing she could do, or say, would protect her from the heartbreak to come.

Chapter Twenty-Three

As they walked inside Rod's home, Abby noticed that things looked perfectly ordinary again, including the patio, visible through the French doors. A moment later Ilse, with her usual smile, escorted them down a short hall into Rod's office.

As Ilse left the room and the door shut, they sat down. Rod gave Preston a thumbs-up.

"So what brings you here?" Rod asked, getting things started.

"After this case is closed, Sitting Tall Ranch will be in need of funds," she said.

"Some of the investments Stan made for me took another wrong turn so I've got some cash flow problems right now," he said. "But I'll be happy to help you with some fundraisers. You could hold some special event here on the estate and charge admission."

"I plan to get the department involved and maybe other city agencies," Preston said. "Of course, we'll have to wait until the case is closed, but it shouldn't be much longer now."

"What's changed?" Rod asked, instantly picking up his cue.

"We've found Carl Sinclair's journal. It's a police matter, so I can't really discuss it, but I can tell you this—although he wrote it in code, we've already cracked the first part and expect to have it all before the end of the day. We have reason to believe the journal holds the name of the man who

came after him and the location of several stolen paintings
Carl kept in hiding."

"So it's all over but the crying," Rod said. "Outstanding."

"I believe that by noon, midafternoon tops, we'll be ready
to make some arrests," Preston said.

There was a soft knock on the door and Ilse came in. "I'm
feeling a little under the weather, Rod, so unless you need me,
I'd like to head home."

"That's fine. Go ahead," Rod said.

After Ilse left the office, Preston held a finger to his lips,
reminding them that the bugs were still in place.

A few minutes later the three of them went outside onto
the patio. Preston's phone rang. It was the patrolman who was
watching the *casita* and Ilse.

"The subject's inside the house, Detective. Currently, she's
on the phone. I can see her walking around."

"If she leaves, call me immediately."

"Copy."

About ten minutes later, as Preston and Abby were leaving
the estate with Preston driving, they spotted a familiar-looking
figure on the sidewalk down the street. Though carrying a
large tote and wearing a hoodie and sweatpants, a far cry from
her designer clothing, the woman's long-legged strides and
purposeful walk gave her away.

"Don't look at her," Preston said. "We'll circle the block
and come back around."

Preston called the patrolman as soon as he turned away.
"She's not there, is she?"

"I haven't seen her for the past several minutes. She came
to the window, looked around and then left the front room.
Let me go in for a closer look."

Preston parked at the curb and waited. A few minutes later
the officer called him. "She's gone, sir. She must have slipped
out the back."

As Preston hung up, Abby looked over. "From the way she's walking, she's got a specific destination in mind."

He pulled out into traffic, then circled the block and cruised down the street. After a short distance, they spotted her again, walking down a graveled pathway among the grass and trees.

"She's cutting across the city park," Preston said. "I won't be able to follow her in the car. I'll have to park somewhere and go after her on foot."

"I'm going with you."

"No. Drive back to the ranch and wait for me." He took off his jacket, turned it inside out to change its color, then put it back on.

"Handy—a reversible jacket," Abby said. She quickly pulled her hair back into a ponytail and fastened it with a rubber band she had inside her purse. "I'm going with you. You're not the only one who wants to know what Ilse's up to."

"All right," he snapped, reaching for the Stetson in the backseat. "I don't have time to argue."

They climbed out of the SUV, leaving it parked at the curb, and started down the same path Ilse had chosen. They remained at a distance, screening themselves whenever possible with the natural contours of the ground, trees and bushes.

Preston kept his eye on Ilse but had to hold Abby back. "The key to tailing a suspect is patience and positioning. Keep them in sight, but always give them plenty of room. We look a little different now, but we still need to maintain our spacing."

"She's going to get away if we don't hurry up," Abby said, urging him on.

"No, she won't. She's headed for the bus station. She took the shortcut across the park because it knocks a couple of miles off her route and she can't be easily spotted by an officer in a police cruiser."

Although there had been no indication that Ilse suspected

they were there, she suddenly stopped, turned around and slowly searched the area behind her for followers.

Preston instantly stepped into the shadows of a tall pine tree, pulling Abby with him. Facing away from Ilse, he pressed Abby's back to the trunk of the tree and kissed her.

For one breathtaking moment, she forgot everything but Preston. His mouth was hard and insistent, and as she parted her lips he groaned and deepened the kiss.

Seconds later, he pulled back. The fire she saw in his eyes made a shiver course up her spine. He held her gaze for a brief eternity, then turned his head and looked across the park.

"She's on the move again. Time to go," he said. "Ilse's not taking anything for granted, and she's watching her back. Be ready for her to make more abrupt stops."

As they continued to tail Ilse, the memory of Preston's kiss burned inside Abby. She could still taste him and feel him against her. She loved him. No one had ever filled her with such strong longings, but Preston would never allow himself to need anyone other than his brothers.

The knowledge stung. With effort she forced herself to concentrate on Ilse. This woman was probably the key to catching Carl's killer and ending the case that threatened the ranch's continued existence. Ilse was the priority now.

As Ilse entered the bus depot, they waited a moment, then stepped inside and sat in an area where travelers were waiting with luggage and backpacks. Preston picked up an abandoned newspaper and handed Abby a section.

Ilse walked toward the ticket counter, then stopped to look around. They lowered their heads, pretending to read.

Ilse waited in the short line, bought a ticket, then stepped away, turning around again to make sure she wasn't followed. At long last, she walked toward the rear wall of the main floor and to the long row of metal lockers.

After one last look around, Ilse fished a key out of her tote and went to one of the larger storage units. She had a problem opening it, but after a moment, they saw her remove one medium-size cardboard mailing tube from the locker. She quickly tucked it under her arm, then started walking around as if bored and impatient.

"Got it," Preston said, lowering the cell phone he'd used to video Ilse's activity. "But if we move in now and that doesn't hold a stolen painting, she'll know for sure that we're on to her, and we'll never get the evidence we need. Let's stay back and watch her for a while longer."

Preston caught the eye of the plainclothes officer who'd been positioned to back him up and held up his hand, signaling him to wait.

"What if she jumps on the next bus? She has a ticket. She might even make an exchange as she wanders around through the crowd and we'll never see it happen."

"I've got that covered. She's on depot surveillance and has two sets of eyes on her. If she makes a move for the loading area outside, I'm arresting her. Trust me—I do this for a living."

Ilse suddenly turned and moved toward the loading zone door labeled Gate 1.

"Stay here, Abby," Preston said. He rose and nodded to the officer, who'd been standing across the room. The plainclothes cop moved over to cut Ilse off. Ilse, who was already on her guard, veered away, picking up speed as she headed for the Gate 2 door instead.

Preston had anticipated the move and was already blocking her way. The minute she saw him, she turned back but soon spotted the other officer.

"Ilse, stop. You're under arrest," Preston said.

Panicking, she looked toward the station entrance.

"Don't try it, Ilse. You'll never make it outside. If you re-

sist, you'll only be making things worse for yourself," Preston
said. "You're already facing serious charges."

The crowd of travelers, suddenly aware of what was going
on, froze and stared silently as he cuffed Ilse's hands behind
her back and informed her of her rights.

"Hang on to the lady, Detective Edwards," Preston said to
the plainclothes officer.

As people started to talk and move around again, suspect-
ing the action was over, Preston turned to go talk to Abby, but
she wasn't where he'd left her. "The woman I came in with—
where did she go?" he asked Edwards.

"Near the entrance talking to the guy in the sports jacket,"
Edwards replied with a directional nod of his head.

Preston turned, worked his way through the active crowd
and saw Stan. They were near the main entrance—Stan holding Abby's forearm in a viselike grip. As Stan's eyes met his,
Preston inched his hand down toward his gun.

Stan shook his head and moved back the lapel of his own
jacket, revealing the handgun jammed into his waistband. For
emphasis, he put his hand down on the butt.

Gesturing by cocking his head, Stan motioned for Preston to approach.

"What the hell?" Edwards muttered, coming up beside
Preston, Ilse in tow.

"She's been taken hostage. Just hold on to the suspect. I've
got this," Preston said, trying to keep his voice normal and
not alarm bystanders. Any increase in the level of tension
could get Abby shot.

As Preston drew near, Stan pulled Abby closer to him.
"Lead the way outside, Bowman," he ordered. "Don't create
a problem for Abby."

Preston opened the door and paused in the entry, looking
back at them.

"Keep moving," Stan ordered. "Walk down the alley to the gas meter, then stop."

Preston saw Edwards start to advance. He held up his hand, halting the detective, and shook his head.

Fifteen seconds later, thirty feet down the alley, Preston stopped. "This is as far as we're going, Stan. We're going to be followed, you know that. Save yourself some jail time. Let Abby go and surrender your weapon."

"Not going to happen. I've got the hostage and I'm making the rules. Follow my instructions to the letter, Detective, or your woman will die. Am I clear?" Stan had his gun out and aimed at Abby's side.

"Yeah," Preston growled.

"Take out your weapon with your left hand *slowly,* then put it on the ground and slide it over to me with your foot," Stan said.

Preston put it on the ground as instructed, but he didn't kick it over. "You'll have to come get it. I've got it set for a one-pound trigger pull, and if I bump it too hard it could go off. A ricochet inside this alley could take any one of us down."

It was only a half-truth, but for now he hoped it would keep Stan from getting an additional weapon.

"You've been made, Stan, and Detective Edwards is already calling for backup," Preston added. "You've hit the end of the road in this alley. Let's make a deal before you have to face down a SWAT team."

Stan shook his head. "Catch." He tossed Preston a set of keys. "Once we get to the end my pickup's parked on the right. You'll drive and Abby and I will stay in the rear of the cab. If you try anything, I swear I'll shoot her in the head." He waved his gun slightly for emphasis.

Stan instructed them at gunpoint to walk to the end of the alley, where his truck was parked against the curb.

"Get in. It's unlocked," Stan ordered Preston.

"I've got Ilse and you've got Abby. Let's trade. That's what you want, right?"

"Not even close. Ilse knew the risks. She messed up, but I have no intention of making the same mistake." He poked the barrel of his pistol in Abby's side. "Now get in."

Preston had no other option at the moment. Stan's hand was shaking, and he couldn't risk Abby's life. He'd get his chance later, after they reached their destination. The department would also be tracking his cell phone. They wouldn't be alone for long.

He climbed into the driver's seat, looking back as Abby and then Stan slid into the car. At the far end of the alley, he could see Detective Edwards standing there, phone to his ear.

"Face forward, start up and drive. Don't look back again unless you want to hear gunfire."

"Where are we going?" Preston asked, inserting the key.

"Pull out into traffic and head west. You'll find out soon enough," Stan said. "One more thing, Detective. Take your cell phone out with one hand and toss it out the window. I'm not about to risk getting tracked."

Preston considered telling him that he didn't have one, but this wasn't the time to argue. He got rid of the phone.

Stan reached into Abby's purse next, feeling around for her phone and keeping his eyes on her and his gun out of reach. "If you both keep your cool, this will be over soon. Detective, you'll drive us out into the middle of nowhere, I'll drop both of you off, you catch the next ride into town and I keep going. No one needs to die."

They all heard Abby's phone beep just as he pulled it out. "Keep driving, Detective," he said, preempting any move from Preston with a wave of the gun toward Abby.

Stan glanced down at the text message. "That kid, Bobby, says he's decoded Carl's journal. He's ditched the guy watching him and is going to get the McCabe painting, 'The

Roundup.' Smart kid. He figured out where Carl hid it," he said. "Changing plans, folks. We're going to the ranch instead," he said, tossing the phone out the window and onto the bed of a passing pickup.

"You leave Bobby alone, Stan. He's just a kid," Abby said.

"Play by my rules and no one will die. You're talking with Crazyman, and I mean what I say," Stan said.

"So that was you sending those emails," Abby said.

"Of course. But I'm after the painting, not the kid," Stan added. "I take it and disappear, and you two go on with your lives."

Chapter Twenty-Four

"Why are you doing this, Stan? I still don't understand," Abby said.

"I grew up hearing all about Carl Sinclair and my grand-dad's fencing operations. Grandpa Miles got a little senile toward the end and Grandmother just assumed I'd think it was all crazy talk," Stan said. "For a long time I did. To me, Carl, the super thief, was just an arch villain/hero my granddad had made up. Then I met Ilse and new possibilities opened up."

"You knew that she'd bugged Rod's office?" Abby asked.

"Not at first. She and I became friends and one night I told her that I'd never meant to become an accountant. I'd wanted a life filled with excitement and adventure like my grand-dad's. When she heard the name Carl Sinclair, she said that he was back in town and told me what she'd overheard—Carl admitting that he'd changed his name. That's when I knew fate had given me a chance. Everything I'd ever wanted was right there just waiting for me to take it."

"So you convinced Ilse to help?" Preston asked him.

"It didn't take much convincing. Initially, she'd hoped to get something on Rod and blackmail him, but we both realized that we'd stumbled onto something much bigger. The paintings that Granddad and Carl had stolen were worth enough to keep us sipping mojitos in the Caribbean for the rest of our lives. We looked for them around the ranch on our own at first. Well, actually, I did while Ilse kept the chief's son distracted. He was always there till late. I wasn't able to find what we wanted, so we went to Plan B."

"You killed him because he refused to tell you?" Preston asked.

"No, man. It was self-defense. We tried to force him to tell us where he'd put the stuff by threatening to kill Bobby and making it look as if he'd done it if he didn't cooperate. He took us to Hank's enclosure, then came at me with a shovel. I wrenched it away from him, and while we were fighting, Ilse picked it up and hit him twice. He went down and stayed down—permanently."

"No one saw you two?" Preston asked.

"No, but that idiot camel wouldn't shut up. He started bellowing like crazy. Lucky for me it was thundering and nobody heard. Then we saw Monroe walking toward the enclosure. Ilse went to meet him and kept him busy, as usual, while I took care of things. I moved Carl's body as fast as I could, hoping that would get Hank to shut up. It did. He quieted down once he couldn't see Carl anymore. I left Carl's body in the horse pen, figuring people would assume the horses had spooked because of the storm and trampled Carl."

"You're not going to get away with this, Stan. Too many people know what you've done," Abby said.

"You also left Ilse standing there in handcuffs, so she'll probably say *you* were the one who hit Carl," Preston added.

"Doesn't matter. I've always had an escape plan. In a few hours I'll have disappeared forever. It's a funny thing about being an accountant. You make friends with all kinds of people, particularly if you're willing to break a few rules."

"Once you have the painting, you'll let us go?" Abby's voice shook, betraying her fear.

"I'll keep you with me until I'm out of town—insurance, if you will. After that, you're on your own."

PRESTON DROVE DIRECTLY to the ranch. He'd left Kyle with Bobby, and the chances of having the kid give his brother the slip for more than a minute or two were zero to none. Sure enough, as Preston pulled up, Kyle and Bobby were standing close by.

"Don't even think of doing something stupid, Detective," Stan said. "If you signal your brother, Abby's brains will be splattered all over the backseat."

Preston knew he wouldn't have to do anything at all. Though Kyle clearly hadn't been told about the situation yet, seeing him driving Stan's truck and sitting up front alone while Abby and Stan were in the back would flag his brother that something was wrong.

Preston climbed down out of the extended-cab four-door pickup as Stan and Abby came out the back. As they did, Preston saw Kyle's shoulder stiffen, then he bent down to talk to Bobby, who was holding something in his hand.

In an instant, Stan pushed Abby out in front of him and allowed Kyle to see his gun.

"If you make the wrong move the woman goes first, the boy second. You get me?" Stan growled.

Bobby froze, his eyes as big as saucers. "That's why two people were riding in the backseat."

Knowing Bobby had spent practically all his life pretending to be a spy, and worried he'd do something foolish with the wrench he was holding, Preston spoke quickly. "Bobby, we're going to be fine, so just do as Stan says."

Bobby nodded and swallowed hard.

"All right then. We're all on the same page," Stan said. "Kyle, put your weapon on the ground along with your radio and cell phone."

Kyle did as he was told, but the look on his face told Preston that he'd take the first available opportunity to rip Stan Cooper apart.

"Give me your handcuffs, Bowman," Stan ordered.

Preston hesitated. He knew what was coming next.

"Do it! Toss them to your brother," Stan ordered, pointing his pistol at Abby.

Preston removed them from the keeper on his belt and tossed them to Kyle. "Sorry, bro."

"Attach yourself to the bumper grill by your right wrist. One of those big bars, so you can't twist it loose," Stan ordered Kyle.

"No," Kyle said.

"Don't push me," Stan said, grabbing Abby and moving the gun under her chin.

Abby closed her eyes.

"All right," Kyle said. "Relax."

Kyle walked past Preston and Abby slowly, and as he did, he met his brother's eyes.

Preston knew that Kyle wanted nothing more than to tackle Stan, but he'd do what had to be done.

After Kyle had attached the handcuff to the big metal grill protector, Stan added, "Now your wrist."

Once Stan heard the click, he went over and took a closer look, keeping out of range of Kyle's arms and feet. "Okay, kid," he said, looking at Bobby. "You said you knew where the painting was. Where is it?"

"I sent the text to Abby, not you," Bobby said, his voice shaky. "Carl wouldn't have wanted you to have it."

"Look, kid, it's a trade. You give me the painting. Your friend Abby and her cop friend stay alive."

"Bobby, do as he says," Preston said.

"It's down there," Bobby said, pointing toward the animal pens.

"Lead the way," Stan said.

Bobby walked toward the barn even more slowly than usual. "The fence post by Hank's enclosure isn't like the other ones. It's hollow. Kyle and I had to go back to get a wrench so we could unscrew it. The top part is hard to move." Bobby held out the pipe wrench.

Preston was already trying to figure out a way to get to it. The wrench wasn't much of a weapon against a gun, but it would extend his reach enough to knock it away.

The one ace in the hole he still had was that Stan didn't know about the new cameras and Daniel, or one of his employees, had undoubtedly monitored their arrival. They'd have plenty of backup soon. All he had to do right now was stall for time and, if possible, try to get the drop on Stan before he did something stupid.

As they reached the enclosure, Hank began to bellow.

"Abby, make that thing shut up," Stan hissed.

"I can't. He won't listen. He hates you. You killed his friend," Abby said.

"I told you it was Ilse. Which post, kid?" Stan asked, keeping his gun on Abby, who was on his right.

"It's the one with the sign telling about Hank," Bobby said. "The sign is attached to a nut screwed into the top of the post."

"All right, kid. Use the wrench to take off the nut," he said.

Bobby tried, but it wouldn't move. "I'm not strong enough, even with the wrench. It's rusty and stuck. You have to do it."

"If you're pulling something, kid…" Stan said, his voice turning deadly.

"I'm not!"

"If that painting isn't there…"

"Carl said it would be!" He tapped the side of another pipe with the wrench and there was a solid metallic sound. Then he tapped the pipe holding the sign. "Listen," Bobby said. "Hear it? Sounds hollow, right? This is where he put it."

"Leave the wrench on the ground, Bobby," Stan said, then looked at Preston. "The kid must have loosened it up a little. Try it with your hands. *Don't* touch that wrench."

It took Preston a few seconds, but he was finally able to work the top loose. A thin wire led down the hollow pipe. Preston pointed it out and stepped back. "Go ahead."

All he needed was for Stan to move away from Abby. The second he reached over to pull out what was attached to the wire, he'd have him.

Almost as if reading his mind, Stan shook his head. "No, you pull it out for me, Bowman."

Working carefully, Preston grabbed the wire and pulled. The wire was connected to a cap attached to a smaller-diameter piece of white plastic pipe.

"Pop that cap off and let's see what's inside," Stan said, looking out of the corner of his eye toward Hank. The camel had come over to investigate.

Preston worked the cap loose. Inside was a rolled-up canvas painting held together by a string.

"Open it carefully. I want to make sure it's the real thing," Stan said.

"I'll need to reach for my pocket knife to cut the string," Preston said.

"Don't even think it. Slide the twine off."

Preston worked the string loose, then unrolled the canvas. He'd expected to see a scene from a roundup, but this had nothing to do with cowboys or cattle. It was almost a replica of the sketch *Hosteen* Silver had left for him. It depicted a small bird of prey protecting its nest from a large owl. Only one element was new to him, and it rocked him to the core. In the canyon below, a young boy watched the sky and a woman knelt beside him. A single blue feather drifted down toward them, though neither seemed aware of it.

As Preston stared at the painting in his hands he knew destiny had found him.

"Aim it toward me so I can get a better look, but keep it away from the fence. I don't trust that camel."

Preston, still searching for an advantage, held the painting so Stan would have to turn his head slightly.

"It's not 'The Roundup,' but that painting's worth twice as much," he said. "It's titled 'Dreams' and is one of his earlier works. Roll it back up."

Preston did, working slowly to buy time.

"Looks like we're all coming out ahead on this. Even you, Abby," Stan said.

"What are you talking about, you weasel? I may lose the ranch."

"Cheer up. You're not as bad off as you think. I've been cooking the books ever since I found out about Carl. How else could I buy you out cheap? You're not rich, but you're definitely in the black. The same goes for Garner. I had to make sure he didn't try riding to your rescue, so I made him think he'd taken some heavy investment losses. Guess you both need to find a better accountant."

"She trusted you," Bobby said angrily.

"Live and learn, kid." Stan glanced at Preston. "Quit stalling and hand me the painting."

Holding out his left hand, Stan poked the barrel of his gun hard into Abby's ribs.

When Abby groaned, Bobby, who'd picked up the wrench unnoticed, smashed it against Stan's knee.

With a cry, Stan swung the pistol around toward Bobby, but Preston grabbed Stan's gun hand at the wrist, shoving it up and back and cracking the man's forehead with his own weapon.

The gun went off, sending a bullet into the sky.

Preston grabbed the pistol, tore it from Stan's grasp and kicked the man in the groin.

Slammed backward, Stan grunted in pain and fell to his knees. As he sagged against the fence rail, Hank brought his head down and bit Stan hard in the shoulder.

Stan cried out and rose to his feet, but Preston, having put the pistol on safe and tossing it aside, moved in. He threw a right cross that connected with Stan's jaw and sent the man tumbling back down to the ground.

Preston wanted this fight. "Get up. You're brave when you're holding a gun on a woman and a kid. Now let's see what you've got when you're fighting someone your own size."

Stan shook his head and stayed on the ground. "Forget it," he said, seeing Kyle and Daniel running up and hearing the wail of approaching police cars.

"I've got him," Preston called out, spinning Stan around and cuffing him with a zip tie, one of several he'd recently put in his pocket.

Abby retrieved Preston's pistol and stepped back with Bobby.

"We'll keep an eye on him for you until the officers arrive," Daniel said, moving Stan away from Abby and Bobby. "Go take care of your friends, bro."

Bobby grinned as Preston came up. "Way to go! I knew we could take him."

Preston looked at the boy and smiled. "And we did, buddy. Teamwork."

Bobby glanced back at Stan as Kyle and Daniel held him away from them. "You, me and Abby. We backed each other up when it counted, just like family."

"You've got that right," Preston said and bumped fists with Bobby. "That painting is still on the ground over there. You wanna get it before Hank does?"

"Sure." As Bobby hurried away, Preston focused on Abby. "He's right, you know," he murmured, pulling her into his arms. "The three of us are family in all the ways that count. Listen to White Wolf's call. Marry me, Abby. After that, we can adopt Bobby and make it official."

She smiled. "A package deal. What more could a woman want?"

"Let me give you a few ideas," he said and covered her mouth in a deep, slow kiss.

"About time," Bobby called out. "Grown-ups take *forever* to see what's right in front of them."

"Just plain stubbornness, if you ask me," Daniel said, laughing.

Epilogue

The cliffs were bathed in the gold, orange and red of late afternoon as Preston and Abby arrived at Copper Canyon. Moments after they parked, first Bobby came out of the house followed by Preston's brothers and two women Abby hadn't yet met.

"This is our last get-together before Kyle leaves again," Preston said.

"Is he coming back?" she asked.

Preston nodded. "By the end of the year. Now come meet some of the family."

Preston introduced Abby to Holly, Daniel's very pregnant wife, and then Gene introduced his wife, Lori.

Before Abby and Bobby could go into the house with the others, Preston took them aside. "I'd like to show both of you a very special place. It was where I first learned about being in a family."

Preston took Abby by the hand and led her and Bobby a little ways up the canyon.

"When *Hosteen* Silver first brought me here to Copper Canyon I had a rough time of it. Life hadn't taught me to trust anyone, so I didn't want to hang out with my brothers. I wanted a space of my own. A tree house seemed perfect. I'd seen one on TV, so I picked out that tree," he said, pointing to a large cottonwood next to the arroyo.

"You built that?" Bobby asked, looking up at the small four-sided boxlike structure.

"Not completely, no," Preston said.

"My idea at the time was just to put in some kind of floor and maybe a length of rope so I could climb up, but I couldn't do any of it alone. The more I tried, the more frustrated I got. One day after I had stormed off, ready to sulk, I looked back and saw Kyle and Gene starting to work together on the place. They were doing what I hadn't been able to do by myself. I went back and joined them. We all shared the work from that day on, and it turned out to be a great place. We used it for a long time."

"I try to do stuff alone, too," Bobby said. "It's hard to count on anyone else."

"My brothers and I aren't related by blood, but we're family in all the ways that matter most, like it is with Abby, you and me," Preston said. "So, Bobby, what do you say? Would you like to make it official?"

"You mean you'll foster me?" Bobby asked, his voice rising in excitement.

"No, I was thinking we could start the adoption process once Abby and I are married," Preston said.

"And we'll live in the big house at Sitting Tall Ranch," she said, "though we're going to have to do some remodeling."

"And lots of repainting," Preston said with a grin.

"More blue?" she said, laughing. "What color do you want your room to be, Bobby?"

"My own family *and* my own room? Who cares what color it is," he said.

"Okay," Preston said. "Now that we've got that settled, let's go back to the house. Kyle's got everything we need, Bobby, including a baseball glove that needs to be broken in. While we're waiting for dinner, you and I can go practice throwing and catching and maybe take a few swings with the bat."

"For real?" Bobby asked.

"For real," Preston said with a smile.

"Can I get in on that?" Abby asked.

"Hey, you're part of the family team now, too—the Copper Canyon crew. We're unstoppable."

As they headed back, Bobby leading the way, Preston placed his arm around Abby's waist and pulled her closer to his side.

Abby looked up at him and smiled. "So what do we do for a second date, Detective Bowman?"

"Get married? I've got this ring in my pocket...."

* * * * *

A sneaky peek at next month...

INTRIGUE...

BREATHTAKING ROMANTIC SUSPENSE

My wish list for next month's titles...

In stores from 16th August 2013:

❏ Glitter and Gunfire – Cynthia Eden

& Bridal Armour – Debra Webb

❏ The Betrayed – Jana DeLeon

& Task Force Bride – Julie Miller

❏ Bodyguard Under Fire – Elle James

& Most Eligible Spy – Dana Marton

Romantic Suspense

❏ The Missing Colton – Loreth Anne White

Available at WHSmith, Tesco, Asda, Eason, Amazon and Apple

Just can't wait?

0813/46

Special Offers

Every month we put together collections and longer reads written by your favourite authors.

Here are some of next month's highlights— and don't miss our fabulous discount online!

On sale 6th September

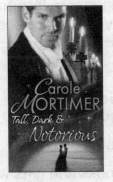

On sale 6th September

On sale 16th August

Save 20%
on all Special Releases

Find out more at
www.millsandboon.co.uk/specialreleases

Visit us
Online

0913/ST/MB433

Join the Mills & Boon Book Club

Want to read more **Intrigue** books?
We're offering you **2 more** absolutely **FREE!**

We'll also treat you to these fabulous extras:

- **Exclusive offers and much more!**

- **FREE home delivery**

- **FREE books and gifts with our special rewards scheme**

Get your free books now!

visit www.millsandboon.co.uk/bookclub
or call Customer Relations on 020 8288 2888

The World of Mills & Boon®

There's a Mills & Boon® series that's perfect for you. We publish ten series and, with new titles every month, you never have to wait long for your favourite to come along.

Blaze®
Scorching hot, sexy reads
4 new stories every month

By Request
Relive the romance with the best of the best
9 new stories every month

Cherish™
Romance to melt the heart every time
12 new stories every month

Desire™
Passionate and dramatic love stories
8 new stories every month

What will you treat yourself to next?